INFILTRATED

MARK A. HEWITT

Black Rose Writing | Texas

ISBN: 978-1-68513-022-0
PUBLISHED BY BLACK ROSE WRITING
www.blackrosewriting.com

Printed in the United States of America
Suggested Retail Price (SRP) $25.95

Infiltrated is printed in Book Antiqua

*As a planet-friendly publisher, Black Rose Writing does its best to eliminate
unnecessary waste to reduce paper usage and energy costs, while never
compromising the reading experience. As a result, the final word count vs. page count
may not meet common expectations.

Also by
MARK A. HEWITT

THE DUNCAN HUNTER THRILLER SERIES

Special Access
Shoot Down
No Need To Know
Blown Cover
Wet Work
Special Activities

OTHER TITLES

Airshow!

INFILTRATED

We enter parliament in order to supply ourselves, in the arsenal of democracy, with its own weapons. If democracy is so stupid as to give us free tickets and salaries for this bear's work, that is its affair. We do not come as friends, nor even neutrals. We come as enemies. As the wolf bursts into the flock, so we come.

Joseph Goebbels

PROLOGUE

Democrat Representatives of the 108th Congress took turns going to the floor of the House of Representatives to introduce House Joint Resolutions; the last Democrat in line moved to the lectern and proposed a Constitutional Amendment to remove the "natural born citizen" requirement for president under Article II of the U.S. Constitution. From their assigned seats, two Republican Representatives observed the proceedings, exchanged glances, and made notes for the Republican leadership. The last of the House Joint Resolutions was given a number: 59.

Later in the year, another Democrat Representative of the 108th Congress went to the floor of the House of Representatives and introduced a House Joint Resolution. He proposed a Constitutional Amendment to make a person who had been a citizen of the United States for at least 20 years eligible to hold the Office of President. Three Republican Representatives who were sitting together observed the proceedings on the floor and made notes for their leadership. The Democrat Representative from Michigan dismounted the lectern and logged in the proposed amendment with the House Clerk; the House Joint Resolution was given number 67.

The proposed Constitutional amendments, HJR 59 and 67 and six others, were never mentioned in the newspapers, and the mundane work of congressmen was not carried on any of the cable news networks. Without fanfare or vitriol, Republican leaders from both Chambers of Congress countered Democrat efforts to remove the "natural born citizen" requirement for president from the U.S. Constitution with their proposed legislation.

The following year, a Republican Senator of the 108th Congress from the State of Oklahoma, introduced a Senate Bill, the *Natural Born Citizen Act*, to *restate*—not redefine—the constitutional term "natural born citizen" as it had been defined in the Naturalization Act of 1790, to wit, "Children born of U.S. *citizens are* natural-born citizens."

Congressional Democrats were mum on who would benefit directly from their proposed amendments to the Constitution. As was their way, that person would not be identified directly. The Republicans in the Congress wondered which Democrat would benefit from such legislation.

At the Democratic National Convention when the keynote speaker took the stage, it became clear to the Republicans in Congress what the Democrats were up to. The junior Senator from Michigan was introduced to all of America and became an instant national figure.

The Senator from Michigan electrified the convention with his presence, style, and eloquence, but more than one Republican member of Congress noted he was not a "natural born citizen," per the U.S. Constitution. He touted his book, an autobiography no one knew anything about. Overnight, he became a millionaire. In his biography, he stated he was born of an American mother and a Muslim father from Africa.

While the proposed Democrat legislation to amend the Constitution appeared to be tailormade for someone like the Michigan state senator, Congressional Republicans dismissed any notion of a reasonable presidential campaign for him. Every one of the eight House Joint Resolutions to amend the U.S. Constitution to remove the "natural born citizen" clause had been referred to the House Committee on the Judiciary and failed in committee. There would be no amendment to the U.S. Constitution.

The Speaker of the House thought the Republicans had killed the Democrat's ideations of making an ineligible candidate for president eligible through legislation.

But he was wrong.

CHAPTER 1

August 3, 2004

On the other side of the Washington, D.C. metroplex, ten days after the Democrat National Committee Convention, a dull and quiet station office which served the Maryland Transportation Authority (MTA) was a hubbub of activity at shift change. Two female MTA Police Officers fresh from afternoon muster and pre-patrol briefings left the building and stepped into the brilliant sunshine. They slipped on dark sunglasses and monitored the eastbound traffic flow.

Vehicles were expected to speed up the steep incline of the Chesapeake Bay Bridge, but the two officers noticed a dirty Toyota sport utility vehicle (SUV) was losing speed. That usually indicated the vehicle was in some mechanical distress.

One police officer commented to the other, "I hope they pull over *before* they become a problem *on* the bridge."

The women had witnessed thousands of vehicles of every shape and size pass in front of the bridge's station office and climb the bridge for the Eastern Shore. Most of the time the flow of traffic formed steady lines, slow trucks to the right, the fast movers to the left, speeders zipped between vehicles of varying speeds. The vehicle in trouble continued to slow as it passed in front of them.

The passenger of the SUV, a woman wearing a traditional Islamic headcover, held a camera to her face.

It suddenly became obvious to the officers the vehicle wasn't in distress; the vehicle was reducing speed on purpose. The woman was videotaping the entrance to the Chesapeake Bay Bridge.

What the? The MTA officers looked at each other to confirm they were not hallucinating. *You can't do that! That's against the law!* They leaped into action and ran to their assigned police interceptor. They used their siren and flashing lights to overtake the slow-moving vehicle and conducted a traffic stop before it reached the apex of the bridge.

The police officers cautiously approached the vehicle and then tag-teamed the couple inside, peppering them with questions. One officer noted the driver wore a sand-colored *thobe* and a black and white *keffiyeh* of the type Palestinians were known to wear. She had seen photographs of the Chairman of the Palestine Liberation Organization (PLO) Yasser Arafat wearing an identical *keffiyeh* of white and black lines and geometric designs. The officers ordered the man and woman out of their vehicle; the two wore sandals and their clothes smelled of goats. The officers were convinced they had seen the man's face before, recognizing his impressive two-tone mustache and beard. But law enforcement officers all across the country knew Khalid Sheikh Mohammad was in Guantanamo Bay, Cuba, dining on three culturally sensitive meals per day. It couldn't be the al-Qaeda mastermind, but his face was eerily similar.

The driver's English was poor, and his attitude was worse. The woman's round face was framed by a black *hijab*. Her English was better. As it became clear they would be detained, she became terrified of her situation. She denied strenuously she had been taking pictures of the bridge. A physical search of the Muslim woman revealed the videorecorder the officers had seen. A search of the vehicle uncovered a notebook filled with Arabic writing was wedged between the driver's seat and the forward console.

Although the man claimed to have lost his driver's license, one police officer queried the national law enforcement database to ascertain the vehicle was registered in Virginia to Ismail Selim Elbarasse. Whether the man was really Ismail Selim Elbarasse was anyone's guess. The woman in the *hijab* had stopped talking altogether. The MTA Police Officers assumed she was related: a wife or sister. She seemed fearful of the man.

The station office dispatcher notified the Department of Homeland Security (DHS). The DHS Rapid Response Team sent a vehicle and security officers to the bridge's MTA station office. They took custody of the woman and the man believed to be Ismail Selim Elbarasse.

Security officers at DHS Headquarters (HQ) contacted the National Counterterrorism Center (NCTC) and informed a counterterrorism (CT) task force officer a man identified as Ismail Selim Elbarasse and an unidentified woman were in custody and were being held in conjunction with videotaping the support structures of the Chesapeake Bay Bridge.

The CT officer at the NCTC who took the call became the temporary head of the new Elbarasse Task Force. He queried the NCTC's Terrorist Identities Datamart Environment (TIDE), the U.S. government's central classified repository for all known or suspected international terrorists and their networks, and immediately retrieved all known biographic and biometric information on Ismail Selim Elbarasse; his full name and aliases, date of birth, photographs, and any derogatory information connecting Elbarasse to terrorism. The NCTC Elbarasse Task Force officer transmitted all known information to the DHS officers via their vehicle's computer. This included a photo of Elbarasse to ensure positive identification. The DHS security officers made the identification even though Elbarasse was clean shaven in the photo.

Since this was a suspected domestic terrorism case, the FBI's Senior Special Agent in Charge assigned to the NCTC informed the Elbarasse Task Force officer the FBI was especially interested in Elbarasse and would assume operational control (OPCON) of him. The DHS security officers transported Elbarasse and his female companion to the Department of Corrections Central Detention Facility, Washington, D.C. The National Crime Information Center (NCIC) warrant database indicated Elbarasse should be approached with the utmost caution; he was believed to be armed and extremely dangerous, although no weapons were found on him or in the vehicle when he was stopped.

Officially, Ismail Selim Elbarasse was detained on an outstanding material witness warrant issued in Chicago in connection with fundraising for Hamas, the terrorist organization and former *de facto* ruling party of the Palestinian government. Investigations establishing the connections between Elbarasse and the PLO were progressing.

Counterterrorism specialists from the FBI processed the images captured by Ismail Selim Elbarasse's woman which included close-ups of cables and other features that were "integral to the structural integrity of the bridge."

With Elbarasse and his assumed wife in an FBI holding cell, the FBI's Washington Field Office sought a surveillance warrant against a suspected foreign spy under the Foreign Intelligence Surveillance Act (FISA). Within an hour, the FBI's attorneys had made their case to the FISA judge on duty and had obtained a surveillance warrant of Elbarasse's cell phone and cell phone records.

CHAPTER 2

August 4, 2004

The presenter with the red laser pointer finished her brief by highlighting several before and after slides. One PowerPoint slide captured a multigrid database chart which showed the names of thirty men, their believed locations, and their associated organizations. She said, "Last year, we had thirty, and now there are twenty." It looked as if she was lining out and excising the names with the laser, but it was only computer graphics. "We are at a loss to explain what happened to these men and why their numbers are decreasing on the *Specially Designated Terrorist* watch list. In fact, CIA sources tell us some thirty designated terrorists have been eliminated over the last twelve months, but there is no known reason for their deaths. SOCOM hasn't taken credit. The Agency denies they were responsible. Obviously, someone is lying."

A man from the audience shouted, "You make it sound as if a decreasing number of terrorists is a bad thing." The comment elicited chuckles from the majority of federal agents. But there were no laughs from the Special Agents who identified as Muslim.

The brief was over; and the auditorium lights came on. About a hundred special agents stood up, shuffled out of the rows of seats, and returned to work.

The newly assigned Special Agent in Charge of the Elbarasse investigation raced out of the mandatory brief. For two years he had been the lead American investigator of sex crimes in Europe involving Americans, and he had just returned from monitoring the contractor who was consulting during interrogations in Guantanamo Bay, Cuba. Link Coffey of the Special Surveillance Group, Washington, D.C. Field Office had received the email notification he was waiting for and was on his way to the United States Foreign Intelligence Surveillance Court. The FBI had determined probable cause to search Elbarasse's residence after Special Agent in Charge Coffey had requested a search and surveillance warrant from the FISA Court.

Coffey wore a dark gray suit and an uninspiring dark gray tie as he left the FISA Court with the search warrant. He wanted to get out of his suit and into his working uniform of black cargo pants, body armor, steel-toe boots, and a navy windbreaker with FBI emblazoned on the back in yellow block letters. It was the uniform of choice for taking down criminals and conducting investigations. Surveillance began on Elbarasse's cellphone and computer.

After a four-hour investigation of the premises, the half-dozen CT Specialists on site concluded there was nothing of interest in the house. Coffey refused to admit defeat. He asked for the building's blueprints and a tape measure. He measured all the rooms and found a discrepancy in the basement.

A cleverly constructed false wall created a sub-basement where Special Agents found over 80 banker boxes filled with files, papers, photographs, and what were believed to be financial records, and other assorted documents on metal racks. A cursory look revealed the records were in Arabic. They also found a fireproof safe with a combination lock. Special Agent in Charge Coffey had the boxes and the safe transported to the largest and most comprehensive crime lab in the free world, the FBI Laboratory in Quantico, Virginia.

As the boxes were unloaded from an unmarked van, Coffey was shunted into a conference room and received an expanded CT brief on Elbarasse. Special Agents, a man and a woman, delivered the brief. The detained Elbarasse was a former board member of the Islamic Association for Palestine and was suspected of being a Hamas activist. He had served on the Palestine Committee, a front organization created by the Muslim Brotherhood in the United States to help Hamas politically and financially. At the time of his arrest, Elbarasse was an assistant to Mousa Mohammad Abu Marzook, a Palestinian senior member of Hamas. Photographs of the suspect were shown on the wall screen.

Coffey knew they had taken a bad one off the streets of America. Now he would learn how bad. Coffey motioned for the presenters to continue. He wasn't entirely shocked his case was now a full-blown counterterrorism case.

One briefer announced, "In 1995, Marzook was listed as a *Specially Designated Terrorist*, an SDT, by Treasury. He remains on the list with all the alternative spellings of his name."

Coffey thought, *The usual suspects. Specially Designated Terrorist. These SDTs probably have STDs....*

The female briefer said, "Two years ago, a federal grand jury in Dallas returned an indictment against Marzook for conspiring to violate U.S. laws that prohibit dealings in terrorist funds. At that time, Elbarasse was a minor assistant to Abu Marzook, but postliminary he was named an unindicted co-conspirator by a grand jury in Chicago. We think what we'll find is that Elbarasse's boxes contain the bank records of Marzook. Justice would like to charge Marzook in a conspiracy that raised millions of dollars for Hamas and the Muslim Brotherhood, but they do not have his records. If these are Marzook's missing records, Justice will assume jurisdiction and try Marzook, even if it means trying him *in absentia*; any questions?"

At the end of the brief, Coffey raced back to the lab. The safe was opened; it contained more documents in Arabic. Those documents were in salmon-colored binders instead of being in folders and files like the documents in the banker's boxes. The papers inside the binders had all been perfectly stacked and secured with thin metal strips that were run through three holes on the sides or two holes atop. The metal binding strips were bent over and locked in place.

Coffey determined all the documents from the banker's boxes and the safe should probably be classified at some point, but for the time being they would be considered "sensitive." Sensitive documents didn't require the special handling or storage requirements of classified documents.

The safe's contents were inventoried and copied. A sample binder was sent to another Special Agent, a native Arabic speaker and practicing Muslim, for translation and transcription. Two days later the documents in the binder were returned with the Special Agent's report: the documents were nothing more than bank statements and old internal Palestine Committee records. There was nothing to connect Elbarasse or Marzook to Hamas or the Muslim Brotherhood.

The official report of transcript baffled Coffey. He sensed something was wrong, but he couldn't see it immediately. Slowly it came to him; *Why did the Special Agent assigned to do the translations and transcriptions take so long?* Coffey had asked for a rush job and the findings in the report made little sense. *If they were simply bank statements and old internal Palestine Committee records, that's a five-minute job. Wouldn't bank records have lists and charts?* Coffey was about to fly into a rage, but he caught himself. *Something isn't right with this. I just don't know what it is, exactly.* He paced in his office. He stopped in front of the window and stared outside, not seeing anything as he allowed his mind to wander. *I think I know, but I must proceed with caution.*

Coffey was careful asking, via email, "Was there anything with Abu Marzook's name or one of his aliases on it?"

The Special Agent who did the translation took an inordinate amount of time in responding. Coffey felt like a downed pilot behind enemy lines firing off a red flare as a last gasp for help. *What is wrong with this guy? What is taking so long?*

The FBI and the whole counterterrorism establishment had once prided themselves on immediate answers to a Senior Special Agent's or FBI seventh-floor executive's interrogative, but the man at the other end of the line responded as if the official request on an active hypersensitive CT case was a joke, like it was a non-graded exercise and not to be taken seriously.

Coffey was incensed at not getting an immediate answer. Completely flustered, he shut down his computer and told his secretary he was leaving the office.

I might regret not thanking Achmed for his translation work. Screw him!

On his way home long after the sun had set, Coffey turned down the music in his 1970 Mercedes 280 SL roadster. He was still incensed and spat out in a gravelly smoke burnished voice, "That's *bullshit!* I just cannot believe it. There is no way those are simply bank statements and internal records! *That* crap would be in those 80 *boxes,* not the safe!" He undid his tie and allowed a thought to permeate his brain. *I should have thought this out. I was too aggressive. Too much of that*

Marine shit in me. I shouldn't have used the.... He couldn't even think the word: *Muslim.* Then he allowed the pernicious thought to materialize: *I shouldn't have used that Muslim for the work. But the records were in Arabic; what choice did I have? I couldn't really ask for a second opinion unless I want to be tossed off this case.*

He sighed as his mind cranked up again. *Maybe they're personnel records. We'd lock up personnel records – but not bank statements and committee records! I...think.... I think...I need...a second opinion.* He rolled his eyes in exasperation, unaware he was driving too slowly for the conditions and was being passed on both sides by furious, finger-flinging drivers speeding south on Interstate 95.

The environment in the enforcement arm of the FBI is so volatile right now, so political... if I do that...I'll get shitcanned faster than a jet launched off the pointy-end of a carrier. They act like they are the personal Gestapo of the Director. He finally accelerated to the posted limit and smiled at the memories of his time in the Marine Corps aboard a flattop, flying the huge mechanical beasts with two afterburning engines that would make the ground tremble...such a long time ago. *Those were magical times. Not like having to work for a living.*

He patted the dash of his Mercedes lightly and remembered. *This is such a remarkable car. You used to see them occasionally, then they all disappeared. As if they had been recalled like Pintos. It seems like this one is the only one left.* When newly promoted Captain of Marines Link Coffey first saw the Mercedes, it was trashed in a junkyard. The engine was disassembled and in the trunk, it didn't have a lick of paint on it. But he could see the beauty of the car. It had become a project for him, particularly in the evenings when some of the other officers of the squadron would come to his apartment with beer and pizzas or burgers. They would use some of their mandatory crew rest working on the disassembled two-seater. Nearly everyone in the squadron loved working on or checking on the progress of the restoration. Now all he had left of those times was the old red beauty they called the *Pagoda* for its distinctive roofline and acres of glass.

He made the rest of the trip in silence; no radio, no mumbling, no cursing. Yet his mind remained active as he toyed with the possibilities – how to get a second opinion. *There is no way I can go into* the deputy director's office and say, "I can't trust your Islamic science experiments for a simple assessment, because if there is any Islamic CT component contained within the investigation, it will be corrupted. You might think you can trust them, but I don't trust them, not for intel, for the truth, for the time, not for anything." Coffey didn't want to resign. He had always wanted to be an FBI G-man like his father, and now he was in counterterrorism. It wasn't what he had expected. The problem was the enforcement branch; they made the whole Bureau look like frat boys with guns and badges on an all-night banger. The counterespionage division was seemingly awash with spies.

Like in all of government, there had been problems inside the FBI, and some of the senior leaders had stopped being leaders, had stopped being law enforcement executives. Not that they had become *spies*, in the sense of the Soviet spy, Robert Hanssen, or *political* in the sense of Mark Felt, aka "*Deep Throat*." Hanssen spied for the Soviets' money; Felt for the prestige, for being famous while remaining anonymous, and because he hated the president.

Now there was presidential pressure on the FBI to back off conducting surveillance of all Muslims. *In this post-9-11 environment, we're supposed to open our arms to them. Work with them. But not in counterterrorism. Maybe they would be useful in counterespionage. Don't these clowns on the seventh floor know the FBI has tried for decades to keep the spies from infiltrating the Bureau? Our fearless leaders have given up all pretext of being the premiere law enforcement agency in the world; now we must be more "diverse," more "inclusive," more "equal." In other words, DIE! Does anyone think for a minute the KGB or the CCP engages in any of that diverse and inclusive and equality nonsense? What horseshit! The FBI isn't a liberal science project. At least it shouldn't be.*

As Coffey pulled into his driveway and waited for the garage door to open, his thoughts continued. *The Bureau has been an exceptional place to work, but the administration has forced us to stop surveilling mosques and forcibly engaging with Muslim leaders. They hired Muslim interpreters and transcribers…I swear they've turned it into the Stasi. These are the wrong people. These Muslims are working for their friends or the Muslim Brotherhood, not for the Bureau or America. I swear if they came within a mile of a polygraph machine, it would burst into flames. But if I go to the Inspector General about this, that would be the end of my career.*

Other agents used FBI tools and resources to check on these Muslims. If they are fired or transferred; the leadership says we are picking on them. This double standard is appalling. The administration cannot see they have opened the doors to spies. Spies from the Muslim Brotherhood. How could they allow this… this… infiltration? He was disgusted. *I need another set of eyes to look at those documents! But who?*

Hours later, a full bladder and an erection woke him up; he stumbled out of bed and headed for the toilet. As a steady stream of urine splashed about, his overactive brain identified one, maybe two Arabic speakers and readers who were absolutely trustworthy. They were not FBI. One was CIA and a special kind of patriot, the only woman in the Agency who had interrogated the worst of al-Qaeda at Guantanamo Bay. *Our FBI Muslims would have found a thousand ways not to interrogate one of theirs.* Coffey remembered she was new to the Agency, but she was exceptional. She was a solid intelligence officer, and she was drop-dead beautiful.

He was embarrassed; she was the source of his tumescence. *I'll only ask her as a last resort. Those legs, those eyes, that face! If she works for me, I'll get nothing done! I'd be like a hound dog – wanting to sniff her neck! But…this is important shit – quit thinking of her! I need answers!* He sighed at the folly of even considering her. Coffey knew if an FBI Special Agent contacted an Agency intelligence officer, especially an analyst, interrogator, or executive, the FBI leadership would find out, and they would raise holy hell. *I swear I'm working for lunatics. If they even thought I was contemplating sharing intelligence with an Agency-type, there'd be grounds for dismissal.*

But, there was another guy. The grandson of one of the most famous former Communist Party spies. John! John Lindell. From the Pumpkin Papers Irregulars Dinner. I was impressed with him, if for no other reason than his grandfather was history, American history, history of communists, the history the Democrats absolutely hate, the history that isn't taught in schools. It's usually only discussed in a SCIF (Sensitive Compartmented Information Facility) or an FBI auditorium "in the theoretical" during a classified briefing. But it was true. The FBI had screwed up again. F Troop rides again!

Back in bed, there was no longer any evidence of a tent pole under the covers. He was thinking of him and not her.

We exchanged business cards; I have his card. Somewhere. A contractor. A Ph.D. in Arabic Languages; Cairo University. His mother held a Ph.D., and his grandfather was the reason we were all there that night, celebrating the victory over the communist Alger Hiss; the man had weaseled himself to the top level of the State Department for the Soviets. The Pumpkin Papers Irregulars Dinner—man, that was a fun night. A convocation of conservatives meeting openly in the middle of the cesspool that is the Washington, D.C. Democrat Party sewer, a place that is full of rats and shit. It was like the French Resistance having a party in the middle of a Nazi concentration camp!

The American people have no concept of celebrating victory over communism, although the Pumpkin Papers Irregulars Dinner was exactly that. Carl von Clausewitz said, "Politics is combat by other means." The Democrats have the press corps as their troops. America thought we were the bad guys. Ah, the power of propaganda. Joseph Goebbels, the onetime venomous Nazi editor, wished he had our media.

Only, Dr. Lindell is a Democrat. Guess you can't have everything. But he's an old school Democrat, like JFK, the ones that are pro-military and pro-police and pro-second amendment. Not like our current batch of idiots.

Coffey stared at the ceiling in the dark. His brain was too active for sleep. He remembered some of the published story, some of the FBI history. *It had been called the Trial of the Century. Dr. Lindell's grandfather had been a communist spy running Alger Hiss, the highest placed Soviet spy in the U.S. government when he defected from the Communist Party. Was it 1937? 1938? Long time ago.*

Dr. Lindell's grandfather fled to Florida with his family and maintained a very low profile. He knew the communists would be after him. The KGB. They called assassinations Wet Work. What evil people do to stay in power.

I bet the commies went berserk when he shook off their collar and leash. Became a Christian. I remember that much from the book. Moscow wanted him to come to the Soviet Union, to Red Square and KGB HQ, to award him a medal. But Stalin was in the middle of purging generals and party members. For some, it was an honor to be called from the United States. For others, it was a death sentence. Coffey sighed. *Isn't that what they did in the White*

House, after September 11th? Purge the FBI leadership for a handful of Islamic leaders with dubious allegiances?

No one in the FBI leadership seriously investigated the situation as al-Qaeda men methodically infiltrated airport security companies across the United States. They let nineteen hijackers walk through the checkpoints with weapons which should have been stopped by the x-ray machine.

The FBI blew it in the worst way. As the Bureau's supreme terrorism experts, we were giving lectures on the KGB and counterintelligence, patting each other on the back, when Islamic terrorism was afoot under our noses. On 9-11, Muslimas working the x-ray machines at the major airports just let the hijackers' weapons pass through the machines at an appointed place and time. The hijackers guided on the hijabs of the women behind the x-ray machines so they knew which line to get into. No one suspected the lowly minimum wage employee was in on it. The hijabs were key; without them and the women wearing them, the weapons needed to hijack the jets would not have made it through the x-ray machine and into the airport's sterile area.

The FBI's leaders wouldn't believe al-Qaeda was that sophisticated, and instead of investigating the reports from the field, they ignored them. They wouldn't listen. Too much hubris.

Muslim men taking flying lessons who were not interested in learning to land. Muslim men and women seeking employment at airport security firms, learning the locations of security cameras and working their way into management positions so they could schedule the x-ray machine operators. The IG (Inspector General) reported after 9-11 more aggressive surveillance of mosques could have stopped al-Qaeda's plans to bring American aviation to its knees. One Presidential Executive Order stopped it all.

We were worried about the Russians, the "reds" and not the "greens." Islamic green. Who would believe they were an existential threat to America? The world? There was something else at the back of his mind, but Coffey couldn't get it to materialize. *Turn over! Sleep!*

Coffey bounced to a better spot on the mattress and glanced at the alarm clock. 4:05. He screwed his eyes shut and demanded his mind relax. He needed a couple more hours of sleep, but his mind would not disengage and turned back to thoughts of Dr. Lindell. *What was the lesson? There was a lesson to be learned.... Ah yes, the FBI leadership didn't believe Chambers; they thought he was a buffoon, someone with a mental* disorder. *We couldn't believe al-Qaeda was a serious threat and anyone blowing the whistle on suspected terrorist activities was dismissed as a conspiracy nut. Who told us that? The Muslims in the FBI. Reassuring us they were not the problem. Islamophobes were the problem. Implying it was a problem of white men without saying it was a white man's problem.*

We have learned little. We were made to look like fools again. Anyone who was part of the operation dismissed al-Qaeda's incursion into the contracted airport security companies either resigned or got fired. By the grace of God, I was away from the flagpole, detailed to Europe, investigating sex crimes and pedophiles. American contractors who arranged for sex with an undercover FBI agent posing as a child had their contracts revoked. Nasty creatures.

Now, no one is going to believe Muslims have infiltrated the FBI. And they're running interference for who, exactly? Those who must not be mentioned, the Muslim Brotherhood or maybe the Islamic Underground? Are there others? Elbarasse?

Coffey sighed, nearly blurting out, *Hundreds!*

He turned over again and deliberately closed his eyes. He didn't want to see what time it was. He calmed himself and remembered.

Before the *Pumpkin Papers Irregulars Dinner*, he had researched Whittaker Chambers' history. When Chambers was ready to talk, the Federal Bureau of Investigation was not interested. The charge was too incredible. Alger Hiss was a State Department rockstar. Politicians liked the cut of his jib. And reportedly, there was no evidence. Nothing had changed with the FBI's corporate philosophy.

Coffey yawned and thought, *It's a travesty; Americans have it so good they always assume the best when they should assume the worst. The power of commie propaganda.*

In May 1942 and June 1945, the FBI interviewed Chambers, but took no action. Those interviews were impacted by the Director of the FBI who stressed the actual political orientation of the United States, which viewed the potential threat from the Soviet Union was minor compared to that of Nazi Germany. In November 1945, Elizabeth Bentley, formerly a member of Soviet Underground, also defected. Special Agents took her testimony, and she corroborated virtually all of Whittaker Chambers' story. It was only then that the FBI began to take Chambers' allegations seriously. The FBI had become serious about investigating Hiss, so Chambers played his trump card. He declared he had proof of Alger Hiss' spying.

The press called them the *Pumpkin Papers*. In a hollowed-out pumpkin on his property near Baltimore, Chambers had hidden microfilmed copies of the secret State Department documents Hiss had given him to photograph for the Soviet Union.

Why did he make copies? Were they insurance of some kind?

When we printed out those documents, it made a stack of paper four and a half feet high. The FBI had again been made to look like clowns on parade. Even the Keystone Kops were a better law enforcement organization when executing an investigation.

Coffey lifted one eyelid and saw the clock read 5:01. In fifteen minutes he would have to get into the shower in order to get to work on time. Thirty minutes more and he would be stuck in rush hour traffic for who knows how long.

He switched thought-gears from the old man to the grandson.

I'll call him to see if he's even interested.

After breakfast in the FBI Lab cafeteria, Coffey tried to call Dr. John Lindell but was unsuccessful. He tried to leave a voice message but immediately received a text message. *Unable to take your call. Am extremely busy. What do you need?*

Coffey was shocked at the immediate response when a loud bout of borborygmus hit him. There was nothing he could do but let his tummy play its rendition of belly bongos. His stomach was overfull, signaling he had overeaten again, an indicator of stress, but he ignored the rumbling in his abdomen and punched buttons as fast as a single finger could. *Would like to invite you to lunch at the FBI Lab in Quantico to look at some papers. I need some help.*

His stomach quieted down. Coffey jumped at the cellphone immediate response. *Give me a date and a time. I'll make time to help you.*

CHAPTER 3

August 5, 2004

The following day over breakfast in the cafeteria of the FBI Laboratory, Senior Special Agent in Charge Coffey laid out his concept of operations to Dr. John Lindell. As soon as they finished their meal, they moved to a conference room where they would not be disturbed.

Coffey handed the first document stack to Dr. Lindell, the same set of documents that had initially been translated as "...nothing more than bank statements and old internal Palestine Committee records." Not knowing what to expect, Dr. Lindell read the documents before making any notes. Coffey watched the man's expression go from impassioned, to concerned, to horrified.

Color drained from Dr. Lindell's face; he trembled a bit as he looked up at the FBI man. Dr. Lindell's speech had always been a few knots slower than the rat-a-tat-tat of Coffey's Virginian burr. When he could form words, Dr. Lindell whispered, "The title of this... is..., '*An Explanatory Memorandum*: On the General Strategic Goal for the Group in North America.'"

Coffey mashed his brows together. He was befuddled. "Ok.... So, what does that mean?"

In a voice just above a whisper, Dr. Lindell said, "Inside this folder is the Muslim Brotherhood's detailed strategic plan to defeat the United States. To infiltrate it. It's a blueprint for conquest."

Coffey raised his head and eyebrows to confirm, "They're not bank statements or old internal Palestine Committee records."

Dr. Lindell slowly shook his head. "No, sir. Copy one of ten. You were told these documents are bank statements and old internal Palestine Committee records?"

Coffey nodded.

"I would not trust whoever told you that. I'm just getting started, but I would say this is incredible. I've seen nothing like it. So, you apparently have more problems than this copy of the Muslim Brotherhood's strategic plan for destroying the United States."

Coffey nodded, then said, "I do. *We* do." *The CIA's working on a translation program, but that could be years away.*

"How can I help?"

Coffey could barely contain himself. "Would you be willing to do some consulting work? We'll pay you to translate and transcribe the documents we have."

Dr. Lindell asked, "*Eighty* boxes? That, I probably cannot do. I have a hard commitment next week; I can give you a week and the weekend and the old college try. For eighty boxes, I think I'll need a month and some help, but you probably don't want me to use your guys?"

"I do not. I'd like to keep this between us for the moment. What do you think could be in the rest of these boxes?"

"After just the first few papers, I suspect the documents you found are the archives of the Muslim Brotherhood."

Coffey liked the assessment. *Bingo!* It was rational and it made sense. It made him feel smugly correct.

Dr. Lindell smiled, "Doing these will be more exciting than what I was doing for free. It will be my pleasure."

They made a business deal with the shake of a hand. "As for some help, if you need some, I was going to see if I can get a woman from the CIA. I think she'd be a tremendous asset if she's available. I just have to figure out a way to bring her in without alerting our fearless leaders. With you, no one cares about a man who looks like he stepped out of an Indiana Jones movie. With her, we'll get no work done. Everyone will want to take a peek."

"A looker, huh?"

He rolled his eyes, smirked, and exhaled. "No, so *incredible* as to not be believed. Platinum green eyes. *Oh.* I'm sure sex with her is so off the charts the neighbors have cigarettes afterwards." Dr. Lindell chortled as Coffey continued with his little act by exhaling as if the breathtaking beauty had walked out of the room thus allowing him to breathe again.

Before Dr. Lindell got back to work, he accused Coffey of a heinous crime. "I want you to know, before this morning, I was a fairly diehard Democrat. I had little use for Republicans. I put up with them, especially the Conservatives during the *Pumpkin Dinners*, but I couldn't conceive of the world they live in. After seeing these documents, I'm having doubts. I didn't know things like this existed. Really existed, as in how evil exists in the world. I never really bought into what my grandfather did, and I gave the benefit of doubt to the Democrats. I believed their propaganda. Do you know what I mean?"

Coffey nodded. *Some can see the evil for what it is and choose to side with the truth. It's called being "red-pilled" and Dr. John Lindell admits he's there. Maybe he has been multi-dimensional red-pilled.* Coffey said, "I do. When you have the clearances and see the evil men can do to others, I don't know how honest men can be Democrats."

"There really are bad guys out there wanting to do harm to us."

"I think it was Secretary of State Henry Stimson who said, 'Gentlemen do not read each other's mail.' In those days, there was a prevailing attitude against spying, that we were all above that. It assumes the other gentleman is actually a gentleman."

Dr. Lindell nodded; he knew where Coffey's mind was going.

"It's like saying 'gentlemen don't need to lock their doors' when they live in a gated compound. Our worldview is Americans can think what they like, but we have to deal with the people who robbed their house." Coffey thought of his work in California and Europe, finding and trapping pedophiles before they had their way with children. "In ways you cannot imagine. The media won't cover their atrocities. The media is their propaganda arm."

"I'm thinking my political beliefs have been in error."

"You were subject to the propaganda. And your guys are the masters. And the media. Most people are unaware they are even being manipulated." Coffey smiled hard and reached out to shake Dr. Lindell's hand. "Like the keynote speaker at the last *Pumpkin Papers Irregulars Dinner* said, 'Welcome to the fight.' And, thank you again. Now let me get out of your hair so you can get back to work." Coffey cringed after he referred to Dr. Lindell's hair; the man had little. *I'm not fit to polish your head. I'm dispicable.*

For six days, Coffey met Dr. Lindell at the security gate outside of Quantico and escorted him inside the FBI compound. Every day Coffey got Dr. Lindell badged, walked him to the cafeteria for breakfast, and then to their Elbarasse Task Force secure conference room. Coffey unlocked a four-drawer combination safe and let Dr. Lindell work in peace until lunch, when they found a remote place in the cafeteria to eat if the cafeteria was open. At the end of each day, Dr. Lindell debriefed Coffey on his findings for the day.

On the last day of his contract Dr. Lindell was exhausted; he nearly stumbled out of the conference room on his way to lunch. Coffey was concerned and asked how he was doing.

"I'm fine and I'm not. This is depressing work. You can see evil at play. Some of those documents in those binders. I'm sorry, I couldn't finish those in the boxes. I gave some of them a cursory glance; not in depth. But most of that stuff is positively frightening."

"Like how?"

"It's not the work of a *madman*, like Kaczynski."

Coffey frowned. *Another FBI failure.*

Dr. Lindell continued, "They have a strategy and an agenda for destroying the United States, specifically our leadership. They have hundreds of plans to make Americans convert to Islam, to do the bidding of the Muslim Brotherhood for them. And not just by flooding the prisons with imams and converting the weak to Islam. The Muslim Brotherhood intends to co-opt the leadership of America. By using propaganda, they will trick them into believing a counterfactual understanding of Islam and the nature of the Muslim Brotherhood. This skewed understanding will coerce these leaders to force the Muslim Brotherhood narrative on their subordinates: that white men are evil, are white supremacists, and must be eliminated from the planet."

Like what they are doing to the FBI? They plan to use propaganda to get people to believe Islam? Use mass hypnosis. Isn't that what they are doing now? Holy crap! Coffey refrained from shaking his head to dismiss the poisonous thoughts. Coffey asked, "Such as, surveillance of mosques must cease so the good aggrieved Muslims will help the FBI in counterterrorist activities?"

Dr. Lindell nodded. "Exactly. Which if you think about it, is a psychological operation. There were other documents that looked like they were fascicles of the *Explanatory Memorandum*, like the undated binder entitled '*Phases of the World Underground Movement Plan.*' It specified the five phases of the Muslim Brotherhood movement in North America. Phase One is the discreet and secret establishment of leadership. Phase Two is the gradual appearance on the public scene and exercising and utilizing various public activities to establish a shadow government within the government."

Establish a shadow government within the government? Jackpot! Unconsciously Coffey crossed his arms. "Anything else?"

"Something so horrible I questioned my ability to transcribe Arabic. Analysis of several documents suggest they believed they could — my term is *brainwash* — they used a word I was unfamiliar with, but the context was clear. They were training children in a madrassa to assassinate presidents. In America, they assumed kids touring the White House wouldn't get patted down and wouldn't be suspected of carrying a bomb. This was written before September 11, 2001 when the security rules changed for everyone."

The extremists used children for a variety of things. Hamas did it to Israel. Kids had to to survive. "That's psycho. Anything else of note?"

Dr. Lindell sighed. "Several things. It looks like there was some significant correspondence between senior members of the Muslim Brotherhood and the entity I had never before heard of, the Islamic Underground. There are documents in here which show they have churches here in the U.S. On the outside they look like regular churches, but on the inside, they are clearly Islamic. I would have never thought that was possible, but it's all part of their plan. There are references of them in Chicago and Detroit. They've learned they can hold terrorist training with no FBI or law enforcement knowledge at a Saint James Boy Scout Camp in Michigan."

Coffey was trying to wrap his head around the news there are terrorist training camps in America using catholic boy scout camps as fronts. *Christian churches as Islamic centers. Incredible!*

Dr. Lindell had confirmed what Coffey thought, the infiltration of the FBI and America by al-Qaeda or the Muslim Brotherhood or the

Islamic Underground was total. There was nothing he could do except what he had already done: copy and scan the documents and get them accurately translated.

Dr. Lindell announced, "There are two more things, and then I really have to get going. There's a letter; it's a complaint from someone not identified that *the reckoning*, what we call 9/11, forced their hands. Muslim expansion in America came to a halt on September 11, 2001, and this group was perturbed with al-Qaeda for screwing up their plans. They have been waiting for the right person to execute their plan and strategy for a long time. Actually, they say 'They *are* waiting for *the one*.' Very curious phraseology. Makes you wonder if they have someone in training."

Coffey relaxed for a moment. "That's the problem with plans—you need someone to execute them." He looked at Dr. Lindell, studying the man. Dr. Lindell had something more to say. "But now they do? You think they do?"

He hesitated to nod. "It's not in the documents *specifically*, but I'm certain they do. What I have read and what I have seen in the papers and on the tube paints a picture. There are hints of evidence but maybe I'm reading too much into it."

What the hell is he talking about? Coffey waited for more information.

Dr. Lindell said, "There's more evidence. Not in your boxes of documents. Kind of like there's another safe with all the answers, or like the missing pieces are in a box at home. Maybe it's like algebra—when you have two known quantities, you solve for the unknown. Connect the dots. Anyway, a couple of days ago, I thought they had someone in mind, maybe someone they have been grooming; they would need a perfect fit. Then today I read they have been waiting for... *the one*...."

"John, what does that mean?" Coffey was puzzled.

"The *Explanatory Memorandum* was written in 1991 by a member of the Board of Directors for the Muslim Brotherhood in North America and a senior Hamas leader named Mohammed Akram. It was approved by the Brotherhood's *Shura* Council and Organizational Conference and was meant for internal review by the Muslim

Brotherhood's leadership in Egypt. It was not intended for public consumption, particularly in the targeted society of white Christian men in the United States. One of the documents from the safe indicates the Muslim Brotherhood was on the lookout for a candidate. In another set of documents someone offered up their candidates, but they were all dismissed by some unknown council."

"Because they already have a candidate?"

"Very good, Link. A very special candidate! They have been recruiting people and testing them and waiting a long time for the right ones to come along. Now they think they have a candidate for the President of the United States, and candidates for several positions they consider the top jobs in government, such as CIA Director. The most recent document I reviewed doesn't name the person they've been grooming for the CIA Director. They may already be running him as a spy."

"You mean like how your grandfather ran Alger Hiss when he was a communist? Do you know who this guy is?"

When grandfather was a communist. Today the Conservatives of the Republican Party celebrate him as a hero. For decades, Lindell hadn't been fond of a grandfather he didn't know and had been embarrassed about the things he did as a communist and as an anti-communist. There had always been something unseemly about his grandfather's life. Now he was seeing his grandfather in another light. *After defecting from the Communist Party of the U.S., when the KGB came for him and my grandmother and my mother to kill them, grandfather kept the family together and the assassins at bay. Off balance. That was when the authorities wouldn't protect him because they didn't believe him. I have been hard on him too, but I shouldn't have been so critical. I assumed the communists were peaceful. Just another philosophy. Just another political party. I believed the Democrat's line. Now I know they were lying. These documents have certainly opened my eyes to what was real. What is real.*

Dr. Lindell turned from that thought, smiled, and nodded. He remembered the question. He said, "Yes. There is correspondence some entity has funded his rise to prominence from afar. It suggests they want to see this senior intelligence officer who converted to Islam years ago lead the Central Intelligence Agency. It may be that he's actually working for them in some capacity to this day."

Coffey was awestruck. *Oh no. I know who he's talking about. Gaspar Rutchek. He famously said during his entry polygraph for the CIA he voted for the Communist Party USA leader Gus Hall when he ran for president, and he still got into the CIA. The FBI had set up wiretaps for Gus Hall and learned how the CPUSA were planning to infiltrate all of our institutions back in the 1960s and 1970s. If he converted to Islam under the pretext he could do greater undercover work for the Agency. Maybe he was doing undercover work for them. Another Robert Hanssen.*

Dr. Lindell kept remembering key items, pieces of intelligence which had fascinating stories behind them he had failed to include in his report. He felt they needed to be discussed. He said, "Link, this is wholly my personal assessment, my opinion only. I'm not a conspiracy theorist."

"You mean you don't believe in *chemtrails*. UFOs?"

"No. This is the observation you can't make any sense of immediately, pay attention to everything going on around you. It's like when the two rail lines were converging at Promontory, Utah in 1869. There were clouds of dust being kicked up from both sides as the railroad workers slowly came together. As the dust settled the workers saw a person standing over the spot where they would drive a nail to join the rails together. That job wasn't given to just anyone. A special person was selected to drive the last spike. It was an acknowledgement of the accomplishment of those special goals a few people worked to complete."

Coffey's brows narrowed. He was more bewildered than ever. He asked, "John, what is it you see?"

Dr. Lindell wrapped his arms around himself. The complex body language registered he really wasn't sure of his analysis. "The body of work strongly suggests they have a candidate they have been grooming for president. A non-governmental organization (NGO) has been providing all the funding, but there isn't a single piece of paper you can point to and say — he's the one they have been waiting for. There is no name."

"Shit!"

"So, Link, while I haven't seen a document, I think I know who it is! Enough time has passed since the *Explanatory Memorandum* was written. I think I could prove it if I had to. It can only be one person. If you look at the documents as a requirements document drafted by their elites and their politicians, I think it's the guy who was the recent speaker at the DNC Convention, Maxim Mohammed...."

"*Mazibuike*?"

"Yeah, I'm sure *that's their guy*. The Muslim Brotherhood's *keystone*, the one person who can make all their plans and dreams come true. If he was the president.... And he has all the credentials. At least the Muslim Brotherhood thinks he does."

Coffey said, "The guy with the Russian first name and Muslim middle name? I saw something that said he was a Christian."

"I checked; he isn't anything. Officially, he's unaffiliated. But the kicker is that after his speech, people starting looking into his business. Not the people who have been buying his autobiographies." Lindell held up two fingers.

"You mean, like the conservative media?" *Two autobiographies? Who writes two autobiographies? Didn't Adolf?* Suddenly he sussed Lindell was probably correct.

"Yes. I know I'm right. If you look at the Democrat's lineup, there really isn't anyone else. He fits their profile of the one who can secretly establish Muslim leadership and a shadow government within the government. And he's already doing Phase Two. They need a president, and not just any Muslim can be president."

Coffey tilted his head. He obviously wasn't keeping up.

"Only a Muslim who isn't a Muslim. Islamic green on the inside and red, white, and blue on the outside. He would have to have allegiance to the Muslim Brotherhood. His father would have to be a Muslim. Allegiance to Islam. That's how it works. Alger Hiss was Communist red on the inside and red, white, and blue on the outside."

Coffey took it all in. He asked meekly, "Phase Two is again?"

"Making appearances on the public scene. He burst onto the scene with a book and the keynote address, and he's already a state senator. There are now millions who want him to run for president. That is the most incredible case of *mass formation psychosis* I've ever witnessed."

Dr. Lindell nearly screamed, "He could be the one to take down America *if he were to become the president!* The night of the convention, the media emphasized he was a Christian, but I think they were taunting the Republicans like when they had some billionaire Arab offer funds to build an Islamic Center at the site of the collapsed Twin Towers. When they conquer someone or something, they erect a mosque at the site of the battle."

Coffey was excited, not in a good way. *Shit! Shit! Shit!* "You think this guy is the Muslim Brotherhood's wet dream?"

"I'm certain of it; *he's their guy,* although there's nothing in these archives that names their chosen candidate. Look at who it couldn't be, and then look at who is left standing. One guy. And if he were to become the president, *he* could do everything in the Muslim Brotherhood's strategic plan and the 'Phases document.' It's a strategic plan for conquest. *Link, he's the guy!* They have groomed him."

Coffey agreed and nodded.

Dr. Lindell continued, "It's as if there is another entity, someone pulling the strings. The marionette. Look at it this way, the Muslim Brotherhood has no understanding of what it takes to be a leader of a country. They do not understand how to be a president. There must be some other feeder entity. Like that group in Europe which screens politicians for all the European governments."

Coffey asked, "The *Ostgut Foundation?*"

"Yes, I'll bet it was the *Ostgut Foundation.* They paid for his education. Radicalized him. There is *no one* else like him in the Democrat Party. There is *no one* else like him on the planet. And they know it. And the *Ostgut Foundation* knows it. And they will protect him like he is...."

"*Damien Thorn?*"

Dr. Lindell mashed his lips in a conspiratorial smile and slowly nodded for effect. He snapped his fingers and pointed at the FBI man. "*Exactly.*" He explained, "You can only see this if you recognize and study patterns. The key to being a chess master is to recognize the patterns of the pieces being moved and devise a counterstrategy."

Coffey could see that Dr. Lindell had figured it out, and it all made sense. *Damned Ph.Ds!* "*Crap,* John. Ok. I believe you. I really believe you. I didn't watch this Mazibuike dude, but I read about him. I'm only tangentially aware of the *Ostgut Foundation*. I respect you and value your word and your analysis. So, for the moment, let's keep this tucked inside our body armor, ok? Let's refer to *him*, Mazibuike as…, um, Maxim Mohammed, um – *3M* from now on."

Dr. Lindell smiled an affirmative. He said, "There's more."

"More?"

"I've been on an emotional roller coaster since my first day."

Coffey was surprised by the admission.

Dr. Lindell nodded, inhaled, and looked toward the ceiling searching for answers to questions not yet asked. "The last box I looked at seemed to be a collection of pamphlets or technical manuals. I suspect they were at one time Army field manuals or maybe even Agency handbooks they adapted for their purposes. I would have worked on all of them if I had the time."

"What were they?"

"Well, I wish I had been able to spend more time on them; they were scary. One was a sixty-page handbook for Muslims living in the West. It was called *Safety and Security Guidelines for Lone Wolf Mujahedeen*; it provided methods and procedures to blend in with Westerners, to avoid looking like a Muslim. The first chapter outlined proven methods for *jihadis* to pretend to be Christians and stay below the radar of the law enforcement and intelligence services. Another chapter outlined how home-grown terrorists can plan for and carry out attacks, since they are less likely to be noticed. Nightclubs full of loud music and drunk people were noted as the perfect places to discuss terror plans without being recorded or spied upon. One chapter focused on how to conduct sabotage at American airports by infiltrating airport security. Another chapter showed how to conduct sabotage at American airports using drones."

Shit! The top secret 9-11 investigation detailed how the Muslim Brotherhood infiltrated airport security and got weapons aboard the four hijacked aircraft. Coffey was getting more disturbed by the second. He meekly inquired, "Using drones?"

"Yes, they provide explicit details on how to bring down a commercial jet by flying drones into the intakes during takeoff. I didn't know the technology was that advanced. I only see those things at the mall — but I haven't been to the mall lately...."

Coffey thought, *Oh my God.*

Dr. Lindell continued, "Another pamphlet referred to sheep and lambs. I initially dismissed that as stupid but I finally figured out those terms are how the *elites* looked at the general population. Very difficult reading — like political glossolalia — they have their own language, apparently. Anyway, my initial assumption was off...."

Coffey thought, *Political glossolalia? Seriously?*

"It was more like a user's manual on propaganda with odd references to things, like the top politicians were the earthly embodiment of 'gods.' One pamphlet that was especially frightening and I could not believe it was real was entitled '*Silent Weapons for Quiet Wars.*' It's about social engineering or the automation of society on a national or worldwide scale."

Coffey's eyes went full-on Marty Feldman. His head was about to burst. "*What?*"

"I think the genesis of this document and the others might have been from — you'll think I've lost my mind."

Too late! But Coffey said, "I won't. I know you're a serious man."

Dr. Lindell spoke like a drug mule going through a customs checkpoint. He leaned in closer to Coffey and in almost a whisper said, "I've actually heard about these, seen nothing like them in my studies. I didn't look at them all, but if I were you, I'd lock them up. From what I could see of the one. I think the originals may have been created at the; you'll think I'm unbalanced...."

Coffey assured Dr. Lindell he wouldn't.

"... at the Nazi's Ministry of Propaganda. But it's possible the Allies created these after the war. I know the Allies got control of all sorts of documents, like the Nazi's rocket program, their heavy water experiments for making atomic weapons, jet engines, medical experiments, and of course the Enigma machines. But if I were to hazard to guess, it looks like they also got into Hitler's and Goebbels' Ministry of Propaganda. It's mind control stuff."

Coffey was taken aback. "*Mind control?*"

Dr. Lindell couldn't stop. "Not just how to trick a Jew to get on a train to a death camp, but how to take over the world. Pass laws that strip people of their citizenship and then you can do whatever you want with them, for example. A how-to book using fear to turn people into sheep; specific words to use to induce *mass hypnosis*. It was…*incredible*. I distinctly remember this: '*This is the secret of propaganda: Those who are to be persuaded by it should be completely immersed in the ideas of the propaganda, without ever noticing that they are being immersed in it.*' Makes Orwell look like a piker."

Oh, my! Quoting Goebbels? Incredible! Coffey couldn't stifle a massive inhalation and said, "John, I knew you were the right guy. I *will* put those aside and I will lock them up. I appreciate all the work. Thank you. I'll make sure you get paid."

"Thank you." The men shook hands one last time.

"Justice has been screaming for your report. They will try Elbarasse and Abu Marzook." He sighed, ran fingers through old fighter pilot hair, and said, "Now, I just have to figure out what the hell all this 3M BS means."

As Dr. John Lindell left the building, Coffey reflected on how much the man had helped him. He had enough counterterrorism work to do for months. Back in his office he slid into his office chair and reflected: *The Muslim Brotherhood. Goebbels quotes and propaganda…. Mass formation psychosis. Don't both parties do propaganda? I need to do more research. Now, where can I find Silent Weapons for Quiet Wars?*

CHAPTER 4

October 24, 2019

I Know You're Out There Somewhere blasted from the speakers in his helmet. Duncan Hunter was on a southernly heading and passed over several ships in the Mediterranean. No one on the deck of the freighters looked up. No one heard or saw the aircraft he was piloting. No one could. It was impossible unless he ran into them.

If the ancient black aircraft were a car, the *Yo-Yo*, as it was affectionally called by the U.S. Army personnel who flew it and maintained it in Vietnam, it would be declared a *resto-mod*. A lot of work had been done to make it quieter, to make it invisible, to make it more effective, to make it deadlier. When the eleven 57-foot wingspan prototypes rolled off the assembly line in 1969 all they had was a night vision sensor and a periscope to see what was going on beneath them. Fifty years after it was stricken from the inventory and declared obsolete, it now had an 80-foot wingspan and was still the quietest powered airplane ever built. But now it had sensors and lasers, a gun, and a coating that was one of the darkest substances known to man; the armamentarium to do battle with the worst terrorists of the world and defeat them.

As the African coastline appeared on horizon on the nose of the YO-3A, *Maverick* reflected on the noticeable shift in his duties. *The Moody Blues* were no help; their songs just kept him alert during the nighttime transit between continents. This was the latest in a series of pop-up missions requested by the CIA Director and approved by the President. *Maverick* had been all over the Muslim world and Africa. It was almost too much for him, but he could never say no to either the President or the CIA Director or his wife, the Director of the National Counterterrorism Center (NCTC). Their desires were his desires, so there really wasn't an issue. However, the president's term was winding down; in a year the man would be gone, and the special access program would end. *No more aerial eradication.*

There had been beaucoup changes over the last year. For over twenty years, Hunter, call sign *Maverick*, had hunted down and eliminated the world's worst terrorists in the Middle East, South America, Africa. Single shots, one terrorist at a time. A new mission every few months. Over the years, *Maverick* had stalked lions, tigers, and bears, but found terrorists were the most difficult prey. Terrorists were aggressive, indiscriminate murderers, targeting mostly civilians, but sometimes political figures. Some killed for money; some killed for ideology, but most of them killed for power. Over 200 of them had died with football-sized exit wounds in their backs. But none were in Egypt or Libya. Too much illumination to work over Egypt, too dangerous to work over Libya.

Maverick used specific intelligence gathered and analyzed by the intelligence community in America and Europe to intercept transnational gangs and groups of international terrorists. These terrorists were hellbent on killing innocents to create chaos and achieve power or on kidnapping girls for the sex trade.

He wasn't home much, for there was work to do. *Radical Islam at work. Not anything you'd find on the five o'clock news.* There was strength in numbers for the criminals. This meant it was imperative for Hunter to find the head terrorist of whatever organization he was stalking. Terrorist leaders were always surrounded by personal security details. Some security details had been fifty-man strong. Gaddafi's personal protection detail had been in the hundreds. After Gaddafi was killed by the Muslim Brotherhood in 2011, going into Libya became a low priority; it no longer mattered.

So, except for Libya and Egypt, he killed terrorists where he found them, and he killed them all. From as few as one to as many fifty-armed bandits. The escalation in requirements made it even more dangerous work, but it also proved to be twice as lucrative.

Having the ability to disable large groups of terrorists to the point of mass incapacitation and then kill them individually was a tremendous and inimitable capability. He left few traces of American or CIA responsibility or of even being in the area. The advantage of surprise rested with the special airplane, its special sensors and weapons, and its special pilot.

This mission was in Algeria. Algeria's national oil and natural gas company, Sonatrach, had dominated the country's hydrocarbon sector for decades. The American oil giant, ExxonMobil, had recently negotiated an agreement to develop the shale gas fields in the Ahnet Basin in southwestern Algeria using the American's special horizontal drilling and fracking technology to extract tens of thousands of barrels of oil every week. But bringing new technology into the oil fields would eventually invite the Luddites of Islam: the *Groupe Islamique Armé* (GIA) or the Armed Islamic Group of Algeria, acolytes of the Muslim Brotherhood in North Africa and one of the principal Islamist groups that had been trying to overthrow the Algerian government for years. Their primary goal was to force the Algerian government to reject or resist any technological help from the United States.

Tonight, like the previous week in Mali and the week before in Somalia, the *Yo-Yo* would find, close with, and destroy armed men from the Muslim Brotherhood or the Islamic Underground and thus save Allies' and American lives. *Maverick* would verify the Agency's intelligence that the men on the ground were *unfriendlies*, intent on murder and mayhem with weapons of war. That they were without uniforms designated they were transnational criminals, or religiously motivated terrorists, or mass murderers out for a good time. He'd deploy the lasers to blind them all. While they were rolling around on the ground or running into each other like cartoon characters, he would use the aircraft's gun to kill them — the counterterrorism equivalent of culling the herd — until his ammunition ran out. Like he had done for years.

Maverick had sixty of the experimental laser-guided *Terminator* rounds. He would use them all to stop the foot soldiers of the Muslim Brotherhood affiliate from overrunning the ExxonMobil compound. It would be an ugly job, but only he could to do it.

Within an hour of being overhead on station, five vehicles approached the oil production compound and drilling rigs from the east. *Maverick* flew out to meet them. He deployed the Terminator Sniper System (TS2), the forward looking infrared (FLIR), an infrared

(IR) laser designator (LD), and the *Weedbusters* laser system out from under the airplane.

The clarity of the FLIR imagery in his state-of-the-art visor was spectacular, approaching photograph-quality. There wasn't a uniform on any of the men, but they all carried AK-47s, the terrorist weapon of choice. The imagery was being recorded and comported with the intelligence received, which meant that whatever Muslim Brotherhood affiliation this band of terrorists belonged to, it would not matter. They were going to die.

When *Maverick* went into attack mode, he put the LD on the radiator of the lead truck and fired an IR-guided round into the vehicle's engine block, instantly disabling the truck. The supersonic crack of the bullet striking the metal within the engine compartment startled the terrorists, confusing the driver and the leader of the group.

As the vehicles stopped in a line to see what had happened to the lead truck, *Maverick* rammed the throttle of the YO-3A to takeoff power for two seconds and then returned it to its minimum power setting. A low growl startled the men on the ground. They looked at each other, and then they looked up.

When all eyes were scanning the skies for a clue what generated the indistinguishable noise, *Maverick* fired off the *Weedbusters* system saturating the eyes of the men with ultraviolet radiation, searing the optic nerve and blinding them instantly. As the terrorists writhed on the ground or in the back of the trucks clutching their damaged eyes, *Maverick* systematically targeted each man, laser designating the sternum and firing the TS2 which launched the experimental laser-guided bullet into his chest.

When all the men were dead and there was no more activity on the road, *Maverick* climbed and circled the killing zone using the FLIR to ensure there would be no attack on the drilling compound that night, there were no reinforcements and no one had escaped. He targeted where he knew the fuel tanks of two of the vehicles were. Laser-guided bullets tore through the metal yielding the thermal signature of a spreading pool of fuel onto the ground.

From a nylon helmet bag beside his seat, *Maverick* withdrew two devices used to start fires. *Maverick* engaged the autopilot and the altitude hold feature, set the timers for each device, paralleled the road where the vehicles had stopped, opened an access door in the cockpit, and threw the *Firestarters* out into the airstream, hoping they would land close enough to the trucks to create a fire.

He climbed slightly then paralleled the road used by the terrorist group to see if he could locate the point from where they staged their attack. In the mirrors mounted along his canopy bow, he watched the terrorists' vehicles erupt in fire behind him.

Covering three miles every minute, he found a likely location where there were similar vehicles in what was essentially an abandoned town of decrepit structures. *Maverick* selected a combination of switches to deploy the thermal imager, lasers and TS2, and then went hunting for men with AK-47s. He killed twenty more terrorists without having to blind them using *Weedbusters*. He dropped more *Firestarters* onto the structures, eventually setting the town ablaze. Satisfied his mission was complete, he retracted the sensors and the TS2 into the airframe and turned north to return to Spain.

CHAPTER 5

October 30, 2019

Rho Schwartz Scorpii was rarely seen out of the hotel, but today had been special. The weather had permitted him to be driven by one of his long-time bodyguards to the Cologne Bonn Airport Executive Terminal to take delivery of the organizations newest corporate jet. Although the temperature was cold, there were no clouds to interrupt Gulfstream Aerospace's delivery ceremony. With the chill, it would have been wise to have the beige convertible top up on the 540K, but Scorpii insisted on having the top down. Roadsters were supposed to be driven without tops. Rudolf Blohm, the security man and driver, complied with the directive; however, he overrode the billionaire's assertion he was warm enough. Against Scorpii's protestations, Blohm quietly bundled up his passenger with several additional blankets. A mile from the hotel, Scorpii was thankful for Blohm's insistence. The car's inadequate heater was augmented by layers of thick wool blankets, but he would never admit he might have been wrong.

The driver of the Mercedes 540K used electronic keys to access the airport security gate as well as the security system installed at the airport's largest private hangar. The new jet had been parked outside of its hangar and had been prepared for delivery with a wash, a buff, and a freshening of the interior.

The Gulfstream G-900 had a 9,000-mile range, by far the longest in the class of aircraft, and had made the transoceanic trip from Savannah, Georgia in record time. Gulfstream's newest jet was the latest and most spectacular corporate aircraft coming to market for the billionaire class. There had been a bidding war for the one-of-a-kind business jet, but American rap stars couldn't compete with a billionaire with hundreds of millions of euros and dollars of disposable income. All eyes were on the G-900 sitting in front of the hangar. It was painted a brilliant white polyurethane with a red stripe. Reports of it selling for over $100 million were true. During the intimate ceremony, Scorpii sat in a wheelchair and covered with a blanket, his gaze drifted on a trio of low-slung vehicles under individual form-fitted car covers at the far corner of the hangar. He tried to remember if there was supposed to be three cars or two. Suddenly he couldn't even remember what was under the car covers.

The acceptance ceremony concluded when the Gulfstream CEO simulated handing the new aircraft's logbooks and keys to Scorpii before handing them to his driver-bodyguard. Blohm transferred the hardware and trinkets from Gulfstream Aerospace to the Mercedes' rumble seat. The Gulfstream crew towed the G-900 inside the hangar under the watchful eye of Scorpii. Once everyone had left the inside of the hangar, Blohm closed and locked the doors.

After returning to the hotel with the top up on the old car, Europe's wealthiest man was helped out of the burgundy 1937 Mercedes-Benz 540K Special Roadster by the driver, who ran around to the passenger's side of the vehicle, with the hotel's concierge. The old man struggled and had difficulty breathing, but after disembarking the iconic two-seater, he took two small shuffles and turned to admire the coachwork of the car as he always did. It was perfection on wheels. The sweeping fenders looked like they had been copied from Michelangelo's notebooks on form and grace.

The burgundy was by far his favorite. The hotel owned and maintained three other 540Ks — a red, a black, and a silver, all with contrasting leathers — for some of the special visitors who stayed at the hotel or had meetings with the Supreme Lord Chancellor, Rho Schwartz Scorpii. Being chauffeured in the two-seat roadster was the benefit of staying at the hotel, especially as many of the remaining 540Ks had been relegated to museums. One of the hotel's latest acquisitions — a silver 540K with dark blue leather — had set a sales record at an auction in America selling for nearly $10 million including buyer's premium. The other car purchased by the hotel and now hiding under a car cover in the aircraft hangar was an electric vehicle, a new, one-of-a-kind concept Mercedes-AMG GT R Pro Gullwing.

Rudolf Blohm helped Scorpii to his room to nap until the doctor arrived for the daily evaluation of the old man.

•　　•　　•

The group of women were waiting in the antechamber of the hotel's executive suite. The women were well-dressed for the occasion; they expected to have an audience with the head of the European Federation. A tall, immaculately attired man left the suite wordlessly, passed between two over-muscled men who were more internal security than house detectives, and entered the executive suite conference room.

The Chancellor didn't like to interface with women, so the Executive Director of Foreign Intelligence, High Captain Maalik El Masri would receive the report, distill the report, and then relay the report to the Chancellor. El Masri was shockingly thin and had lips like a woman, but he was a good-looking man for his age, which was somewhere north of sixty.

Maalik El Masri had been educated in Cairo at the Egyptian Special Operations Academy and Sophisticated *Thunderbolt* Course. He had moved up the ranks to be considered for promotion to intelligence officer for service in the intelligence branch. When he was being given a polygraph for the top-secret clearance required to work in the intelligence branch, in an unguarded moment, he had mentioned that, "…he could see the viewpoint of the Muslim Brotherhood."

The Muslim Brotherhood was viewed as the sworn enemy of Egypt's ruling class. The comment was traitorous; he was immediately suspected of being a spy trying to infiltrate the Egyptian intelligence service. He was summarily dismissed from the *Thunderbolts*, banished from Special Operations, and told, "You have offended Allah." Before an elite group of assassins from the *Thunderbolts* could organize a search and destroy mission to ambush him, El Masri ran. He escaped with his life, found his way to Germany via an Islamic Underground railroad, and took up shelter in one of the men's clubs in Berlin. There he met his savior and benefactor, Rho Schwartz Scorpii. That had been decades ago.

The security men also had decades of experience protecting Scorpii.

El Masri would do anything for *his* Chancellor. Meeting with Scorpii daily, El Masri was given the position of Executive Director of Foreign Intelligence. He spent a great deal of time welcoming the men and women, Muslim or non-Muslim, homosexuals and lesbians who had been purged from NATO and America's intelligence agencies and their Federal Bureau of Investigation. He may have found NATO's and America's rejects odd, but they were experienced.

Nearly every other day, El Masri deposited a dozen compact discs of surveillance videos of NATO officers on a shelf in the Lord Chancellor's vault. He logged the new videos, the Lord Chancellor and El Masri still referred to them as *tapes*, affixing colored markings on each tape for quick reference. When he was done with his chores, he closed the vault door.

El Masri's prime directive was to deliver *Die Lage, The Situation* to the Lord Chancellor daily. *Die Lage* was the daily summary of high-level, all-source information and analysis on international intelligence and political issues captured, collated, and produced for the Supreme Lord Chancellor. El Masri also functioned as the Chancellor's emissary for official and unofficial matters, especially with international clients seeking sensitive, delicate, and secret meetings. It was perfect cover for the Executive Director of Foreign Intelligence whose power was growing every day.

El Masri also met with activist groups from around the world who came begging for money and approval of their plans. The exception was the American women. They came for money and plans for revenge. El Masri signaled the women to enter. The ladies jostled each other to be first to shake his hand. They ignored the security men, for they might have been with the organization for decades, they were the lowliest on the status totem pole.

The security men had seen all types of people come and go in the twenty years they had been guarding the Supreme Lord Chancellor. They reciprocated the indifference of the women, for they weren't the least interested in them. The security men made eye contact with each other. They didn't comment, didn't react, didn't judge. They were the muscle of the facility, if muscle was ever needed to protect a discriminating clientele or the greatest liberal philanthropist to emerge from the war.

The women were more aware of the hotel furnishings than the hotel security. They raved over the amenities of the Althoff Grandhotel Schloss Bensberg; everything about the suites at the Bensberg was Lucullan. The three women, lesbians sexually, lawyers professionally, were in Germany to deliver their report.

Without a lengthy preamble or the slightest hint of an accent, El Masri welcomed the women to Bensberg then came to the point. "What is the status of the racial and anarchists' organizations?"

The spokeswoman took a deep breath, "There are two prominent groups that operate in tandem and are run by dedicated Marxists who seek to destroy America — its governments, its houses of worship, its monuments to historic figures, and its flag and national anthem. They are on track to double in size in a year, just in time for the election."

"That is good. The economy?"

"We are ahead of schedule in disabling free enterprise. The weekly supplies of petroleum are trending negative. Sabotage and regulation are suppressing exploration and pipeline building which is preventing growth in those areas of the economy. We've followed your guidance of renaming solar and wind energy resources as renewables."

"That is good. Education?"

The woman didn't look up from her notes. "Our agents are replacing the standard pedagogy in schools with Marxist ideals, what we are calling Critical Race Theory in the United States. We are definitely ahead of expectations. This strategy will breed generations of Marxist revolutionaries for decades to come. White America doesn't look to prevent an overthrow of their local school boards and governments. They are not engaged; the suppression is working. We are making titanic strides."

"Very good. Very good. Local politics?"

"Today, we have reports of looting and burning of businesses, government buildings, and churches in twenty states with plans for another four. Robbery, assault, and murder are trending positive. Your funding of Democrat district attorneys, mayors, and governors across the nation is having the desired effect. We progressives have zeroed in on electing prosecutors as an avenue for criminal justice reform, and your foundation is providing the funds."

"We must quietly overhaul the U.S. justice system."

The woman continued, "Marxist Democrats are winning elections, controlling cities, counties, and states. They are aiding the destruction by removing all obstacles to violence. As planned."

"That is very good. Police?"

"With your guidance and funding, prosecutors are denying police the means to stop rioting, looting, arson, assault, and murder. If these people are arrested, they are released without bond or charge."

"Without charge? That is fantastic!"

"Yes, we are advancing one of the progressive movement's core goals—reshaping the American justice system. Democrat attorneys general and state prosecutors can limit the charges brought against violent felons, so they avoid execution and long prison sentences. Felons are back on the streets in no time, definitely years before ordinary sentences. Your funding of district attorneys and prosecutors who refuse to prosecute felons in the face of withering criticism of the locals has had a major effect."

"That is good. Very good. What about the courts?"

"Your generous investments are paying off in ways we couldn't imagine just a few years ago. Today there is virtually no protection of the public or justice for crime victims. We have activist groups protesting judges at their homes; judges are retiring in record numbers. All efforts to undermine the criminal justice system are progressing well. If I might add, we learned much from advocating against the American Psychiatric Association and inducing them to change their despicable DSM." (*Diagnostic and Statistical Manual of Mental Disorders*).

"I'm familiar. This is good to hear. Any feedback on our methods?"

The woman finally smiled. It wasn't a pleasant smile. "What we can say is the propaganda has been effective. Successes beyond our imaginations. Before we applied the silent tools, our successes were uneven or nonexistent. With a little bit of social justice *juice*, we have seen voting majorities, many of whom mistakenly think social justice means fair treatment. They have spearheaded efforts for criminal justice reform. Those they elected, as you predicted, have condemned the United States, the Constitution, and the criminal justice system. We have turned them onto their own tails. It's as if our dreams have come true."

"Very good. Funding?"

"We thank you for your most generous donations. Your direction has been on target. We have financed dozens of these tertiary-level politicians. The Justice and Public Safety PAC has been very effective, as were some non-profits. Your funding of American Psychiatric Association protests will ensure more mental disorders are removed from the DSM. We know you want to render that document obsolete."

"Success brings more funding."

"With your help, our pilot program of investing $1 million per state to elect prosecutors and district attorneys who are committed to avoiding prosecution of criminals has paid off in Virginia, California, Maryland, New Jersey, Connecticut, North Carolina, Illinois, and Michigan. They are no longer prosecuting prostitution, public camping, public urination, and other quality-of-life crimes, exacerbating lewd and lascivious behavior, drug abuse, trespass, theft, and unsanitary conditions throughout the cities."

"Very good. Do you have examples? The Chancellor loves to hear success stories."

"We now have prosecutors in California who seek to change the charges for having personal relations with minors from a felony to a misdemeanor. It's the first step. In another area, these states changed the law and now won't prosecute any theft of property of less than one thousand dollars U.S. We have disadvantaged people stealing necessities in broad daylight with no police response. Those investments are very fruitful in Marxist Democrat leaning states and the large cities, regardless of overall political affiliation. A prosecutor we funded in Detroit refused to prosecute a worker who staged what the Americans call a hate crime. We view it as a success story, but we wish she would do more."

"What has she done?"

"Well, she has dropped only 30 percent of all felony charges, including those for murder. We could have seen 100,000 accused individuals go free, but she only dropped charges on 25,000."

El Masri filled his lungs, smiled and said, "Work on her. She needs more encouragement. The wind is at our back; we are reaching the tipping point. We cannot allow the restoration of law and order in America. To do so would allow America's silent majority to become vocal again, and they would vote out those responsible for the emasculation of the police and the support of Marxist revolutionaries. I will report your successes and request for additional funding to the Chancellor. We will be back to you soon. In the meantime, enjoy the furnishings of this grand hotel. You must check out the spa. It's to die for, quite remarkable."

·   ·   ·

The physician's report was delivered to El Masri as the women left. After reading the physician's diagnosis and completing his synopsis of *Die Lage* for the Supreme Lord Chancellor of the European Federation, the impeccably dressed El Masri snapped polished heels at the foot of the conference table and left the meeting room.

The doctor's report was foremost on his mind; it was devastating. The Lord Chancellor was living on borrowed time. Morphine was to be administered to control his pain. This was news that had to be controlled and suppressed. The Lord Chancellor's personal security team would have to dispense the medication every few hours. El Masri could trust no one else with such information. Knowing the path of the future and what must be done, El Masri would do whatever was possible to make his mentor comfortable. He waited for his next assignment not knowing if it would be his last.

He didn't have to wait long. Scorpii's suit didn't fit... *properly*. It was a typically over-engineered German business suit that would have made a Savile Row tailor blush; it was so intricate. The Supreme Lord Chancellor was nearing eighty and had been steadily losing weight, so the tailor's latest effort didn't fit as it should. It would have a few days ago. Now, it simply hung on him. It must be made to fit him much better.

Scorpii waved away the team of tailors and received the High Captain alone. El Masri quickly read the summation of the situation in America. The ancient man nodded uncontrollably. El Masri didn't know if the almost 80-year-old Supreme Lord Chancellor was agreeing with the intelligence analyses, if he was experiencing minor tremors, or both. The daily intelligence brief was complete. The conversation moved from intelligence to politics.

The High Captain El Masri, a distant relative of the Muslim Brotherhood's founder, Hassan al-Banna, could barely hear the Supreme Lord Chancellor. *"Das Amerikaner?"*

"Herr McGee, mein Kanzler?"

"Ja...."

El Masri explained the intelligence analysis, "They believe the Director of the *Cee ah a* will seek the presidency. If he does, he will announce soon. He will have the backing of the president, his party, and his race." His words had a slippery butyraceous consistency that were incongruous of his military demeanor.

"Chancen?"

El Masri replied, "For *das Amerikaners*, McGee is the perfect political candidate — there is no question he will defeat all competitors. Our informants are concerned. Their political intelligence is true and accurate... and when *das Amerikaner Cee ah a* Director formally announces his candidacy as we expect, he will be a formidable candidate. He will win, barring unknown external factors, such as interference, opposition research, and political headwinds. He's under close surveillance."

Scorpii said, "He was responsible for the death of our friend, General Roustaie."

"Jawohl, mein Kanzler!" El Masri reflected on the general's annual visit of the Lord Chancellor. He had been the leader of the IRCC until *das Amerikaners* killed Roustaie in Iraq. Obliterated him with a missile. Reportedly, there wasn't enough left of Roustaie to fill a shoebox. Roustaie had been the real brains behind aviation terrorism in the United States starting in the 1980s. He saw the potential of commercial

airliners being perfect traps; each one a long tubular prison cell where hostages couldn't escape. El Masri thought, *That man had such vision!* The greatest aviation achievement was the creation of the Anglo-French *Concorde*. And unquestionably General Roustaie's greatest spectacular was planting a bomb on an Air France *Concorde* and blaming an American jet for its crash.

"*Die Frau?*" Scorpii asked again, "*Die Frau?*"

El Masri recovered from his reverie. He knew "the woman." He quickly said, "*Mein Kanzler*, you expected she would be named his replacement. It's their way. She's under close surveillance but there is much we do not know. We believed we knew where her residence was but there is only a young woman living there now. We do not know where she sleeps; we have tried to find her residence."

Scorpii continued to nod, then sat up straight. After several seconds of catching his breath, he stood up. He held on to the edge of the table for support, then shuffled to the picture window. The morphine dulled the pain but also dulled his senses.

El Masri followed Scorpii to the window, hoping the old man wouldn't stumble or collapse.

Rho Schwartz Scorpii, the Supreme Lord Chancellor of the European Federation of socialist and communist nations committed to the destruction of capitalist nations everywhere braced himself. His chest heaved as he struggled for oxygen. He was about to say something; he took his time. Something had energized him; he appeared to be stronger than when he had first risen from the chair. He turned and said, "*Der neger muss gestoppt warden.*"

With a heavy Berlin accent, Scorpii continued, "*Der neger* tried tricks to find me. He cannot be allowed to take that post. Continue all efforts to… surveil him. We have the assets in the country. If we need to move those assets, move them…." He took a few breaths and turned back toward the window; then he said, "Stop him. Do not fail me." Once the ugly directive had been uttered, Scorpii turned back toward El Masri and said, "I want a brief on *die Frau*. I sense *die hündin* isn't who she pretends to be. I sense *die hündin* requires closer surveillance. *Die hündin* cannot be allowed to take that post when *der neger* vacates."

The bitch? El Masri was surprised when the Supreme Lord Chancellor switched languages and swore. He had been through so much, but rarely let anything bother him. *The CIA tried to find him, find us.... The lawyer took the bait, but found the antenna in the watch box, the latest addition to the Chancellor's collection of watches of the famous. Did the Amerikaners actually think the watch gambit would work? It wasn't clever, very clumsy.*

The Supreme Lord Chancellor was correct; *the CIA executives must be stopped. They must be eliminated. We will stop McGee. We have stopped the others. And we will update the information in the woman's exiguous file.* High Captain El Masri snapped his heels; "*Jawohl, mein Kanzler!*"

Supreme Lord Chancellor Scorpii waved the younger man away. As El Masri departed, the next group of officers of the European Federation took their positions at the table. Scorpii left the window and wearily returned to his seat. No one spoke until he was in position. With a nod, the Bensberg Conference Director handed out a list of attendees of the upcoming annual Bensberg meeting between the communist and socialist leaders of Europe and North America.

Scorpii reviewed the list and said nothing. The pain was returning....

The group's unstated agenda was bringing down the United States of America and Israel, by destroying their free market Western capitalism and its legal and intelligence systems. The group's stated goal was to ensure chief executive officers of U.S. industries would be protected under a one-world government.

Scorpii raised a finger and the Bensberg Conference Director began his spiel. "Besides the world's top 300 billionaires, we have political leaders from thirty countries, Islamic leaders from Africa and the Middle East, and Marxist and Communist leaders. This year we told the managers at the airport to expect 1,000 aircraft."

"*Das ist gut. Sehr gut. Sehr gut.*" Supreme Lord Chancellor Scorpii congratulated the man and dismissed them all with a wave of his trembling hand.

They were running early. He had one more meeting. El Masri escorted the Secretary General of the North Atlantic Treaty Organization (NATO) to the Supreme Lord Chancellor's office. Except for his personal attorney, the Secretary General would be the last official visitor for the day.

As the Supreme Lord Chancellor was meeting with the Secretary General of NATO, El Masri sat in the outer chamber. He recalled it had been about eighteen months ago that *Herr* Scorpii's private attorney had bid on a rare wrist watch for Scorpii. El Masri thought the attorney was something of a popinjay. But he had learned to give the men Scorpii handpicked for special projects and activities a wide berth, for they possessed power he didn't have.

When the attorney visited, he was always in a fresh pressed Saville Row double-breasted suit, Gianni Versace tie, and Crockett & Jones handmade shoes. He and *Herr* Scorpii always compared notes about their attire. Scorpii's clothes seemed to shrink, while the attorney's needed to be let out. The men would laugh — it was the only time El Masri had seen the Supreme Lord Chancellor laugh — about the style and fit of their suits.

The attorney had brought the rare Autavia *Jochen Rindt*. As Scorpii had fondled the timepiece, the attorney remarked the CIA had tried to track him with the watch box. Scorpii laughed heartily when the attorney said he had disposed of the counterfeit box in the Chunnel.

The attorney had also brought several gold timepieces that escaped the melting furnaces of the German extermination camps. The Jews had valued their pocket watches more than their lives as they were marched to the gas chambers. They were the finest examples of originally Jewish-owned timepieces to have survived.

After bidding the Secretary General of NATO "Auf wiedersehen," Scorpii rang for his security team. The pain was increasing. One of the men dispensed a few drops of the liquid morphine. Grateful the relief was nearly instantaneous, Scorpii dismissed the men without thanking them. Dealing with the pain tired him. Scorpii was exhausted, but he had things to reflect on before he forgot them. He withdrew a black leather-bound journal from the desk's center drawer and wrote down the day's events. He knew he had to hurry. He wanted to sleep before the pain returned.

CHAPTER 6

October 31, 2019

Lovely, statuesque, complete with a husky voice and a British accent, Director of Operations (DO), Nazy Cunningham, concluded the special edition of the President's Daily Brief (PDB); for the *President's Eyes Only*.

Before returning the *Disposition Matrix* to the DO, the President of the United States scanned the list of terrorists one last time.

Mohammed Ali Hammadi 1985 TWA 847
Ahmad Khalid Saleh Hashash 1988 PanAm 103 Bombmaker
Ahmed Jibril 1988 PanAm 103 Planner
Ibrahim Salih Mohammed Al-Yacoub 1996 Khobar Towers
Abdullah Ahmed Abdullah 1998 Embassies, Tanzania, Kenya

Nazy Cunningham said, "It's been two years, Mr. President. Al Jazeera and the Revolutionary Iranian Guard Corps (IRGC) have finally confirmed what we have suspected. We have removed four men from the *Matrix*. Now there is one." She handed the President an updated *Matrix* with a single entry:

Ahmad Khalid Saleh Hashash 1988 PanAm 103 Bombmaker

Javier Hernandez, the President of the United States accepted the document. *Now just Hashash…. Two years to get confirmation! That was a long time coming.*

CIA Director Bill McGee said, "Two and a half years ago, General Mostafa Javad Roustaie, the leader of the IRGC was at the top of the list…."

"… and was removed by *Noble Savage*," said President Hernandez.

McGee said, "Instant confirmation by our Chief of Station in Baghdad."

Nazy nodded and continued, "After General Roustaie was removed from the battlefield, these other men moved to the top of the FBI's Most Wanted Terrorist list. Now there is only one."

President Hernandez looked up. A modicum of pleasure registered on his face. "Remind me, General Roustaie's crime...."

Bill McGee said, "Mr. President, Roustaie helped plan the 1983 Hezbollah operation that killed 241 Marines in Beirut."

President Hernandez intoned, "That's right. Please continue, Nazy."

Nazy said, "Mr. President, regarding Hashash, we have heard nothing on him in many years."

The President nodded and asked, "What is your confirmation on these other terrorists on the *Matrix*?"

Director McGee's eyes glanced over to Nazy Cunningham. He said, "Mr. President, triple confirmation. A defector and an Al Jazeera announcement with photographs authenticated their demise. Their burial was aired on Iran's Bushehr TV and translated by MEMRI, the Middle East Media Research Institute."

The President nodded and said, "Thank you, Director McGee. Nazy. A couple more questions."

"Of course, Mr. President."

"Dr. Ashraf?"

Miss Cunningham said, "Mr. President, Dr. Ashraf is at a safe house in the Appalachians. He has not yet been debriefed, but he will be soon." Mahmoud Ashraf, a senior intelligence officer of the Central Intelligence Agency, had been sent to Iran before the turn of the century as a faux defector to sow disinformation about a powerful Islamic Revolutionary Guard Corps officer. He had been missing for over fifteen years until he contacted a covert CIA operations officer in Teheran and requested an extraction. Duncan Hunter, the master at extracting defectors, was dispatched and flew into Iran.

Satisfied, the President said, "Algeria. *Noble Savage*." It was more a question than a statement.

McGee pivoted his massive head to see what Nazy would say.

"Mr. President, the *Noble Savage* asset prevented the Armed Islamic Group of Algeria — the GIA — one of the more violent acolytes of the Muslim Brotherhood in North Africa, from penetrating the ExxonMobil compound and the Algerian drilling sites. There were no American casualties, and there was no damage to Sonatrach's facilities and pipelines."

"Other casualties?"

Nazy said, "Mr. President, there were no casualties; the raiding party and their base camp were neutralized."

Director McGee said, "And, consumed by fire. At one-tenth the cost of a *Hellfire*."

President Hernandez nodded, palmed his knees, and turned to McGee. With a grin he said, "Bill, send Exxon and the Algerians the bill." With a smile he asked, "Iranian's National Biosafety Laboratory?"

Bill McGee said, "We have confirmation it and the Ayatollah Khomeini Institute of Virology were destroyed, Mr. President. Also consumed by fire. We found Rho Schwartz Scorpii's picture at the top of their board of directors' organizational chart. We suspect he had been funding gain-of-function research there, trying to turn a simple virus into a lethal coronavirus."

Nazy said, "Our initial assessment was that the Khomeini Institute's biological weapons activities included population-specific research on germ weapons capable of attacking ethnic groups."

"But you have updated your assessment?"

Nazy said, "Better analysis, Mr. President. We reinterviewed several of the women who were rescued from the institute. Those interviews suggest the Iranians and Chinese were conducting biological experiments on ethnic minorities. In consultation with the experts at our bioweapons laboratories at Dahlgren, their efforts could be designer viruses that attack certain ethnic groups."

President Hernandez tried to get clarification. "You mean Christians. And Jews. They're always on their target list."

McGee and Nazy nodded in agreement. "Yes, Mr. President."

"Nazy, an exceptionally admirable brief as always. Thank you. Can I have a few minutes with the boss?"

"Of course, Mr. President." The former Muslima anticipated her early dismissal. A gold Rolex Ladies *President* slipped down her wrist and a scintillating three-diamond wedding band glinted on her finger; trinkets of wealth not normally associated with civil servants.

Agency executives had become especially conscious of any ostentatious display of wealth after CIA intelligence officer, Aldrich Ames, made the mistake of driving a new $50,000 Jaguar to work when his salary was only $60,000. The FBI investigated the source of Ames' newfound wealth and discovered he had been paid handsomely by the KGB for compromising virtually all Soviet agents of the CIA and other American and foreign services. Ames had compromised more highly classified CIA assets than any other officer in history until Robert Hanssen's arrest seven years later.

President Hernandez and Director McGee knew the source of Nazy's wealth. Her husband was rich.

Nazy Cunningham removed a wrapped box before returning her papers to the black Halliburton Zero briefcase. In one uninterrupted movement she wordlessly handed McGee the box. With her ankles together, briefcase shut, her hands full, she stood and unconsciously shook her hair free. The length and volume of her hair, tinged with a few random strands of gray, would have made Diana Ross proud. Painted lips turned up slightly, and tasteful diamond earrings festooned her delicate earlobes. A ribbon cross was suspended from her neck. Christian Louboutin heels crushed the pile carpet of the Seal of the United States of America under her flowing silk jacquard polka dot dress which was more expensive than it looked. It wasn't a surprise how *soigné* she looked.

The President wasn't concerned about Nazy's red-bottomed shoes leaving marks in the carpet. He wondered what was in the box.

The men didn't overtly watch Nazy leave the Oval Office.

"She's incredible. I don't know how you get any work done."

"Yes, Mr. President. People stop and stare when she walks the halls of the Agency. She's the eidolon of femininity and isn't bad looking either." They chuckled. "When Duncan's in town, you see the Apollonian side of her delivery; it's rational, scientific, serious, and conventional. She wants to get the brief over with. She has a husband to see. They would be inseparable if it wasn't for the CIA."

"Do you know her story?"

More than you could possibly imagine. "Mr. President, she's absolutely unique and that has nothing to do with her looks. When she was at Guantanamo Bay interrogating detainees, they would become enraged that she was even there—they came from a culture where women are not allowed to be in the same room with men until they are called for. Nazy wore a *naqab*, the head and face covering with a slit for the eyes. But she has green eyes which are usually the mark of Persian royalty. The Shah of Iran had vivid green eyes."

"When she was in disguise, they saw a traitorous Arab woman who could hypnotize them with a look. To make matters worse, she had been educated and could speak better than they could for she was trained as a lawyer."

McGee continued, "Terrorist men had the same mindset regarding women as slave owners did of their slaves, that if these people ever got educated, they would lose their dominance. The left always seeks ways to manipulate people for their own gain and dominance through fear and domination."

"So, Mr. President, you can imagine when they would see Nazy and those green eyes were going to be their interrogation officer, they became frightened and enraged and didn't want to be interrogated. When they lost their cool, she exposed them and picked them to pieces. She could manipulate them so thoroughly they spilled their guts. She never touched them but she was psychologically savvy. They had a fear, a psychosis, they could try to hide their secrets but they knew she had the power to get them to tell them."

"Not all, of course. She knew what they were thinking and what secrets they were hiding. To them she was the anthesis of a Muslim woman and a demon. In the interrogation room, American psychologists would approach interrogations academically. Military men approached them rationally. When U.S. armed forces were deployed to the Philippines in 1927, the *juramentados* immediately carried out suicide attacks against U.S. forces. American officers were aware of the Spanish's use of behavior modification and propaganda tactics, and found the practice of using swine offal and blood an effective *deterrence* to the unprovoked suicide attacks."

"When American soldiers killed these religiously motivated suicide attackers, their commanders held very public funerals for them. Since the Mohammedans were to have no contact with swine and especially not its blood, the American soldiers threw the dead *juramentados* into a grave. Pig's blood was splashed over the dead from head to toe. Once the dead pig was thrown in the grave, the burial was complete. The scene shocked any captured *juramentados*. Soon the word got out to not attack the Americans."

"General John 'Black Jack' Pershing reported his soldiers sprinkled captured *juramentados* prisoners with pig's blood and set them free to warn others. He was quoted, 'Those drops of porcine gore proved more powerful than bullets.' General Pershing controlled the minds of the *juramentados* with threats of being immersed in pig blood. This was a raw battlefield behavior modification technique and it had the desired effect. For American soldiers, the religiously motivated suicide attacks stopped. Politics is combat by other means. This was a classic *psychological operation*."

Politics is combat by other means? President Hernandez said, "These are the things that drive the left crazy."

"Yes, Mr. President. We've been conducting psychological operations in the field and post-war for a long time. Nazy was given a little training but soon mastered the methods to influence their emotions, motives, and objective reasoning, and ultimately the behaviors of these men."

"That's why they hate her."

"Yes, Mr. President. Among other things. Nazy knew these men grew up believing they were the kings of their world and women were sheep. She knew the Sheikh Khalid Mohammads viewed themselves as infallible, utterly dominate mentally and were sensitive when their deficiencies were pointed out and emphasized. Sheikh Khalid Mohammad planned to blow up ten jumbo jets over the Pacific. Vainglorious to a fault; they needed hundreds of followers just to plan something of that scale. And those people talk. The leaders of terrorist groups all suffer from a narcissism disorder. And the men of terrorism hate white men for their inventions, especially aircraft. That is why terrorists attack them with a fever but our Muslim allies fly our front-line fighters. The difference is terrorists have a mental disorder and the men and officers of the Jordanian, Egyptian, and Saudi Air Forces do not."

"So, what you're saying..."

"Mr. President, you have to screen out the mental disorders. Something your predecessor failed to do; he injected them into our defensive organizations. You have to screen out the riff-raff. The Muslim nations have found it's easy to identify the potential terrorist for everything Americans do is an affront to Allah, especially conceiving of and building machines that can travel faster than a bullet."

"It's all in the questions?"

"Over there and here, the only way to find them is to polygraph them. Which we've been doing at the CIA. The FBI is completely infiltrated."

"So Nazy knew what they would say, what they would do, and how they would act. She knew how they liked to dominate women and the ultimate domination is to treat and sell women like sheep. She's something of a psychological *Rosetta Stone*."

"That's the essence of it, Mr. President."

"He pulled off another one. Two. I guess that makes the top five you and Duncan have eliminated."

McGee said, "Yes, Mr. President. But I'm afraid there will be hell to pay. We hit Iran incredibly hard and we can expect retaliation."

"I'm surprised they haven't already tried."

McGee continued, "Yes, Mr. President. We have to be on our toes."

The President's eyes fell to the box beside McGee.

McGee smiled. His eyes panned the office and briefly fell on a Lucite display case with a white Stetson *El Presidente* inside. He remembered it had been a gift from Burnt Winchester before the President nominated him to be the Attorney General of the United States and tasked him to overhaul the U.S. justice system. *Another Navy man.... A Judge Advocate General officer (JAG).* McGee then looked into the eyes of the President. "Mr. President, I haven't heard if he had any troubles. We are using him now in ways that would have given my predecessors nightmares. They were cautious back then. We had good men, but the technology held them back. Pictures of Soviet missile sites were about all they wanted to stick their necks out for. If the truth could be told, Mr. President, we wouldn't have done half the things we have done if it hadn't been for your leadership."

President Hernandez responded, "Did you know I met Duncan when he was in the Border Patrol? That day, I could tell there was something special about him. We've known each other a long time. I could tell then he was a point guy. Duncan views difficulties as a challenge, which adds spice to his work. I'm grateful for his talents. Things would have been much worse without him."

"We would have a hundred names on the *Matrix* instead of one. He's dynamic and fearless, and he gets the job done. It fits him." A somber McGee nodded while looking at the President. He added, "These are activities that cannot be done by unmanned platforms. The Agency has tried for decades. The airplane is a silent weapon, and the pilot is brilliant. An incomparable capability that interrupts the opposition's efforts to fund terrorism and chaos."

The President replied, "But we haven't been able to eliminate that funding source. Scorpii."

"Scorpii," McGee confirmed. "Virtually impossible nut to crack. He not only finances the Democrat Party dark money machine; he funds the part of Islamic terrorism Iran does not."

President Hernandez, suddenly mischievous said, "Some would say they are the same."

McGee had one final thought before he shifted thoughts of Hunter aside. He said, "Duncan is a man of letters but he isn't regarded as a good candidate for a desk job."

"I wanted him as my National Security Advisor."

"Duncan knows his place and limitations. He really is the only person who could have gotten us to this point."

President Hernandez smiled in agreement and said, "The *Matrix* is virtually empty."

McGee smiled; nodded. "Yes, Mr. President, it is, and Duncan wanted me to give this to you." He handed the President the wrapped box; McGee knew what was inside. President Hernandez had an idea.

As the President struggled with the Kraft wrapping paper, McGee paused for a few moments and thought, *Hunter said once we expunge the riff-raff from the Matrix, I should run for president. There's only one we haven't been able to get. But we are going to get him! Even if we have to hire crows to pick the bastard's bones clean....*

President Hernandez was stunned when he saw the green Rolex presentation case. He was like a kid at Christmas who had gotten something he would never buy for himself. Not wanting to appear too eager, he took a measured approach and carefully opened the Rolex box as McGee spoke, "Duncan thought it would be appropriate to celebrate the elimination of the names on the *Matrix*. You know he has a thing for Rolexes." The 18k gold *Daytona* was identical to McGee's which was also a gift from Hunter. The inscription on the case back read. *A Grateful Nation Thanks You for your Service.*

The CIA Director ignored the President's emotional response and tried to continue the brief, but President Hernandez said, "Help me put this on." After all the tags were removed, McGee demonstrated how the clasp worked. The President slipped the *Daytona* on his wrist and admired it. "God, that is beautiful."

"It is, Mr. President. It is. Duncan said to reward you for the fight."

President Hernandez placed the watch's display case in the *Resolute Desk*. He tried to keep his eyes off of the gold timepiece, but the weight on his wrist constantly reminded him this Rolex was not a cheap imitation. The men continued from where they had left off.

The *Disposition Matrix* was a list of the CIA's and the FBI's top 100 terrorists in ranked order. Through their contacts on the ground over the past twenty years, the CIA had found the bad boys of the disparate terrorist organizations worldwide. They had cataloged them, racked and stacked them, then prioritized them for eradication as if they were individual species of vermin.

Only four people knew of the existence of the *Matrix*: the CIA Director, the President, Nazy, who compiled and updated the list for them, and the program manager, Duncan Hunter.

The only name left was Hashash who built the bomb that brought down an American jet over thirty years ago. It had been decades since he had been seen in Europe. Some intelligence had him dead; other embassies reported possible sightings, "in dispatch." McGee knew Duncan Hunter had never cared who was on the *Matrix*, with the one exception of the old bombmaker.

When the CIA got good intel on terrorists, Hunter's job was to locate them and eliminate them. At night. One by one, sometimes in twos. McGee lamented Hunter was now being asked to engage and interdict terrorist operations; work that had once been reserved for Special Operations Forces.

Sometimes it meant killing the forty, fifty, or sixty-man security detail of a terrorist warlord. Sometimes the target was a raiding party. Hunter did it all from his ancient surveillance aircraft from the Vietnam era. A former CIA executive heard the Army was sending the prototype aircraft to scrap, and he snapped some up before they were lost forever to the salvage man's crusher.

President Hernandez began talking about presidential campaigns, while McGee was still thinking about how some terrorists had spent years on the *Matrix*, effectively hiding from the Agency's intelligence officers in the field. Until there came a day the terrorists screwed up; when they momentarily took their personal security for granted. Maybe they wanted to be with a woman alone, and the deviation was recorded by an insider, an informer, *an infiltrator* and transmitted to CIA Headquarters by dispatch. But if the target was in Europe, it was always a no-go. No Socialist European president or prime minister would grant the U.S. a hunting license for an Islamic terrorist in their country. It was just as well. Hunter always vetoed any *Noble Savage* operation over Europe for fear of discovery.

The CIA Director took no glee in updating the *Disposition Matrix*. It was part of the business. But the President took a measured bit of glee lining out a terrorist's name, celebrating a little schadenfreude around their demise. These were men who had killed Americans and allies, who believed they could murder with impunity, who believed they would never be found. And they were correct until Duncan

Hunter turned the tables on them. He began finding them in Africa and the Middle East and killed them without compunction.

McGee turned his attention back to the President.

President Hernandez asked, "Any regrets about leaving the CIA?"

McGee narrowed his lips, nodded, and said, "Mr. President, yes. I was unable to convince Congress to outlaw the Muslim Brotherhood. And there are still thirteen sailors buried in Libya. They've been interred in Muslim lands for over two-hundred years; I thought we could repatriate the officers and crew of the *USS Intrepid*."

The President was unaware of the story.

McGee told the high points, "President Jefferson had been at war with the Barbary Pirates and had refused to send any more monetary tribute to the Muslim caliphate. He sent Sailors and Marines to negate the agreement. But the *Intrepid* blew up prematurely and killed all thirteen men on board. The sailors' remains were discovered onshore the next day. They were abused by the enemy and partially devoured by a pack of stray dogs before Capt. William Bainbridge and other Navy prisoners in Tripoli were allowed to bury them."

President Hernandez was shocked.

"Mr. President, these men, America's first sailors, didn't get an honorable burial; they were dragged through the streets, fed to wild dogs, and dumped in mass graves."

The President said, "Tripoli is hardly Normandy." *Normandy with its manicured lawns and serene cemeteries. No presidents before me did anything? Why?*

"No, Mr. President, those men are not honored there; they're *stashed* there as if they were some bizarre trophies. I thought after the ouster of Gaddafi in 2011 we would bring them home. There was a lot of interest. The Senate was on the brink of passing legislation that would have required the Pentagon to seek the return of their remains. I spoke before two committees. And then, nothing."

"I don't know what I could do. I don't think there's anything I can do."

McGee shook his head to show it was a lost cause. "No, Mr. President, I thought if it was going to happen it would be because of me. But we are at war with our own State Department and the FBI. I'm lucky to get the time of day from them."

Several seconds passed, then President Hernandez asked, "Do you think Nazy will make a good replacement?"

"I do, Mr. President. She will get the time of day from them. She's got the brains and temperament for it, but Duncan will need to be convinced. He won't like Nazy being the Director; he'll think we are unduly exposing her to the Muslim Brotherhood. And he's probably right. If they had something like a *Disposition Matrix*, she would be at the top of it. She has hurt them in multitudes of ways...."

"They almost killed her." The President shook his head.

I know; more than anyone.... "Yes, Mr. President. Multiple times. They hate her. To them she's an apostate. She defected from Islam. She showed Muslim men that escape is possible and that living in freedom is achievable. She's the one who got away and she'll require protection until she dies. But as for Duncan, he will support her decision."

He looked at the gold on his wrist then said, "Bill, so what you're saying is you're going to do it."

"I am, Mr. President."

"That's fantastic. I have been afraid it was over. We cannot get anything done in Congress and the Democrats have found ways to cheat and win elections. But I also believe we have a chance. If America is going to survive, it's got to be you. The country needs a champion. We need a *nautical man*; we need you to turn this ship around. America needs a different kind of leader. America needs you to be the next President of the United States."

Bill McGee clenched his jaws momentarily, nodded, and exhaled. "Yes, Mr. President, the situation isn't lost on me."

"Over anyone else in government. You're a rare leader. I'm glad you're on our side."

"Thank you, Mr. President. I wouldn't last two seconds as a Democrat. Thank you for your support."

"Our generals and admirals are not up to the task. It seems they have forgotten how to lead."

"They're Mazibuike holdovers. Duncan has written about it—an Eastwood essay in the papers. I agree with him. Your Democrat predecessors injected gays, transvestites, and transgenders into DOD for one purpose, to destroy those tenuous cultural bonds soldiers must have when they train or go to war. No one's military — not the Russians or the Chinese — allows mental patients anywhere near their sane rational people and military equipment. But our generals and admirals allowed Mazibuike *carte blanche* to do exactly that. Now it's difficult to remove them from the military and the intelligence community. If I'm in, they will be out."

"You have been very successful at CIA. I've tried, but my generals and defense secretary have no political will. They tell me to my face they will do it, but they do nothing."

"Mr. President, you did the best you could. Those generals and admirals and senior civilians slow rolled you with promises of studies. All they did was fail to support you while covering their asses. I'll get them out of there."

"I know you will, Bill. I know you will."

"We need new generals and admirals. The current crop of flag officers profess loyalty to you, but when there is the least bit of pressure, they break in favor of the opposition party. It's a form of infiltration. We assume they are apolitical and will give good advice, but they really are *dark state,* working in the shadows to undermine a Republican administration."

"They came so highly recommended...."

"That was because of that TASC think tank. They were an underground communist network. They should have never been trusted. Those generals have been grossly unfair to your administration. Some would call it treasonous, although that is a word which makes one recoil in disgust and incredulity. You give them orders; they pretend to follow the orders, then blame you for their poor results. That is a classic propaganda bait and switch tool. I believe America is in a propaganda war with the left's best propagandists in the intelligence business, yet it's hard for us to see it."

"Bill, you're on target. How did we get to this point?"

"Mr. President, we don't get to talk much on domestic policy...."

"We should. This has been enlightening. You're absolutely right."

McGee said, "Mr. President, these apolitical generals don't know how much trouble we are in. They should have been studying *counter-propaganda*. It isn't good enough to be apolitical. We have to choose and stand up for what is right. They are not serving the Office of the President very well."

The President nodded. McGee's and Nazy's private brief had suggested Republicans were not good at *counter-propaganda* either. They wouldn't fight back unless their backs were against the wall. Those on the left understood the proclivities of the right and laid mines to force the Republicans to retreat under a withering assault of charges of racism. While the problem was coming into better focus, it was also time to move on to another subject.

The men faced each other, elbows on their knees, hunched over. For the first time today, they were afraid to say what was on their minds. For an instant, McGee found the walls of the Oval Office fading like cheesy special effects from a 1950s science fiction movie.

President Hernandez said, "Some things are just obvious. *Counter-propaganda*? The left's propaganda is ridiculous, and they are killing us. Other than you, we don't have a person of such stature to deliver a counter argument. You know more than most, Admiral."

After hearing "Admiral," McGee blinked. He was nonplussed to find the Oval Office walls back where they should be. The PDB had been a comprehensive intelligence brief, now with that requirement out of the way, their conversation could be one between friends. Between Republicans. Between Conservatives. It was time to talk of the things they never talked about, *specifically*, domestic enemies.

McGee responded, "The left, the Democrat Party, and all the special interest groups are trying to nibble at the U.S. in order to bleed her, eviscerate her, and bring her down. It's as if the left has discovered the keys to the secret silent weapons locker from Goebbels' Ministry of Propaganda and are using them against America and the Republican Party."

McGee's next thought frightened him a little. *And...if they had access to them and started...sharing... them. Heaven help us. I'm trying to save our nation, spiraling out of control, besieged by Communists, Marxists, Socialists, and Islamists had taken its toll. America is at a turning point.*

President Hernandez replied, "If anyone can lead America and negate the left, you can. You have a lock on the subject, you have studied it extensively, you have made the most of your time at the CIA, and you know what the CIA and the communist countries have done in the way of secret research. You know their playbook. You know where Goebbels' files are, and where the Soviets and Eastern-bloc counties buried the bodies."

"But will that be enough?" McGee asked. "America is purposely being turned into a horror show. Riots funded by leftist and communist organizations like BLM, belligerent leftist mobs in all the major Democrat-controlled cities. Democrat-controlled city councils are defunding police departments and implementing no-cash bail programs. In Democrat-controlled cities murders and crime are rising stratospherically. Television networks, radio stations, and newspapers all blame you or capitalism; the classic leftist propaganda tropes."

"The *dark state* propelled a senator who was ineligible straight into the White House. The *dark state* is still irrepressibly loyal to former President Mazibuike. They continue to wage political war, a silent propaganda war on you, Mr. President and on all Republicans."

During the last election Marxist and Muslim Brotherhood Democrats had regained the majority in Congress. Laws had been passed to ensure close elections would flip in favor of the Democrats, that recounts and audits would be managed by the *dark state*, and challenges to election results would take years to be resolved. After being sworn in, the new Congress tried every month to remove President Hernandez from office on some nonsensical charge.

President Hernandez agreed, "I know all this excessive vitriol between the parties can be traced to the CIA file on President Maxim Mohammad Mazibuike. The left say it should never have seen the light of day, instead of being released by an unknown *whistleblower*, it should have been burned or shredded. Not that it was true or accurate mind you—just that it should have been trashed. Destroy the evidence so there is no proof. The Marxists in the Democrat Party had been riding high; President Mazibuike's agenda was being implemented, even if it was strange for a self-professed Christian to devote so much time to Islamic issues."

"Then the Democrats and their emotionally incontinent media were toppled from their horses when Mazibuike resigned and the vice president died in the apparent murder-suicide. Washington Democrats weren't impressed with the vice president, but they didn't want him killed because that meant as the Speaker of the House of Representatives I would ascend to the presidency. In the blink of an eye, the Secret Service had me at the White House to be sworn in as President of the United States."

Democrats could explain Mazibuike's resignation and sudden departure. They knew he was never eligible to be President, he wasn't a "natural born citizen," and the CIA file proved Mazibuike was not the man he claimed to be—but they would never admit those things. But they couldn't explain the vice president's death. It smelled like a mob hit, but the heads of the crime families said they hadn't done it. There had been no contract for the vice president. Which meant there had to be another political player. Whoever had done it had to be extremely accomplished and lethal.

"Some thought it was about time Republicans fought back."

President Hernandez thought, *What an odd choice of words from someone who speaks so precisely.*

CHAPTER 7

October 31, 2019

President Hernandez pivoted to ask McGee what his wife Angela thought about him running for office.

"She's doing what wives do when their man takes their family on the fast-track road to perdition. Hold on tight and enjoy the ride. She said the country had given us so much, and I was probably the only one in America who could lead Americans out of the darkness of this Democrat Party tyranny *and* their shadow government."

The President nodded at the reference to shadow government. "She's a smart girl. You know she's right."

McGee quietly nodded. *Isn't it sad the only man who could bring America to her knees was the lying, cheating Mazibuike, a black Muslim man, and now the only man who could get America off her knees was a trustworthy black Christian man?* He shared his perspicacious thoughts with the President who agreed.

"Bill, the Founders and I know you're the right man, at the right time for this job. And let's not overlook the *Insiders* pushing for a one-world government...."

McGee said, "They sell their ideas as utopian, but the natural state of man is freedom. Their goal is to destroy freedom. They are American Communists trying to pass themselves off as patriots in the struggle against oppression."

The President nodded, "They are dangerous, but they cannot do it — this one-world bullshit nonsense — without a defeated United States. You and I know we can stop them. We've stopped most of the chaos associated with Islamic terrorism — Muslim Brotherhood terrorism. We're close to stopping their one-world agenda."

These were somber times and the men spoke matter-of-factly. President Hernandez said, "I asked for a brief from the Justice

Department on how it was possible for Mazibuike to get elected. Attorney General Winchester assigned a special prosecutor to find out. What the FBI would have determined had it not been fully compromised and infiltrated was that it looked like the Muslim Brotherhood spent a hundred million dollars, funds everyone in this business knows they didn't have, to groom him for the office."

"A hundred million dollars: tuition at Harvard, bribing Congressmen to change the Constitution, and airtime on the networks to shape the narrative. Mass hypnosis. America is suffering from mass formation psychosis."

McGee said, "They used every tool in the Joseph Goebbels propaganda toolbox to make Americans ignore the facts and believe he was a natural born citizen and therefore eligible to be president. That's not the work of the Muslim Brotherhood, that's... the work of Rho Schwartz Scorpii." *Socialist Marxist multibillionaire....*

The President didn't mind the interruption. "Yes. Scorpii. And the Democrats he funded did everything in their power to change the law, because the citizenry will still follow the laws, regardless of how bad the laws are."

McGee said, "Mr. President, Hitler got the German legislature to change the law to strip the Jews of their citizenship; these clowns are trying to strip white men of their rights. It's the same thing. Control."

"Exactly. I asked the Attorney General where the FBI leadership stood on the topic of the Muslim Brotherhood. The AG asked the FBI for an investigation three years ago, all he got were blank stares. So, he went with a U.S. Attorney, named him a special prosecutor, and he got to the bottom of it. That confirmed our perspective of the FBI."

"They are not on our side anymore." After a pause, McGee added, "Mr. President, I also asked the AG to investigate TASC—the Trans-Atlantic Security Council think tank. I was interested in the people they recommended. He found, as I suspected, none of them had the qualifications listed on their CV (curriculum vitae). TASC excluded any reference to liberal, social, Marxist or communist affiliations, conferences attended, keynote speaking engagements at socialist meetings, or their travel to socialist and communist countries."

President Hernandez said, "I'm completely unaware of that investigation."

"Mr. President, I asked Attorney General Winchester for a favor. We were interested...."

"We?" The President's curiosity was piqued.

McGee smiled. "Mr. President, Duncan, Nazy, and me—we. Apparently, our pilot has a lot of time on his hands when he's flying and, as he said, he looks at things we may not have considered fully. Duncan brought up the issue, and I asked the AG to investigate TASC. Duncan looked at the consequences of TASC's recommendations for high-level posts in government. Our government and European governments. These people worked more on socialist issues than freedom or capitalism. President Mazibuike's TASC-appointed executives completely upset the balance of power with his Muslim Outreach."

President Hernandez said, "In other words, Duncan put a face on the *dark state*. Exposed Mazibuike's holdovers."

"And TASC maintained the fiction with wildly fantastical bogus CVs that those people would be *fantastic* candidates for the top jobs in the new administration, but they...."

President Hernandez said, "...had no allegiance to the United States or European governments, they hid their allegiance to leftism, liberalism, socialism, Marxism, or communism."

"Yes, Mr. President."

"That's why you didn't go to the FBI. Scorpii spent a hundred million dollars to get Mazibuike elected—he must have funded the rest. Muslims in the FBI...."

"Yes, Mr. President." McGee thought, *The FBI's totally infiltrated. They would be the wrong group to investigate anything; a modern-day version of asking the fox to protect the chicken coop. And a hundred million dollars to groom one person. To the Insiders, the wealthiest men in the world, a hundred million dollars is pocket change. Could they be bankrolling the Muslim Brotherhood too? We've collapsed the main terrorist networks but are we certain the Muslim Brotherhood doesn't have money problems? Our Muslim allies are fighting them with everything they have. They are not funding them. That's got to be Scorpii.*

McGee knocked the thoughts away, pressed his lips, and nodded. Reality was setting in. *Now the dark state will really try to kill us all. My kids…. It's their way to keep us in line….* "Mr. President, it's not that there are too many Muslims in the FBI; there are too many Muslims whose allegiance is to the Muslim Brotherhood and maybe even al-Qaeda or ISIS instead of the United States. That is just one major part of the problem. Just the other day, the FBI Director fired a Muslim special agent who was caught deleting the files of several U.S. Congressmen and women of Islamic heritage and the Muslim faith."

"I didn't get that brief — Bill, do you have more?"

Not my purview. But…. "Mr. President. I'm sure the AG will be on your calendar soon to tell you the result of that investigation. I am aware only because this was exactly what Mazibuike's infiltrators did when they got access to the Agency. I understand the deleted files at the FBI were primarily background investigations which had been conducted by the Department of Homeland Security. They showed that several state and U.S. Congressmen, some in office and some running for office, were engaged in marriage for convenience schemes to obtain U.S. citizenship. DHS said it wasn't their job to investigate the prevarications of senators and congressmen. They don't want to investigate what they see are minor administrative infractions. The problem is they don't look at these events as *infiltrations* by an adversary inimical to the U.S. Attorney General Winchester said there was even a file on a Congresswoman who had secretly married her biological brother to gain U.S. citizenship."

"That is unbelievable."

"Republicans in Congress were disturbed to discover FBI special agents — *Muslims* — were systematically looking the other way on any issue of *Muslim* men and women who were trying to fraudulently achieve citizenship. We would not have known these immigration documents existed if they hadn't been bragging to Republican staffers…."

President Hernandez interrupted, "There's that Goebbels quote. He said, '*We enter parliament in order to supply ourselves, in the arsenal of democracy, with its own weapons. If democracy is so stupid as to give us free tickets and salaries for this bear's work, that is its affair. We do not come as friends, nor even as neutrals. We come as enemies. As the wolf bursts into the flock, so we come."*

"That's right, Mr. President. We look at that quote as a warning; Democrats look at it as 'that's us and our unstated aim.' No allegiance, only conquest. Infiltrate as far as they can. Take out the weakest link."

"And then America. The Democrats used to be partners with a different view. Attorney General Winchester must be tearing his hair out over at Justice."

Hmmm. Mazibuike's holdovers. Dark State. He's sounding like one of us…. Fighting the Spartans at the Battle of Troy. "Yes, Mr. President. Just like the documents at DHS, Justice, and the FBI, the Mazibuike documents did exist at the CIA. They showed the nature and the extent of the help Senator Mazibuike received along the way to inauguration. More proof has been revealed from the secret DNC archives thanks to *Whistleblowers*."

President Hernandez said, "That's kind of a Whittaker Chambers moment." The discussion of spies, secret documents, and shadowy governments unsettled the President.

The men knew Washington Democrats and the media were active participants in the conspiracy to whitewash those documents. It was as if they were the leaders of a band of domestic terrorists. The release of the DNC documents by *Whistleblowers* had been likened to the U.S. Attorneys having the mafia's archives dumped onto their desks, or the Muslim Brotherhood and Islamic Underground's *Explanatory Memorandum* being found in an Annandale basement and transcribed into English.

McGee said, "*Whistleblowers* provided the part of the iceberg that couldn't be seen, that they…."

The President re-emphasized: "*We do not come as friends, nor even as neutrals. We come as enemies.*" Then he remembered, *Domestic enemies.* He said, "They said it every day, but we didn't believe them."

"Another one of Goebbels' silent weapons. They say something so outlandish, but it's the one time they tell the truth. You never know when they are lying to you."

"Be glad, Bill, most of them are in Washington." The men laughed; the laughs turned to grins; the grins turned to the next topic.

The President asked his CIA Director, "What is on your agenda? When will you make the announcement?"

"Actually, Mr. President, tonight I'm the keynote speaker of the *Pumpkin Papers Irregulars Dinner*. Duncan will be there in disguise, and Nazy too, of course...."

I remember going to those Dinners too. The President understood; nodded.

McGee said, "And Colonel Eastwood will be the first reporter to cover it, because the left won't send anyone to our program. I'll give him some exclusive comments."

The President said, "I expect it will be a barn burner. Afterwards, you'll need to spend time touring the country, building your political reputation and campaigning to get the nomination. I have no qualms you'll make Conservatives comfortable with who you are; you're America's greatest hero. You bring so much experience to the campaign it cannot do anything but increase the izzat of the campaign. You'll be unstoppable if you run on a platform to stop America's retreat before world Communism and Islam."

"I know you'll run an exciting campaign, and I'll help where I can, you only need to ask. Make yourself acceptable to Republicans and independents, and we'll see if we can peel off votes from the Democrats. Our goal is to raise you from political oblivion and make you President of the United States. I will introduce you to the money men; not the controlling types but patriots who have made their fortunes and are waiting for their leader. It will take a Herculean effort to raise the billion dollars you'll need for this campaign. You know the Democrats will throw everything they can at you and your family, so be prepared. My campaign network is still intact; your announcement will invigorate them. I'll get them to jump into the pool with you. What do you think?"

McGee smiled, "Just another day in the life of the future President."

President Hernandez jumped up and raced to his desk; the *Resolute Desk* was a gift from Queen Victoria to President Rutherford B. Hayes. It was built from the oak timbers of the British Arctic exploration ship HMS *Resolute*. As a desk, it was imposing as it was spectacular. He hurried back to a dazed Director McGee and gave him a file folder. "Bill, inside, is an Executive Order I don't believe you have seen. It looks like Mazibuike issued it a year before he resigned. It appears to have been given to all the secretaries and heads of our agencies, but curiously not the CIA. I know you're leaving, so I'll share it with Nazy, too. I would appreciate both of your inputs."

McGee nodded, removed what looked to be a signed copy of the EO. He read the header: *Using Behavioral Science Insights to Better Serve the American People.* He looked up at the President with incredulity. *If that's not an Orwellian title for controlling the minds of all Americans, I don't what is.*

President Hernandez said, "There is no record of it in the Federal Register or in our official White House records. The AG stumbled onto a copy. When he found it wasn't in the Federal Register, he smelled a rat. My secretary called the other department head secretaries. They claim they have it in their administrative folders, and it has been implemented as directed. But not the CIA. Isn't that strange?"

McGee pulled on an ear as he read a few lines of the EO. He asked, "This is bullshit lawyer language; it's Project *Bluebird* brainwashing all over again. It says a Social and Behavioral Sciences Team would issue guidance within 45 days of the date of this order. And how does everyone else in government know about it? Mr. President, do you know what this really is?"

President Hernandez shook his head.

McGee said, "Mr. President, this is *dark state* communications. Recall from the Muslim Brotherhood's *Explanatory Memorandum*; they wanted a candidate who could secretly establish Muslim leadership and a shadow government within the government. If you have one, I will bet there are others. Just to regulate the acolytes of the *dark state*. Amazing."

President Hernandez said, "It's no wonder Democrats went ballistic when I was sworn in."

McGee rubbed an eye that was about to burst a blood vessel. When he took his big thumb out of his eye he said, "You interrupted their plans. This is raw government-sanitized propaganda. You would expect something like this from Nazi Germany. Not the U.S."

The two men faced one another, like tag-team thinkers. McGee said, "I had no idea Mr. President. It looks like this might be a founding document…for their secret government? I think we have to see what came out of your office and what we received at CIA. Could there be more of these same type of EOs that were issued? Could be a job for the IG or Security. Since we were not part of the cabal, I'll have the deputy take this for action."

"You're going to be busy."

"I am Mr. President."

President Hernandez shook McGee's hand and McGee left the office.

•   •   •

McGee and Nazy rode back to CIA Headquarters and discussed the contents of the EO. "I thought I was reading a Soviet pamphlet on injecting Beria-type propaganda into the government. Now I see why schools around the country are implementing Critical Race Theory into the classrooms. You can bet school boards were given a copy of the EO, and the states ran with it. Democrat states were more than willing to comply with a 3M executive order."

Nazy asked, "What are you going to do?"

"Think on it."

"Think on it?"

"Yeah, I now know what I'm going to talk about at dinner. What I'm going to do."

Nazy was concerned. It wasn't like Bill McGee to be coy. "Which is?"

"Oh, we'll see after dinner if you approve. You invited Eastwood?"

"I did."

McGee said, "He wouldn't come for me. You're my secret weapon."

Nazy was taken aback. "I swear Bill McGee, that is the most sexist thing I've ever heard from you!"

"Am I wrong?"

Nazy broke out in laughter. "No. You're right. It's just a little odd you felt you can be truthful with me on a thought or concept like that; most men would never admit women have certain powers."

"You have super powers, Nazy and you and Duncan and I are a team." There was no sexual tension, just friendship and professionalism.

Nazy smiled at the man who saved her life and said, "We are that."

CHAPTER 8

October 31, 2019

The bar area for the *Pumpkin Papers Irregulars Dinner* was packed; standing room only with overcrowding that would send fire marshals into conniptions, except the fire marshals and fire chiefs were also invited. One short wall was dominated by a long portable bar with nine or ten attendants in white coats and black ties. They could and would concoct any drink and serve champagne without limit. The patrons filled the tip jar with Lincolns, Hamiltons, and Jacksons. The opposite wall featured an author of espionage thrillers, autographing copies of his latest, *Special Activities,* for an adoring crowd. Some took pictures with the dashing old pilot.

McGee, Nazy, Hunter, and Eastwood formed a small knot near the author's table. If there were other correspondents besides Eastwood, they didn't make themselves known. Publicity would be on the CIA Director's terms. Rear Admiral McGee abominated the press; he considered them little more than political agents of the Democrat Party. Fifth columnists. Pains in the ass.

He told Duncan Hunter his disguise made him look like leech bait. The men laughed; Nazy was not amused.

A former Secretary of Defense (SECDEF) and the current Attorney General, Burnt Winchester, were slowly making the rounds, squeezing through the masses of Brooks Brothers and tailor-made suits all appropriately accessorized with a bevy of unique orange ties until they found who they were looking for, Bill McGee. The men shook hands and held on like an umbilicus, conveying respect and reverence as they quietly exchanged comments. The old SECDEF, the Attorney General, and CIA Director had been Eagle Scouts and Navy men together: SECDEF a pilot, the AG a JAG officer, and McGee, a SEAL (Sea, Air, Land). The SECDEF concluded his visit with accolades and a warning to stay out of politics. The Attorney General laughed.

McGee said, "Too late." McGee and the SECDEF laughed at each other heartily and vowed to stay in touch. McGee told Winchester he would see him around campus.

Nazy had been so busy admiring her husband's suit she hadn't been able to catch Duncan's eye and give him their sign. She was certain the suit was identical to the tailored gray "Cary Grant suit," the best suit in movie history. Finally, he looked at her when everyone else was looking away, so she slowly tugged on an earlobe with a diamond-rich earring; it was her non-verbal way to say she loved him.

Duncan Hunter smiled and slowly dragged the back of his finger across his brow to show message received, and I can't wait to get you alone. He thought, *Oh, Baby! You look so good in black!* Even at sixty, he could be an imp. After sincerely eyeballing the beauty of his wife from behind one of the CIA's most realistic disguises, he found the dynamics between the old SEAL and the even older SECDEF amusing. He smiled outwardly and thought, *Is there a more perfect person for CIA Director? Did I do good sticking that bug into the ear of the President?*

Hunter thanked Eastwood for his articles and asked him what he had been up to.

Dory Eastwood said, "After *Escape from Devil's Hole*, I've been intrigued with the whole problem of the child sex trafficking trade. It's hard to get anyone to talk about it here in the U.S., but it's a huge problem in Europe. I'm hoping a couple of the mental health clinics will vouch for me so I can interview survivors, victims."

Nazy had listened intently said, "Those poor people."

Quarter-million kids missing every year in Europe. Hunter said, "Good luck with that. If you need me for anything, let me know."

Nazy, Hunter, and Eastwood watched the parade of people who each took a few seconds with McGee, shaking his hand or offering an anecdote of past meetings McGee couldn't remember. Then above the din they heard, "Excuse me, Ms. Cunningham?"

The CIA men and Eastwood assumed some level of tutelary services as they unintentionally and unconsciously surrounded Nazy, who was wearing a moderately low-cut gown for the occasion. The men turned their eyes to the interloper. He looked vaguely familiar to McGee and Eastwood, like an older ruddier Charles Ingalls character from the *Little House on the Prairie* television series. Eastwood thought the man was likely somebody who had been important once upon a time, as they all were to one degree or another when they wore younger men's clothes. But age had crept up on them all. Only Nazy was winning the fight against Father Time. The strands of gray in everyone's hair—those who had hair—showed no one was truly winning the age race.

Duncan knew who the man was immediately, and it created a dilemma for him. *Former Marine Captain Link "Chain" Coffey. Still has a little of that Michael Landon thing going on. Still has hair. Nazy will turn him into a blubbering fool. Now what do I do?*

When the man introduced himself to Nazy, the scrubby gathering of men was duly impressed. "Miss Cunningham, Link Coffey, formerly Assistant Deputy Director of the FBI. We were at GITMO together, I think 2003-2004." He was showboating and struggling to keep his eyes above her chin.

Nazy thought, *Oh, yes, I remember, a nice fellow with all the instincts of a scorpion. I suppose I have to introduce him to everyone. I dislike this. No one was supposed to know I am here.*

McGee raised an eyebrow and waited for Nazy to respond to the breech in protocol; she shook the man's hand, smiled politely, and introduced the men in her entourage. "Oh yes, I remember, good to see you again. This is Director William McGee, Colonel Eastwood, and Dante Locke."

Duncan Hunter watched Coffey's eyes go wide open when Nazy said she remembered him.

Unaccustomed to being introduced at all, especially in disguise, Hunter shook Coffey's hand wondering if the man would try to get into Nazy's space. He frowned as Coffey fiddled with his suitcoat and tugged at his shirt and tie, subconsciously trying to get Nazy to notice him as a potential suitor. She waited for him to say something else.

Hunter thought, *Some things don't change. Next thing he'll tell Nazy she looks nice although she's looking unbelievable tonight.* A sensible and civilized husband doesn't object to other men admiring his wife; he can even comprehend her returning the admiration. But the men surrounding her and Nazy's own body language flashed *KEEP AWAY* signals to other men; when Duncan touched her arm, she lovingly moved into his touch. Coffey was breathing hard; Nazy had that effect on men, and his old acquaintance was so enamored of her he didn't take the hint.

Hunter refrained from speaking, keeping his distinctive low rumbling voice in check. That would be a dead give-away. *If I told Coffey to quit the primping, she's married to me, he would faint. I could have some fun with this.*

Several lifetimes ago, he and Coffey had been in the Marine Corps together, flying F-4s and serving aboard ship. But *Maverick* had been a loner while Coffey had lots of friends, especially when he was buying beers at the strip-clubs. The other pilots hit the bars and clubs; Hunter played racquetball and took graduate school classes. Consequently, they were never close friends but more than mere acquaintances. Their interests converged as Coffey had an old car he was restoring, and Hunter raced an old Corvette around the country.

Hunter had been flying as a contract pilot for the CIA for over 20 years and had lost track of his old squadron mates, as is often the case in military relationships. Before flying for the CIA, he had been an airport security manager and directed the Border Patrol's national aviation program. He had also taught grad school for a bunch of Air Force instructor pilots and eventually became a big shot in the Air Force aircraft maintenance leadership structure while working as a contract pilot for the CIA. During those years in aviation maintenance, Hunter had met and become friends with a retired CIA executive; now his life was dedicated to the CIA and the U.S.A. He was totally out of touch with the Marines he had known.

But not being in touch wasn't the same as not being informed. Hunter knew Coffey had traded a jet for law school. When he heard Coffey had gone to the FBI, he was shocked. Hunter had figured Coffey would open a bar in Key West or a college town like Missoula, Montana to be near the girls.

Hunter noticed Coffey was still struggling to keep his eyes off of Nazy. She wore a long-sleeved black gown and black heels. She accoutered herself with thousands of dollars' worth of diamonds around her neck and suspended from her ears. Her gown showed little cleavage, mostly to hide the ugly scar from McGee's extemporaneous field surgery. The men who had rescued her knew that while little black cocktail dresses were favored by the other women in the room, Nazy favored modesty, length, and sleeves to hide the scars.

Having just returned from a mission overseas, it was hard for Duncan to keep his hands off of his wife, but they would soon be alone. He perused the room. Everywhere he looked people were surreptitiously staring at Nazy. She was the most striking woman in the room. It didn't matter if they looked. No one in this crowd would be so moronic as to make a pass at her, especially since she was protected by the three amigos, McGee, Eastwood and him. She would go home with him. Duncan politely nodded and returned his hands to his pockets. Voices and hands are difficult to disguise effectively.

Coffey had his own internal turmoil. *I thought I'd never see her again. She's still so striking. Oh, how I wanted her to want me, to have that profound connection. I couldn't tell if she was younger or older; all I knew was she was breathtaking. She was in a class by herself, and I didn't have what it took to enchant her. I wonder who did, and why she's here tonight.*

Nazy sensed there was something amiss. Duncan was not saying anything, he had tensed up. *There was something about Coffey which obviously disturbed him. Was Duncan jealous?*

When Coffey recovered from his Nazy-induced trip down memory lane, he introduced Dr. John Lindell, the grandson of Whittaker Chambers and the real reason for the assembly of people at the *Pumpkin Papers Irregulars Dinner*.

Director McGee said, "Dr. Lindell, I believe we are at your table."

Eastwood wondered if that meant he would be banished to a table in the kitchen, but Dr. Lindell said, "It's an honor Director McGee. You're a man of extraordinary talents. And Colonel Eastwood, I have read about your exploits. I've seen your television specials, and I listen to your radio show whenever I can. You have the knack for radio."

"Thank you, Dr. Lindell." Eastwood wanted to ask for an interview. He lifted a finger to make a point when Dr. Lindell said, "I've already checked on the seating." He made a little swirling motion with a finger, alluding to, "…we're at the same table and the four of us will face the podium." He panned a delicate finger across the CIA people, McGee, Nazy Cunningham, Hunter (Dante Locke), and included himself.

Eastwood and Coffey both thought, ...*which means my back will face all the goings on. Sitting at the big table in the cheap seats. Again.*

McGee smiled; he was used to getting the best seats.

Hunter, alias Dante Locke, one of several cover identities the Agency had given him, remained quiet. His Colt *Python* was suspended from his shoulder holster and his Kimber 1911 rested at the small of his back. In large groups, his training demanded he have a plan to kill everyone he met at tonight's assembly, but these were people who had been vetted. With few exceptions, they were senior members of law enforcement and the intelligence community (IC). It was one of a few times where McGee was without a personal security detail. That was one of Hunter's jobs for the evening.

These *Irregulars* were playfully referred to as *The Resistance*. It was an informal, clandestine counter-espionage organization of older men and women that operated under the surface of government when it was necessary. Newcomers couldn't permeate the tight-knit *galère* until they had spent their time in counterterrorism or counterespionage and become senior members of the intelligence establishment. The average age of line troops was the twenties. The average age of Special Operations warriors was late thirties to early forties. The *Irregulars* members' average age was the mid-fifties to early sixties. The men who were most responsible for the Conservative movement in the United States were in their seventies and eighties.

Eastwood's head was spinning. He knew of virtually everyone in the room, but his mental organizational chart was fuzzy. *I'm completely out of my element. This group resembles Fifth Columnists but are so different it's safe to say they are something else entirely. More clandestine, more effective, more.... Older? What can old people do? So, what are they; hell, who are they?*

Coffey quietly announced, "Fifteen years ago Dr. Lindell translated the *Explanatory Memorandum* for the FBI. It's the Muslim Brotherhood's strategic plan to defeat America."

Hunter thought, *Well, that's interesting. I will wager my Ferrari the Muslim Brotherhood doesn't know that! And, that makes Dr. Lindell a patriot. And probably Coffey too. I had no idea.*

Director McGee held out a giant hand and shook Dr. Lindell's hand. He asked if he could announce that bit of FBI history.

Former Assistant Deputy Director Coffey said, "There shouldn't be any problem, Director McGee. It wasn't ever classified. I was the Special Agent in charge of that investigation."

Thought Hunter, *Damn Link! Now I find out you're a real patriot. You must have been one of those "late to light" guys.*

McGee said, "Thank you. I will mention it when it's my turn to speak." Everyone in the group smiled.

For those who were unaware, Coffey stated, "Dr. Lindell's work was instrumental in the government winning its case in court against the Muslim Brotherhood and the Holy Land Foundation. The documents he translated were copied and forwarded to the Justice Department and the National Counter Terrorism Center (NCTC)."

This info elicited a wry grin from Eastwood. He made some notes.

The Director of the NCTC, Nazy Cunningham, continued, "Director McGee declared the Muslim Brotherhood a terrorist organization. The Holy Land Foundation's sole purpose was to raise funds for the Muslim Brotherhood to overthrow the U.S. I remember seeing those documents when I first came to the NCTC. That archive was incredibly large. Nothing like it had been seen since the war."

Nazy smiled and all the men nodded and smiled with her.

Eastwood saw it was another remarkable display of courage and leadership by the CIA Director. Even when their own documents proved the Muslim Brotherhood was a terrorist organization and not some unregulated Middle East militia, the FBI steadfastly refused to designate the Muslim Brotherhood a terrorist group. Even the Congress refused to make that declaration. They were too concerned it would inflame the FBI's Muslim Outreach employees.

Eastwood jotted some thoughts. *Most of the U.S. government is propounding the BIG LIE: that the Muslim Brotherhood isn't a terrorist organization. The FBI and the Democrats in Congress say the Muslim Brotherhood is simply a misunderstood group of people wanting to help others. McGee used the truth, facts, and figures to expose the propaganda hidden by Congressional and FBI personnel. He knew the IC had to fight the Muslim Brotherhood propaganda with counter-propaganda.*

When America's most celebrated terrorist killer had been sworn in as the CIA Director, there had been some seventy terrorists on the FBI's Most Wanted Terrorist List. After three years there was only one. Director McGee, former SEAL Team Six Commander, was not to be messed with. Some Republicans in Congress believed he was a larger-than-life hero, while others, mostly Democrats, believed he was the brother of the devil. Those he left alive on the battlefields of Afghanistan believed he was the devil incarnate.

Coffey had left the Bureau when it became obvious the FBI had been compromised, infiltrated by Muslims with a covert obeisance to the Muslim Brotherhood and the Islamic Underground. At President Mazibuike's behest, nearly all the countries of Europe voluntarily took in millions of Muslim refugees from North Africa and the Middle East. Mazibuike's actions were predicted by the *Explanatory Memorandum* and required for Muslim Brotherhood dominance.

Counterterrorism specialists warned their superiors President Mazibuike was upsetting the balance of power in Europe. Then he opened the southwest borders to illegal aliens and told the Border Patrol to effectively stop doing their jobs and stand down. The action gave hundreds of thousands of Muslim refugees from North Africa and the Middle East free passage into the American heartland.

Coffey was intrigued by the man who wasn't saying anything.

McGee sensed the G-Man's curiosity. He offered Duncan a modicum of cover with, "Mr. Locke is...."

Hunter interrupted at half-volume, "Do you still have the *Pagoda*? I believe it was a 71 280SL." McGee, Nazy, and Eastwood snapped their heads in incredulity; their eyes bulged like Peter Lorre in a horror flick. It wasn't like Hunter to break his cover.

Nazy thought, *Oh Duncan, you shouldn't have done that.*

Eastwood puzzled, *What's going on here?*

McGee wondered, *Who owns a Pagoda?*

Coffey couldn't believe the bourbon-soaked bass coming out of the old man's mouth. *That's familiar! Where have I heard it before? How... how could you possibly know about the Mercedes? Who are you?* He recovered enough from the shock to ask, "Do I know you?"

Hunter put a finger to his lips to convey *Say nothing more on the subject*, then made a "V" sign, the victory sign with his fingers; he held them horizontally and flexed them twice.

As a SEAL, Director McGee had used hand signals in the field. He observed the silent communications, and perceived Hunter was purposely outing himself. *Oh, Hunter, you must have a good reason.*

Nazy, Eastwood, and Dr. Lindell were trying to make some sense of what Dante Locke was doing with his fingers.

His head swirling, Coffey couldn't believe what his eyes were telling him. He reached out to steady himself on the end of the table of the author selling books and then sat down on the end of it. He scrutinized the man. With the salt and pepper hair and beard and dark mustache, he looked remarkably like the Marko Ramius character from the Hunt for Red October, just in a gray suit. *I think I know who that could be but… he's dead.*

Above the din of the happy hour room, Hunter leaned into the circle of friends, withdrew a Moleskin notebook from his suit coat and scribbled a note. He showed Nazy, McGee, and Eastwood the note: *We know each other. I told him who I was if he remembers.* There was a cartoonish quality as the group of four pivoted their eyes from the man who registered as Dante Locke to Coffey. Dr. Lindell remained bewildered. He hoped someone would tell him what was going on.

Before anyone could ask *"How?"* the concierge stepped into the bar area and began malleting a Deagan Dinner Chime: G, C, E, and G over and over, signaling the crowd to take their seats in the dining area. The crowd silenced immediately as the concierge continued around the room, herding the patrons into the dining room like a sheepdog.

By thoughtfully positioned name cards—Eastwood verified he and Coffey would have their backs to the podium. Coffey remained seated on the author's table, as he tried to reconcile *Maverick was alive.*

Captain America isn't dead. With two fingers, he flashed his Rocket number – seven seven! Did anyone else in this room know how fighter pilots counted with one hand? Maybe the SEAL. Two fingers vertical was "Two," two fingers horizontal was "Seven." Only military guys like Maverick would know that, and he would know about the Mercedes. But that face isn't Maverick's! That is one of the harried faces of a Sean Connery character. Then the obviousness struck him. It wasn't surgery. *It's a mask!* Coffey headed toward the dining room trying to make sense of it all.

At the table, Hunter removed a *Growler* from a suit pocket and palmed it; he was grateful for the interruption. *Saved by the bell! I'll have to talk to Coffey, but this isn't exactly the right place to divulge to the FBI or a retired FBI Special Agent I'm on a special access program.*

Coffey hadn't counted with one hand since the Marines. He had questions. *Why would a resurrected Maverick be wearing a mask? What the hell is that green thing? What is going on?*

Then Hunter switched on the green device activating several LEDs around its circumference and toggled through different flashing modes. Coffey was bewildered and scrutinized the round contraption from a distance. Maybe it was a road safety flare—but it was green and not international orange like others he had seen at trade shows—which made no sense. Why would Hunter bring an electronic road flare to dinner? That made no sense either. McGee, Nazy, and Eastwood ignored Hunter's actions with the *Growler*.

Eastwood guided Dr. Lindell to the keynote speaker's table. Hunter took Nazy's arm, led her to her seat, and sat next to her.

Coffey was approaching the table when he noticed the wedding bands and assayed Cunningham and Hunter were probably married. *Now I understand. He was marking his territory. Message received. Lucky dude! Can't make any cracks about her now!*

Hunter quietly placed the light-neon green rubberized device with flashing green lights in the middle of the table and covered most of it with a copy of the evening's orange program. Nazy and the CIA men knew well when activated, the *Growler* generated a bubble of electronic noise and prevented anyone and anything from electronically eavesdropping on their conversation. Anyone using a *Growler* could speak without concern that their words were being recorded. Hunter fiddled with the device so it would not interfere with the emcee's microphone. When Eastwood placed his smartphone near the *Growler* Hunter cautioned him, "Dory, can you put your cell in your pocket? I won't be responsible when it bursts into flames."

Eastwood complied. Coffey was slack jawed. Dr. Lindell was simply at a loss.

Coffey kept glancing at *Maverick*. *That's a mask, but I've seen nothing that realistic.*

Coffey and Dr. Lindell noticed "Dante Locke's" activities with the green device but said nothing. They were in the company of CIA personnel and some things were better left unspoken. Their indifference to the *Growler* suggested they knew exactly what it was for and that was the most fascinating thing of all.

Coffey had read that *Maverick* — in the squadron they called him *Captain America* behind his back — the famous Duncan Hunter, the generals' *Golden Boy* who beat them all at racquetball, the man who escaped a bad ejection from an F-4, could not cheat death on a commercial jet. *How? Maybe the better question was Why?* He had seen an announcement in the *Marine Corps Gazette* Hunter had been buried at Arlington maybe a decade ago. *The Marine Corps Gazette article stated the only people at his funeral were the President, and the CIA Director before McGee.* Coffey sucked wind. He had thought that odd at the time. *That's not Marko but Maverick, but not really. Is he part of the McGee's security detail? He's not anyone's security detail. He's a pilot. But if he's carrying a weapon…. What the hell is going on with Maverick?*

Maverick; the man behind the mask kept smiling. It was as if he were saying, *It really is me. I don't have time to explain, but I'm on assignment. Capiche?*

The old FBI special agent feebly nodded and gave Hunter a thumbs up. *I'll wait until Maverick gives me a clue.* Coffey pointed at the *Growler*; *Maverick* winked at him. Intelligence Community silent lingo.

The show was about to start. The Master of Ceremonies took the lectern. There were pumpkins in the dining area and a monster pumpkin next to the lectern. The programs were orange, and nearly all the conservative activists wore orange ties. Someone at the head table was wearing a mask for the occasion. It was Halloween after all. Everything was as it should be for what was going to be the best *Pumpkin Papers Irregulars Dinner* on record.

CHAPTER 9

October 31, 2019

At her first *Pumpkin Papers Irregular Dinner*, Nazy was intrigued with all the men's orange ties. Everything was orange; the tablecloths, the napkins, the programs. She watched the movement happening on the podium, the emcee was making ready his remarks. The atmosphere and surroundings were more extraordinary than anything she had ever experienced; it didn't evoke the bar scene from *Star Wars* or anything from the mind of Charles Addams who had created the macabre yet debonair characters of the *Addams Family*.

Things could have been considered weird, maybe bizarre for some. One thing was for certain, everyone was enjoying themselves.

Proudly displaying a prominent orange pumpkin patch tie, the emcee began, "The term *pumpkin papers* carries special significance for anti-communists, national security experts and analysts, and today's anti-terrorists. It's a reference to Whittaker Chambers using a pumpkin to hide microfilm copies of secret and stolen State Department documents given to him by State Department official Alger Hiss for transmission to the Soviet Union. Those canisters of film constituted absolute proof of Hiss' guilt and role as the highest placed Soviet spy in the American government. We applaud and celebrate Whittaker Chambers breaking with the Communist Party. Those who know the story are familiar with how he tried repeatedly to get someone at the FBI to believe him. He eventually did, and Hiss was tried and put behind bars."

As the *Irregulars* erupted in boisterous applause, Nazy was quietly shocked speechless. *So that is where that term comes from! No one could ever tell me, and now I know. She looked at Duncan to tell him. We would send teams out to recover diaries and journals and personal papers. When those teams returned to Headquarters, the Chief of Diaries, before I became the Chief of Diaries, would ask them if they got the pumpkin.*

Duncan could see something had amused his wife, and so he stuck his face into Nazy's hair and whispered directly into her ear: "What's so interesting?"

She whispered, "When we send intelligence officers out to get diaries, papers, journals, microfilm, or personal documents, we say 'Did you get *the pumpkin*?' I had no idea where that came from."

He laughed quietly and squeezed her hand.

The emcee continued, "The '*Pumpkin Papers Irregulars Dinner* is held every Halloween to pay tribute to Whittaker Chambers and those anti-communists and leaders of the Conservative movement who follow in his footsteps. It was no less than the late exalted President Reagan who said Chambers' autobiography, *Witness*, was his favorite book, after the Bible, of course. *Witness* was about Whittaker Chambers' conversion from communism to Christianity and the cause of fighting for freedom, how we must learn from the past, and why democracy requires civic virtue and eternal vigilance. Conservative activists now fight America's domestic enemies in the courts and in Congress."

"This august group of patriots knows Whittaker Chambers wrote a letter to his children. He told them he considered the Alger Hiss case a basic conflict of faiths; Communists versus the Capitalists; atheists versus the believers. For the *Irregulars*, this is the fight of our day."

"Here, here!"

Throughout dinner a passel of speakers paraded to the lectern and delivered short spiels. A political dissident and a defector from the formerly communist country of East Germany lit a candle and placed it inside the huge carved pumpkin next to the lectern.

Eastwood was next. As he approached the lectern the emcee provided, "Before our keynote speaker, the highlight of this evening is an old anti-communist war hero, Marine Corps Lieutenant Colonel Demetrius Eastwood. He will announce the nominees for the disgraceful 'Victor Navasky Award.' Representing sheer indifference or blindness to the evils of totalitarianism, a ten-watt bulb pretending to be a spotlight, the award is named after the publisher emeritus of

The Nation. It was Navasky, in a fit of egregious dumbassery, who famously asked the question regarding the Alger Hiss case, 'Espionage, is it really so wrong?'"

The *Irregulars* erupted in laughter and applause.

Hunter thought, *And the Democrats think, "Pedophilia, is it really so wrong?"*

"Among his various positions in the Marine Corps, Colonel Eastwood served on the National Security Council and made a run as a presidential candidate. He has produced several fascinating award-winning documentaries, such as *Escape From The Devil's Hole* which won an Emmy. He's a radio talk show host and a distinguished war correspondent. You can find his penetrating and timely articles in the *Washington Times* and the *New York Post*, and in newspapers across the country. Ladies and gentlemen, I give you Colonel Eastwood."

Eastwood introduced his remarks about the Navasky award and the nominees, mostly Washington, D.C. Democrats in the House and the Senate by saying, "This is all done in good humor; we don't want the thought police barging through the doors." His energetic speech was a combination of jokes and serious warnings about national security problems and the people who caused them.

"One of the runners up is Sandinista and Cuba worshipper, the Mazibuike-backed Democratic progressive mayor of New York City. We know the mayor has a soft spot for Islamic terrorists, and has vowed to dismantle the New York Police Department's outstanding counterterrorism program. But the winner of the Navasky award is former President Maxim Mohammad Mazibuike who isn't available to accept the award. There was a rumor President Mazibuike was incompetent, but then we learned he was actually the Muslim Brotherhood's preeminent spy. He was a little like a five-year-old pyromaniac setting fire to everything he touched."

The crowd erupted in applause, and Eastwood returned to his table.

More speakers took turns at the microphone, giving updates on the war on communism and radical Islam. As the tables were cleared, the emcee mounted the dais one last time and announced their next guest needed no introduction, but as it was rare for such a distinguished gentleman from government to be part of their festivities, he felt obliged.

He began with a moving encomium, "There are some men who have made incredible history, such as Charles Lindbergh, General Charles Yeager, Neil Armstrong. They made their mark in the light of day, in the open, trying to conquer something greater than themselves. But there are other men who are even more accomplished in the service of our country than Lindbergh, Yeager, and Armstrong. Their names rarely grace the pages of newspapers or are the subject of television specials or biographies."

"These are men who, on the strength of their intellect and character, led American troops to incredible things. They continually engaged with America's enemies in the most inhospitable locations. Names you likely have never heard, like Admiral Roy Davenport and Marine General Chesty Puller, both awarded five Navy Crosses for heroism, for gallantry, for valor. Rear Admiral William McGee, the son of a Tuskegee Airman, received the nation's highest award, the Congressional Medal of Honor, five Navy Crosses, *and* two Distinguished Intelligence Crosses making him by far the most decorated man ever to wear a uniform for the United States of America. Indeed, we are blessed tonight; we may never see another so decorated American patriot as Admiral McGee. Currently, Rear Admiral McGee serves as the Director of the Central Intelligence Agency. Ladies and gentlemen, I give you Director Bill McGee."

Led by Duncan Hunter, a.k.a. Dante Locke, the assembly of men and women stood and clapped as Bill McGee took the lectern. The *Growler's* light kept flashing; it was the only thing in the room that didn't care what was going on.

McGee took a moment to relish the applause; gripping the sides of the podium he smiled to the *Pumpkin Papers Irregulars*. They clapped and whistled and didn't look like they would stop, so he quickly polished his round glasses and returned them to his face. Smartphones slipped from suitcoats and purses to capture the event. They clapped for three minutes as McGee rumbled into the microphone, "Thank you" and waved his hands trying to get the crowd to sit down. "Thank you, thank you. Apparently, you have nothing else to do tonight. I appreciate it. Well, that's all I have. You've been a marvelous crowd! Thank you. Thank you."

The crowd chuckled with salubrious approval. When Hunter and Nazy took their seats, the rest of the dinner crowd sat down.

McGee thanked the master of ceremonies and the other speakers. He singled out Colonel Eastwood for his dedication to truth and honor and Dr. Lindell for his continued efforts to keep his grandfather's remarkable achievements alive, exposing communists who had infiltrated the government and lived to talk about it. He said, "There's someone you may know at our table. I think we have Captain Marko Ramius, straight from the movie *Hunt for Red October*. He doesn't do autographs, and he's not wearing an orange tie. I suppose he favors Egyptian blue. He appears to be the only one who didn't get the memo.... Maybe he has been overseas or under the seas."

Polite clapping from the other tables. Hunter was mortified. He wondered, *What the hell was that for?*

McGee continued, "Before there was a Witness Protection Program, defectors from communism had to have their wits about them to keep themselves and their families safe. The KGB had *wet work* teams in America—assassins, courtesy of the First Chief Directorate of the Kremlin."

McGee spoke about the CIA and their international challenges without divulging secret material or airing the Agency's dirty laundry. He spoke of domestic issues, BLM riots in major cities, of illegal immigration, of energy production, and technology. "You know as I do, decades of Democratic rule have ruined some of our finest cities."

"This Democrat Party isn't the Party of Jefferson or Kennedy. This is a communist Democrat Party. There are more people, including children, who are enslaved worldwide than ever before in history. The goal of the Democrat Party is to neutralize white men in the United States and to malign white men. They have manufactured crimes, a mythology of racism and white supremacy that distract the minds of Republicans and Conservatives while philanthropist billionaire Rho Schwartz Scorpii funds...."

The *Pumpkin Papers Irregulars* booed and hissed at the mention of the socialist billionaire's name.

At hearing "Scorpii," Hunter involuntarily lowered his brows and looked down to conceal his thoughts. No one paid him any mind; they were all focused on McGee. Hunter tuned out McGee's comments. The CIA had tried to locate Scorpii a couple of years ago with bait they hoped he would take, but nothing came of it. He also recalled an article by Eastwood months ago. *Scorpii is a billionaire oil tycoon with close ties to European leaders, including the Russian president. He was among two dozen European oligarchs and officials who were sanctioned by the Treasury Department several months ago. He has been investigated for money laundering and accused of "threatening the lives of business rivals, illegally wiretapping a government official, and taking part in extortion and racketeering."*

Hunter considered, *How many of the terrorists we eliminated did he fund? Without his money the world's terrorist problem would have been manageable, maybe it would have died on the vine. Would this group believe we're in a silent war with an eighty-something year-old billionaire hiding out in Europe? This is a culture war. A war of infiltration instead of invasion, intimidation instead of free choice, of psychological forces so insidious we come to believe the idea of doing our part by giving up our rights is our own.*

Bill McGee smiled at the interruption, then continued, "… in the U.S., Scorpii funds Democrat informants, he funds Democrat studies, and he funds Democrat Party candidates. Through third party law firms, Democrats can cite studies on public policy with the predictable outcomes: Republicans and Conservatives are racists and white supremacists. Now I know Democrats are easily confused, but what does that make me, exactly?"

The *Irregulars* erupted in laughter and applause.

"They see things in terms of color; we view things in terms of freedom. Law-abiding people fleeing tyranny come to America for freedom."

The *Irregulars* applauded, again.

"What they really want is to strip our citizenship from us, to outlaw Republicans and Conservatives. They want a one-party system. We desire a colorblind society; we are willing to live in peace. They desire revenge."

It was incongruous for a black man to speak about how the left vilifies white men, Republicans, and Conservatives. McGee talked about controlling behaviors. "It's simply incredible 50 black editors of black newspapers in large cities went to Moscow in the 1950s for propaganda training. Within ten years, they had flipped the African American vote to the Democrats. This is the power of learned propaganda. After almost 100 years of Republican representation, African Americans voted for the party of slavery and the KKK, and I might add, the party of propaganda. We can see those editors learned mass hypnosis."

"Propaganda, you say? Doesn't everyone engage in political propaganda? Let's review the record. The *Pumpkin Papers Irregulars* and the leaders of the Conservative movement are incredible historians. In the final days of World War II, the Office of Strategic Services, what is today our Central Intelligence Agency, secretly acquired the records of Joseph Goebbels, the Nazi's Reich Minister of Propaganda. They also obtained the records of many of the doctors serving in the Ministry of Propaganda. Americans may have heard of Josef Mengele but actually know little about the German *Schutzstaffel* (SS) officer and physician. Maybe they have heard of his notorious sobriquet, the *Angel of Death*. He's mainly remembered for his actions at the Auschwitz concentration camp where he performed physical experiments on prisoners. But hardly anyone knows Joseph Goebbels and his doctors also performed experiments, but on the minds of prisoners."

The *Pumpkin Papers Irregulars* interrupted McGee with booing and hissing. They were not fans of Mengele or Goebbels.

"The only purpose of the Ministry of Propaganda was to control the minds of the people. That is actually a quote from Goebbels. All Marxist, Communist, and Socialist countries have a Ministry of Propaganda. It may be called the Political Office in Russia or Cuba or Venezuela or China. We are not surprised the Democrats are clamoring for their own Ministry of Propaganda, of course, under a different name. Such as a Diversity Office, led by a Diversity Officer."

The *Irregulars* applauded the CIA Director's insight.

"And, that isn't all. Are you aware of the Presidential Executive Order: *Using Behavioral Science Insights to Better Serve the American People*? I'd like you to think about that—and no, that isn't a President Hernandez executive order, but a President Mazibuike EO."

Many of the *Irregulars* pulled out their smartphones to fact check the CIA Director.

McGee continued, "I can see some of you are checking up on me. Every day we are manipulated and controlled by the left's propaganda, and we must break the left's hold on us. The former president directed the government to use propaganda to control the way you think and make decisions. Let me repeat that. President Mazibuike directed the government to use propaganda to control the way you think and decide. Period. Full stop."

The *Pumpkin Papers Irregulars* booed the former president.

"Let's look at the CIA's declassified *investigative* projects such as *Artichoke*, *Bluebird*, *Mockingbird*, and *Chatter*. Essentially these projects asked, 'Can you program or use propaganda on a person to get them to do something they would not normally do?'"

"Allow me to state for the record, these studies were accomplished in the 50s and 60s, before Marxist, Communist, and Socialist policies had been able to infect the U.S. government. Project *Artichoke* was a derivative of a Nazi Ministry of Propaganda investigation. Its purpose was to determine whether a moral person could be made to perform an immoral act involuntarily, such as *attempted* assassination. Have you read the book or seen the movie, *The Manchurian Candidate*? Richard Condon, the author, ignored the established boundaries of that area of *dark psychology* with his story of sleeper agents, brainwashing by hostile communist forces, and the ability to turn an assassin *on by a specific command*. He used a queen of diamonds from a deck of playing cards as the triggering mechanism. Very creepy stuff."

"But Goebbels was researching these same things in the 1930s and 1940s in an attempt to send someone to London to take out Churchill. Hitler also wanted someone to come to Washington, D.C. to remove FDR permanently. Another was to go to Moscow to eliminate Stalin. In the end, those programs were too difficult to do. We have Goebbels' diaries that substantiate the Ministry's projects. But there were other projects, many others. When it looked like Germany would fall, the SS, the *Schutzstaffel* reportedly boxed up their research on propaganda, killed the Ministry's researchers, and Goebbels committed suicide."

"Goebbels knew his days were numbered. He was quoted as saying, '*There will come a day, when all the lies will collapse under their own weight, and truth will again triumph.*' He knew even the best master manipulator would fail over time."

"Why am I talking about some old Nazi propaganda programs? Let's not be duped into thinking the media or the Democrat Party hasn't used Goebbels' practices and methods directly. We know they used them during the run-up to the election of Maxim Mohammad Mazibuike. They used mass hypnosis techniques on Americans to help ensure he became president. Then with his secret executive order, he moved to control Americans through propaganda."

The *Irregulars* booed and hissed.

"Most Americans have heard of Pavlov's dog. The dog was trained to respond to the sound of a bell which presaged the delivery of food. The dog was being conditioned to salivate on command. That's a mind control experiment. You're aware of psychological experiments, but you're probably not aware they have been used as weapons for a century. They are called the silent weapons for quiet wars."

Coffey and Dr. Lindell exchanged stunned looks.

"The old Soviet Union's Lavrentiy Beria was the Joseph Goebbels of his day. He said, 'Show me the man and I'll show you the crime,' Let me talk about Beria for a few seconds. Or maybe you're ready to go home?"

The *Irregulars* were emphatic: NO!

McGee smiled. "Truth be told, I don't want to go either."

There was thundering applause which inspirited McGee to continue.

"Beria was one of the most despicable humans to ever walk the face of the earth. During World War II he was in charge of the 4th Special Department, what we call the Directorate of *Wet Works*: assassinations and sabotage operations. He administered the vast expansion of the Gulag labor camps and was primarily responsible for overseeing the secret detention facilities for scientists and engineers known as *sharashkas*. His men beat these educated men, forcing them to conduct research. After Stalin's death, Beria formed a troika with Georgy Malenkov and Vyacheslav Molotov. They led the country until the coup d'état by Nikita Khrushchev. Beria was removed from power, arrested, tried for treason, sentenced to death, and executed. During his trial there were allegations he was a serial sexual predator of boys. As I said, a nasty one, but a master in propaganda and mind control."

"Then there is the Machiavelli quote from *The Prince*. Instead of reading it, I want you to take some time and *consider* it. *Things must be ordered in a such a mode that when men no longer believe, one can make them believe by force.*"

"Is it any wonder we cannot trust the media? Anyway, when we discuss propaganda, we must also accept it's the sole focus of political warfare. Clausewitz stated *politics was combat by other means.* Goebbels said in his diary: *Propaganda has only one object – to conquer the masses.* And there have been secret U.S. Army Field Manuals describing the *silent weapons for a quiet war.*"

Link Coffey and Dr. Lindell snapped their heads again, suddenly exchanging worrying glances. *Silent Weapons for a Quiet War!* Slack jawed, they were stunned the CIA Director had repeated the name on the old pamphlet Lindell had translated. Mention of the document made them more focused on the speaker.

McGee continued, "And *silent weapons* mean the tools and different forms of propaganda needed to conduct a political war. All of our adversaries know the United States cannot be defeated militarily, but through propaganda the U.S. can be destroyed culturally. Once the American culture is demolished, the cohesive culture of our wonderful military will be ripped asunder, and then there will be no one left to protect us. That is their plan."

The *Irregulars* were strangely quiet.

During the pause, Dr. Lindell quickly leaned over to Coffey and whispered, "Did you ever figure out what the silent weapons of quiet wars were?"

Hunter's eyes followed the action at his table and overheard Dr. Lindell's question to Coffey. Hunter withdrew a vertex pen made from a banksia pod, turned over an orange program and scribbled a few words on it. When McGee began speaking again, he indicated to Eastwood to pass the program to Coffey. Coffey and Dr. Lindell looked at what Hunter had written: *Anything that induces FEAR.*

Coffey looked at *Maverick*, then at Dr. Lindell. *They leverage fear as a weapon?*

McGee stood fast at the lectern and allowed a thin smile to appear. "Ladies and gentlemen, the election of Mazibuike was a clear demonstration of *dark psychology*. The media and the Democrat Party engaged in the mind control techniques of Goebbels and his henchmen to get Mazibuike elected, they induced fear and mass hypnosis to convince you he *appeared* to be eligible to run for president. Remember? They leveraged the media to convince Americans that questions about Mazibuike's father's birthplace were racist. Not that they were disqualifiers but if you asked that question you must be a racist. Over time, in many Americans minds, Mazibuike's father wasn't from a foreign country, which apparently made Mazibuike eligible for the office, so said the ladies from the *View*."

Duncan Hunter and Link Coffey exchanged glances when McGee mentioned Mazibuike wasn't eligible to be president. They shared the same thought: *Of course he wasn't! Some Americans were convinced it was a conspiracy theory. Others could prove the Democrat Party and the media had used propaganda against Americans and usurped the Constitution to elect Mazibuike, but no one would listen. It was a complicated story. McGee knew and he had the answers.*

McGee added, "Remember how the media leveraged their evil propaganda. If you wouldn't vote for Mazibuike, you were deemed a racist. If you criticized a black man, you were deemed a racist. There is no more powerful tool of propaganda than calling someone a racist. There is a fear to be called a racist. Racism would be dead in America today if it were not for certain people on the left and leftist institutions. I mean Democrats, the media, and the American education system."

The *Pumpkin Papers Irregulars* howled and applauded. The light on the *Growler* kept beating.

Duncan Hunter softly applauded. He thought, *So true. If it weren't for double standards, they would have no standards at all. Racist is the ultimate magic word – accuse a moral person of being a racist and their fear turns them into a blubbering fool. They will do whatever the manipulator requires of them to prove they are not a racist, like voting for someone they found deplorable, as McGee intimated. Propaganda doesn't work on everyone; but not everyone is needed to sway an election.*

CHAPTER 10

October 31, 2019

McGee accepted the applause; he took a drink of water to moisten his mouth. He had debated with Nazy if he should reveal the next block of information. The *Irregulars* were having an excellent time. No one wanted to leave, and they seemed to be eager for more. He looked at Nazy, who nodded.

The CIA Director began, "I'm going to change gears ever so slightly. There was a time, long ago, when the GDR or officially the DDR, the *Deutsche Demokratische Republik*, sought a higher level of international recognition. They were East Germany, and they had a nasty reputation as communists. I should say, the East German *secret police*, the *Stasi*, gained that nasty reputation by how they controlled political opinion in the DDR. And just how did they do that? They used the conventional methods of gulags and torture. But to seek better recognition *internationally*, they needed a lower-profile method of suppressing opposition to Communism. So, in 1976 the *Stasi* came up with a strategy and a means of psychological oppression and persecution for those people who expressed opposition to communism. They published a top-secret document called the *Disintegration Directive*. This was their official guide to crush dissent, even potential dissent. It specified a covert, psychological approach to maintaining the Communist monopoly on ideological discourse."

"In other words, *psychological operations*. Let's look at who was specifically targeted in East Germany. As outlined in their *Disintegration Directive*, the goal of the *Stasi* was to destroy dissidents and potential dissidents socially and emotionally without resorting to arrest and imprisonment. How did they do that? The *Stasi* collected private information about the victims and processed that info into something deleterious, then *disintegrated* their careers and their family and private lives."

"In these cases, we are dealing with coordinated attempts by the *Stasi* to harass and humiliate individuals, insinuate they were pedophiles or criminals in order to break them. There weren't a lot of guys who looked like me in East Germany. So, if you were not being manipulated by charges of racism, then they insinuated you were pedophiles. Eventually the victims admitted they were wrong in their thoughts, their writings, their readings. They were ridiculed into believing their existence was harming the collective and their comrades. Everyone has a breaking point, and they were trained to push their victims to that point."

"Sound like anything we know? Social media, for instance?"

"Can anyone see this is what the Democrats did to Mazibuike's Republican opponent—ripped a page out of the *Disintegration Directive*? Can anyone see where this is going in the age of social media? If they can't use racism, they use another silent weapon, unfounded charges of pedophilia. When that occurs, people don't want to have any dealings with you. The social media giants are a propaganda tool disguised as a free service. There's your answer to the Democrat Party's Ministry of Propaganda—it's the social media giants and their media. Now look at President Mazibuike's executive order allowing the government to conduct psychological operations on Americans to 'help them make better decisions.'"

McGee continued, "Remember, the stated goal of the *Disintegration Directive* was to destroy the reputation of the targets. It was done covertly, and often victims weren't believed even if they discovered what the government was doing it to them. Who's going to believe someone charged with being a racist or a pedophilia?"

"Now I want you to imagine the Joint Chiefs of Staff being put in the position of either communicating support for the president's controversial political ideas—not military ideas, *political ideas*—or risking being destroyed by social media. In days gone past, if they didn't support the agenda of the President of the United States they would resign without comment. But today, the social media CEOs ensure any general who gets out of line will be destroyed. He was a racist; he was a pedophile. After thirty or forty years of serving our country, suddenly social media determines if his continued employment is justified. In the past, senior officers who would have resigned in protest over a controversial presidential decision now cannot do so without the risk of being attacked and destroyed through psychology manipulated by social media. Social media threatened to blackmail them as racists or pedophiles. So, a controversial presidential decision is approved because these yes men will do anything to save their careers. If you're a victim of the left's *Disintegration Directive*, the depression and rejection you're feeling are exactly what they want in order to shut you up, control you, and make it appear you fully support their narrative. Remember the Machiavelli quote, that they can make them believe by force."

Hunter reached across the table and retrieved the *Growler*.

McGee said, "One final thought on the subject. Professor Carroll Quigley of the Foreign Service School at Georgetown University said in his five-pound book *Tragedy and Hope*, 'I know of the operations of this network because I have studied it for twenty years and was permitted for two years, in the early 1960s, to examine the *Insider's* papers and secret agenda. I have no aversion to it or to most of its aims and have, for much of my life, been close to it and to many of its instruments. I have objected, both in the past and recently, to a few of its policies...but in general my chief difference of opinion is that *it wishes to remain unknown*, and I believe its role in history is significant enough to be known.' As your CIA Director, I can state emphatically, America is under assault by forces Americans do not know and cannot comprehend."

"It's not only the domestic enemies like the Marxists and Islamists in the Democrat party, but the international enemies too. Like the *Insiders*, or whatever they call themselves this week. Who are the *Insiders*? Senior Democrat leaders, Marxists, and Socialists, and Communists, a few men from the Islamic nations, and a few hundred of the world's top billionaires who all get together once a year—it's very hush-hush—to discuss your future and the future of the planet. Are you going to be racists this week or pedophiles? Their leverage can be incredible."

Hunter was interested in this topic. *Insiders*. He focused more on McGee than Nazy.

"Americans must be told and shown they have been lied to and manipulated by a single political party in order for *the Party*, the Democrats, to maintain their political power in the United States. This won't be an easy thing to do. Propagandists know there are two ways to be fooled. One is to believe what isn't true, the other is to refuse to accept what is true. The propagandists also know it's easier to fool someone than to convince them they have been fooled. The *Insiders* intend to fool the masses with propaganda, induce fear and mass hypnosis, and increase their political power in the world until all nations bow to them."

"Here is where we are today. The Democrat Party leadership will deny they are part of the One-Government crowd, but the evidence is overwhelming they seek one party rule in the United States. They don't have to manipulate voting machines to win elections because now they believe they can use the instruments of propaganda. *Mind control*. This is America—the *bullshit* they are peddling isn't only propaganda, it's unadulterated communism."

The *Irregulars* gave McGee their loudest approval of the night.

Hunter was listening to McGee, admiring his wife, holding her hand, and playing a little innocent high school-footsie under the table. If only the boss would wrap it up.

There was a Ciceronian elegance to Bill McGee's words and Nazy was enthralled. Duncan's mind had drifted off to what he had left behind in North Africa. Pushing that business aside for the moment, something Bill said made him rummage through the attic of his mind for a scrap of information. Why was the big guy bringing up the subject of a propaganda war with the Democrats? He knew Bill had to have a reason; he just didn't see what it was. Hunter didn't want to think of propaganda and communists. He looked at Nazy. She was what he wanted to focus on.

Duncan thoughts changed directions again. He looked around cautiously. All eyes and ears were on McGee. Hunter withdrew a challenge coin from his trouser pocket and reached over the table to give it to Coffey.

Coffey didn't appreciate the interruption. McGee was a fascinating speaker and the topic was sensitive, borderline secret squirrel stuff. *A coin? You interrupted me for a stinkin' coin? I have a thousand of them!* Then Coffey looked carefully at the larger-than-a-silver dollar-sized enameled coin. He recognized the shield and wings, and it sent his eyelids aflutter. *It's identical to the Air America patch, but instead of "Air America" spelled out in the shield, it reads "Air Branch."*

Coffey looked up at Hunter and narrowed his brows. He had actually heard about the coin Hunter had just given him. The Air Branch coin was the rarest challenge coin in existence according to the world's largest on-line auction; by far the top coins bought and sold across the planet were from the Agency's many offices and divisions. There were some poor quality photographs of an Air Branch coin, but no one knew who had made them or how many had been made or given out as trophies. Every collector wanted the rarity; but no collector had a single example. Now Coffey had one. It was an exceptionally well-machined and lacquered coin. Further inspection revealed it was numbered. His was number 0006.

He again glanced at Hunter. Hunter's smile was full and arcuate; there was deviousness in the air. *Air Branch? Of course, Air Branch! The guys who conceived and developed the U-2 and the A-12! Mere flying pogues like us in the Marine Corps saw getting assigned there had to be the best job in aviation – but you had to be in the Agency and be a pilot! So, Hunter is working at Air Branch? Doing what? Flying another incredible aircraft no one knows anything about? But what could that be? Everything is a drone nowadays. At least that is what I assumed.*

Coffey ignored McGee for the moment and stared at the intricately cut, brassy black and red enameled coin. He looked to the ceiling and remembered when he was at the FBI, he had tried several times to get access to Air Branch to talk about their unmanned systems. The CIA's Special Activities Division (SAD) was reportedly spending the equivalent of the national budget of South Africa to make every clandestine aviation program unmanned. He checked the heft of the coin and while doing so recalled the FBI had bungled several high-dollar ransom cases and thought the use of the CIA's unmanned aircraft might have been able to help. The problem with the FBI's unmanned systems was they were loud; even the short-range electric ones.

He remembered a case, one where the FBI actually got it right and looked good in the process, really good. *That kidnapping case involved a little girl and millions in ransom. Somehow the girl was found alive, and the Bureau captured the culprits and recovered the money. No one in the FBI knew how it had been done, and it embarrassed the rank-and-file Special Agents who had spent hours working that case. Unlike all other cases, there was no feedback, no lessons learned, no hot wash. The whole thing left a disgusting taste in my mouth....*

Coffey looked at the coin again and wondered. *I heard a rumor it was the only time the FBI Director ever asked the CIA Director for help. The CIA was prohibited by law conducting domestic operations.* Coffey slowly raised his eyes to Hunter. *We always screwed those up. If there actually was help.... I always thought there was another reason.... No, the rumor mill was that the Agency was no closer to making the perfect flying robot than those billionaires were to making electric cars that didn't catch fire.*

Coffey gave Dante Locke a thumbs up and resumed listening to McGee. It was about time the Agency had a patriot in charge, but Coffey wondered if Air Branch was back in the business of secret black airplanes no one was supposed to know anything about. *What are the chances of that?*

With his decades of law enforcement and investigations training, Coffey noticed Nazy and Hunter had moved their seats a fraction of an inch to better view Director McGee. She was unconsciously leaning into him and he into her, the marks of lovers. *They are trying hard not to show it but they are definitely husband and wife... and in love. Now, how is that even possible? I'll make Hunter tell me one day.*

Duncan Hunter's mask was starting to itch. He couldn't wait to get the damn thing off. It was easy to blame McGee for ruining his sex life with work, work, and more work. Nazy was just as dedicated to the cause as McGee. Yet Hunter fully appreciated their efforts to keep him out of the bright lights of Congressional oversight hearings and away from the assassins of the Muslim Brotherhood. Officially, Duncan Hunter no longer existed. The Agency had killed him in the name of national security and buried him with honors at Arlington to complete the illusion. A standard white marble headstone was inscribed with the deceased's name, rank, branch of service, date of birth, and date of death.

While Hunter appreciated all the special activities designed to keep him out of a sniper's crosshairs, he didn't appreciate McGee singling him out like he had at the start of his comments. *Did it hurt anything? Probably not. And McGee was having a momentously stately time.*

Hunter knew his work of finding and killing terrorists overseas was ending. There wasn't anyone left on the *Matrix* save one long-time resident: the bombmaker. A place-holder who may or may not be alive. And it could be years before Al Jazeera declared him dead.

Hunter also knew there was a man who would never appear on the list: Rho Schwartz Scorpii. The prime financier of terrorism was reportedly in bad health in Germany. When he died no one was expected to pick up the torch and fund progressive and terroristic causes. But maybe that was wishful thinking.

Plus, President Hernandez was a lame duck President. He had provided the ultimate cover for the special access program and was at the end of his two terms. When he left office, McGee and Nazy and Duncan would all be out of a job. No more CIA, no more quiet airplanes, no more Democrat Party dirty looks.

McGee's baritone caught Hunter's attention again. "The stated goal of the *Disintegration Directive* was to destroy the reputation of the target and make him or her so preoccupied with their personal difficulties and emotional turmoil that he or she had no will to question the government."

Hunter thought, *Oh, that's new.*

"After the fall of the Soviet Union, several communist regimes of Eastern Europe largely disintegrated. But communism hasn't disappeared from the continent or the minds of the ruling elites. We have to remember how these communist regimes work; the ruling class desire control above all else. They kill their dissidents. They control the industrial media complex, and in doing so portray capitalism and America as an evil monster. They are masters of propaganda and must make their population afraid of the capitalist United States."

"Fear is the most pronounced motivator of the masses. Fear is also an oversized lever to convince judicious people to give up their freedom because they believe the people in power will protect them, as they say they will. They ignore Goebbels' line, if you tell a lie often enough, people begin believing it. The Australians gave up their weapons believing their politicians would protect them. The day will come when they will regret that decision to capitulate their freedom for the liberals' siren song of promises. Liberals and leftists have an agenda, and they have been at it for decades. They cannot be trusted. We cannot let them take control of America again!"

"The greatest threat to mankind is the same today as it was a thousand years ago. We are ruled by parasitic psychopaths who plunge us into war, manipulate us against each other, and flood our mind with fear, hate, bigotry, and ignorance with every chance they get."

"We see where the evilness of communism has failed. Now a new set of masters, dictators, and totalitarians rise, ready to take over. They are already impacting our world. Humanity must not harbor any belief that we can co-exist, for if you offer a hand, they will cut it off with a sword. Communist regimes are criminal regimes buttressed by propaganda, and they think of nothing but conquest. Theirs is an evil forged by hate, degeneracy, and revenge."

Rear Admiral McGee said, "I'd like to tell you a little story, just recently declassified." He looked over to Eastwood as if to say, *Pay attention to this*.

The room was eerily still. Even the servers who had been refilling glasses of water stopped to listen to McGee. "Operation *Charlemagne* was a Nazi Ministry of Propaganda project designed to see if they could get the vote of people who would not normally vote for them. Remember the Nazi Party was hardly anyone's first choice. Sometimes we hear 'Hitler was elected.' In other words, it was the German people's fault; they chose Hitler and in choosing Hitler they chose fascism. Hitler's Nazi Party was the single largest party and voting bloc in Germany in 1932–33 and Hitler became Chancellor through constitutional means—he was *appointed* to the office by Hindenburg, Germany's president." All eyes were on McGee.

"To maintain their power, dictators have been obsessed with the idea of stealing elections by whatever means necessary. The Nazi's had a theory that if you can get someone to vote against their normal will, you wouldn't have to manipulate ballots. Our story begins with a certain Marine Corps officer, a captain, working for the Office of Strategic Services and assigned in France to lead the French Resistance. At the time, he lived in a world of rubble. He had left the mountains of France for a prisoner of war camp. His name was Captain Peter Ortiz...."

CHAPTER 11

October 31, 2019

Demetrius Eastwood nearly fell out of his seat. *I was just thinking of Captain Peter Ortiz!*

Hunter and Coffey looked at each other and mouthed, *"Big Bird?"* The one-of-a-kind call sign; the *nom de guerre* of *another* Peter Ortiz who flew in their back seats when they were F-4 pilots over a quarter century ago. Only *their* Pete Ortiz was a *Junior. Was it possible Big Bird's dad was the famous OSS hero Pete Ortiz?* McGee had their undivided attention.

McGee continued, "I have recently declassified these files and tens of thousands of photographs; hundreds that have never been seen. They show the extent of collaboration the Nazi's had with the Grand Mufti of Jerusalem, Amin al-Husseini. We have a Marine Corps officer to thank for these records. This is just one of his stories."

"Some know Captain Peter Ortiz was assigned to the French Resistance, the *Maquis*. OSS Director Donovan expected the Reichministry of Propaganda would fall as the Nazi Reich was falling, and Donovan wanted Goebbels' research and diaries. To get them he needed a man of unusual talents."

"Captain Ortiz was given two simple orders from the OSS Director, William Donovan: *Do not allow the Nazis to destroy the files from the Ministry of Public Enlightenment and Propaganda. Do not allow the Red Army to capture those files.* Those succinct and precise orders came from the head of the OSS via the OSS Station Chief in Geneva, who subsequentially became the first civilian and longest serving Director of Central Intelligence, Allen Dulles."

"Captain Ortiz, whose father was American and mother French, was a master of languages and disguises. How he made his way to Berlin hasn't been recorded, or at any rate hasn't been declassified. Here's what we know. When Ortiz arrived in Berlin, he reported he found several of the Reichministry of Propaganda's buildings on fire and the Soviets in the Reichministry. They were about to leave in three troop carriers. What happened afterwards is the stuff legends are made of."

"Marine Corps Captain Peter Ortiz and two Special Operations Executive NCOs, all dressed as locals, chased off the Soviets and entered the Reichministry. Ortiz found thousands and thousands of papers, files, and documents inside. Some were smoldering. The Red Army had emptied the file cabinets of their contents and had taken the empty file cabinets. They had also left the Ministry's heavy office safes. The Soviets had gotten to the Reichministry of Propaganda before the Americans, but the troops of the Red Army had made it easy on themselves by taking only the easy stuff — empty cabinets. They left all the good stuff — the Reichministry of Propaganda's papers, studies, and research."

The *Pumpkin Papers Irregulars* howled with laughter and applauded America's good fortune.

"Ortiz used whatever he could, bedsheets and tent canvas and tarps to bundle up Goebbels' papers, documents, and files. Now Captain Ortiz had once been a race car driver before the war. He commandeered three Nazi trucks which, in the parlance of war means *he stole them* and raced them 500 miles to Paris, France."

"If that isn't incredible enough, Captain Ortiz presented a letter signed by FDR *and* Churchill directing troops to assist him in his top-secret project. And the Americans did. One American who assisted eminently was General Patton. Now, General Patton wasn't impressed with Captain Ortiz's letter, but he wanted to see what Ortiz's OSS were spiriting out of Europe."

"The story goes General Patton climbed into the truck bed with Captain Ortiz; Ortiz unfolded a tarp and withdrew a file. The top document was the original law signed by Hitler and several other Nazi officials in 1933, entitled *Law for the Safeguard of German Blood and German Honor*. This was the document that barred marriage between Jews and other Germans and changed the citizenship status of German Jews to that of Jews in Germany. This document legally established the framework which eventually led to the Holocaust."

"Patton was so impressed Captain Ortiz had *captured* the Ministry of Propaganda's archives that the general assigned some aircraft to expedite the removal of the documents from Europe. In appreciation, Ortiz offered General Patton signed copies of what became known as the *Nuremburg Laws*, but not before Ortiz used a Minox subminiature camera to photograph them for the OSS. These were the cornerstone documents that allowed the legalized persecution of Jews in Germany. The most important of the *Nuremburg Laws* was the one which stripped German Jews of their German citizenship."

"The general accepted the documents. The original signed *Nuremburg Laws* had been in General Patton's family since Captain Ortiz gave them to him. A few years ago, they were given to the Library of Congress. Also, in the CIA's Museum, there is a copy of the receipt for 25 Minox cameras purchased by the Office of Strategic Services and Captain Ortiz's Minox camera is on display."

"Within days, two C-47 *Dakotas* transported the Ministry's records across the Mediterranean Sea, across the Sahara to Monrovia, Liberia. From there, two of Juan Trippe's Pan American Airways flying boats flew the files to South America and then to Baltimore."

"Maybe some of the Goebbels files were shipped to Moscow and maybe some were destroyed. All we know is some were scattered underfoot until Captain Ortiz collected them. They were still in their German-type office folders. You know, those thin metal strips in the salmon-colored binders that were run through holes punched in the paper; you bent the metal strips over and locked the papers in place. Just the German efficiency you would expect from the Nazis."

Twittering laughter burst from the tables. Some part of McGee's narrative tweaked Hunter's psyche, and he reached for his wallet. He fished out a gold coin he had been carrying for decades since he was just a kid; his dad was stationed in Germany.... Hunter remembered.... *I thought they were just dull yellow coins scattered on the ground. I was ten and a coin collector. I filled my pockets, thinking I had become a thief.... It was exciting, but I felt bad.* Hunter gazed at the face of evil embossed on a coin. A *gold* coin that wasn't really a gold coin. *I remember it was as big around as my mother's silver dollar necklace but twice as thick.* McGee was talking of Nazis; Hunter studied the crude Nazi emblem—eagle and swastika—that was unevenly embossed in the coin. Below the emblem was 1943.

Hunter nodded. *I had fifty of these until I went into the Marine Corps. And I still carry this reminder of my first unreal adventure as a child. When I became an adult, I understood that it was my first encounter with evil. I'm certain this coin was made from the gold teeth of Holocaust victims. Even today it has an alien, eldritch aura to it and reminds me that the fight against evil is never done.* He returned the coin to his wallet; McGee's voice brought Hunter back to the present.

McGee said, "Ortiz could read German. A considerable number of fragments of what we later discovered to be Goebbels' diaries were found in the courtyard of his ministry. The diaries, and yes, there were more than one, had evidently narrowly escaped burning; some pages were singed. Virtually all the documents recovered by Ortiz smelled of smoke, and he was worried they would combust after they wrapped them up in tarps. Those documents had been locked up for decades."

The *Irregulars* clapped for Captain Peter Ortiz.

"Now, somewhere in the 2002-2003 timeframe during a routine inventory of archived files, the Nazi Ministry of Propaganda file on Operation *Charlemagne* and the corresponding research was found missing. This was just one operation of hundreds Goebbels and his henchmen performed. This project used propaganda—*in 1933*—to manipulate people who would not normally vote for Nazi candidates to vote for Nazi candidates. You should ask yourself 'why?'"

"Remember, these records come up missing in 2002-2003 before any of us heard about State Senator Mazibuike. I now put this in the context of the election of President Mazibuike. Some in our Agency made the case the Democrat Party had received the original Nazi's Operation *Charlemagne* file, for they followed it to the letter during the last election. Everywhere across America people were turned into barking-mad mind-numb robots. It's called mass formation psychosis. You remember the refrain from the media and Hollywood. If you don't vote for Mazibuike, you're a racist. If you criticize a black man, you're a racist. That is propaganda; that is mind control. That is how the Democrat Party used the silent tools of propaganda to win that election."

It was deathly quiet in the dining room. People were transfixed by the McGee's comments. No one had ever spoken to them like this.

McGee smiled, "Ladies and gentlemen, we are living in perilous times. Goebbels said, '*This is the secret of propaganda: Those who are to be persuaded by it should be completely immersed in the ideas of the propaganda, without ever noticing that they are being immersed in it.*' Since the late forties the left has been using newspapers, television, and leftist universities to persuade the American population. Has anyone else noticed the most racist institutions of higher learning are run by white leftists in cities run by Democrats, in states run by Democrats?"

The Pumpkin Papers Irregulars applauded again.

"Not liberals; full blown leftists. We have to assume the liberals and the leftists in the Democrat Party and the media have that file and maybe others like it. Maybe Russia is feeding this information to them. Maybe some other entity...."

Hunter's eyes shot up. *Maybe some other entity? Bullfrog, pray tell, what are you intimating? Are you saying Democrats or Insiders or both? Maybe Scorpii?*

McGee continued, "The evidence is compelling. They recognized the awesome power and used the special silent weapons, the instruments of propaganda, to elect Mazibuike. If they can use secret and powerful propaganda techniques to get Americans to vote for *their* candidate *en masse*, they don't need to hijack the innards of voting machines to steal U.S. elections. You'll be blackmailed into voting for a Democrat candidate. Otherwise, you'll be labeled a racist or a pedophile. Mazibuike said the Democrat Party will design policies to help you make better decisions when you're in the voting booth. That better decision will be to vote for their candidate – if you know what is good for you. This is what Mazibuike left us. I wish I were only joking."

"Finely tuned propaganda allows a manipulator to essentially reprogram the brain. If we allow it, they will use those same techniques to pass laws that delegitimize our citizens. Hitler canceled the citizenship of the Jewish people in Germany. You can count on the Democrats to try something similar. Maybe they will strip people of their weapons, turn them into undesirables, and make them targets for elimination. Now think of the possibilities of an immoral political party, a party leadership that does whatever is necessary stay in power. You might start to see the scope of this problem. *We* are not the problem, although the left screams that we are."

"Let me pay homage to our Founders, for they were brilliant men. I believe these farsighted men knew America could be enslaved by the criminal left, so they gave Americans the ultimate right, the ability to protect themselves. The right to keep and bear arms shall not be infringed! The Second Amendment exists for all Americans. The glorious and sublime Thomas Jefferson said, 'The tree of liberty must be refreshed from time to time with the blood of patriots and tyrants.' Things in America have reached a tipping point. I believe we will see Americans versus Communists." McGee panned his hand across the room and said, "This little band of conservatives shall not be shoved to the sidelines. We value freedom. We must win."

"We are conservative men and women who believe the Republican Party needs to stand for something, and we will fight to keep this the greatest nation ever conceived. Together, we are up to the task. This is why I'm announcing tonight among you, my friends and supporters, I will seek the Office of the President of the United States."

Applause erupted everywhere.

Duncan had his girl beside him and his closest friends around the table. McGee could have been spouting national secrets from a firehose, but Hunter wasn't really listening until the *Irregulars* went wild.

He said what?

The applause and cheering were deafening. Nazy had tears flowing down her cheeks as she clapped like a madwoman. Hunter was the last to stand. *Did I hear that right?* Someone had cued up the music, *Hail to the Chief!* He looked at his best friend on the podium. The man he had entertained at the Naval War College with crappy jokes. The man who had needed a little help to extract Osama bin Laden from the Middle East. The man who had rescued his wife from murderous troglodytes in a medieval hell. The man who had rescued him from an insane Muslim convert with a thing for swords and other instruments of torture.

Eastwood was furiously scribbling notes. It was obvious now why McGee wanted him at the *Pumpkin Papers Irregulars Dinner*. Why Nazy asked and not McGee.

Coffey and Dr. Lindell exchanged observations. Eastwood leaned close to Nazy, "The Democrat Party has never shed its racist past. As a conservative and a Republican, Director McGee will give them fits. I don't see how they can defeat him. What is the left going to say? You were hypnotized to vote for a black man but McGee is different? He's truly the candidate we've been waiting for."

Eastwood then turned to Coffey and stated, "He plans to expose the left's propaganda...."

Still applauding, Coffey yelled, "That is what it sounds like."

Dr. Lindell shouted across the table, "It's obvious. Director McGee is the strongest candidate the Republicans could have for the presidency. And if he plans to fight their propaganda with a positive message, expose their *BIG LIES,* then he could very well win and win big. I've suddenly become a fan." Coffey concurred, recalling Dr. Lindell had said something similar fifteen years ago of Mazibuike: "If he ever became the American president, he was the only person on the planet who could lead the Muslim Brotherhood to glory."

Hunter thought McGee would make a good president, but Bill had never been interested in the politics of things. At the Naval War College McGee had told Hunter the main reason he would retire as a Captain was he would not play the politics required to make admiral. He was an operations guy, a field warrior. When it was time to walk away from the field, he would go home and spend time with his family. There would be others to pick up the baton and protect Americans from the enemies of America. He had done his part.

Hunter stood clapping, thinking.... *But that was when there was a Democrat in the White House. In this Republican administration, he has flourished. Now I get it. Now I get him. They use race as a weapon to divide Americans; he will use his race to destroy the hypocrisy of the racist left and unite Americans. Look at this group — they love him! Not because he's black but because he's a patriot!*

I suppose he's not done yet.... I suppose God has more plans for him. Hunter continued to stand in awe. *Holy crap — what was that line...?*

Some are born great, some achieve greatness, and some have greatness thrust upon them. That's the one.

That was the moment Hunter knew something had changed. McGee and President Hernandez must have talked. It was 9/11 all over again. America was in trouble again, and the President called McGee. *Holy shit, Batman! It must be really bad if Bullfrog was running for president.* This will be like fighting fire with a flamethrower.

As the clapping and the side conversations continued, Hunter thought McGee would be the strongest candidate the Democrats had ever had to contend with. The Democrats wouldn't need to steal a few battleground states; they would need to control the election results in all fifty states. *But how can McGee neutralize the left's lock on propaganda? They own the media. Ah, but he had access to all of Goebbels' files; our side has the alternative media. AM radio. Counter-propaganda.* McGee wasn't another Hitler. He was the altruistic Lone Ranger, complete with the *William Tell Overture* playing in the background.

McGee looked over to their table and smiled. Hunter gave him two thumbs up. *That was dynamite, my friend!*

Would this mean four more years of flying for the CIA? *I think that is exactly what it means.... Now I'm definitely going to need help.* He looked at Coffey and wondered about possibilities. *It wasn't time to wake the sheep, it was time to wake the other lions.*

McGee was speaking again. "When I step aside, I'll be turning the CIA over to someone so well respected, so revered inside the Agency you'll be proud to call her your Director of the CIA. She's a remarkable woman...."

Hunter's head was about to explode. *He just hired Nazy! He just hired Nazy! I thought Hernandez was done and Nazy could retire. She and I would ride off into the sunset.... You have so screwed me, Bullfrog! But.... But.... But.... Aww crapola, we are with you Bill, 100 percent.* After a moment of reflection, Hunter remembered the last line in the Declaration of Independence and nearly choked up: "*And for the support of this Declaration, with a firm reliance on the protection of divine Providence, we mutually pledge to each other our Lives, our Fortunes and our sacred Honor." I'll give Bill anything I have. It won't matter; if we lose the country, the left will come for all my stuff.*

McGee looked out across the *Irregulars* and said, "America will find out just how special she is. She interrogated the worst terrorists in Guantanamo Bay, Cuba. It has been rumored for years, but I will confirm here tonight she found the elusive Osama bin Laden in Pakistan when my SEAL Team was looking for him in the Tora Bora of Afghanistan. When the Democrats and the left said they didn't exist, she located Saddam Hussein's weapons of mass destruction after the fall of Iraq. She grasps the nature of the terrorist and has been in the middle of it all, like you, loving this country and fighting for this country. Over anyone else in the intelligence community, she knows the faces of the enemy and knows how to defeat them. The Acting CIA Director will be Miss Nazy Cunningham. When we win the White House, it will be my distinct honor to swear her in as the Director of the CIA." He gestured to Nazy and introduced her. The crowd of *Irregulars* stood and applauded. McGee encouraged her to stand, and although a little embarrassed, she did.

Hunter was mortified. The men and women of the crowd had finally gotten an unimpeded view of her and could see just how stunning a woman Nazy really was. They were enchanted. Suddenly it became unbearably hot under the mask, and his head was pounding from a sudden spike in adrenaline. McGee just outed Nazy, and the Muslim Brotherhood will try to kill her with new vigor. He turned to look at Bill McGee. It wasn't like him to question the longtime SEAL and CIA Director; he trusted him. *But why, Bill? Why?* McGee had to know what he was doing. *So, this is what fighting for America really looks like. Sometimes, I just wish someone would tell me the whole plan. Maybe he did...I was playing with coins; I wasn't paying attention.*

McGee returned to the table with a smile. He looked at Hunter as if to solicit his approval.

Hunter said, "You're going to need a jet. And some pilots."

"Know any good ones?"

Hunter wanted to chortle. "Yes and no; I'm all out of pilots, but I know a few. I'll see what we can do for you. And you'll want the new jet."

That made McGee smile, and he nodded his appreciation. He leaned into Hunter and said, "We nearly got it all done; there's one left on the *Matrix*, and my guys are in still in Libya. Unfinished work."

Hunter grunted and growled, "Oh, yes, I remember, good sir. Out of sight, out of mind." He nodded and was suddenly deep in thought. "A baker's dozen. Now I'll work on it." They shook hands.

McGee's toothy grin said it all: *Thank you*. McGee shook hands with almost everyone around the table; the exception was Nazy who hugged him. Everyone wanted to hug Nazy; not everyone got to hug Nazy. For McGee, a hug from Nazy was an unexpected gift, an expression of love and respect—like getting kissed and hugged by his daughters after they had grown out of that stuff. It was the culmination of an outstanding day.

CHAPTER 12

November 1, 2019

Home, safe inside the 7 World Trade Center apartment in Manhattan, an exhausted Demetrius Eastwood closed the door and squelched the security system with the correct number combination; something he could remember, *the last four of his social.* He was physically spent. He had taken the red eye from Washington's Union Station to New York Grand Central Station, then a mob cash cab instead of a union taxi or an Uber. He had made good use of his time on the train, writing the script for the morning's broadcast and posting his exclusive of McGee's announcing his run for president. It would appear in the *Washington Times* and the *New York Post*. He expected front page coverage above the fold in the morning edition.

The *Washington Post*, or as it was known among Conservatives and Republicans, the *Washington Daily Worker*, would not touch it and neither would the *New York Slimes*. The *Washington Post* presented itself as an adversarial newspaper; the *New York Times* thought of itself as the newspaper of record, the standard in journalism. That may have been true once upon a time, but it was no longer the case. Now, it was nothing more than a Stalinist propaganda outlet. He had told his radio audience ninety percent of today's newspapers are controlled by six corporations with virtually 100% Democrats in leadership positions. They are biased against truth and fairness and engage in propaganda. They consistently defend the interests of the Democrat Party. It made no sense for Eastwood to spend the energy to dance with them.

He was excited. The chief editors of the *Washington Times* and *New York Post* stopped the presses to ensure Eastwood's article was the headline. A lot of Republicans were on those corporate boards.

After a trip to the bathroom and kitchen in the corner suite on the 26th floor of 7 World Trade Center, Demetrius Eastwood walked past the 1957 Herman Miller Eames lounge chair where he usually edited his work and sometimes napped for a couple of hours. He stopped in the middle of the spacious room deciding his next course of action.

The floor area could accommodate hundreds of people but the only furnishings were in his office space. One wall featured parallel planks of lumber recovered from the floors of railroad boxcars. Hanging in the middle of that wall was a rustic frame of barnwood surrounding a worn and slightly faded Texas flag. The antique Leopold office desk of tiger oak held multiple monitors and a desk phone. A black judge's chair rolled effortlessly on a glass chair mat. *Objet d'art* lamps from a bank that had failed in the financial crash of October 1929 warmly illuminated the working area. Freestanding partitions were strategically placed around the office windows to prevent surveillance from adjacent buildings. And there was a butcher-block table with three archaic typewriters — gifts from Duncan Hunter — under hard transparent plastic casings. The décor was also Hunter's doing; sort of man-cave on loan to Eastwood.

Around the corner in a room whose entry door couldn't be seen from the adjacent building was a recording studio where Eastwood broadcast his radio show. With the financial backing of Duncan Hunter, Eastwood hadn't only founded a right-wing American news, opinion and commentary website but also his own radio station. He accepted Hunter's sagacious counsel and investment to create the *Unmasked & Unspun Network*. It provided unfiltered and free-of-spin political news the left-wing media would never report.

After a career in the Marine Corps which ended in a failure and a presidential run that flamed out, the former infantry officer with a top-secret security clearance had only landed part-time gigs with the television networks. He had tried his hand at writing articles, but the checks for those barely augmented his retirement income. Eastwood could hardly pay all the bills incurred in his fledgling war correspondent career. Over the years, he had offered hundreds of articles to newspapers and news aggregator websites. Only a fraction were ever published, and not all of those paid money.

A chance encounter with a conservative news network host had resulted in a little work as a subject matter expert and frequent guest spots on some conservative television shows with a military theme. It was good exposure, but living in New York City, the city that never sweeps, with rats as big as cats living in the trash with the homeless and where all the newspaper and network action occurred was very expensive.

To Eastwood it was obvious the country needed a counterweight to the media's lock on left-biased reporting. Some of his old contacts eventually volunteered to vouch for him so he could secure a White House, DOD, and a DOJ press pass. An attack on a consulate's office in Libya that killed the U.S. ambassador hadn't impacted his journalism career, but following a group of terrorists across North Africa and warning the embassies before the Muslim Brotherhood could strike had put him in good stead with the State Department, the Embassy staff, and the CIA Chiefs of Station. Networks then wanted him as a subject matter expert; newspapers demanded weekly editorial pieces.

After assisting Bill McGee in Nazy Cunningham's rescue in Algeria, he was rewarded a rare CIA press pass approved by the former CIA Director, Greg Lynche. With gratitude from Duncan Hunter, money began flowing into his bank account. Hunter provided him with an armored vehicle from his armored car business and the use of this office space in downtown New York. Eastwood became the go-to guy for network specials on terrorism and terrorists in the Middle East and Africa.

During the early days, the reporters in the press pool shunned Eastwood and his cargo pants with zippers on every pocket, and a white long-sleeve Levis® shirt. They despised everything about him.

His work uniform at the time included a crushable, goose turd-green Tilley atop very short, very white hair; titanium-trimmed rimless glasses, and a khaki Orvis shooting jacket with padded shoulders. He was tall and broad shouldered; his voice was distinctively hard-core Marine Corps, resonating presence, fearlessness, and confidence like a Broderick Crawford police character.

That was then. Now the Tilley was gone as were the Merrill® boots with the Vibram® lugs. Everything had been replaced by Brooks Brothers and Johnston Murphy leathers. He was supremely fit for 75, courtesy of fifty pullups every day and an hour on a mechanical stair climber. Eastwood's doctor told him he needed to slow down and let the youngsters play war correspondent because if he broke something in the field, he'd be days from a competent medical team and sufficient spare parts. There was a higher chance of fixing a young stud who could take a lickin' and keep on tickin' than an old fart who had worn out his body and was on a waiting list for titanium replacement parts.

Eastwood yawned as he entered the recording studio. He energized the transmitter, cameras, and microphones and got to work. In coordinated motions he turned dials and flipped switches like a pilot in a jet fighter ready for takeoff. He donned headphones and checked the output of the microphone. He made final adjustments to the equipment. Eastwood didn't read from a script, but used his standard opening remarks to launch his radio show.

"Thank you for tuning into this episode of *Unfiltered News* and welcome to the only true American on-line news network. In the formerly elegant city of Washington, D.C., where there is no difference between the communist message and the Democrat Party's message, the propaganda arm of the Democrats is at it again. Every week we review the newsworthy events you likely heard nothing about. We'll comment on anniversaries, good and bad, and we'll thank our growing list of sponsors that make this on-line telecast possible. I've got much to discuss. This is Demetrius Eastwood. Let's get this show rolling!"

"I was privileged to attend the *Pumpkin Papers Irregulars Dinner* last night in our nation's capital with CIA Director Bill McGee being the keynote speaker. I've attended several of these dinners that celebrate the victory of Whittaker Chambers over the communist Alger Hiss, but none were as incredible as last evening. The Director of the Central Intelligence Agency, Bill McGee, announced he would run for president. He put the Muslim Brotherhood, the Islamic Underground, and the communists in the Democrat Party on notice Americans will no longer allow their evil ideology and propaganda to infiltrate America and manipulate Americans. It's war."

Eastwood paused for effect. "I have to say, it's about time we had an ass-kicking patriot seeking the White House! As the leader of SEAL

Team Six, Bill McGee responded to the call after nineteen murderers killed over 3,000 innocent people on 9/11. Now, American cities are in flames, terrorists and Marxists are pushing their ideologies, and Bill McGee is again responding to the call."

Eastwood talked nonstop for two hours. It was time to wrap it up for the day.

Eastwood left the recording studio for his desk and chair. He leaned back and yawned; he had fallen asleep in it several times over the years but would not tonight. It had been a long exciting day and tomorrow would be another ballbuster. From the center drawer he withdrew a green fabric covered MEMORANDA journal and entered the day's activities and the key players. Satisfied with the entries, Eastwood returned the journal to its place in the middle drawer, shut off the lamps on the desk, and stumbled to the sofa where he fell asleep in minutes.

CHAPTER 13

November 1, 2019

Loads of soft soap and hot water ensured the glue that held Hunter's disguise in place was slowly coming off in the shower. It was beyond steamy inside. Nazy playfully insisted Duncan had to be clean and glue-free. She would inspect him to ensure that he was. And when he was…. Well, she had been waiting for that moment all night.

Five o'clock in the morning found the lovebirds in the Presidential Suite at the JW Marriott rubbing legs at the bistro table over a breakfast of coffee, juice, eggs, bacon, and toast. Nazy loved bacon; thin, thick, crispy, limpy; it didn't matter. Ten years ago, the former Muslima only tolerated bacon, but no longer. When they were in Texas or Wyoming, both of them feasted on bacon and country ham and pork tenderloins—the three little pigs. Bacon and cheese on toast for picnics. Bacon, bacon, bacon!

But there were more serious matters to discuss this morning. Hunter said, "Those clowns who call themselves correspondents and cover the intelligence community from the café across the street from the Agency and the Department of Defense know, my darling bride, the Director of Operations is a frequent visitor of the McGee household. What they don't know is that you live there. They may know you and Angela go shopping or sailing, and Bill barbeques bacon cheeseburgers. We know that makes it easier on security."

Hunter continued, "The networks' CEOs and the chief editors of the major newspapers had seen many of these relationships between Democrats. They know Republicans are more loyal and dedicated to their spouses and don't have sexual identity disorders. As much as they hope to find something between you and Bill, they know that if there was something, someone would have already raised the issue with the IG, or it would have been caught during a polygraph. Here, there's not even a bit of smoke. You and Bill have history; it's just something they could never comprehend. It's also something they should never know because they would find a way to use it against you." *He saved your life....*

Nazy finished a strip of bacon and said, "If they look into my transactions, they would see I'm buying things for a man. Maybe I'm no longer a bachelorette. Maybe me and the McGee family are simply the best of friends."

Hunter offered, "You have been going to the homes of CIA Directors for a long time. Greg and now Bill."

"Bill's tenure was always going to be temporary and you bought the house where we stay. I'm certain the media thinks he rents it. Security knows I stay there."

"Baby, he's a political appointee. And Greg retired a second time from the Agency. My point is they will pry—to whom is this breathtaking creature, Nazy Cunningham, married? What lucky man found the woman of his dreams and married her? Then they kept it secret—for what purpose? I see the media making trouble. You and Bill agree; you're the best choice to replace him. If he wins, we will just live with it as best we can." He smiled and reached across the petite table to kiss her and gently rubbed his nose with hers.

Nazy concurred. "It's likely the media already have a file on me as I have been delivering the President's Daily Brief for a long time. I had been going in and out of the White House and the Oval Office daily long before Bill McGee."

Hunter noted, "The networks have offices across the street with cameras trained on the White House 24/7. They know who comes and goes. They have probably conducted ten years of research on you. I bet they even have paid informants with access to the White House or McLean or Langley. There is nothing of substance to find."

"Of course, there was one television journalist who came up with the concept that Nazy Cunningham probably wasn't even your real name. There comes a day in intelligence officer's lives when they no longer need a cover name in order to work. But for you, you crossed the Muslim Brotherhood and the Islamic Underground. That work must not be uncovered, or you'll have the Muslim Brotherhood on your delightful callipygian ass."

Three hours ago, they had fallen asleep from exhaustion in an oversized bed. They nestled together like puzzle pieces. The pulchritudinous princess was the Director of Operations at the CIA and could have called in sick, but the professional phenom wouldn't abuse her position. Nazy wouldn't be late to work.

Although her freshly sprayed cinnamon-vanilla cologne was giving him carnal thoughts again, as well as wondering where the nearest Cinnabon store was, Duncan dutifully helped Nazy with the form-fitted spider silk body armor. She held her arms high as he precisely fastened elastic Velcro straps to ensure her torso and all of her essential organs were protected from a close-range gunshot. They were toe-to-toe as Duncan then helped Nazy into her blouse and buttoned it. The ritual wasn't necessary but was an intimate touch when he was in town to send her on her way to work. It was his way of protecting her when he wasn't going to be with her.

As she left, she stuck her head back in the door and tugged her earlobe. The door closed behind her leaving Duncan with a hang fire — he had been a little too slow on the draw and reciprocate her *I love you*. Nazy followed her security detail to the elevator. She was wearing white sneakers with a navy Burberry suit. She was surrounded by her security detail until she entered the middle of the Agency's three limos, then the black Suburbans headed for CIA Headquarters. She left her thoughts of the previous night behind.

She was heading toward new ground. She didn't know exactly what to expect when Bill stepped down and she became the Acting Director. Nazy had spent an inordinate amount of time in the corner office of the seventh floor, but not a second behind the big desk. It was revered territory. Even when Bill left her in charge while he was out of town, she managed things from her own desk in another building at Liberty Crossing as the Director, National Counter Terrorism Center or down the hall at Headquarters, as the Director of Operations. She couldn't do all three jobs; she would have to give one of them up. The obvious career choice was the NCTC Director. But that was her baby; that was where she had solidified her reputation as an analyst.

As the Director of Operations, she knew most of what was going on in the Agency, but not everything. Some things were the sole purview of the Director, like some special access programs. Nazy knew Bill would tell her when the time came for him to leave. Duncan was in one such program, *Noble Savage*. It was for the Director and the President's eyes only. She was especially curious about what was in the Goebbels' files because of McGee's reference to them. She wondered what was supposed to be in there, what was missing, and how was it that it no longer existed in the CIA's archives. It reminded her of the file that had started the resignation of a president.

It was an unauthorized and unofficial CIA file on an American citizen. Highly illegal in officialese; a science project informally. Because files on Americans were the sole purview and responsibility of the FBI, the CIA wasn't allowed to capture and maintain data on Americans. But if an intelligence officer at the CIA didn't follow strict Agency protocols and procedures, and captured and maintained data on an American as if he were acting on behalf of himself and not the government.... And that is what happened, the Chief Near East Division used his position to collect damaging secret documents on the Senator from Michigan before he became the President.

That intelligence officer wouldn't log open-source materials onto an inventory sheet or account for them in a drawer safe as required by the Security Office.

Nazy let her mind float back to the day she had found the president's file in her new office as Chief Near East Division. *Mazibuike's file.*

Duncan asked me to look for it. I thought it had to be a figment of his overactive imagination. If it was real — where would I find it? I stumbled upon it on a shelf of non-fiction books, biographies, and autobiographies. Books from the former Chief. Everyone was looking for a secret file; where do you keep files at the CIA? In a safe, of course. But that would have been too obvious. My predecessor was a genius. He replaced the pages of the man's two autobiographies with documents from the president's file, and put those books on a shelf out in the open. When I found them, I got them out of the building. And then Duncan released the pages and stopped Mazibuike, stopped the infiltration of the Muslim Brotherhood into government offices, and stopped the Muslim Brotherhood's building new mosques in America. *I've seen their internal documents... those that made clear their strategy of subversion waged by stealth was only until such time as Muslims were powerful enough to progress to violence for the final conquest.*

As the driver turned onto George Washington Memorial Parkway, Nazy wondered what Duncan and Link Coffey would talk about when they got together. It's not that she didn't trust Coffey; she barely knew him and knew very little of what he did. *Curiously, he knew Duncan years before I did.* Nazy remembered what it was like in Guantanamo Bay; Coffey and the other men were obviously interested in her, but she wasn't the least bit stimulated by any of them. They weren't like Duncan. They could never be like Duncan.

She knew Duncan was getting a little concerned about finding someone to fly with him. If McGee were to be elected, Coffey could replace Duncan on the *Noble Savage* special access program. Nazy stared ahead in deep thought, *...but if that doesn't happen, I'll be assigning Duncan targets from the Matrix. A wife shouldn't have to do that, send her husband off to kill other men.... Even if they're terrorists. Is it a conflict of interest? Having Duncan punish the men who hurt me? No, I would do it only if it was necessary, and the President approves all targets. Lord knows what will happen if Bill becomes the President. He has a little of that "Kill them all and let God sort them out" mentality.* She rubbed her eyes. *I wish Duncan would find someone else to do that work. Maybe he has.*

Pulling into the CIA Headquarters complex, Nazy anticipated the reactions to Bill's announcement. She checked her BlackBerry for the CIA's *Early Bird*, a daily roundup of intelligence, military, and defense news stories from around the globe curated by the CIA's public affairs office. The top item was a *New York Post* article; they had run Eastwood's exclusive on the front page. *All of Washington knows. Everyone will know Bill's leaving, and I'm moving into the corner office. Temporarily. The other newspapers and the networks will pick up the story. It will be mere minutes before they criticize us, if they haven't started already.*

The mockingbird media were not interested in the truth or the facts, only how quickly they could destroy or wound an opposition candidate. They also knew for members of the IC, the rules were different; the media had to have an informer, someone with direct knowledge of the topic. Like the infamous former FBI Deputy Director William Mark Felt, Sr., *"Deep Throat."* Described by the media as the anonymous government source who had leaked classified information to *Washington Post* reporters, he was a partisan and hated President Nixon. Felt should have been prosecuted for espionage, for aiding and abetting the enemy, for passing classified information to members of the media who didn't possess the simplest of clearances and were not authorized to see or possess classified information.

Then there was the issue of McGee's secret life as a Navy SEAL. Not just any SEAL, but the U.S. military's primary Tier 1 special mission unit tasked with performing the most complex, classified, and dangerous missions directed by the National Command Authority. As a member of one of the five publicly disclosed special mission units, the Naval Special Warfare Development Group (DEVGRU), SEAL Team Six had conducted various specialized missions such as counterterrorism, hostage rescue, special reconnaissance, and direct action against high-value targets.

Captain Bill McGee had been the Commanding Officer of DEVGRU, the U.S. Navy component of the Joint Special Operations Command (JSOC). After the aircraft were flown into the World Trade Center on September 11, 2001, the first telephone call from the JSOC Crisis Action Center was to Captain Bill McGee. He was told to get his spurs on and saddle up. He and his men were going to Afghanistan to play *cowboys and terrorists.* There was much confidence in McGee's ability to find and capture Osama bin Laden. Everyone from the President of the United States on down thought it would be done in days. The SEALs would come home with OBL's head on a pike.

But that didn't happen.

•   •   •

After his stint in Afghanistan, publicly available records showed the McGee family had left Newport, Rhode Island, where he had been a student and instructor at the Naval War College. McGee and family moved to Fredericksburg, Texas. He became the CEO of a scientific group, a huge training facility near Hondo, Texas that may also have been a CIA front company once upon a time.

The media titans ordered a complete dossier, domestic and international on McGee. They would also look into periods when McGee was away from Texas and times when McGee and Cunningham's paths crossed. The media would love to use the propaganda tools of insinuation to destroy McGee and Nazy.

Bill McGee had been on the media's radar for some time, because he was on the Democrat Party's lists of potential Republican presidential candidates. They all knew if he ran he would make a formidable candidate. Republicans keep lists of the world's worst terrorists and try to neutralize them. Democrats and the media-maintained lists of potential Republican candidates for high government office and do whatever is necessary to disqualify them.

It was well known in conservative media circles Republican candidates sought to protect all of America and Americans. Democrats seek to protect their party and their members like mobsters from an Edward G. Robinson film. Both parties have a top-secret name for their top-secret list of their top-secret targets managed by their most senior political official in their party. Each political party called the document a *Disposition Matrix*.

On top of the Democrat Party's *Disposition Matrix* was Bill McGee, the CIA Director. He was their worst nightmare. He was considered unimpeachable and unbeatable, and he was African American. The Democrats and the media were almost against everything McGee stood for. He was a huge political counterweight; to force him to drop out would require a huge scandal. If the Republicans ran Bill McGee, they would need no one else to round out their slate of candidates. Bill McGee the war hero and most decorated military man would dominate any debate scenario.

•   •   •

When she reached the top floor of the headquarters in the New Office Building, Nazy was a little surprised to find McGee's security detail waiting for the elevator. She acknowledged the secretaries with a wave and entered McGee's office.

He said, "We have to talk." He got up and moved to the conference table. He didn't take the seat at the head of the table.

After she closed the door, Nazy said, "I know."

McGee motioned for her to sit at the head of the big table, and she did. He began, "I'll dispense with the obvious. Nazy, you know most of what goes on here is above the water line."

She nodded. *What an interesting choice of words...above the water line....*

"We have little time. I talked about it a little last night; America is in for the fight of its life. That isn't an exaggeration. The President and I agree, I must win the White House if the country has any chance to survive. From this day forward, they will be after you and me with a vengeance. If we can stay alive and I win, our work will have just started. The *Insiders* know what we have done to them; Duncan has removed all the terrorists from the Matrix. The Muslim Brotherhood and the Islamic Underground in Africa and the Middle East are so disorganized right now they have no leaders as the head of their affiliates — well you know...."

Without referring to notes, Nazy said, "They're blaming others within the Islamic Underground for their failures. Islam grows only through conquest. Duncan has made it impossible for the Islamic State to grow or for al-Qaeda to make any headway. The President has isolated Iran, buttressed the militaries and economies of Muslim nations that defy the Muslim Brotherhood, and convinced more countries in Europe to reject the Muslim invaders. After years of Mazibuike's influence, we are steadily making gains."

McGee nodded. "We must have a strong leader to continue the resistance movement." His face reflected the seriousness of what he was saying. "With me going to campaign, I can no longer do my part. I don't have any other choice." McGee reached over with a hand the size of a catcher's mitt and squeezed Nazy's hand. He said, "Nazy, you're incredible, one of my dearest and talented friends. This isn't a job for former SEALs or NCS, and we both know that. This requires strong, thoughtful *analytical leadership*, and there is no one else...."

McGee quickly smiled and said the obvious, "… other than that husband of yours who we need right now. I will say we are blessed to have you as one of the heads of *the resistance* to lead this fight. The CIA is constrained from domestic issues by charter, but the FBI is MIA! Missing in action."

"They're infiltrated."

"They are, so we must be very careful. Nazy, be very, very careful."

So, we are the Irregulars. Nazy smiled without flashing her teeth. The former Muslima, the woman who rejected Islam for Christianity, the former Muslim spy who became one of the CIA's most effective operations officers, squeezed back with a delicate hand and said, "Your confidence in me means the world to me. Thank you, Bill. I won't let you down."

"I know you won't, Nazy. Now, let's try to stay alive."

CHAPTER 14

November 2, 2019

Lieutenant Colonel Demetrius Eastwood, *Dory* to his friends, was having a field day with his exclusive news piece about Bill McGee running for president. Director McGee had done him a huge favor by inviting him to the *Pumpkin Papers Irregulars Dinner*, although officially he had been invited by the Director of Operations, Nazy Cunningham.

When Nazy asked, there wasn't a man alive who would refuse her dinner invitation—even if it meant having to ride the train from New York City to Washington. And back again.

On the Acela going back to Washington, Eastwood thought, *Women may try to suppress their desires as they get older, but the ones who look best are often a bit untamed. Hunter must have asbestos sheets because that girl is still so hot even after all these years.*

It was hard not to think of when he first met her. One-minute Nazy had been one of the girls sharing a drink with the guys in the cafeteria, and the next she had been caught in the middle of a Muslim Brotherhood assault on the embassy. After the Algerian armed forces had secured the U.S. Embassy and begun the investigation, some bombmaker from al-Qaeda or one of the Islamic Underground affiliates had used enough explosives to blow a hole in the side of the embassy's security wall.

That evening after dinner, Nazy had excused herself, saying she had a phone date. She had left the cafeteria and was halfway to her apartment to call Duncan when the bomb had gone off. Debris from the blast had torn much of her clothing away and peppered her exposed skin with rubble from the concrete wall. The shock wave had slammed her to the ground and rendered her unconscious. She had turned her head away before the blast, so her face was miraculously and virtually untouched.

Intelligence suggested it was likely radicals from a Muslim Brotherhood mosque and an imam inimical to the United States who had set the bomb. Documents recovered years later in Libya, showed al-Qaeda in the Islamic Maghreb (AQIM) had taken credit for the assault which blew a hole big enough to drive through before they stole the senior CIA officer laying in the yard.

Eastwood thought, *The most extraordinarily thing was McGee knew intuitively what had happened, and we followed him without question. That is the kind of leader he is.*

Eastwood held his chin, transfixed as he relived that evening. *We commandeered an embassy car and chased down the men who took Nazy. When they entered what they thought was a safe house, McGee went in right after them. They wanted to destroy that beautiful face; destroy that body. They were raping her and one had started to cut off her breast as a trophy. She was leaking blood from hundreds of shrapnel wounds on her arms, torso, and legs. I assumed McGee was killing every terrorist in the building. I didn't ask. I heard the shots and McGee carried her out. He had covered her with a sheet and directed us into the truck. McGee sewed her breast back on; I cleaned and closed wounds as best I could. We were drenched in her blood.*

I was convinced she was going to die on that makeshift operating table, McGee's lap. That Nazy is alive today is a testament to McGee's bravery, and his skills in combat first aid. Remarkably, she's back at work and is still as beautiful as that first day I met her. She knows how to hide the wounds she endured that night. He exhaled and stretched his neck. Eastwood rarely recalled that evening on purpose, but seeing Nazy again was a reminder of McGee's heroism and the actions they took to save the life of Hunter's wife.

He rubbed the stubble on his head. *The truth is McGee needed me there at the Papers dinner to file my exclusive report and make the announcement on my radio show. I feel like I'm in a CIA counterintelligence operation. The Democrats and the media have already tried to kill the announcement and have started the propaganda machine to neutralize McGee as a candidate. Oh yes, McGee is going to run his campaign like a counter-intelligence operation. And I'm going to help. Every day; every week.*

But first, the President's Press Conference.

CHAPTER 15

November 2, 2019

After Nazy's detail took her to work, Hunter checked to see if there was Muslim Brotherhood surveillance on their house along the Potomac River where his daughter lived. It was too hot for Nazy to visit or live, necessitating her to live in the mother-in-law's suite at Bill McGee's heavily-guarded residence in Annapolis. Confident there wasn't any, he paid the cab and extracted his daughter's up-armored Hummer2 from the garage and headed to Marine Corps Base Quantico. The Hummer was only driven when Duncan was in town and there wasn't any clumsy surveillance. Nazy had a late-eighties Mercedes SL coupe Duncan had taken from a terrorist group in Boston. Everyone from that group was dead; they couldn't use it anymore.

Hunter met Coffey at the FBI's combat or fighting pistol course near Quantico; Hunter without his disguise and Coffey without his Dr. Lindell. Coffey's first thought: *Well, I see the old Ray-Ban Aviators have been replaced by Maui Jim's.* Hunter wore an understated Moose Drool ballcap, some wrinkles radiating from the corners of his eyes, and a couple of scars from past endeavors.

Coffey explained, "The course isn't a competition shooting range; it's geared towards survival on the modern urban and rural battlefield. We'll use our own pistols and gear."

For Hunter, it was a refresher of the combat mindset, threat identification, techniques of tactical shooting, and shooting while moving. Laser sights on the Colt *Python* made aiming and trigger control a snap. The .357 magnum rounds turned the wooden targets into flinders. In an hour the men went through 250 rounds each. They worked up a sweat and an incredible appetite.

Hunter was thankful for having the opportunity and said, "Lunch is on me."

They drove to Tun's Tavern, a boozer's boozer named for the birthplace of the Marine Corps. It was located near the town's railway station in the bantam on-base town of Quantico. Hunter ordered a Diet Mountain Dew and so did Coffey. They talked of the old times in the Marine Corps.

Coffey said, "I remember the ship went nuts when you challenged the Soviets to a duel."

Maverick smiled at the old memory and said, "I wouldn't call it that. If you remember we were cruising off the coast of Korea when a Russian voice came over the Guard frequency, 'Unknown aircraft, you are in Soviet airspace. Identify yourself.'"

"I said, 'This is a United States aircraft. I am over international waters.'"

The smile on Coffey's face was growing with every passing second.

"The Soviets argued with me and said, 'You are in Soviet Union airspace. If you do not depart our airspace, we will launch interceptor aircraft!'"

"And all I said was, 'This is a United States Marine Corps fighter pilot, graduate of TOPGUN in one of the greatest aircraft ever made, the F-4 Phantom, also known as the most efficient distributer of MiG parts on the planet. Send your girls up, I'll wait!'"

Coffey laughed until he coughed and choked. *What a great story. Before his accident.*

He remembered reading how Captain Duncan "*Maverick*" Hunter had ejected from a crippled fighter that killed his back-seater, *Geek*. *Maverick* had endured multiple surgeries to fix his broken body. More than a pilot, *Maverick* was a legend. There was a rumor. Coffey would ask if the opportunity arose.

Maverick's face had aged, but he didn't have many wrinkles, just some nasty old scars on his cheek. *He must work out like a madman. I knew he was a monster on the… racquetball courts – that was his game. And I remember there was something about his watch. It was famous; I don't remember why. The pilots who flew with him said he flew that jet better than anyone, and that included the Skipper. That's probably why everyone in the squadron called him Captain America. I think I was just intimidated.*

As they waited for their food *Maverick* shared new information. "A week after *Geek* ejected us from the F-4, my parents were returning from Europe on a PanAm jumbo jet. It was December 22, 1988, Flight 103. A CIA press release said a Libyan bombmaker had created a device to target several Agency executives who were returning to America on that jet. The bombmaker planted the altitude-sensitive explosive device in a radio in the checked baggage of someone who never got on the jet. After the investigation, laws were passed to prevent anyone from checking their bags and not getting on the plane. If someone didn't board, their bags were removed."

"For decades it was thought the bombmaker was living in the remnants of old East Germany under an assumed name and occupation. He was radioactive—no one wanted to deal with him or hide him. America's intelligence community were after him until there was a change at the CIA. When the new Director called off the dogs, he went so deep he disappeared."

Coffey said, "Gaddafi had no compunction about killing a planeload of people just to take out Agency officers who were aboard. Counter-terrorism in the late eighties, early nineties, was a different ball game. Politicians didn't know how to deal with it and didn't want to. They didn't want to spend the money to protect Americans and consequently nothing was done. Not until after September 11, 2001." *Sometimes politicians had to have the shit slapped out of them to get their attention.*

Maverick concurred, "You're right. I was in the hospital for months and was livid the whole time. I was trying to figure out how to stop terrorist's plans against aviation so no more innocent victims would die like my parents did on that flight. I was the Marine Corps' newest washed-up fighter pilot; I really didn't know what to do. Test pilot school was gone, NASA was gone. My whole life was gone—I couldn't even play racquetball like I used to. But I learned something about human nature. After I was injured, all the people I played over the years wanted to get me on the court for a little revenge. Maybe a lot of revenge. I didn't blame them; revenge can be a tremendous motivator."

"After I got out of the hospital, I started exchanging ideas with a couple of engineers in my graduate school classes, and we designed the ultimate obstacles for terrorists. Even won a patent for a system that knocks out hostile UAVs that steer into the intakes of jets. We sold a bunch of those systems to airports."

Coffey smiled—he was impressed. *That explains so much.*

"I knew I would never get back into the cockpit of a jet, so I needed a plan. While I completed my contract with Uncle Sam, I changed my major from aeronautical engineering to economics and political science. I studied why people become terrorists. I started thinking of ways to make air travel safer before I retired."

Hunter didn't tell Coffey that most of all he wanted revenge. Figuring out how to make airports *terrorist-proof* was a lucrative distraction from hating the bombmaker, and it had made him a millionaire several times over.

Maverick continued, "My education into why terrorists mass murdered civilians was grossly lacking. On the day I was discharged from the hospital, I didn't believe I would ever find the man or men who had killed my parents. Yet I promised my dead mother I would do everything humanly possible to chase him or them to the gates of hell and take revenge. An eye-for-an-eye meant dismemberment or decapitation, and since those are concepts an Islamic terrorist appreciates and accepts, I was agreeable with that. I didn't realize it then, but I became so focused, so preoccupied with revenge that I probably could have been diagnosed with a personality disorder and classified in the *Diagnostic and Statistical Manual of Mental Disorders.*"

What the hell is that? Coffey didn't have a clue but responded, "That would not have been good." He wanted to change to a lighter subject so he said, "I remember you were an animal on the racquetball courts. You beat everyone, and they all said you played a game they were unfamiliar with."

"That's probably because I played a game they had never seen before." Hunter told him a story. "I played in a lot of tournaments and saw a lot of truly incomparable players. There was this guy, Jimmy Lowe. Army. Skinny as spaghetti. Faster than a bullet. And he beat everyone. He was the best military racquetball player to have ever played the game. Played pros; crushed them with hardly any effort. He was number two in the nation one year at the National Singles. So, if I wanted to be world class, I had to learn to play like Jimmy Lowe. That meant I had to change my game from reactive to proactive. Ninety-nine percent of players respond to the ball coming off the front wall. Jimmy watched his opponent and anticipated where he would hit the ball. He could read the body language of the other player, because every racquetball pro telegraph their shots no matter how hard they disguise it. Jimmy made a beeline to the spot where the ball would hit the wall and with lightning-fast reflexes hit unreturnable shots. He played in the front of the court while everyone else played in the back. That's what I learned to do. Once I could master those anticipatory skills, which is another way of saying *thinking in a different way*, I was nearly as tough to beat as Jimmy."

For a moment Link Coffey considered the wisdom of being proactive rather than reactive in sports. *That's not braggadocio; it makes perfect sense.* He confided, "I was never all that athletic. I was just glad to be out of the cockpit. It was a great assignment, but the pressure to perform was incredible, and it nearly gave me ulcers. I did my time in uniform, but then it was time to move on to what I was trained to do — law enforcement. My degree was in criminal justice. You actually inspired a number of us in the squadron to continue our education. I heard the FBI loved cops with Ph.Ds. or JDs, so that is what I went after. Law school was the copestone of my life. You showed us we could be more than just pilots. I suppose, being proactive rather than reactive."

The copestone of my military life was learning to fly the F-4 Phantom II. Two J-79 afterburning monsters. Different strokes for different folks. Hunter smiled and asked, "What did you do in the FBI? Somewhere, I heard you got a law degree and then nothing. I'm impressed you were the guy who found the *Explanatory Memorandum*."

The retired Assistant Deputy Director of the FBI said, "Well, I got my start like a lot of newbies, doing dirty work. I investigated sex crimes. Child trafficking. Pedophilia. I hunted down pedophiles before transferring into counterterrorism."

And I hunted down sexual predators in the Marine Corps after being released from the hospital.... That is incredible. Maverick tried not to raise an eyebrow. He asked, "Pedophiles?"

Coffey nodded and continued, "They're the worst of the sexual predators. Very difficult to catch and charge with a crime. The child sex trade is enormous; probably $150 billion enterprise. European laws are geared to facilitate the exploitation of children. In America, there are states now trying to reduce the penalties for pedophilia, proposals to drop terms like sexual offender, saying it has a negative connotation. Across the country there are thirty or so ballot initiatives to change the penalty from a felony-stupid, go-directly-to-jail, to a misdemeanor. Slap on the wrist, get let go, and do it all over again. States are changing laws to lower the age of consent. Lower the age for marriage. Sexual activists are trying to scumble the sharp lines in the law." Coffey didn't want to admit they had failed to find the thousands of missing boys, over a hundred thousand in Germany alone, the targets and victims of pedophiles.

Maverick thought again, *Pedophiles.... I wonder.... I think we look at them as a minor problem...but in Europe..... He* took some time before responding. "Here, they will have to get the DSM changed, get pedophilia removed—like the sexual activists did with homosexuals, transvestites, and transgenders. Once they get those terms eliminated, then they can claim to the world what they do is normal. I used to think their real goal was *acceptance*." He shrugged and added, "Now I think it might be revenge. Revenge against those who have called them abnormal."

Coffey said with a grin, "Or they're just clinically attracted to children and would do anything and pay any amount to have access to children. I'm astounded you know so much on the topic."

After a few moments of reflection, *Maverick* added, "Link, why weren't you guys more successful?"

"In Europe, I think it's because they're socialist and secular with no Christian values; they pass laws that benefit the criminal. So often, our hands were tied and we abandoned those initiatives. American law is Christian-based and sees the exploitation of children as a crime. In Europe after the war there were so many children without parents, and the laws were so weak. There was no political will to interrupt the cycle or incarcerate pedophiles. In the absence of laws, those guys came out of the woodwork like termites."

Hunter responded as if the topic was painful to discuss. He asked, "Did they congregate in towns? Like how the gays took over Provincetown and Key West?"

"What the gays have over there in the cities is a large network of mens clubs dedicated to a sybaritic lifestyle. Think Provincetown times a thousand. They created an illusion they're mostly harmless. That what they do is rare, infrequent. Pedophiles are a completely different variant of sexual disorder. Some are predators. Some are something other."

Hunter's surprise was obvious. He thought, *Some are something other? Well, that's an interesting comment....* "What do you mean, something other?"

Coffey continued, "There was evidence some of them had turned their self-absorbed predatory impulses into more radical areas, such as counter-Christian cults, like Satanism and child sacrifices. At abortion clinics where the trafficking of aborted fetuses was legal, there seemed to be competition between the biotechnology labs and the pedophiles for aborted baby parts. In other cities, pedophilia was viewed almost as a rich person's *sport*. We heard there were Satanic rituals held in castles." Coffey's eyes asked, *Why?*

Maverick grinned, "Oh, once upon a time I thought there was a link between the people in the DSM and those who were susceptible to propaganda, like how do you radicalize someone to be a terrorist? Start with the understanding that terrorists who will fly jets into buildings have mental disorders; they're easily hypnotized and can be easily manipulated. Not everyone can be hypnotized. Bin Laden got nineteen men to fly into buildings for revenge with no concern for their own lives. I thought pedophiles might be like that, obvious mental disorder, easily hypnotized, and manipulated. But listening to you I see I was locked in a paradigm; that was clearly my American outlook. Europe has a different paradigm regarding pedophilia."

Coffey nodded his head and agreed. "They do."

Hunter startled Coffey with a final thought, "You know *acceptance* and *revenge* are some of the silent weapons of propaganda."

"I didn't know that." *Wait, there's that term again. The silent weapons of propaganda.*

Hunter continued, "Being susceptible to propaganda means being overly sympathetic, being overly conscientious, being extremely disgusted, being despondent, being in despair, those who are overly repentant and those who want to atone for the sins of everyone. Those are well-understood dispositions from the umbrella of propaganda. Whatever their preoccupation in life is. I'm sure I'm not the only one who noticed that people who are not susceptible to propaganda are not susceptible to peer pressure, either. They cannot be swayed into pedophilia or toward the radicalism of religions like Islam."

"That's heavy."

Maverick nodded, "You know that Goebbels' quote? *'This is the secret of propaganda: Those who are to be persuaded by it should be completely immersed in the ideas of the propaganda, without ever noticing that they are being immersed in it.'* I thought there might have been a correlation."

Coffey suddenly grasped the significance of what his friend had said. *Maverick* had made an incredible leap in logic. *Who wouldn't notice they're being immersed in propaganda? Those who are preoccupied with their personal issues. That… is… incredible.* Coffey nodded. *And that explains much. Captain America, I'm glad you're on our side.*

Before another word could be spoken, their meal was served. They spoke of lighter subjects as they ate.

After the plates had been cleared, Coffey wanted to return to safe topics but his inability to find the perverts in that assignment was like acid on his tongue. He couldn't escape the failure. He hadn't experienced the trauma of a bad ejection, like Hunter. He hadn't experienced the emotional trauma of having his parents murdered by a terrorist's bomb, like Hunter. Then it occurred to him to ask, "Why the hell were you in disguise? And it was a good one. I had no freaking idea it was a disguise. You messed with my mind when you spoke and flashed your rocket number. I couldn't believe it was you. I read you had died."

"I didn't. I said, 'Make me dashing,' and they made me a Russian."

Coffey ignored the attempt at levity and noticed *Maverick* hadn't answered the question. He asked, "How?"

"Before I answer that, what are you doing nowadays?"

"Not a damned thing. Collecting my retirement. I do some public speaking when they call me; I'm in a speaker's bureau. I'm an adjunct instructor—I teach maybe one class every few years, and I take trips to places the Marine Corps never took us. I hike the most fascinating places: Iceland, Ireland, Finland, Greenland. Meet a few girls." *But I'm bored.*

You still have your hair and your face isn't all scarred up. "I bet you still drive all the girls wild." Hunter smirked.

Well, there was one I didn't drive wild. Coffey nodded and sniggered, "And when I come home, I don't even have a bag. I buy all the clothes I need while I'm on the road. I have nothing but the clothes on my back and my passport when I go through Customs. Why do you ask?"

"Want a job?"

•   •   •

They blew out of the Manassas Regional Airport in Hunter's G-550 heading to Elmira, New York. Coffey figured Hunter would ride in the back in the expensive seats; he was astounded Hunter actually crawled into the pilot seat. He would have flown solo if Coffey hadn't been with him. In the security of the jet's cockpit, Hunter explained the rationale for being disguised in public places. He was dead, after all, and in certain public venues he couldn't afford to be recognized. In the relative safety of the FBI's Combat Pistol Range, Quantico Marine Corps Base, and Tun's Tavern, there was no need for a mask. He was among friendlies.

It was the first time Coffey had been behind the controls of a jet in almost 30 years. The skills quickly came back to him. Flying the brutish F-4 *Phantom II* had been work. It was uncomfortable with helmets, oxygen masks, torso harnesses that would crush your nuts, G-suits, and straps to keep your legs tight against the ejection seat, if you ever had to use it. Easing into the Gulfstream's cockpit with Honeywell's state-of-the-art Symmetry Flight Deck, featuring 10 touchscreen displays, active-control side sticks like an F-16, and other advanced avionics was pure luxury. *Now this is how to fly a jet!*

Maverick said, "The aircraft has an air-purification system, large oval windows and low-altitude pressurization systems. Taking control in the cockpit's like slipping behind the wheel of an Aston Martin *Gran Turismo* dressed in a silk suit. Functionality and comfort are engineered to perfection. About $63 million of perfection in this configuration."

Coffey asked with the impetuosity of a thirty-year-old fighter pilot, "Where's the afterburner?"

Ten minutes into the flight Coffey spoke into the microphone and asked, "Where did you get this?"

"Officially or unofficially?"

Coffey replied, "Both."

Hunter turned to him and grinned, "Well, *officially*, I acquired this because it was *abandoned*. It was brand new and hadn't been registered to anyone. So, I claimed it."

A $60-70 million jet and you just took it? Oh, that's bullshit! Coffey was almost speechless but could ask, "What's the unofficial version?"

"Well, seeing you're not read in on that specific special access program and any disclosure by me would be a violation of federal law...."

Special access program? Damn Hunter, what are you really doing? Nothing says drop the subject like uttering those three polysyllabic words: Special access program. CIA secret squirrel stuff. Programs so secret that divulgence would likely lead to someone's death.

Hunter said he was interested in Dr. Lindell, so Coffey told Duncan the whole story, how they — the FBI — had attained the archives of the Muslim Brotherhood in America. Coffey said, "Dr. Lindell translated most of the documents in those boxes, and one of those documents was this thing called the *Explanatory Memorandum*. When Dr. Lindell looked at all the information he had read and transcribed for us, you might find this *provocative*, he said he was *convinced* Mazibuike was the *de facto* leader the Muslim Brotherhood had been looking for, waiting for."

Hunter was not surprised and agreed, "He was right."

Coffey was nonplussed. "Conservatives and Republicans' conspiracy theories. There's been no proof."

"Link, you're FBI. Please. At what point does a dump truck load of evidence constitutes proof? Proofs are solved mathematical formulas. Q.E.D. and all that. Forget proof, prosecutors convict on evidence. Everything he did, and you think that isn't evidence?" Hunter had become surprisingly testy.

"It's like what is official and what is unofficial. Officially, according to the media who cannot be trusted any further than I could lob a 57 Buick into a lake, Mazibuike was as pure as the driven snow. Unofficially, everyone in the intelligence community knew he was crooked and wasn't eligible to be President, but he got elected and pushed Muslim Outreach initiatives through his administration like you jamming a side of beef through a meat processor."

Coffey was a little shocked at the response. "I sense there is more to that story."

"That bastard tried to kill me."

Coffey looked at Hunter with disbelief. *No friggin' way!* "What? How? When? Where? That's virtually impossible to believe."

"He had reason to hate me. He was on a mission and I interrupted his plans. The *elites* don't like it when you interrupt their plans."

Hate you? Captain America? Elites? Coffey was taken aback. *What does that mean, "They don't like it when you interrupt their plans?"* He asked, "Plans? What plans?"

"The plans in the *Explanatory Memorandum*. I released his file to Congress and the press. I stopped his ass cold. He could no longer implement his Muslim Outreach programs across the government and the planet. He saw himself as the second coming of Mohammad. People would commit murder for him if it was necessary, just like Damien Thorn. He was livid he had been outed, but there was a modicum of self-preservation in him. The coward resigned and ran away. He suspected someone would be on to his ass, like Delta or SEALs or maybe some of your guys, except the FBI had been infiltrated long before 3M. Which reminds me, what the hell happened to the FBI? It used to be so great."

3M? That's what I called him. Incredible. Coffey had the proverbial deer in the headlights look before the freight train obliterated Bambi. "What happened to the FBI? It had been on a downward trajectory long before 3M. The Bureau's standards had been the highest in law enforcement circles and their standards had stayed that way because of their culture of excellence. I believe that culture was reflected in the quality and accomplishments of their work. The FBI of old hired the best, trained to be the best, and got rid of the rest. Then they started hiring substandard people. After 9-11, someone got the bright idea we needed to hire Muslims, and that single action did more to undermine the Bureau than anything."

Hunter said, "You guys were feared by organized crime for achieving what no other enforcement agency could do: hunt down, arrest, and convict mob leaders. I saw the FBI bringing justice to those who would terrorize the United States, both foreign and domestic."

Coffey grinned. "Yeah, the FBI's original charter of promoting integrity throughout government by ferreting out corruption fell apart. Oh, there were spies getting caught, and bought off politicians were nabbed as well. The old FBI created a deterrent that said public corruption came with real risks."

"Yeah, I thought the Bureau had a well-deserved reputation as the world's premier law enforcement agency."

"That's why I went there out of the Marines. To be associated with the FBI was a thing of pride. That was then. Being a part of the FBI is no longer a thing of pride. Many retired agents admit to being embarrassed and ashamed of what the Bureau has become. In preventing crime, the FBI has dropped the ball far too many times. The FBI leadership allowed itself to be compromised."

Hunter said, "Your place and the CIA were forced to take Muslims to destroy the IC culture, DOD was forced to take gays and trannies to destroy the warrior culture, but the CIA saw the light and kicked their Muslims out. The FBI remains compromised."

Maverick always gets to the heart of the issue....

Hunter stopped slamming the FBI and returned to his interaction with Mazibuike. He continued in a monotone as he looked through the pilot's windscreen, "Somehow 3M found out it was me who released his file. They could never figure how I could have done it. I don't have that kind of access to those files or offices. But I'm sure a former CIA Director suspected me and told him. A couple of years after he left office, he found me and tried to kill me and hundreds of other passengers on a jet. So, I chased him to Dubai and I killed him. I cut his head off and threw it and his body from the top floor of the Burj Khalifa."

CHAPTER 16

November 2, 2019

You released his file? You hunted him down and killed him. Not possible. I'm waving the bullshit flag! It took a few seconds for Coffey's brain to process what he heard. His eyes rolled to the back of his head and his heart started slamming in his chest. He looked at *Maverick,* who was calm and cool, adjusting this and that in the cockpit. *That's not possible! Captain America is a murderer? This has to be a joke!* His brain shifted into hyperdrive. He knew the FBI had investigated. They spent months trying to figure out how the CIA could have created the file and how a CIA file could have been spirited out of the complex. He also knew the CIA's document control procedures were legendary, the best in the business. Hell, the CIA even tried using behavior modification experiments from the archives of the Nazi Minister of Propaganda, Joseph Goebbels, to prevent Agency employees from providing intelligence to adversaries. *That was Project BLUEBIRD; I remember....*

Every lead had been a dead end. None of the special agents found anything other than the intelligence officer who had informally collected documents and intelligence on Mazibuike. The Chief Near East Division was found in his back yard with a hole in his chest you could drive a Mack truck through. That bit of intel the FBI knew, but not the details. Coffey asked for more.

Hunter gave an impassioned lecture on how the former president had people who loved him and still supported him. There was one guy in Oregon the FBI investigated after the fact, after he was killed, also in...*Dubai.* "Tamerlan al-Sarkari was a non-practicing Muslim, which meant he drank and chased girls and drove a Porsche—but more than that. He was the prime software engineer for Boeing and Airbus. Ph.D. in software engineering. Brilliant but not radicalized at that point. He liked girls, not goats."

"Then something happened. He started *deviating* from the norm....
He wrote a program within a program which could be accessed via
satellite during the automatic engine and aircraft position updates.
When it was activated, al-Sarkari programmed the jet to shut down
the jet's pressurization system, knock everyone out, turn to fly way off
course, then crash. Big ocean. Never to be found. It was the perfect
terrorist tool. I was on one of those jets, and 3M knew I was on that
Qantas 747 heading to Australia. We think al-Sarkari must have
hacked into the airline's reservation system, because he found me.
Mazibuike commanded al-Sarkari to shut down the jet; Mazibuike
thought he had killed me."

"But, but...."

"Military jet aircrew trained in a pressure chamber have sharper
sensate abilities than mere mortals with no training. That training
saved me and about half of the passengers. I have never been
susceptible to losing consciousness at altitude. I sensed the loss of
pressurization without losing my faculties. I saw a kid's balloon had
expanded to the size of a medicine ball. That's when I knew why my
skin was tingling and why it was difficult to breathe. I didn't panic, I
looked for secondary indications. In the flight kitchen and the cabin,
the crew were all out."

Knowing the cockpit of a 747 was virtually impenetrable, he asked,
"*How*...how did you get in the cockpit?"

Without hyperbole or braggadocio, Hunter told him. When Coffey
realized the simplicity of the solution, he knew he was in the presence
of genius. "The co-pilot was toast, but the pilot was still alive. I put
him on bottled O2. I needed him to land the jet. We barely had enough
fuel to make the former Clark Air Force Base. Tamerlan al-Sarkari, the
brilliant software engineer, was especially wicked—not only did he
shut down the pressurization system without tripping the
pressurization alarm, he also commanded the jet to dump fuel. That
was a murderous boy who knew how to cover his six." Hunter related
the rest of the story, how he took the identity of the co-pilot, flew to
Dubai, and found Mazibuike. He briefly described how he decapitated
the former president, how he defenestrated his head and torso, and
how he was covered in Mazibuike's blood.

That doesn't sound like Captain America.... Coffey said, "He really was Muslim Brotherhood?"

Maverick nodded and said, "You meet all kinds of crazies in this job. You come into contact with the evilest people on the planet. Yes, Muslim Brotherhood; Islamic Underground, most likely. I'm afraid you and your friends at the FBI were under the influence of propaganda, the propaganda of Muslim *infiltrators*. I would bet a form of *mass formation psychosis*. Mazibuike had his fingerprints on things, stepping on the scales of justice. I don't think your guys could have found a burning *Qur'an* in the middle of a mosque at midnight. I'll bet the FBI leaders listened to the *infiltrators* and not the rank-and-file guys like you, so they did nothing. The Muslim *infiltrators* knew exactly what they were doing. Their leaders understand psychology, and their acolytes have flown jets into buildings or made suicide attacks on U.S. forces for a hundred years."

Coffey was dumbfounded. This was validation from *Captain America*. He had been thinking this for decades.

Maverick turned to face Coffey and continued, "There is a big lie that is being promoted. It says Muslims tried socialism, Baathism, pan-Arabism, Marxism, leftism, and liberalism, and the result was always destruction. The Muslim *left* says, 'Let political Islam have its chance for once. Let the Muslim Brotherhood have its chance to be in charge.' But it isn't true political Islam never had its chance. That's propaganda. Political Islam rules Afghanistan to this day through the Taliban. Political Islam has ruled Iran since 1979. Political Islam has ruled Iraq since we turned the country over to the Iraqis. Political Islam dominates Lebanon, Gaza, Sudan and what has been the outcome?"

"It's like when leftist Democrats are in charge. They get elected, they steal the treasury, they fight to maintain power, they create failed states in the U.S. and failed cities. Ask, 'Is this the outcome they wanted?' The Algerian and Jordanian governments are continually on guard against Muslim Brotherhood interference. The Jordanian King has put the Muslim Brotherhood in a cage, and consequently Jordan is running well. The Muslim Brotherhood doesn't want the current Algerian government to move forward with their oil extraction and development projects, because that makes the government stronger and more independent of the Muslim Brotherhood. Every day the people of Algeria show they're better off without the Muslim Brotherhood."

"Just as most of the problems Islam is experiencing today are because of the destructive totalitarian policies of the Muslim Brotherhood, most of the problems America is experiencing today are because of the totalitarian policies of the Democrat Party — leftists have taken over the Democrat Party. The goal of the Muslim Brotherhood is to infiltrate the highest levels of government: the U.S. government and the FBI. They tried with Egypt and Jordan but failed."

Coffey's knew there was more than a bit of truth in what *Maverick* said. *For years I said the Muslims in the FBI were infiltrators. They were the most adamant that Mazibuike wasn't Muslim, wasn't Muslim Brotherhood. He was a Christian. A radicalized Muslim cloaked with the tincture of Christianity is like a cloak of invisibility in American government.*

The FBI leadership took the assessment of the Muslim Special Agents who had contacts and insight into those mosques instead of the assessment of line Special Agents. But they didn't have proof…uh, evidence either.

Hunter set the jet up for landing and offered Coffey the controls. He said, "She's just a big baby. Easier than an F-4 *Phantom II*. I won't let you get into any trouble; worst case, we'll take it around. If I say, 'My jet…'"

Coffey said, "Hands and feet off the controls." *And just like that, we are off on another topic.*

"You'll be surprised how easy it is."

Coffey handled the jet as if he had been flying it for years. *Pilot feel returns in an instant, just like riding a bike.* Coffey's command of the aircraft impressed Hunter. The landing was as precise as if Coffey had only been out of the cockpit for three days instead of thirty years. *Maverick* had made all the instrument checks, radio calls, and said, "My jet" as they straddled the runway centerline of the Elmira Corning Regional Airport and decelerated under 100 knots. *Maverick* taxied the aircraft to an old aircraft manufacturing business that had been bought out by Lockheed Martin over a decade ago. A new white

LM-130J sat on the ramp. On its tail were the gold and red letters and the logo of Quiet Aero Systems. The new owners of the facility.

Coffey had little idea what was coming next. A couple of men waved their arms to guide *Maverick* to a stop. They chocked the wheels as he shut down the engines.

Duncan Hunter jumped out of the cockpit, opened the cabin door, and lowered the airstairs. Coffey followed. It was freezing outside and he hadn't brought a coat. As they walked across the tarmac, Coffey tossed the challenge coin Hunter had given him the night before into the air, thinking, *What is going on???*

Hunter's Rolex *Submariner* with the bright blue dial sparkled in the sunlight. It hid the scar where his hand had been surgically reattached. He wasn't ashamed of that scar because it was evidence he was stronger than the man who tried to kill him.

Maverick came to a hangar door that looked to be every bit as secure as any FBI building Coffey had been in. Hunter took a pair of access cards from his wallet, inserted one into a reader and scanned the chip embedded in the other card. The door unlocked; Hunter pushed it open and allowed Coffey to pass before closing it behind them. They walked down a hall until Hunter stopped and threw a few light switches. He announced, "This is my other ride."

Coffey was taken aback, not by what he saw but by what he didn't see. He sucked a lot of wind, like a man who had been struck in the solar plexus. He approached cautiously and softly asked, *"What the hell is that?"*

"This is a YO-3A. It's a quiet airplane. You can see the huge oversized canopy and wheels and the aircraft's basic outline, but you can't see the airframe, the wings, or the propeller. It just looks like a black void, no definition. You can't hear it—it has a double muffler system on the other side. A reduction gearbox turns the prop so slowly that it generates just enough thrust for the plane to stay airborne...."

"No shockwaves off the prop tips?" *Incredible!*

"None. This is Lockheed's other spyplane, number nine of eleven prototypes delivered to the Army in 1969. The U-2 and A-12 blackbirds got all the press; this one does all the work."

Even as he got closer to the airframe, he couldn't see panel seams, rivets, or screws. Coffey asked, *"What is this stuff?"* He could feel them; he just couldn't see them. Everything was just black. As he looked at the silhouette of the airplane he realized, *That's how they did it! That's how the FBI rescued that girl!* He flipped around to look at Hunter with a look that said, *I know how you did it. You've also done some work for the FBI…. You're the mysterious Maverick who rescued women in the U.A.E. and jets in Africa! You really are Captain America! Holy moley!*

Maverick encouraged Coffey to touch the black coating which was playing tricks on his eyes. Hunter knew that touch helped and said, "It's one of the darkest substances known; the marketing materials indicate it absorbs up to 99.96% of visible light. It's made in the U.K. and comprises vertically aligned carbon nanotube arrays. It doesn't look real, does it?"

"It's…*beyond* my powers of description."

"And it's quiet."

Coffey was so preoccupied with the coating he ignored the three cars under covers along the furthest wall and forgot Hunter had highlighted the airplane's two mufflers and reduction gearbox. He asked, "Is it electric?"

Hunter said, "Electrics can't do what this airplane does."

"And what does this airplane do?" He was beginning to see how extraordinary the airplane was. If the external technology was off-the-charts secret, then there was no telling what was inside.

"Link, if McGee is successful in his bid for the Presidency, and there are no changes to what I'm doing, I will have my hands full. I will need help."

"Doing what?"

"Hunting down and killing terrorists. In this. In one of these."

CHAPTER 17

November 2, 2019

Coffey shook his head violently. The career FBI Special Agent took over. "There isn't an organization in American government that allows the murder of men, even if they're terrorists in another country. Geneva Convention. Nuremburg Laws...."

Hunter turned to the YO-3A and put his hand on the airplane that the U.S. Army once had considered obsolete. "The president or emir or prime minister of the countries where terrorists operate, convict and sentence these mass murderers to death *in absentia*. They authorize an emissary of the President of the United States to conduct special activities, as necessary, to prevent the murder of additional innocent life in their countries. Protection of the public may require the neutralization of the terrorists. In other words, authorized shoot-to-kill orders. Publicly, the leaders of all the countries involved disavow any knowledge of these efforts."

That was unexpected. You're an emissary of the President? You have authorization to enter a country and execute their condemned mass murderers – as long as it's not made public?

"Are you serious?"

"I'm dead serious. That's 99 percent of the time. There are special circumstances where I conduct special activities as required."

"What the hell does that mean?"

"Take, for example, there were five terrorists we – the U.S. government – have been seeking for a long time. Three had killed American servicemen, but we couldn't get to them. Two were involved in the downing of a commercial airliner. They couldn't be found and couldn't be brought to trial. We've been chasing Islamic terrorists at the top of the FBI's Most Wanted Terrorist list, but we couldn't get access to them either. Some of them had been living in or hiding in Iran."

Coffey's narrowed his brows. He knew of the men. They had gotten away with murder.

Then an impassioned *Maverick* rattled off their names. "Mohammed Ali Hammadi was convicted in a West German court of law for air piracy and murder for his part in the 1985 hijacking of TWA Flight 847. Hammadi had murdered U.S. Navy diver, Robert Stethem and dumped his body onto the tarmac in Beirut, Lebanon. Ibrahim Salih Mohammed Al-Yacoub had been indicted and tried *in absentia* for his part in the 1996 bombing of the Khobar Towers military housing complex in Dhahran, Kingdom of Saudi Arabia. Nineteen U.S. Air Force personnel and a Saudi local were killed. Abdullah Ahmed Abdullah had been indicted and tried *in absentia* for his involvement in the 1998 bombings of the U.S. Embassies in Dar es Salaam, Tanzania and Nairobi, Kenya. Two truck bombs killed 224 people. Ahmed Jibril had been indicted and tried *in absentia* for leading the 1988 plot to down Pam Am Flight 103. He was paid millions of pounds to mastermind the attack. Ahmad Khalid Saleh Hashash was secretly tried *in absentia* for making the bomb that brought down Flight 103 in 1988. Those five men were at the top of the FBI's Most Wanted Terrorist list. You know as well as I do, now there is but one." *And no one has seen him for years....*

As Coffey ran the concept through his head, Hunter explained how he did it. "Our labs in Texas developed fist-sized silent drones. We called them *Blackwings*. They don't have any of the skirr you would normally associate with spinning rotors. Continuous harmonic balancing cancels out noise propagation. If I could locate the murderers of our troops, I was authorized to employ those drones."

Coffey was dumbfounded. He sputtered, "How... how... *how?*"

"How do they work? First, I plug a USB cable from my laptop to each of the Lilliputian rotorcraft drones and download the photographs of the terrorist's faces. The artificial intelligence makes it easy; all I have to do is drop them over the target area where they should be. They either find the terrorists, match their faces with the facial recognition software and kill them, or they don't."

Coffey couldn't believe what he was hearing. He stared at *Maverick* in disbelief.

"It's simple. When the *Blackwing* locates its target, it hovers until the optimum attack profile is achieved and then it rams the forehead of the person. A one-ounce, shaped-charge warhead detonates and penetrates their skull. Death is instantaneous...."

Maverick paused for a moment to reflect on just how lucky they had been that night. It looked like finding Hammadi, al-Yacoub, Abdullah, and Jibril was going to be an abject failure, and we were going to be captured or die trying. I had seen it coming, the day when the YO-3A and all of its quiet and stealth technologies would be defeated by terrorists who had been studying how a hundred of their compatriots had been killed in the middle of the night in some of the most remote locations on earth. It didn't take a genius to figure out the intelligence community had weaponized unmanned aircraft, then we were also likely to have other secret nighttime capabilities that could find and eliminate the enemies of America with a single bullet. Or a tiny drone no one could hear. Blackwings.

Coffey thought, *Impossible!*

Maverick chuckled. "Al Jazeera reported their deaths, meaning the technology worked. But Hashash is still on the loose."

Coffey took several deep breaths. He had to admit he wasn't up to date with the state of weapons development. He asked *Maverick*, "So, technically, all you have to do is download their photographs and drop the *Blackwings* over the target?"

Maverick nodded. "If I can't use the aircraft's TS2, drones give us other...*opportunities*."

Coffey tried to speak. *TS2?*

Hunter continued, "There are still some technical challenges. Ethical issues. They could go stupid and kill kids. I have to be sure they're only used against terrorists."

Coffey found his tongue and peppered his friend with questions. "How far can they fall before they come alive and start flying? Can they be swatted away? How much battery life do they have? How long have you been doing these *special activities*?

Maverick ignored the technicalities. He said, "Twenty... twenty-five years?"

It then occurred to Coffey, "Ohhhhh, that explains how the men on the Most Wanted and *Specially Designated Terrorist* watch lists were systematically removed from those lists.... Without comment. No one knew how. No one told me. We didn't have a need to know. I didn't have a need to know."

Maverick rubbed the coating and patted the airframe like it was a faithful horse and said, "Now you know."

Coffey thought, slack jawed, *That's incredible!*

Maverick said, "The explosive charge collapses a metal foil liner inside the warhead to form a high-velocity superplastic jet of liquid metal. The brain is destroyed, cooked in its cranium by hot expanding gasses. They cut off the heads of infidels, we shoot eyeballs out of their sockets. I love American ingenuity!"

Maverick moved to the canopy and Coffey followed. *Maverick* gave him a descriptive tour. "The original YO-3A had long wings and a short fuselage. Conformal antenna. Monster transparencies for exceptional viewing and situational awareness. Everything that would be found in the airstream of a normal aircraft was engineered to be smooth and internal so it wouldn't make noise. This one and its sister have been modified extensively. New cockpits, sensors, wings. Optionally manned. It has ATLS, Automatic Takeoff and Landing System. The original airplanes had fixed wings; these have removeable wings like gliders. It was originally placarded at 135 knots max speed, but with improvements and the right propeller it has a dash speed of two-o. It makes noise at that speed—propeller tips are supersonic—but in mission mode the throttle is retarded, the reduction gearbox is engaged, and the prop turns at just enough RPMs to maintain flight."

The right propeller? What does that mean—there are more than one? Coffey barely nodded. Somehow, he knew this airplane contained more technology than he could conceive.

Maverick said, "We use it in ways that could never have been imagined in 1969. The *Yo-Yo* is equipped with the latest sensors; FLIR, laser designators, a laser eradication system we call *Weedbusters*, and a gun. Not just any gun, mind you, but a Terminator Sniper System, TS2, one that uses experimental laser-guided ammunition...."

Coffey's eyelids fluttered. He was taken aback. "Hold it! *Laser-guided* ammunition? Like, *laser-guided bullets?*"

"That's right. When I need them, the sensors and the TS2 fold out from underneath the aircraft. It has forty years of weapons technology built into the airframe. I can't be seen, I can't be heard, and I can't be picked up on radar. I can put a bullet into an ace of spades at five miles in the dark with the IR, infrared laser designator. P-sub k approaching 100. (Probability of Kill.) Beyond five miles, the laser spot gets too big for something as small as a playing card. Max effective range is about ten miles head-on. It has thermal radar and a thermal gunsight." *And I've even shot down a drug smuggler's plane. He never knew I was there. I've done a lot of crap in twenty years....*

Coffey had difficulty keeping his eyes off of the black coating and *Maverick* admonished him, "Stop looking at the coating. They coated a Beemer a year or so ago. It's about $50,000 a gallon. All the non-black parts look like they're hovering, stuck into something that is unreflective."

"That would be pretty cool. You know, you're friggin' demented."

"You have no idea. We also have flight suits made with the stuff. Those are about a hundred grand apiece."

Not believing any of it, Coffey retorted, "Those must be the most expensive flight suits on the planet."

Maverick said, "Scientists at the Lawrence Livermore National Laboratory developed a breathable, protective *smart fabric* that responds to biological threats like viruses and bacteria, and chemical agents, like sarin gas, and the material neutralizes all of them. It's a special infused fabric that combines breathability and protection to microscopic dangers in a biological environment."

Biological threats?

"When you see it and touch it, you'll know it's not a Nomex® flight suit. It's a multi-layered multi-functional material with carbon nanotube pores, graphitic cylinders with diameters more than 5,000 times thinner than a human hair."

Coffey suddenly understood, "You mean *nanotubes*, like the paint on the *Yo-Yo?*" *It's like the coating on the YO-3A only in a fabric! I suppose that material would play tricks on the eyes and induce vertigo. And there was a wearable version? Totally incredible.*

Maverick continued, "The real magic is that the nanotubes trap and block biological threats. The middle layer is a threat-responsive polymer that enables protection against the even tinier chemical threats which can fit through the outer layer's nanotubes' pores. Throw it into a dryer with UV lamps and the UV kills the trapped pathogens stuck in the nanotubes. The material is triggered by contact of the chemical or biological threat with the polymers on the surface of the membrane."

Coffey was speechless.

Maverick smiled, nodded, and said, "What's really cool are the new helmets. Rather than waiting until I had a neck problem, I asked my engineers to develop a lightweight next-generation helmet which includes a mount for night vision goggles (NVG) for night flying. I had been using standard ANVIS-9 Aviator Night Vision systems with all of its acuity shortfalls. I fly in some pretty nasty places. Remember we wore cloth skull caps in F-4s, and they kept our heads cool. But first-generation skull caps aren't a good solution in hot environments, and my head got nasty sweaty pretty quickly. Sweat ran down my back all the time. ANVIS-9 were heavy. Good imagery but not great, especially during landings. I wanted something that was light and ventilated, and with better acuity. They came through bigtime."

"You remember how hot it was in Yuma. We lost buckets of water before we even got in the F-4's cockpit. It's like that; flying over the desert of the Middle East or equatorial Africa."

"This helmet is more comfortable than the old helmet?"

"It is. After two days of getting fitted, I couldn't even tell it was on my head."

"Incredible."

"And it has a pair of lights mounted on its sides. The best part is how you turn them on—you use your jaw muscles."

Coffey was confused. "Jaw muscles?"

A smile confirmed the claim. "There's a switch on the helmet that barely touches the jaw. It has different settings—a short clench, followed by a long clench and that activates the lights on the helmet."

"And that lights up the cockpit?"

Maverick nodded. "And there's improved noise cancellation technology. You need it to block out the reduction gearbox roaring in front of you. The old helmet had a counterweight, NVG mount, and noise cancellation. It was integrated, and it was all helpful, but it was heavy. That is old-school that I save for the training airplanes."

Old school? Training airplanes? "We had nothing like that, but then again, we weren't flying a few feet over the ground on NVGs."

Maverick continued, "This fifth-generation cockpit's now a technology hub. We just installed digital visible, low-light level, and infrared cameras, as well as image processing and display component technologies and integrated systems."

"Meaning?"

"Meaning in this cockpit we now have reconfigurable, full color displays with high resolution and brightness. Now I don't have to wear the heavy ANVIS-9 night vision goggles. The image processing hardware displays what I would see with night vision goggles directly on my helmet visor. And it even has the capability for enhanced augmented reality."

No NVGs? You can see in the dark without night vision goggles on your head? Imagery is on your visor? "You mean like those things you see gamers wearing?"

"Those are commercial-grade, first generation stuff. Our systems are the product of an Intelligence Advanced Research Projects Agency, IARPA, contract. About twenty years ahead and a hundred times more powerful. The digital night vision technologies are integrated into the helmet and projected onto a substrate in my visor. No more looking down into the cockpit for information when I'm flying low level and need to have my head out of the cockpit. The new visors allow a heads-up security posture by presenting all relevant battlefield and air data to the pilot's visor. Airspeed, altitude, terrain, attitude, heading—comm and nav symbology. This is the second aircraft to receive the improvements and upgrades."

Coffey had been speechless. When he found his tongue he asked, "What does something like that cost?"

"Each helmet costs more than a Ferrari. *And not a new Ferrari.*"
They laughed.

It was obvious *Maverick* had an apodictic knowledge of the aircraft and its capabilities. As he walked around the aircraft and talked, Coffey followed. "The first-generation aircraft had a FLIR. Scopes in both cockpits. We used it to locate the FARC, the *Fuerzas Armadas Revolucionarias de Colombia.*"

Coffey said, "The Revolutionary Armed Forces of Colombia."

"Si. We find terrorist and narcoterrorist groups and their hostages in the mountains of South America, Somalia, Mali, probably all of Africa, and a lot of terrorists in the Middle East. In an aircraft the bad guys can't see or hear, they think no one is around. Perfect time for intel gathering. The next generation, we deployed a laser designator and could get in close enough to make positive IDs on terrorists hiding under physical countermeasures, like overhangs and canopies. They learned how to defeat satellites and cameras on UAVs. You know how Osama bin Laden's hideout was constructed with large overhangs to defeat satellites and high-flying UAVs with their fantastic optics and cameras. I fly so low I can look under those canopies and see right inside those houses. I put the LD on the target and a UAV operator sees the laser-designated spot and fires a missile to take out the terrorist and his buddies. It requires a positive identification, otherwise there is no launch. And all engagements are on tape."

"Incredible." Coffey turned 360 degrees to admire the building's surroundings.

"The Agency has to develop the intel necessary so I can get to that spot on the planet to make a positive ID. The next generation technology was the incorporation of *Weedbusters*. The CIA advanced the technology of aerial eradication by thirty years."

Weedbusters...sounds like a bad comedy movie. Coffey pointed at the three cars under covers and a contraption on a stand with a cover on it in a corner of the hangar. "What are those and what is that?"

Maverick grinned, walked over to the gray vinyl covering, and removed it. He turned his head to see Coffey's mouth agape. *Maverick* said, "I use a jet pack... *for special problems.*"

"A…jet pack…*for special problems*…." Coffey repeated as he shook his head continuously. Once the awe had worn off, he helped Hunter replace the covering.

Maverick said, "Even though it's not quiet, it was our only solution to get inside the Burj Khalifa *after hours*…." *The problem that night was getting to the top floor without using the elevator. The building panels of the world's tallest building were designed to muffle the natural winds at 2,000 feet. If they could suppress wind noise, they could suppress the exhaust noise of the jet pack. And they did.*

What Coffey was seeing coupled with what Hunter was intimating was too much to comprehend. *I read where the jet pack used by James Bond had a twenty-second range. What fuel could they be using?*

Maverick and Coffey walked back to the YO-3A. "A pilot wonders what fuel it uses."

Coffey nodded, slightly afraid of the answer.

"Pellets of *metallic* hydrogen." Hunter grinned at the thought, *In the 1930s, the Hungarian-born Eugene Wigner predicted that metallic hydrogen may potentially be a highly efficient rocket propellant. We proved it!*

Coffey's eyelids fluttered as he tried to force his brain to comprehend what *metallic* hydrogen could actually be. Not being an engineer, he gave up. He pointed to the covered cars.

"You have a *Pagoda*. Those are 1957 Mercedes 300 SLs, two black, one blue; a Gullwing and two roadsters. This hangar is heated." Maverick pulled the cover off of one.

Coffey was speechless. He walked around the black Gullwing. He looked up at *Maverick* and said, "This is a million-dollar car."

"I'm well paid." Maverick and Coffey replaced the cover gently.

He apologized for interrupting *Maverick's* brief and asked, "What does *Weedbusters* do again?"

"We irradiate drug crops. We kill them with ultraviolet light. In the beginning I flew into Afghanistan and we killed about 5,000 hectares of mature opium poppies in a week. Now I can kill half-a-million hectares of new sprouts in a single night and put the Taliban completely out of the opium business. We destroy their funding stream. If we ever leave the country, the Taliban and the Muslim

Brotherhood will be back in the opium business again. Every year they put in a crop and every year I come around and destroy that crop." *Maverick* snapped his fingers to emphasize the drug lords' tenacity.

What an interesting comment. Does he know something the rest of us don't? "They...."

Maverick filled in the missing parts of the conversation. "Yeah, they never know what hits them. The drug cartels still think they lose their crops to a virus or some biological weapon. So they keep trying."

"But it's just light?"

"UV-C. Doesn't leave any residue as evidence that I've been there. We use the C-band of the ultraviolet spectrum. Of course, the secret is in the dwell time and altitude."

Of course.... Coffey didn't actually know anything about laser-killing systems but was suddenly intrigued.

"The rising temperatures triggers the opium poppy's erumpent activity. Over the years we found out we only have to make the baby plants sick enough in the beginning of their growth cycle to damage their ability to put up a mature harvestable opium bulb."

"But...."

"Would you kill baby Hitler or Goebbels or Mengele if you could, knowing what they would grow up to be? Here, we know exactly what baby opium plants grow up to be: mature opium plants. The difference is we damage them as they're emerging from the ground so their little baby brains don't develop and mature. As sprouts, they're fragile and can be damaged easily. I don't need to spend a lot of *dwell* time to kill plants like I used to. UV-C isn't found in nature and has the shortest wavelength. It kills everything: plants, bugs, even coronaviruses. To achieve maximum effectiveness, I fly low at a precise speed which allows for maximum radiation of the target."

That is so incredible as to be impossible! Who would have thought of using a laser to kill or maim plants? Maverick, apparently. Was that one of his patents? He said he has patents...equipment designed to thwart terrorists. Plants too? Apparently! Coffey wrapped his arms around his chest and asked, "But don't the drug lords put kids in the fields...? To counter aerial eradication programs?"

"Yes, they do when there is spraying of a mature harvestable crop. We use a laser when the plants are just emerging from the ground, and if the FLIR shows there are kids in the open field, I program the fire control computer to block the area around them and irradiate around them as they sleep. Since we have been killing baby plants, I have seen no children in the fields. But if there were, I wouldn't wake them up. I don't expose them. In the old days some plants were left untouched, unirradiated around the kids. It wasn't enough to make any commercially appreciable amount of opium, but if the kids had woken up, they would have known something was happening."

"Really? How's that?"

"In those days when *Weedbusters* was engaged, the mature poppy plants would *fluoresce*. Before we coated the plane with the *black*, the fluorescence would illuminate the belly of the *Yo-Yo*. That doesn't happen anymore. No reflections."

"How would you know something like that?"

"Beside the fact the plants I irradiated beneath me lit me up like the background of a neon sign? What you really want to know was how did I think of it? *Weedbusters*."

"Yeah...."

Maverick grinned. There was no way to describe the rush of excitement he got with every mission so he didn't try. The challenge of killing unrefined dope or finding and killing bad guys kept him coming back for more.

He said, "I was in a dental office, probably twenty-five years ago, and I saw an article about how the ozone layer had become so large over Antarctica the tip of South America, Patagonia, was experiencing virtually no plant growth. With a small ozone hole over the South Pole everything in Patagonia had been green. Trees, bushes, grasses, plants. Green. But with a big hole, everything in Patagonia was now dead. Dead and gray. The additional unfiltered, naturally occurring UV-B killed all the plant life in Patagonia over days...weeks. I asked, 'Why couldn't we use a UV laser to kill or maim poppies in Afghanistan?' The State Department had an aerial eradication program—nine countries, two billion dollars over ten years. I thought we could do it for far less and with an insignificant footprint. And I was right."

"Can you hit coca or marijuana?"

Maverick nodded and said, "All the time. Poppy is a once-a-year crop, coca and the marijuana are year-round. Coca is hard to kill, like whacking cardboard, but whack it enough and it will die. It turns brown like prickly pear cactus that has been frozen. Sometimes I want to drop a *Firestarter* in the middle of a patch and burn the coca."

"*Firestarter?*"

Maverick nodded and continued, "Let's see. You know the basic construction of electric vehicles; they have a big flat battery tray between the tires. Now the contents of that battery are under extreme pressure and are well protected. But if a metal fragment punctures the partition that keeps the components separate or if the battery is punctured, the lithium reacts vigorously with the water in the air and produces a fire. Hotter than a magnesium fire. Now, I wanted that kind of spontaneous energy as a method to start a fire, but not any fire. If you noticed in the YouTube videos, once an electric vehicle catches fire, even fire departments cannot put them out. That's what I wanted as a programable grenade; something with a built-in timer I could set to go off or maybe go off on impact. Selectable. I would toss one out the aircraft if the situation arose. Our lab boys came up with a device I call *Firestarter* and I figured out the ballistics to get a *Firestarter* near a target. It helps to be a decent bomber in F-4s. Anyway, they burn so hot and fast a couple of them can literally burn down a building before the fire department can arrive." *And if you stuff one into a dead man, no dentist would be able to use teeth to identify a victim.*

Coffey said, "You sound like you have experience being an arsonist, too?"

Maverick turned to him, grinning like a pyromaniac.

Coffey continued, "That would mean you would have a strange and exotic chemical fire that can't be contained by usual means. What a novel weapon."

Maverick nodded. "Exactly. I love them but I don't get to use them as much as I could. Often, I do not want to leave any traces I had been there, and *Firestarter* prevents those missions. But there are others. There are times I thought I could take out a drug lab when I flew over one, but we feel it's more important to maintain our anonymity. Many times, it's better to give the local militaries credit."

Coffey said, "I understand we lost some Marines in Vietnam to magnesium fires when their helicopters crashed."

"I think our lithium-based *Firestarters* burn hotter and faster than magnesium or phosphorus just because of where they are on the periodic table. But the UV is the silent killer and you can do so much with it as long as you have the right altitude, as in above ground level. Marijuana is easier than poppy. They take a lot of water and are so susceptible to the UV-C that the plants' leaves almost melt when it's hit with the laser." As he led Coffey through the high security door, *Maverick* concluded his brief on the YO-3A with a comment all of their aerodynamic smoothing and conformal equipment generated sixty percent less drag than comparable-sized aircraft.

Getting Coffey out of the hangar was like dragging a six-year-old out of a candy store. On the ramp, *Maverick* said, "Now I have two aircraft that are also fully *optionally* manned. Takeoff and landing, basic FLIR work; I can program them before or during flight." He stopped and pointed along a row of hangars. "Our cover is in these hangars where World War Two warbirds are in various stages of repair and refurbishment. It's a twenty-year-old business, Quality Fighter Restorations. Ten Oshkosh champions, three-time Rolls-Royce Heritage winners. Authenticity is our specialty. The hangar is a natural purlieu for pilots and aircraft mechanics and unusual aircraft. We mostly do single-engine aircraft work, but occasionally twins with radials. Each aircraft they work on has a particular haecceity."

"I'm afraid I don't know what that, haecceity means. Your vocabulary was always out of this world to mere mortals like me."

Maverick grinned. "Link, that's what haecceity means — the aircraft they work on are often the only one of its kind. Like a Fokker *Dr.1*, if I can ever get my hands on one. I have my eye on a stunning black and white one with an original rotary engine. I made him an offer he shouldn't refuse."

Rotary engine? Don't you mean radial engine? Coffey smiled broadly and laughed to himself. *Maverick misspoke. At least I think he did.*

Maverick refused to point to the Supermarine *Spitfire*, basking in the sun in front of the hangar. Real pilots can recognize the early dogfighters from a time zone away. "Like the *Spitfire*. There isn't another one anywhere like it; it's a flying museum piece. Better than when it left the factory. I can't fly a high-performance jet like the F-4 *Phantom II* anymore, but I can fly a warbird—and I don't have to go out on a mission so I get to enjoy just how thrilling it is to have that power at your beck and call. That's what my guys do so I can do...*stuff*. That's here. I have a place in Texas where we do custom, antique cars as well as armored car conversions."

Coffey shook his head. "And you want a *triplane*?"

"Officially, it's a *dreidecker* and it has the original rotary engine that spins and throws oil everywhere."

"An engine that spins?"

"Oh yeah, all nine cylinders. There's only a few of those engines remaining from the war. One hundred-year-old technology; if you see one it's usually in a museum. Not on an operational airplane. The centrifugal forces of a spinning engine on the front of such a light aircraft have to be incredible. There's a reason old Manfred von Richthofen could do a flat-turn."

Coffey thought, *I only thought I knew airplanes.*

Maverick continued, "So, over there, we have old mechanics with experience on antique aircraft as well as a bunch of disabled troops from Vietnam and the Iraq and Afghanistan wars working on refurbishing aircraft. They won't stop until whatever they're working on is perfect. They're craftsmen and specialists doing museum-quality work." He pointed to a pristine Douglas DC-3 in polished aluminum and original Pan American Airways livery parked out front. "We just took delivery of that *Hummer*. It's impeccable and I can't wait to fly it."

Boys and their toys.... Coffey said, "I don't know what to say."

"Tell me you'll think about joining our little enterprise."

"I have a couple of questions." *First of all, you know you're human carbon monoxide—the silent killer?* He chuckled at his unspoken witticism.

Maverick was surprised Coffey had questions. "Go!"

"There was a rumor that on your first flight in the F-4 you flew the jet better than your instructor."

"True. He accused me of being an Air Force *Phantom* pilot, but the *Skipper* set him straight."

"How could you do something like that? We all took off like the Space Shuttle on our first flight."

"Well, I cheated."

"You cheated?"

"I'm always cheating, but in a good way. The CO wanted to know, so I told him. I was the gradebook officer, and all the student grade sheets crossed my desk. I put them into each student's folder."

So? Coffey didn't understand.

"I would read what the instructor had to say about each student; what they did well and not so well. Like you said, everyone's first takeoff was a disaster. I scheduled myself for simulator time until I figured out how to takeoff like the instructors. I told the Skipper before my first flight I had 200 hours of simulator time practicing how not to do what everyone else did. I took off at eight degrees, flat as a board, and then flew the rest of the hop like I was an expert. I cheated."

I could have done the same thing, spent more time in the sims, but I chased girls. Coffey changed directions. "Who are the *Irregulars*, really; is it a secret organization?"

Hunter smiled and said, "The *Irregulars* are not a secret organization although they fight evil; think of them as the Justice League of Communist Fighters who battle against the crime syndicate that is the Democrat Party. We simply meet once a year and enjoy everyone's company." *That's probably a "good-enough" answer.*

"I don't get it."

"You're familiar with 'politics is combat by other means.'"

"I am. Clausewitz."

"As an FBI Assistant Deputy Director, you know today's battles are done in court. Lawsuits are not *tea and crumpets*; they are battles. Most of the *Irregulars* you saw at dinner fight the important Constitutional battles with Democrats, liberals, commies and professional lefties in the courts. Their lawyers and our lawyers draft legislation. We fight them at the ballot box. Read an old *Covert Action*

Information Bulletin and you'll see the professional left has considered us domestic enemies, racists, and domestic terrorists. White supremacists, KKK, whatever. They're clowns who get masters' degrees in red rubber noses."

"But McGee.... A quarter of the people at the *Dinner* were African Americans, and there were other minorities, too."

"The professional left wants to make any discussion about race because they know it's the perfect propaganda weapon, and they believe shouting *racist* gives them an advantage. It's the prime silent weapon of propaganda that can inflict pain, stop a conversation, and kill a movement. Conservative *ideology* is color blind—doing the right thing is color blind. The left wants to make it about race to gain an advantage, but the right knows it's about ideology. Christians versus atheists. Most Americans are unaware U.S. Senator Hiram Revels from Mississippi was the first African American to serve in the United States Congress. The first twenty-three African American Congressmen were Republicans. Freemen. That's history the Democrats don't like, and their media won't cover."

Coffey now nodded and grinned. "That makes sense. But Mazibuike was the first African American to be elected president, and he was a Democrat."

"He wasn't eligible. I'll tell you the rest of the story later."

One of these days you'll tell me the rest of the story? What rest of the story? You already told me you decapitated him and threw him out a window. What more could there be?

Hunter asked, "Anything else?"

"Are you and Nazy married?"

The question caught *Maverick* off guard. He lifted his left hand and admired his wedding band and said, "You know Link, I'd rather not answer that question right now. Maybe one of these days I'll tell you."

Coffey stopped walking on the airport ramp. *That's obviously a 'yes but I can't talk about it' answer. Fair enough, Maverick.* He turned to look back at the YO-3A hangar and said, "You're telling me many more things than I would have told anyone."

Maverick had expected the statement. The observation. "You're clean. We were Marines. Phantom drivers. Law school. Madrassas were not part of your education. You didn't hang out with the anarchists of the Weather Underground; you didn't vote for the Communist Gus Hall for president. You didn't make excuses for Marxism or socialism. You chased pedophiles. It takes a certain kind of patriot to do dirty work."

He has done a background investigation on me. "Why me?"

"I said I need help. This isn't a job for snowflakes. You're not a snowflake, and I think I can trust you, even if you're FBI. We are in the middle of a fight against the left to save America and probably the world. You know me. None of that is hyperbole. It takes a certain level of training and education just to see what the left is doing."

"Like what?"

"Like in order to understand and solve quantum physics equations you have to have a Ph.D. in physics and mathematics. Einstein saw the world differently and others had to work at it for a long time to get to a point where their minds could catch up before they could understand the whole E=mc² thing."

Coffey nodded.

"We have known each other a long time, and you were glad I was still alive. When we were in the Marine Corps, you saw Air Branch as I did—if we were there, we would fly the most incredible aircraft in the most difficult missions. I put up with the discomforts of flying a fighter because it was the most exciting thing I could think of; you looked to the FBI because fighting criminals was the most exciting thing you could think of. Am I right?"

"You're right." Coffey grinned.

Maverick grinned. "So, you have seen the silent weapons we use against terrorism. The left uses a different set of silent weapons for the next quiet war; we believe they need to be stopped."

Coffey said, "I thought I was familiar with that term but I'm still not sure what silent weapons means."

"So, we have a quiet airplane, FLIR, LDs, *Weedbusters.* Their silent weapons are the tools of propaganda. Goebbels and his ilk were masters of psychology, specifically *dark psychology.* Mind control methods and procedures. Actually, the very precise use of specific words to gain an advantage. Best example, the Nuremberg Laws.

Hitler stripped the citizenship away from German Jews. With the stroke of a pen, he rendered all Jews non-citizens, *persona non grata*. Ready to be deported or worse. Words on paper to manipulate them, to make them move or do something they didn't want to do. Why do you think the Democrats work so hard to abolish the Second Amendment? Zimbabwe passed laws that outlawed white men owning anything. That was the hunting license blacks needed to exterminate the whites from their country."

Link Coffey's eyes fluttered.

Maverick continued, "There will be time to explore the whole panoply of *dark psychology* and propaganda tools at a later date. Yeah, we need you to understand who we are fighting against, but first I think we need to get you back into a cockpit. Not one that is loaded with weapons systems and is challenging to fly like the F-4, but one that is easier *physically* to fly with sensors that give us a tactical edge. I'm pretty sure this work will be more rewarding than anything you ever did in the Marines or the FBI."

"I'm interested. And I can pass a flight physical."

"Perfect! I'll train you to fly the long-wing birds. We'll go up to the National Soaring Museum for some slow flight. That's Harris Hill over there; they have a runway on top. We have a simulator here, and you should know the work requires night vision goggles. We use my old NVG helmets. But it will be like your first cat shot, the ones after are a snap. We'll get you back into the cockpit in no time. We'll fly dual when we can."

"Sometimes you can't?"

"Some missions may require an empty seat going in, and some require an empty seat coming out. My time isn't really my own. But it has its fringe benefits."

Coffey thought, *Like sleeping with Nazy....* After a few moments, he said, "In other words, sometimes you bring someone out and sometimes you insert someone into the country. You're an on-call service."

Maverick nodded and said, "I'd like that to be, 'We, Kemosabe.'" Just then his BlackBerry went off. There was a single number in the display. *CIA Director's office.* Hunter excused himself, walked back toward the hangars, and answered the phone. Believing it was Bill McGee, he said, "Oh captain, my captain. What can I do for you this beautiful and exquisite afternoon?"

Acting Director of the CIA Nazy Cunningham cooed, "I need you."

CHAPTER 18

November 2, 2019

The White House Press Secretary called a press conference that was not on the schedule. After allowing the members of the White House Press Corps to take their seats, the President of the United States, followed by the Director of the Central Intelligence Agency, the White House Chief of Staff, and the Vice President entered the White House briefing room. President Hernandez mounted the podium and took the lectern. "Algerian terrorists, the Armed Islamic Group of the Muslim Brotherhood organization, have attempted to destroy the ExxonMobil compound and Algeria's national oil and natural gas company, Sonatrach."

"Algeria is one of our Islamic allies and has been for several years. Using American horizontal drilling and fracking technology they extract thousands of barrels of oil every week and contribute to the national security of Algeria and her neighbors. Members of the U.S. military and Special Operations Command in concert with the Algerian military protected the Americans and Algerian oil workers. Are there any questions?"

There were no questions on Algeria. The press corps wanted a statement from the CIA Director. President Hernandez yielded the podium. As Director McGee commanded the lectern, press photographers included the Presidential Seal in all of their photographs. Those images would be broadcast to every television around the country: the distinguished African American presidential candidate in a black Brooks Brothers suit and bright red tie at the lectern with the Seal of the Office of the President in front of him.

The positive press and tailor-made photo opportunity infuriated the leftist media. They wouldn't put that video of Bill McGee on the air. If they were forced to do so, they would use only an official stock *headshot* of the CIA Director with part of the soundtrack.

Bill McGee called on Colonel Eastwood for the first question.

Demetrius Eastwood of the independent on-line news network, *Unfiltered News*, stood as he addressed the CIA Director. His sleeve slid back when he held up his notepad to reveal a Tudor *Black Bay* with black face, red bezel, and a leather strap. "Director McGee, kudos to the SEALs of SOCOM for another successful interdiction mission. There was a time when Americans abroad would never have been molested, assailed, or murdered. This episode marks another successful interdiction mission in North Africa. Americans would like to know just how much help the CIA gave the Algerians to ensure this ambush would fail?"

McGee regripped the lectern, "Colonel Eastwood, the leadership of the Muslim Brotherhood and other terrorist organizations will soon recognize it's not in their best interests to engage in terroristic behaviors because America stands ready to protect her interests and her allies."

President Hernandez stepped forward and added, "I believe it was John Wayne who said, 'Life is hard; it's harder when you're stupid.'" McGee and the President smiled at each other. McGee said, "You have to be incredibly stupid to threaten Americans abroad. The President has repeatedly said he has no qualms about using the full force of America's military might to destroy the criminally stupid when they take up arms to murder or menace our citizens. Thank you for the question. Colonel Eastwood, did you want a follow-up?"

"Yes, Director McGee, you announced yesterday you would run for the Office of the Presidency. I think America would like to hear about the plans of the nation's most awarded military man. Is this your last official act before hitting the campaign trail?"

"Colonel Eastwood, this is about the nation's business, and I'd like to stay on topic. I will discuss our campaign with you on your radio show — sometime next week; will that work?"

"Thank you, sir. That certainly will." Eastwood was ecstatic; as the mainstream media sat on their hands, he was going to interview McGee and help propel his candidacy down the road.

President Hernandez replaced McGee at the lectern. McGee retired and stood against the wall. The President asked if there were any other questions. He called on a reporter from one of the cable news networks. She asked, "Isn't murdering destitute Africans a clear sign America is to its core a racist country?"

The President said, "That is disgusting. You need to get some new material. You asked that same ridiculous insipid question a few years ago. Western intelligence officials haven't turned a blind eye to reported human rights abuses, and no one murdered destitute Africans. It's that type of inaccurate reporting which makes you and your network look like fools."

"We know Algeria's opposition parties fear Algeria's growing economic influence in Northwest Africa. We are skeptical of certain elements in Algiers that portray al-Qaeda, AQIM, or the Muslim Brotherhood as helpful, misunderstood elements of political Islam. But let us be clear, the Muslim Brotherhood in all of its forms and through all of its affiliates is a major threat to regional stability. Our troops prevented your destitute Africans who had taken up arms against the Algerians from committing murders on Americans and Algerians. For trying to engage in cheap propaganda, for trying to besmirch our troops and make excuses for terrorists you have exceeded the bounds of decent journalism and are no longer welcome here. Press Secretary, pull her press pass and get her out of here. Can I get a Marine to escort this poor excuse of a journalist off the White House grounds? Director McGee, could you finish this press conference? Thank you." And with those final words, President Hernandez and his entourage exited the White House Press Room, leaving CIA Director McGee to approach the lectern again.

Eastwood and the other members of the White House Press Corps were stunned. *There's nothing like a former Wellesley College women's studies professor spouting angry communist tropes on camera.... And was the President feeling his oats?*

Eastwood noted President Hernandez wouldn't accept the reporter's premise that U.S. forces were doing anything but protecting the lives of innocent Americans and her allies. Non-state actors do not care about the rule of law. Their only desire is power. The men of al-Qaeda, AQIM, and the Muslim Brotherhood were terrorists, international criminals, not destitute law-abiding people.

Director McGee said, "I believe we speak with a single mind on this subject. If international criminal elements like al-Qaeda, AQIM, the Muslim Brotherhood, or any of the organizations of the Islamic Underground choose a life of intimidating, threatening, capturing or killing Americans in an effort to hold them hostage or in an effort to extort funds from Americans or American companies, retaliation will be swift. Retaliation will be total. They will be annihilated in a place and manner of our choosing. When evil strikes Americans, whoever they are and wherever they are, the evildoers will be held accountable, and the country from which they operate will be held accountable. That is the end of this press conference."

As he stepped from the microphone, Director McGee finished his last official act as an unelected public servant.

CHAPTER 19

November 2, 2019

Duncan Hunter's face changed instantly, "What a pleasant surprise *Director* Cunningham. I expected *Bullfrog*, but got the beautiful matriarch of Langley."

Nazy was all business. "I have your position in Elmira; I'll have a PPR (Prior Permission Required) for Andrews for you soon. Meet you on the ramp?" Nazy had talked to the U.S. Air Force Chief of Staff for airlift and he confirmed a cargo jet would be at Joint Base Andrews.

Hunter rolled his eyes; he wanted to talk to Nazy, not the Acting CIA Director. *I just got home and now you're sending me out again? I do not like this!* He asked, "Just like that?"

Nazy knew assigning her husband for a mission could have a deleterious effect. They would have to talk about it. But for now, all she could answer was, "Yes. *Ramrod* out."

Like an exhausted marathon runner, Hunter shuffled his feet over to where Link Coffey was admiring the different WWII fighter aircraft in the hangars. The Supermarine *Spitfire* and P-51C *Mustang* with a red painted tail were immaculate; their restorations were perfect. Hunter said, "Link, we have to go. Duty calls."

Coffey turned, and they walked to the Gulfstream. Hunter walked around the jet, inspecting the engines for oil leaks and the landing gear tires for proper inflation. None of them looked like they needed nitrogen, but they would need to be changed soon. *Maverick* was back in pilot mode as he kicked the chocks away from the front of the tires. Coffey followed a pace behind, as if Hunter was showing the junior aviator the procedures for performing a preflight inspection.

Once safely airborne, *Maverick* transferred control of the jet to Coffey. "Your jet."

"My jet." After leveling off at the assigned altitude, he asked, "I take it you have a mission."

Maverick nodded. He was distant.

"But you're not taking the blackbird."

Maverick grinned. He knew which aircraft Coffey meant. "Its twin is en route...." *Should I tell him more?* Hunter wasn't angry at Nazy; she was only notifying him about the mission approved by the President. It could be anything. If he saw a C-130 on the ramp it would likely mean unimproved runways and a few days to get into position. If he saw a C-17, the giant jet cargo jet of the U.S. Air Force, that would mean an expeditious trip. Time sensitive targeting. You couldn't land a *Globemaster II* just anywhere like you could a *Hercules*. He would receive the tasking from the Director in a double wrapped envelope. *I guess that means Nazy now.*

Maverick looked at Coffey and knew he hadn't given him an answer. So, he asked again, "Are you interested in a job?"

Coffey smiled and said, "I didn't think you were serious."

"When can you start?"

"When do you need me?"

"Now."

"Now?"

"Now."

"I don't have a bag."

Hunter reached for the satellite telephone on the bulkhead behind the pilot's seat and dialed the CIA Director's office. He told Nazy he was bringing Coffey aboard, "...and that means NDAs (non-disclosure agreements) and some favors if I'm to take him with me."

The encryption technology delayed their conversation for a second. Nazy gave Duncan the PPR number then asked what more Duncan needed.

Maverick repeated Coffey's measurements for flight boots, traveling clothes, shoes, socks, skivvies, shaving kit, sleeping bag, noise canceling headphones and a sleep mask all for his go bag.

Nazy took everything down and called her secretary into the office. "I need the paperwork to read-in someone on a special access program." The secretary called security to reactivate Coffey's clearance and to send someone shopping for a pop-up.

• • •

Hunter knew what was in store for him when he saw the C-17 on the Navy side of the field. He was directed to park the Gulfstream at an adjacent parking ramp. On the ramp near the C-17, he saw the Director's car and the vehicles used to transport her security detail. *Maverick* had the base operations van take him and Coffey to the Navy Base Operations building for bio breaks before blasting off. When he emerged from the building, Nazy stepped from the blacked-out Suburban and walked to intercept Hunter. Hunter directed Coffey to the Agency limo to take care of *paperwork*.

Coffey tried to keep his eye on Hunter and Nazy as he walked to a matronly woman stepping from the black vehicle. He did a lot of bowing, trying to convey some level of gratitude for the spontaneous request for provisions on his behalf. They exchanged pleasantries as he stood at the hood of the vehicle and signed NDAs and other required documents. As he was busy affixing his signature to papers he had no time to read, the woman removed shopping bags, clothing bags, and a shoe box. She collected the signed papers and said, "I've got these. Can you carry a dozen pizzas?"

Pizzas?

The two of them walked to the jet with their hands full. Coffey introduced himself; the woman did not. He didn't know if he had signed over his life savings to the nameless woman or merely boilerplate documents, the tools of the intelligence trade that needed to be validated with ink.

In the middle of the tarmac, it was cold and breezy, and Nazy did her best to keep her hands off of Duncan. He was perpetually warm and she would warm her hands on him when the temperature dropped. But she behaved because they were in the company — eyeshot or earshot — of other Agency personnel. It wouldn't do to have the CIA Director, acting and future, leaning into him inviting his hands to encircle her waist while she threw her arms around his neck feeding him one kiss after another and melting the buttons on his shirt. It was better for everyone she and Duncan remain professional, everyone except Hunter and Nazy.

Winds swirled around on the ramp continually blowing her long black hair across her face. She handed Duncan the double-taped envelope, shook his hand like he was the next-door neighbor who had just mowed her lawn, and turned toward the Suburbans. She adjusted her earring to tell Duncan she loved him. Hunter reciprocated with a fingernail across his brow and sighed with disappointment as Nazy walked away. *Even in running shoes she has the best legs in Maryland.*

Maverick turned and entered the cargo jet's door. Inside he saw several standard 463L pallets stacked with ice chests, boxes, and crew and passenger's baggage under taut cargo nets. *The boys have been busy.* In the center of the jet the YO-3A's non-standard shipping container was lashed down with chains.

Three decades ago, he had traveled on Air Force C-141 *Starlifters,* and when he didn't have a troop seat he rode in an unattractive, overly worn, fuel-smelling, semi-reclinable gray seat mounted on a standard 463L pallet. He was glad there had been substantial improvements since then. The seats were still mounted on standard 463L pallets, but now they were reclinable gray *faux leather* seats. One pallet of seats was occupied with what *Maverick* surmised were weapons-toting Air Force security personnel. As he looked around, *Maverick* realized the jet was configured to transport VIPs when the white-top executive jets with the authentic leather seats and bedrooms in the rear were unavailable, or when they needed more room for a security detail.

This was a first. *Coffey's going to think this is the normal, I'll have to break the news to him.*

Before they were airborne *Maverick* introduced Coffey to the mechanics of the operation. There were the septuagenarians, Bob Jones and Bob Smith. They looked more like ZZ Top roadies with beards and tattoos than the wealthy men that they were. Bob and Bob were two of the original U.S. Army mechanics who had worked on the YO-3As when the aircraft were introduced in Vietnam in 1969. This was their last trip with Duncan. *Maverick* then introduced Coffey to the new mechanics, also former U.S. Army mechanics, early fifty-somethings, Joe Thompson and Tom Barraclough. *Maverick* explained, "Tom and Joe worked for me when we were with the Border Patrol a long time ago. They're incredible mechs whose talents and clearances were being underutilized at the Border Patrol."

The four mechanics all stood at a modified "At Ease" as *Maverick* talked. Military training runs deep.

He pointed at the new guys, "At the Border Patrol, I told Joe and Tommy they should seek employment elsewhere, and they went to work for the Department of the Interior as inspectors. I think it's fair to say a change in venue doubled their pay. They're thorough, have a keen eye, and their attention to detail is nonpareil. Bob and Bob have done their part in the defense of our country; no one else could have done what they did for as long as they did. I truly wouldn't have been able to do what we do had it not been for them. Joe and Tom, you have big shoes to fill, but we were together for a few years. You're vetted, and you're two of the best mechanics I have ever met. You'll make the next phase of this noteworthy adventure a snap."

The men snickered at how the Army was still helping the Marines do their missions. *Maverick* added, "I asked Bob and Bob to check out the new guys before they retire to their log cabins in Montana and Alaska."

Maverick moved to the front of the security detail's pallet to inform them they had brought pizza. "But before anyone runs off for pizza, could we be lucky enough to have a combat meteorologist among you?" A young attractive woman in BDUs and short brown hair raised her hand and said, "I'm a special operations weatherman."

He was taken aback, for she looked like she was ten. Hunter instantly felt old. He sighed with a smile and walked to the uniformed woman. They spoke for a minute, then *Maverick* reached down and put a couple of pieces of pizza on a paper plate to ensure she wouldn't be the last person to get some.

After pizza and sodas, the mechanics took one side of the jet, and the pilots moved to a pair of troop seats along the other side. The aircrew flipped the cabin lighting from white to red. *Maverick* withdrew a cigar-sized flashlight and cut open the package. There were three envelopes inside; they were numbered indicating three parts and three priorities.

The immediate priority was an extraction from Iran. *Maverick* filled his lungs and exhaled through his pie hole. *An extraction. These are the worst. I hate flying over Iranian missile batteries. I know the black coating works, but it's just scary landing in Iran. I bring help this time and he cannot go.* Hunter looked over at Coffey and said into his ear, "We'll talk about this one. It's an extraction. There's a lot going on under the water, if you get my drift. They're not fun."

Maverick handed Coffey the top-secret document to peruse. He moved to the second envelope, wondering what was *second prize.*

As *Maverick* again unfolded a Buck Kalinga Pro knife to cut the tape away from the second envelope, Coffey read the first sheet. Once he reached the end, he realized he may have been too quick to say he would be a part of the SAP. *Flying into Iran? From Iraq? That is batshit crazy! Weren't extractions, recoveries, renditions, and rescues performed by the National Clandestine Service if they were even considered? And wasn't Air Branch part of the NCS?* Coffey looked up to find *Maverick* reading another document. *I hope there's not a test at the end....*

Maverick looked up again to check the aircrew and airmen were out of earshot. Ensuring they were alone, he said directly into Coffey's ear, "A couple of years ago, ISIS, um, the Islamic State in the Sahara, rolled in on the Mozambique port of Mocimboa da Praia. It handles LNG. Liquefied natural gas, some oil. A few American petroleum workers work offshore, but the industry is dominated mostly by oil giants like *TOTAL*—French company—on the ground. The intel had them barricaded in their compound."

Maverick continued, "When I got there the last time, ISIS was already in the port. They were all carrying AK-47s, and I thought I erased them all. Apparently, that ISIS group now calls itself *Ahlu Sunnah Wa-Jama.* They're back with a new name, and they brought reinforcements. Anyway, they're on the move and have the port in their sights again. Mozambique forces and ISIS-wannabes have been fighting on the border for a few days."

Coffey turned to speak into *Maverick's* ear and asked, "What is Mozambique?"

Maverick surmised he meant what the national religion was. He leaned into Coffey and said into his ear, "It's mostly Christian. U.S.

foreign aid under Mazibuike mandated they tolerate a limited group of Muslims, and the government of Mozambique capitulated. They hoped their nearly unnoticeable Muslim population would assimilate. When you're being dragooned by the U.S. dollar, you forget these guys are like a virus. A meager group of radical Muslims can become a large group of murderers who are drawn to the dark side of ISIS in a matter of days."

Coffey then asked something only a counterterrorism expert would consider. He spoke directly into *Maverick's* ear, "Is that a Democrat Party thing?"

Maverick nodded. "It is. There are a lot of Christian NGOs in the country. Democrats hate Christians wherever they are more than they hate Conservatives in America."

He continued, "So, the Christian Mozambique president is trying to rid his country of radical Islamic influence, but Washington Democrats don't like that. They tie U.S. foreign aid to government acknowledgement of gays, trannies, communists, Muslims—all sorts of cats and dogs and stray critters. When we are in power, Republicans provide foreign aid in order to help their economy. American oil workers help out with oil and gas extraction. We provide military training and equipment so they can protect themselves, and we buy airport equipment for Liberia, Congo, Senegal, the list goes on and on. The lefties at home work real hard that Americans never see 'Gifts from the People of the United States' painted on the side of all that equipment. It's hard to believe I may have to go back."

Coffey shook his head. "Are you saying this isn't a one and done mission?"

"The fight against evil requires constant vigilance. As a law guy you know that. These guys do not give up, so yes, sometimes you have to keep whacking them. Mostly when ISIS fails in their primary mission, and let me state for the record I didn't leave any ISIS alive when I was last there, they reconstitute with a larger more violent force. So, someone is providing reinforcements. I should say someone is paying for reinforcements. Kind of like how al-Qaeda tried to topple the World Trade Center Towers in 1993 but failed; they learned from their failures and then they came back with a new plan in 2001."

Coffey said, "And that's how they spread."

Maverick said, "It is. That's their goal. Growth through conquest. But the economy in Mozambique is getting better. Women have little businesses; kids go to school. Where there are no Muslims, there is safety. Although Muslims pour over the border from Zimbabwe all the time to escape the poverty there because...."

"I understand that leadership... of Zimbabwe. Trillion dollar bills to buy a loaf of bread."

"...they got exactly what they wanted—they passed laws that allowed the extermination of white men in Zimbabwe, and now that place is in the toilet. Anyway, before my last trip to Mozambique a couple of dozen ISIS soldiers waving their green flag overran the military base in Cabo Delgado Province. They shot up the place; I killed them before they started a big fire."

Coffey had not been to a developing country recently and didn't have any experience with the scale of things. "Is it a large port?"

Hunter grinned. "The port is large enough to facilitate multiple cargo ships and an LNG tanker. The main problem in Africa is the commercial enterprises grow faster than the militaries. The military is always understaffed, underfunded, and underequipped to defend their strategic sites from assault. Seaports, airports, border crossings, ports-of-entry. If there were no assaults from ISIS, they could live in peace. Republican foreign aid provides EDA—excess defense articles—surplus aircraft, helicopters, weapons, arms, ships and boats to help their military control their radical Muslims. ISIS targets the seaport because terrorists can be incredibly entrepreneurial as long as they can steal what they want and take a few sex slaves as payment."

Maverick leaned into the FBI man and added, "This crap has been going on a long time. Hitler and Tojo wanted to base submarines in Mozambique or in the French colony island of Madagascar. The Ayatollah Khomeini funded terrorism everywhere when he was alive and Iran continues that policy."

Maverick handed the document to Coffey and cut open the third envelope. Coffey was fascinated with *Maverick's* knife and held his hand out to invite a closer look. Hunter, inculcated by the Boy Scout protocol, closed the blade into the handle then handed it to Coffey.

As Coffey admired the one-of-a-kind pocket knife, especially the scales and the exotic wood pieces which formed the handle, Hunter read the proposed mission. Somali pirates had been stopping boats on the open seas, boarding them, kidnapping the crews, and demanding ransom. Again. The real problem was the ships' owners refused to pay for full-time armed security detail aboard their ships. They hoped for the best and paid the ransom if a vessel was captured.

Maverick explained how this one would go down if they were given a green light. The C-17 would proceed to Djibouti, specifically Camp Lemonnier, the U.S. Naval Expeditionary Base and the only permanent combat-capable U.S. military base in Africa. "Camp Lemonnier once belonged to France and is home to several thousand American troops whose primary role is carrying out counterterrorism operations in the terrorist-rich failed-state of Somalia. There is a growing contingent of Chinese on the base, and McGee doesn't want to give the Chinese an opportunity to spy on our operation. Mostly we don't want them to see our YO-3A being offloaded. If we land, there will be 500 Chinese cameras covering our every move."

"How is it that there are Chinese there?"

Maverick said, "It seems we didn't sign an exclusive use contract allowing only NATO members and African countries to use the base. I hear the Chinese pay five times the going rate to be there, so for Djibouti it's a moneymaking deal. Our State Department argues over pennies while the Chinese outspend us at every turn."

He continued, "If this one goes, we'll land at the Ambouli International Airport for fuel while the aircrew gets their crew rest. We'll crash for the night in a high-security, high-rise hotel outside of the base. I have no confidence this one will go because of the continued Chinese presence. But we plan for the contingency."

Coffey nodded and returned the knife to Hunter. He had one more question. "*Maverick*, I remember you having a rare Rolex." Pointing to Hunter's wrist, "That *Submariner* is beautiful, but everyone in the squadron knew about the *Daytona*. I remember thinking I couldn't afford that watch when I first saw it on your wrist. I was ready to accuse you of wearing a counterfeit. Do you still have it?"

Maverick smiled and shook his head. "It's where it belongs, in the Smithsonian Air & Space Museum. I set the time at the moment the Apollo 11 lunar lander first touched down on the surface of the Moon on July 20, 1969." He told Coffey the story of how President Nixon had commissioned three special and distinct watches for the historic mission. "Chevrolet had gifted the Apollo astronauts with Corvettes. On behalf of all Americans, the President gave each of the Apollo 11 astronauts a Rolex *Daytona* Cosmograph. They were uniquely constructed to withstand high levels of vibrations and the intense magnetic fields expected during spaceflight. Neil Armstrong reportedly hated it, not because it was too complex but because it required winding daily." Hunter held up his wrist. "He traded it for one like this. So, I guess you could say I still have his Rolex."

It was a wonderful story. Coffey had another question. In fact, he had thousands of them. He hesitated before asking, "*Maverick*, is the YO-3A a product of *Skunk Works*?"

Pointing to the shipping container, "That isn't a product of *Skunk Works*; but it was run through the Helendale radar-cross section (RCS) measurement facility after we had the black material applied. Lockheed was not overjoyed to test the Agency's airplane. It's as stealthy at low altitudes as their most complex and secret shapes are at higher altitude. It was built by Lockheed, but they disowned it. The initial quiet-airplane concept was a Navy physicist's idea."

"Navy?"

"Yes, the Navy wasn't interested, mainly because it wasn't a carrier airplane. But the Army was all for it; the initial program was for forty-four aircraft. Somehow the program manager, an Army colonel, got eleven prototypes made at Lockheed *Burbank* and had them shipped directly to Vietnam."

"It started out as a secret proof-of-concept project; a one-man glider with an engine in the back seat and a torque tube that ran over the cockpit to drive the propeller. Weirdest damn thing you ever saw, but it was deliriously quiet and effective. MIT ran acoustics tests on the propeller—which is the biggest noisemaker on a prop plane, not the engine. What you see here is the culmination of fifty years of work to improve on the basic quiet airplane idea."

"Lockheed *Skunk Works* and the others just want to play in the very high-dollar, labor-intensive stealth arena. They design electronically stealthy aircraft for high altitudes. Communist missile defense systems are designed to find the high-flying stealthy birds. We are low and slow, flying above the weeds. They may pick us up on radar for an instant, but the operator will think their equipment is malfunctioning. It's like a silent tool of propaganda; we don't want them to know there are aircraft that can go low and slow, are silent and invisible, and that can cut their heart out."

"That's why it's secret."

"More than secret. It's an unprecedented Agency special access program—SAP. For DOD, special access required—SAR. The aircrew and security personnel are all cleared and approved for special access required programs. Like this one."

"That's commendable."

"And here we are. An Agency front company modest enough it can be hidden from view."

"I really think you laid a gift at my feet, *Maverick*."

Maverick smiled broadly and said, "You're absolutely right, Link. But it's time for sleep. We have to get it when we can."

Coffey nodded. In the red light of the cargo jet's interior, Coffey watched *Maverick* prepare for sleep. Hunter manipulated the seat controls like a pro and in seconds it was in its lie flat configuration. He spread his sleeping bag across his body, placed a black eye mask over his eyes and a set of noise canceling headphones over his ears.

Coffey knew he wouldn't sleep. He had been going ten miles a minute since breakfast. Now over the Atlantic he wondered, *What the hell am I doing here with Maverick? We were never close, although he brought pizzas and beer over to the house a couple of times to help with the Mercedes. I remember hearing some of the troops and aircrew went to the racetracks to be the pit crew for his race car, and he paid for all of their expenses. Motel rooms, meals; I heard he put money in their pockets. He had money. From patents? He's always had money and I didn't. Maybe that's my problem. And he married the woman of my dreams. I have plenty of reasons to dislike him, but I cannot.*

He's doing things I could never imagine, like he has been several steps ahead of me for a long time. Maverick really is Captain America. He treats me like we are old friends. I'm ashamed I didn't make the time to go see him after he wound up in the hospital. And then I lusted after his woman. I'm pathetic.

CHAPTER 20

November 3, 2019

To: Chief Editor, *Washington Times*

The CIA Director completed his final act as America's top spy with a press conference at the White House. Now he's running for president. Some Americans know of him but few know him like the men and women at the Central Intelligence Agency do. What follows are their stories. I respectfully submit this article for consideration.

Title: CIA Director Extraordinaire, William "Bill" McGee

By: Demetrius Eastwood

He never walked across the CIA symbol on the floor of the Agency's headquarters in Langley, Virginia. Bill McGee always walked around. His reverence for the CIA is something special.

The CIA's Director, William McGee, described by his colleagues as *legendary*, is running for president.

Who is he, this Bill McGee? Director McGee was nicknamed *"Bullfrog"* in his days with the U.S. Navy SEALs. In the Tora Bora of Afghanistan, he was *"The Black Shadow."* The men and women of the Agency reverently referred to him as *"Darth Vader*, Prince of Darkness"* during his tenure at the CIA as the top political appointee of President Hernandez. The most highly decorated man to ever wear America's uniform was granted a waiver by President Hernandez to work at the CIA after he reached the mandatory retirement age.

McGee's presidential campaign announcement was first reported by the *Washington Times*. "Bill has had a long and distinguished career serving his country," a group of Special Operations warriors and CIA personnel told Colonel Demetrius Eastwood of *Unfiltered News*, "We are grateful for his decades of leadership in Special Operations Command and in some of the most difficult issues we face at CIA."

McGee has run the Agency since 2016. National Security Agency officials credit McGee with eliminating what could only be called spies and infiltrators left over from the Mazibuike Administration. He revolutionized the CIA's terrorist hunting efforts that eviscerated al-Qaeda and Muslim Brotherhood leaders on multiple continents.

Before McGee came to the CIA Congress was highly critical of the CIA's drone program that saw more civilians killed than terrorists. During the Mazibuike administration the Agency conducted over 500 strikes using armed drones. They killed thousands of civilians but few militants. Critics questioned the legality of the program and decried the civilian deaths, though CIA officials say the Agency was careful to avoid taking innocent lives.

After McGee was sworn in as the Director, the CIA's drone program was significantly curtailed. Civilians were not killed and there was a dramatic reduction in the number of terrorists on the FBI's Most Wanted Terrorist List. Director McGee demanded better.

As terrorists were removed from the FBI's Most Wanted Terrorist List, McGee was considered the *Grim Reaper* of the enemy. "He was the most lethal leader in the U.S. government during his tenure," said a former senior CIA official. Another senior CIA official said, "There is a reason Director McGee sat in the galley for the State of the Union and received all the accolades."

McGee's biography and habits have become part of his legend. The soft-spoken, professorial figure was notorious for keeping the lights dimmed in his office; the amateur body builder spent hours exercising in the Agency's gym, and the subject matter expert relished lecturing operations and intelligence officers in the Agency's auditorium. Once there was virtually no one left on the FBI's Most Wanted Terrorist List, counterterrorism specialists were quick to give credit where credit was due. With Director McGee at the helm, the CIA functioned like a continuous, rolling decapitation operation for Muslim Brotherhood and al-Qaeda leaders. With no civilian casualties.

A former senior Agency official said about Director McGee's leadership, "There came a point when the life expectancy of an al-Qaeda or Islamic State chief of operations was about a month. Whenever these terrorist organizations named a new guy, bam, he was gone."

Muslim Brotherhood and al-Qaeda leaders in Africa and the Middle East became so terrified of the CIA *Black Shadow's* ability to magically remove their friends from the FBI Most Wanted Terrorist List they feared promotions or advancements. Rumors persist in the halls at Langley that a CIA outpost once picked up signals intelligence, a radio conversation between two senior al-Qaeda officials in which one man declined a promotion. He was worried the *Black Shadow*, Bill McGee, would find him and kill him. The man from al-Qaeda said he didn't want to die; he was blessed where he was. This was when there were no missile-carrying drones in Afghanistan. It makes one wonder how McGee could achieve such effectiveness as the *Grim Reaper* that al-Qaeda and the Muslim Brotherhood couldn't stick their heads out of a hole without getting whacked.

McGee said, "In the final analysis, there are a handful of Salafists, like al-Qaeda, who are unrepentant mass murderers. They were so evil that, like some pedophiles, they couldn't be rehabilitated in a thousand years. They have significant personality disorders and have fallen under the spell of the dark side of propaganda. There are few things more worrisome than an aggressive personality disorder with a weapon. They're like mad dogs; they have to be put down. Their crimes of committing mass murder were so heinous they were evil personified. They were a public health threat."

Former officials commented that Director McGee's dedication to his work was unsurpassed. He often pulled 12- or 14-hours days, six or seven days a week. He would sleep in the office and read cable traffic at 3 or 4 a.m. These former officials described McGee as demanding but fair. Those who worked under him and survived the encounter were fiercely loyal. Director McGee would take the time to mentor the Agency's junior officers, citing his own earlier mistakes as examples to be avoided.

Several intelligence officers who contributed to this article concurred with the view that Bill McGee fixed a badly damaged CIA, and America is a safer place because of him.

End of Article.

CHAPTER 21

November 4, 2019

Nazy finished delivering the President's Daily Brief in her usual thorough and professional manner. After questions, she could return to her sprawling corner office on the seventh floor of Central Intelligence Agency's Headquarters. The first ten minutes of questions were totally unrelated to ongoing CIA operations. Another ten questions were more the purview of the Secretary of State, but she answered them adequately.

President Hernandez then asked, "How long does the Agency expect Somalia's latest piracy efforts to continue?"

Nazy repeated a response she had given earlier but added, "We received information this morning the shipping companies whose ships and crews were held hostage by Somalia's pirates paid the requested ransom. We have no further intelligence other than the ship and the people have been released. When these pirates receive their ransom, there is no incentive for them to stop, but Special Operations Command have eliminated the pirates' capabilities to commit high-sea hijackings."

"Also, Mr. President, Admiral McGee spoke with the CEOs of the shipping companies and reminded them that having armed guards aboard their ships is less expensive than paying ransom. The CEOs have reconsidered to have the armed guards aboard again."

The President said, "If Admiral McGee has taken care of the situation, I do not see any need for us to expend any energies in that area."

Nazy understood the direction. The Presidential authorization for Hunter to eliminate the pirates was rescinded. Duncan wouldn't proceed to Djibouti or Somalia.

The National Security Advisor, a Marine Corps general, asked Nazy for any intelligence on Mozambique. Nazy said, "There has been no change in Mozambique's military posture, but Tanzania seems to have decimated the ISIS contingent to where there is no immediate threat on the port."

The President looked over his bifocals and said, "I don't want us to expend any energies in that area unless it's necessary."

Nazy again understood the direction, pinched her lips and nodded slightly. The Presidential authorization for Hunter to eliminate ISIS was rescinded. Duncan would return home after the extraction in Iran. She maintained her professional attitude even though her heart sang. The meeting was not over. Nazy hunched forward and turned to the Chairman of the Joint Chiefs of Staff. She gave him a look that said, *Don't you have something to add, General?*

When the old man in uniform offered nothing, Nazy thought, *Duncan and Bill were so right about some of these generals being members of the dark state. Sometimes they let down their defenses and it becomes obvious, especially when it involves helping our allies and protecting America!* She refrained from shaking her head. *Bill McGee has been exposing the activities of the dark state generals, and now I'm going to have to do the same.*

The Chairman of the Joint Chiefs of Staff finally turned to the National Security Advisor, and reluctantly announced, "It might be possible to send a signal, a battalion of Marines to conduct training or war games. We have done it in the past. Goodwill visit. If they are in the area, whatever is left of ISIS will crawl back under the rock whence they came. We can send some EDA items; some armored trucks to help fill out their army. I will work it." He didn't look at Nazy to complete the transaction.

Nazy thought, *There, that wasn't so hard, now was it?*

The President asked for a few minutes alone with the CIA Director. Nazy left her position at the conference table and moved to the seat vacated by the Vice President. President Hernandez's new gold Rolex *Daytona* stuck out from under his cuff adorned with a Presidential Seal cufflink. As he slid an unmarked envelope across the table he asked, "Is there anything new from *Noble Savage?*"

She looked at the envelope questioningly. President Hernandez whispered, "Thank you card for Duncan."

Nazy nodded and put the invitation-sized envelope into her notebook. She continued, "There is weather moving into the area that may delay or cancel the lift. I'll know more when I return to the office. Does the President want a new protocol for being informed on the status of *Noble Savage?*"

He replied, "Nazy, not really. I wanted to talk about the remaining person on the *Matrix*. Can we get him before I leave office? Is it an issue of resources?" When he shifted his arm his watch slid further down his wrist. He admired the Rolex for an instant then turned his attention back to Nazy.

Nazy uttered the man's full name for the first time in years. "Ahmad Khalid Saleh Hashash was secretly tried *in absentia* for making the bomb that brought down Flight 103 in 1988. We have unverified reports of him in Europe, but there is also a new, single report he's hiding in the Casbah of Algiers."

"Casbah, like the old movie? Ahh, Hedy Lamarr, Hollywood's most beautiful woman of the 1930s." Then he let a loose a thought that would surely get him into trouble if articulated. *Good God, Nazy, you must be the intelligence community's most beautiful woman!* He exhaled and smiled.

Nazy nodded. When she and Duncan were home in Wyoming, they curled up on a sofa and watched old black and white movies of espionage and spies. She and Duncan watched *Algiers* every year. And *Casablanca* and *The Conspirator*; another Hedy Lamarr picture.

The President asked, "Nazy, can you find out? I remember from the movie it was the perfect place for the criminal—what was his name?"

"*Pepe Le Moko* or Charles Boyer?" she asked in a slight Cockney.

"That's right, Charles Boyer. He was a criminal hiding out from the law. But that was the movie, obviously."

"Mr. President, I'll put some more resources on it to determine if Hashash is still alive and if he's hiding at the Casbah. We'll find out where he really is."

"Thank you, Nazy. Might I ask how you found this Hashash?"

"Mr. President, that is a long story, and I know you're incredibly busy. I can have a briefing paper drawn up...."

"Nazy, I have plenty of time, and you can be succinct. I'm interested."

She was a little uneasy delivering an impromptu brief. It wasn't the CIA way, and she was afraid she would miss something. *Maybe this is what Directors do when they're alone with the President.* She filled her lungs and said, "Well, Mr. President. How about I give you a flavor of how we do that? Not so recently, when our analysts began seeing signs Saddam Hussein could fall from power, we sent a group from NCS—National Clandestine Service—to Iraq to observe Saddam's palaces to see if there was any movement of Saddam's private documents."

President Hernandez said, "That sounds dangerous."

Nazy nodded. "Mr. President, through analysis and probability we believed Saddam's private documents were likely being held at his fortified palaces. We were interested in documents that would show, for example, who Saddam had engaged to conduct terrorism, who he had contracted for bombmaking, and who he had assigned to what they called special operations in Iraq and around the globe. We believed the names of the individuals and groups who were conducting *wet work* abroad, I'm sorry, *assassinations*, sabotage, and terrorism internationally and the propaganda used to control his people would be found in the documents."

"In previous document recoveries we have learned the names of bombmakers and special operations forces' leaders, the location and numbers of secret bank accounts, and where the gold and antiquities were hidden. Saddam would want that information close at hand. We wanted to know if he had people who had infiltrated the U.S., NATO, Congress, and Parliament. Saddam was a special case. We also expected those documents to show which NATO members had been providing Iraq with weapons and other defensive systems during the embargo years. That information can be extremely useful when our diplomats are negotiating trade deals and such."

"That's commendable."

Nazy continued without the formal protocol. "My analysis determined Saddam had a general, his chief supply officer, who was loyal to him. He went to the USSR and Europe with a letter signed by Saddam which was essentially a promise of illegal Iraq oil deliveries. We believed this general purchased equipment from the old Soviet Union, and from some of the NATO members for off-the-record weapons systems, and we believed he kept receipts."

President Hernandez's eyes got wide.

"And we were right. After Saddam saw he had lost the country, the last thing on his mind was his papers. When he ran out the door, we ran in and captured his personal papers. We got *the pumpkin* out of the country before Ba'ath party members could get to them. After Saddam was ousted from power, we found that general had escaped, like most of the Ba'ath Party senior leaders did, to an apartment in Jordan. We set up a meeting and bought the contents of his two storage lockers for the price of a vehicle and a stipend. In those documents we found what they had purchased, and we found Iraq was funding what could be construed to be a nuclear, biological, and chemical weapons capability. The general told us where to find the missing weapons of mass destruction...."

The President said, "...that the media claimed didn't exist."

Nazy continued, "There were some chemical weapons, but really nothing else."

"Nazy, why didn't their nuclear, biological, and chemical weapons programs take off?"

"Mr. President, may I answer this way? When Hitler and Stalin tried to replicate the Manhattan Project, they were informed on the level of effort needed, but they thought the U.S. was using propaganda against them. We had over 500,000 scientists, engineers, tradesmen, and such on the project. That was a number they couldn't believe or comprehend; they had spies everywhere and knew it to be true but still thought it was disinformation."

"America spent about two billion dollars."

"Yes, Mr. President. The Nazis and Soviets couldn't believe the effort required, and they didn't have enough professional people.

They could only muster up about 30,000. Which meant, their programs were only for show."

"That's spectacular. The power of American manufacturing."

"Yes, Mr. President. And, the power of freedom. Free people work harder to solve problems. American ingenuity. Our National Clandestine Service raided Saddam's palaces and found and extracted his personal and private papers. He kept meticulous notes."

"As for the Libyan documents, when our analysts' assessment was Muammar Gaddafi would fall soon because President Mazibuike's pushed the Muslim Brotherhood into Libya and forced him out of power, we got people into Libya to assess the most likely location of Gaddafi's personal and private documents. Again, NCS found his private documents. They got *the pumpkin* out of the country, and our analysts evaluated them."

Nazy continued, "Gaddafi's papers showed who he had on the payroll in their secret police and the intelligence service, as well as who the bombmakers were. That's how we found Hashash's name and the secret account numbers from which he was continually paid, and his whereabouts."

"That is truly spectacular! You do document recoveries; various forms of document recoveries. That makes sense."

Nazy nodded. "Mr. President, you may not know one of my collateral duties is *Chief of Diaries*."

The President was interested in this new topic. He sat back and gave Nazy a little gesture to continue. She was the best-looking thing in the room, and he was in no hurry to have her leave.

She said, "We have a facility close to headquarters where we maintain the diaries, journals, research papers, and documents of influential people, like dictators and generals, kings and billionaires, Soviet officials and religious leaders — priests, rabbis, ministers. But also, inventors, scientists, mathematicians, and engineers. Sometimes our document recovery teams cannot get to the archives we seek, as when a leader suddenly dies in office or falls from power and his papers are confiscated before we can get there."

"Their papers are confiscated?"

Nazy nodded and continued, "Yes, Mr. President. Oftentimes. We have people and the opposition have people who recognize the value of acquiring the papers of someone who dies. As an example, when Nikola Tesla was found dead in 1943 in a New York City hotel, the government's Office of Alien Property seized many of his papers. Tesla had claimed to have invented a Death Ray weapon, so rather than risk Tesla's technology falling into the hands of our enemies, the FBI and others took possession of the documents in his hotel."

President Hernandez asked, "Death Ray?"

Nazy said, "Mr. President, it was the mathematics of making collimated light. A laser. The technology and engineering to make a laser didn't exist. But Dr. Tesla knew exactly what he had discovered."

President Hernandez nodded and said, "But that was before the CIA was even created."

"Mr. President, General Donovan...."

"...of the OSS...." The President's attention was piqued.

Nazy nodded and continued, "While everyone was running around New York City, General Donovan took the initiative and boarded a train and somehow obtained Tesla's journals from his laboratory in Colorado Springs. He thought they would prove valuable one day. They were the first journals taken by an OSS member, and they resided in a safe in his office until he was released as the OSS Director. Those journals ultimately became the seed stock for our *Library of Diaries*."

"Remarkable."

"When a leader dies in office or falls from power before his papers are confiscated, Mr. President, one of the last things they do, if they think about it, is destroy their records. Sometimes, they're distracted by trying to save their lives or their fortunes. They often fail, and their papers usually fall into the hands of their secret police. If we want them, we have to buy them. It may be a bidder's market, but often a seller doesn't want to sell to us so we use a contractor. Someone who specializes in recoveries, typically stolen luxury items."

President Hernandez was shocked to learn the CIA used contractors for the delicate work. He wanted to know more, but she had moved on.

Nazy continued, "It's surprising how many of these men keep diaries. We find that while they are considered informal unregulated, and unsanitized documents, they are incredibly accurate, truthful, and valuable. They have information you cannot find anywhere else. And there is something going on psychologically; several diaries and journals are written in *violet ink*. Communist men almost exclusively use violet ink in their diaries. We have diaries of Soviet generals written in violet ink. One worried he would be cashiered after several cosmonauts died during secret attempted orbital missions in 1960, a year before the successful orbit of Yuri Gagarin in April 1961. Then there were Molotov's memoirs; every part of them was in violet ink. He claimed Lavrentiy Beria announced to the Politburo he had 'done Stalin in' and 'saved us all.' Nikita Khrushchev launched a blistering attack on Beria and had Beria killed."

"So much for saving them all."

"Yes, Mr. President. He then removed Beria's picture from official photographs and had his wife and children sent to a gulag. Beria demonstrated he knew how to force professional people to work against their wishes, but he found their work lacked discipline and accuracy. No one knew if it was good or not, and no one cared."

President Hernandez was dumbfounded. He wanted to know more about the contractors the CIA used for document and diary recoveries but he asked about *pumpkins*.

"Mr. President, we ask the teams when they return if they got *the pumpkin*, meaning the collected works of these people: their diaries, journals, papers, manuals, etcetera. *Pumpkin* references the Alger Hiss case in which Whittaker Chambers led federal agents to government microfilms supplied to him by Hiss that he had hidden in a pumpkin on his farm."

Now I remember! Pumpkin Papers! President Hernandez smiled and added, "It's also in the movie, *North by Northwest*. One of the bad guys says, 'I see you've got *the pumpkin*,' meaning Van Damm's statue containing some microfilm."

Nazy nodded with a disarming full smile. "When our diplomats travel abroad, they carry diplomatic materials in orange bags."

It was time to move on. She said, "Mr. President, you've asked about Rho Schwartz Scorpii. After World War Two some connections were simply incredible. Recently our contractor secured Erich Honecker's papers. He led the German Democratic Republic, East Germany, until shortly before the fall of the Berlin Wall in 1989."

"You have Honecker's papers and your contractor provided those?" asked an incredulous President.

"Yes, Mr. President. Honecker's personal and private papers were filled with the names of East German spies in Europe and the United States. Unlike Islamic nations, the European communist countries maintained files on how the Communist Party managed pedophiles in East Germany and how their secret police used propaganda to control their populations. They injected some 2,000 pedophiles into the church."

Pedophiles? Did I hear that correctly? "Well, that's incredible."

"Yes, Mr. President. Apparently Honecker had his own social engineering projects. The East German government allowed single gay men to act as foster fathers to boys, and the East German government ensured there were gay priests in the churches."

President Hernandez became serious. The conversation had suddenly turned dark and ugly.

Nazy continued, "On the propaganda front, the *Stasi* published documents and pamphlets, essentially means and methods designed to crush dissent. They called that program, the *Disintegration Directive*. It was one of hundreds. It was a targeted covert psychological approach to maintain the Communist monopoly on ideological discourse. In the U.S., the left uses the term racist as a tool against the right. They used the term pedophile to control their dissidents."

"So, the leveraging of these words are simply psychological operations?"

"Yes, Mr. President."

President Hernandez shook his head. *What about Scorpii, or did she just forget?*

"Mr. President, when our special operations warriors took down Osama bin Laden, we took his laptop and all of his notebooks. When Dr. Nikita Zhavrazhinov committed suicide after the Democrats lost the election, we rushed a trusted agent from our contractor to Connecticut to remove the DNC Chairman's diaries and papers."

"They got *the pumpkin!*" The President was pleased with himself.

She smiled; she wouldn't give away that Bill McGee was that person or that the contractor was Quiet Recoveries International. Essentially, Quiet Recoveries International was a CIA front company with retired Agency intelligence officers, FBI Special Agents, and military officers, but it was registered and incorporated as one of Duncan's companies under the Quiet Aero Systems line of businesses. She remembered it was run by one of Duncan's friends, Colonel Bong, and Bong drove a Porsche.

"They must have been valuable."

"Invaluable, Mr. President. They can be incredibly dangerous, too. That is why only a few people know about the *Diaries* or have access to them." *Like the people our contractor hires, Quiet Recoveries International.*

"Mr. President, there is one more example I'd like to share with you."

"Go ahead."

"When we recovered the papers of the former DNC chairman, Dr. Zhavrazhinov, he had documents we called *the Kennedy stories*. He knew the Agency's counterintelligence chief had a habit of turning up in the houses of dead people, people with CIA connections, certain leaders of the DNC, or someone the president or his chief of staff might be concerned about."

That's interesting.

Nazy continued, "Mr. President, the DNC Chairman had a file on Mary Pinchot Mayer. She was a mistress of President Kennedy. She was killed by a Soviet assassin presumably to punish President Kennedy for Cuba and the removal of Soviet missiles. The FBI was tracking the KGB assassins; they lost them and within an hour she was found dead. Executed by a Russian caliber. We had men trying to sanitize the crime scene while the counterintelligence chief broke into Ms. Mayer's apartment and took her diary and other personal papers that may have linked her to the President."

The information forced President Hernandez to suck wind. He crossed his legs and tugged on his chin. He was thinking and not about Nazy's looks. The distraction of Nazy's beauty had been overcome by intense counterintelligence work. President Hernandez asked, "You must have hundreds on staff with all the different languages."

"Mr. President, we now have tools that allows English-speaking users to search through foreign language text. An Intelligence Advanced Research Projects Activity program allows us to search foreign language materials and translate those documents into English. The program allows us to understand context and meaning without having to speak the language."

"Can it be used for any foreign language?"

"Yes, Mr. President. Low-resource languages like Farsi, Bulgarian, Georgian, Kazakh, Lithuanian Pashto, Somali, Swahili and Tagalog present a particular challenge to retrieval and translation technologies. The tools and techniques developed under the program boosts our ability to find, examine and analyze foreign language content without needing to learn the language. It also means we can process diaries quickly."

President Hernandez reflected on the new material.

After a few seconds Nazy said, "We have something new on Scorpii." She removed a file from her briefcase and passed it to him. "Mr. President, from the documents we recently purchased from a former senior East German intelligence officer we uncovered... *a Stasi connection.*"

Nazy sat quietly. *Duncan's recommendation to create a dossier on Scorpii suddenly looked to be prescient.*

The President leaned back, donned his cheaters, bypassed the official header, and counted a four-page analysis on Rho Schwartz Scorpii.

In 1942, the SS began operating brothels in some of the concentration camps. Camp authorities exploited the women to reward male prisoners who met or surpassed production quotas. Some 100 women forced to work in the brothels were prisoners from the Ravensbrück camp. Some dozen boys had been removed from their mothers upon arriving at Ravensbrück and were forced to work in special brothels.

The convergence of pedophiles in the extermination camps was a deeply hidden secret. Nazi officers and senior staff of the Reich had a thing for boys. Virtually all the children en route to or in the extermination camps were violently abused as slave labor and perished at the hands of the Nazis. But there were many who were taken from their families and served in the prostitution houses.

Scorpii was one of the missing boys, the smallest and youngest of the Holocaust survivors from the Ravensbrück extermination camp about fifty miles north of Berlin. Scorpii was separated from his family early in the classification process and was assigned to the special brothels. Children were traumatized by being separated from their parents and preyed upon by the pedophiles in uniform, but Scorpii found a way to survive.

SS doctors carried out experiments on women and children at the Ravensbrück camp to develop an efficient method of sterilization. There was a single entry in Goebbels' diary stating he had transferred surgically castrated children from Ravensbrück to the Reichministry in Berlin for a special investigative project. One of Goebbels' office diaries – not personal diaries – indicated the Ministry of Propaganda wished to conduct experiments on children to see if a boy could be programmed or brainwashed to carry a gun or a bomb in a suicide attack. Analyses of Reichministry documents suggest Goebbels and others believed they could brainwash a child to assassinate Churchill, but they had to get close to him. In their analysis, they believed the best avenue of approach was an ambitious malleable young male prostitute.

Entries in his office diaries say the child chosen was given the designation of "S." The unusual timing, the novel prisoner transfer, and analysis suggests one of the children targeted to undergo the behavior modification training to assassinate Churchill was Scorpii.

They were programming children to hate Western leaders. What are the chances they never grew out of that programming? It would explain much. The President nodded almost imperceptibly and asked if he could keep the document in his hand.

"Of course, Mr. President."

"Ok Nazy, what's your assessment of what is in Scorpii's journals?"

Nazy said, "Their plan, Mr. President?"

He nodded; she exhaled. *Nothing like being put on the spot.* "Mr. President, we believe the European Federation's agenda is world domination through radical climate change legislation. The next Bensberg Conference will kick off the program."

President Hernandez asked if it was real?

"Mr. President, the annual Bensberg Conference is promoted by a multitude of billionaires, international leaders, and the heads of left-wing organizations. Several of our politicians from the Democrat Party are slated to attend. They believe they're getting closer to their most important point, which is the strategic defeat of the United States. They're convinced they need to destroy the global economic dependency on carbon-based fuel supplies, oil, gas, coal, etc. In order to destroy something of that scale, the energy program for the entire world, something massive is needed to change the entire world approach toward energy production. Something is needed to create the crisis that provides the origin for the process to begin."

"Do we know what they think that triggering mechanism is?"

"Yes, Mr. President. A bioweapon. A virus created in the lab. A genetically modified version of a deadly coronavirus probably released overseas would induce subsequent panic in America. They believe with social media managing the narrative they will create social structures that will facilitate the global acceptance of an entire new economic system that will be designed around saving the planet."

"How do they plan to do this?"

Nazy smiled. "Mr. President, they must have a Democrat president and majority in Congress."

"So, we really need to elect Bill McGee to save America and save the world."

Nazy clenched her jaws and nodded.

President Hernandez stood up.

The meeting was over. Nazy left the Oval Office without comment. How the CIA found Hashash would wait.

CHAPTER 22

November 4, 2019

Talil had once been the temporary home for hundreds of airmen and Marines, their helicopters, and their jets. The former U.S. Air Force Base in southern Iraq was abandoned and had been renamed Imam Ali Base. It was the perfect location from which to conduct an incursion into the Islamic Republic of Iran.

After landing at Imam Ali Base under brumous conditions, Hunter and Coffey monitored the offloading of the YO-3A into one of the aircraft bunkers Saddam Hussein had built to house a single Soviet-manufactured Iraqi Air Force MiG-25 *Foxbat.* During the Second Gulf War, Operation *Iraqi Freedom,* 2,000-pound JDAMs (Joint Direct Attack Munitions) penetrated the tops of ten-foot-thick concrete bunkers and destroyed the Iraqi's *Foxbats* hiding inside. When U.S. and coalition forces returned home about 80 percent of the bunkers remained unusable.

The CIA crew had commandeered one of the intact bunkers and had assembled the YO-3A inside in advance of the movement order. Shortly after all the cargo had been moved to the bunker it rained. The security troops donned rain gear, grateful someone remembered it does occasionally rain and even snow in Iraq in November.

Standing at the mouth of the bunker watching the rain, *Maverick* said to Coffey, "I have been running a 98-99 percent mission completion rate because of good weather—Mother Nature usually helps out and keeps the puffies away until after I'm done." He had talked to Nazy on the satellite phone earlier. She had told him without explanation the missions in Somalia and Mozambique were canceled. He told her the extraction from Iran looked to be in jeopardy because of the weather. *Maverick* thanked her for sending a weatherman.

Within an hour the rain stopped and a black Cessna *Caravan* touched down at Imam Ali Base. The *Caravan* parked next to the C-17, kept its engine running, and disgorged a tall, thin, balding man in a cheap suit. *Maverick* strode from the bunker to intercept the man's obvious trajectory. They met in the middle of a taxiway; both activated *Growlers* and talked. When they finished *Maverick* shook the man's hand. The suit reboarded the *Caravan*. The special operations weatherman made her way through the line of security people to tell *Maverick* the weather between them and the target was now favorable.

The mission was a go.

Maverick deactivated his *Growler*.

•　　•　　•

When demonstrating the properties of the nanotechnology coating, the manufacturer showed one side of a posterboard-sized sheet of aluminum was severely crinkled and twisted. When they showed the opposite side of the metal, it just looked black. The human eye couldn't discern the hills, valleys, and twists from the obverse side. It really was the darkest material on earth and the nearly square shape of the black three-bladed wooden propeller was the oddest thing Coffey and the new mechanics had ever seen. They knew when the aircraft took off into the night, no one would see it or hear it.

•　　•　　•

Maverick took off on an easterly heading. The GPS symbology in his helmet indicated the instant he crossed the Iraqi-Iranian border. Using the enhanced night vision systems in his helmet, he located the thermal image of a Russian-made S-400 *Triumf* anti-aircraft battery. It hadn't moved from its position from his previous excursions into Iran. The site had always been a lights-out, reduced illumination operation but this time the missile battery was unexpectedly lit up like a Las Vegas casino. Maverick didn't think it was too odd. *Maybe they were having a field day or the site was out of action for parts. Maybe the site's leaders were gone, and the mice were playing.*

Regardless, *Maverick* turned to fly directly over the Iranian anti-aircraft missile radar antenna confident the nanotechnology black coating would render the YO-3A invisible to radar. He also reminded himself radars are not designed to detect aircraft directly above the antenna. That gap is known as the *cone of silence*, a technical term commandeered for the *Get Smart* television shows.

Once the compound was safely behind him, *Maverick* had a couple of hours of low-level flying to get to his destination. It gave him a period to relax and pump some music into his headset. After ten songs Hunter realized he could be accused of choosing Pink Floyd, Moody Blues, Beatles and other British artists based on Nazy's British accent. He snorted as he remembered being in West Germany as a kid and hearing The Beatles, the Rolling Stones, and the other British bands before any of them became household names in America. That was also the time he became infatuated with British race cars: Bentleys, Aston Martins, Jaguars.

It was cloudy with no moon to illuminate the land when it was time to set up for the extraction. The new helmet and night vision systems integrated in his visor displayed the complete battlefield in shades of green. He would pop over a hill, and gain some additional altitude to see if there were any vehicles on the road. He rose in elevation; there was nothing in view. At twenty miles out, *Maverick* deployed the forward looking infrared and laser designators. If all went well, the thermal image of the person to be extracted would be the only thermal signature projected onto his visor.

Maverick reduced his speed and slowed the aircraft. At the target speed, he engaged the reduction gearbox to make the YO-3A silent. The three-bladed propeller provided just enough thrust for the aircraft to maintain altitude. One more hill to go. The FLIR imagery in his helmet displayed there were no yellow, orange, or red hotspots anywhere.

As he crested the final hill the FLIR image in his helmet came alive with color. There were at least a hundred yellow-orange-red thermal images of soldiers moving in the green background of hills and trees. The thermal image of the defector was in the prone position as briefed, his arms configured as directed by some unknown Agency contact.

Maverick frowned. He observed the actions of the troops. Their focus was on the defector, not on him. The extraction had been compromised. Obviously. *Maverick* had choices to make. He could turn around and leave Iran; no one would ever know he had been there. He could shoot the defector, but killing him assumed he was the one who informed the authorities the Agency was coming to get him. Or he could call an audible at the line.

Maverick mulled over what to do. It was apparent no one knew he was there. No one would blame him for abandoning the lift when there were a hundred troops in the hills with AKs, rocket-propelled grenades, RPGs, anti-tank weapons, and machine guns. He searched his memory for other extractions that didn't go off as designed, but he could remember nothing like this. He didn't want to go home empty handed. *Sometimes you get dealt bad cards. The wise poker player knows when to hold 'em and when fold 'em.*

Maintaining altitude he finally remembered. *There was something like this! There had been a kidnapping involving millions in ransom, and the kidnappers had dozens of men with long-range weapons in the hills overlooking the drop-off point, off of a road that bifurcated the valley, ready to kill FBI personnel who tried to follow them. Some of the men in the hills night had night vision goggles. But they were looking down on the target checking the avenues of approach for vehicles. If they had looked up, they would have seen the YO-3A's green shadow in the air.*

In over twenty-five years only one person had ever looked up. It's natural to look ahead, to the side, or behind. The only one who had ever expected an interloper was Abu Manu along the Algerian coast, and Hunter was certain he had been briefed to look up constantly to see if someone was observing him from an airplane.

Maverick silently climbed to get a better view of the entrance road to the shallow valley. Dozens of vehicles on the other side of the hill displayed on his visor in shades of green, but there were no thermal images of anyone in or near the vehicles. And the soldiers weren't wearing night vision devices, just helmets. *Maverick* concluded he had the advantage. He deployed the *Weedbusters* drug crop eradication laser system into the airstream.

The additional drag required more power; he bumped the throttle slightly to add RPMs to maintain altitude. He placed the laser designator dot on the back of the defector and programed the fire control system to make a hundred-foot eye-safe circle around the man. The fire control computer would blank the designated area and not allow a laser beam to enter the eye safe area. With the aircraft configured for offensive maneuvers, *Maverick* rammed the throttle to the firewall for two seconds. This propagated takeoff power RPMs that rumbled into the valley. He perfectly anticipated the increase in torque with rudder inputs.

The sudden noise surprised the men in the hills. It appeared to be coming from the center of the valley, but higher up, in the air. As if the men's movements had been rehearsed and choreographed, they all looked up at the same time to locate the origin of the noise. *Maverick* engaged *Weedbusters*, electronically swept the valley with infrared radiation, and irradiated the eyes of the soldiers.

The effect on their optic nerves was instantaneous; they were blinded by the white-hot energy of the invisible laser. Many screamed and wailed; all they could see and feel was an angry hot white, like being exposed to the arc of a welder's torch at point-blank range. The men panicked for they were certain their eyes had been damaged beyond repair.

Maverick swept the area with UV-C again before retracting the eradication system into the airframe to prepare for landing. He swept the FLIR across the piedmont to see if there were any soldiers whose eyes hadn't been damaged by the unseen laser beams. Confident the ambush force had been neutralized, *Maverick* switched to a visible laser designator and programmed the computer to make letters on the field.

•   •   •

The wailing and crying in the valley coupled with the brilliant red laser near his head made the defector jump up. As he got to his feet he was presented with a pulsating dazzling red message at his feet: SHOW THE SIGN.

The defector kept his head down and raised his thumbs above his head.

The letters on the ground quickly changed to read: LIE FACE DOWN.

Maverick deflected the control stick to move the YO-3A in a gentle right turn, maintaining altitude and speed. He swept the FLIR around the valley again. He saw thermal images of the soldiers holding their hands to their faces. They had discarded their weapons in favor of trying to soothe their eyes. After some seconds analyzing the thermal imagery of men in despair, *Maverick* assured himself none of the soldiers would be a threat to him.

• • •

Duncan Hunter and his passenger landed at Imam Ali Base an hour before sunrise. The Baghdad Chief of Station was waiting and ushered the defector from the back seat of the black aircraft into the Cessna *Caravan*. Before the Agency man entered his aircraft *Maverick*, sans helmet, provided a quick debrief. "They were expecting someone. I'm sure they thought it was going to be a helicopter, maybe one of the stealthy ones used to remove OBL from Pakistan. There were about a hundred soldiers, all armed. I could have returned to base or killed him, but I got him out. The problem is I left a calling card. They know we were there. They don't know how, but they know their guy is gone and their assault force was neutralized. I don't know if the problem is on their end or ours. Either way, you have an issue."

The Chief of Station hung his head and nodded. It was an extraction, but it may have unintentionally ruined any further extractions and infiltrations using that locale. *Maverick* knew the Chief of Station, the COS, was a patriot and would do whatever was humanly possible to find out how the breach of intelligence occurred. He pressed a challenge coin into Hunter's palm as he shook Hunter's hand. *Maverick* told him, "Thank you. Hey, I think we might have a greater problem. I'm glad I got him out because when I talked to him, he had some hard intel. He said the Iranians are livid General Roustaie was killed. They want revenge, and are organizing to assassinate POTUS."

The COS looked as if he were staring into an abyss.

Maverick continued, "Last year we took out the top four terrorists on the planet, those on the FBI's Most Wanted Terrorist list during a rally commemorating those who had attacked Americans. And as you know because you were here, we took out General Roustaie. Iran says they won't tolerate American bullying. They want revenge."

The COS knew that Iranian rhetoric against the U.S. and Israel had been more fiery than usual in recent weeks due in part to the anniversary of the killing of Iran's Quds Force top commander, General Mostafa Javad Roustaie in a drone strike at the Baghdad International Airport, 350 kilometers away.

Wordlessly the COS nodded, turned, and walked to his aircraft. After a few minutes, while the pilots completed their checks and got their clearance, the Cessna departed Imam Ali Base. The Cessna *Caravan* was first to takeoff to avoid the wake turbulence of the C-17.

While *Maverick* talked with COS, Coffey watched the magic unfold as the YO-3A was disassembled and covered in sheets. It was transferred to the rear of the C-17, tailwheel first. One of the aircrew used the jet's cargo winch to pull the aircraft up the incline of the ramp. Once the airplane was inside the *Globemaster II*, the mechanics secured the sheet-covered aircraft into its container for the ride to the U.S. By the time the Cessna was airborne, the C-17 had started engine number one and was working on a clearance to depart.

Once they were at cruising altitude, Coffey thought, *After bringing a defector out of Iran, suddenly killing the former president doesn't seem out of the question.* He said, "So you got him out."

Maverick said, "Now it's up to the Agency to see he stays alive. The Islamic Revolutionary Guard Corps will have their friends in the Islamic Underground in the U.S. on the lookout for him. To kill him."

Maverick thought, *To get him out of there, I ruined the eyesight of a hundred Iranian soldiers, maybe forever. That's an inconsequential price to pay for all the Iranian bombs that have killed U.S. troops in Iraq and Afghanistan. But now the White House and the CIA know Iran means to kill our president.*

CHAPTER 23

November 6, 2019

As he boarded the Gulfstream G-550, Bill McGee saw one of Duncan Hunter's three-of-a-kind, genetically modified spider silk, bulletproof vest on his seat and thought, *There are advantages to having wealthy friends. I will definitely use that!* He and Hunter had made several trips in this aircraft, but this time McGee rode in the cabin and occupied one of the generously overstuffed leather lounge chairs.

McGee reflected riding up front in the cockpit would have been definitely more fun. Now he was one of *those people*. A passenger. It was another acknowledgement he had moved on. He had to work to get elected. No more fun-filled joyrides with spectacular views; no more *Maverick* and *Bullfrog* packing the cockpit and carrying on like schoolkids.

McGee knew Duncan had provided three of his most prized possessions: the newest of his two business jets, his motor coach, and his experimental spider silk body armor. President Hernandez and Nazy were the other recipients of the spider silk body armor.

Before leaving for his mission, *Maverick* had blue-over-gold streaks painted from the jet's nose to its tail to reflect the Admiral's U.S. Navy service. He had even provided pilots for the jet in the interim. Two of his former Air Force graduate students who had been fighter pilots in their own right jumped at the opportunity to fly for the war hero. They were experienced Gulfstream pilots who had delivered their company's newest jet, a G-900 with the latest interior designs, to Europe's wealthiest man and had come straight from Gulfstream Production Certificate Operations to provide immediate, yet temporary flight support for the campaign. Three other retired lieutenant colonels, also former students, had started ground school and simulators to get certified to fly the G-550. Hunter's parent company, QAS, contracted for qualified Gulfstream pilots through a flight service. It wasn't hard getting Gulfstream pilots; it was a challenge getting some who could pass a polygraph.

•   •   •

One of the biggest surprises for McGee, once they arrived in Elmira, was Hunter's longtime ranch foreman, Carlos Yazzie and his wife, Therese, were also arriving with Hunter's lightly armored motor coach and a long, matching trailer all the way from Jackson, Wyoming. Interstate 90 to Erie, Pennsylvania then a right turn to Elmira, New York. McGee wondered how the Yazzies planned to return to Wyoming. That was when Yazzie dropped the rear door of the coach's lengthy trailer and backed out an armored Hummer2. McGee thought, *Of course, Hunter doesn't go anywhere without an armored H2. Or two. He thinks of everything.* Carlos Yazzie repositioned the second Hummer2 in the trailer so it was centered over the tailer's wheels. He then handed McGee the keys, and he and Therese climbed into the H2 and headed back to Wyoming, citing they had chores to tend to.

Demetrius Eastwood had arrived in Elmira a few hours before McGee. He had volunteered to report on the candidate's daily activities. The other reporters assigned to cover the new presidential candidate weren't too delighted to see Eastwood. It would be more difficult to control the narrative with a conservative correspondent on the campaign to refute their biased reporting.

Dory Eastwood was under no illusions about the congeniality of fellow journalists who wanted to cover the presidential candidate. Their reporting would be anything but sincere. They had all voted Democrat. They were chosen for the assignment based on their politics, and they would fearlessly report the Democrat Party version of truth before stooping to accuracy.

Before departing to his first campaign stop, McGee walked over to talk to the dozen men and women of the media who were trapped behind the airport's security fence. He took control of the situation immediately.

Rear Admiral McGee said, "Hello Fourth Estate, Fifth Columnists. In Nazi Germany in 1933, the Nazis passed *the Journalist's Law* which made all newsmen servants to the state and subject to licensing. I would be surprised if every one of you *isn't* a Democrat Party operative since you all vote Democrat. In my book you do not differ from the Nazis' media of 1933, newsmen servants of the Democrats who report what your masters tell you to report. Some of you will do whatever you can to damage this campaign. Good luck on being on the wrong side of history. You can cover our rallies any way you see fit, but this is how *we* are going to conduct interviews."

"I will make a series of statements. You'll have some time to digest my comments and may ask questions before I depart for our next campaign rally. I won't tolerate unscrupulously fabricated stories alleging atrocities or mistreatment committed by patriots or conservatives. If you lie, you'll be rebutted immediately and thoroughly. I'll expect you to confine your reporting to my remarks only. You will not report on my family."

"You won't join us on this jet or any campaign jet, because you're the purveyors of media propaganda. In this campaign you're viewed as the enemies of the state, and your Fifth Columnist reporting is influenced by Communist, Marxist, and Socialist forces I have spent a lifetime fighting against. So, those who are so closely aligned with the enemies of America will be allowed nowhere near our aircraft or our people. You want to cover me, knock yourself out; get your own damn transportation. Colonel Eastwood may come aboard. He's an honest broker."

Some wag from the reporters group hollered, "What's your definition of honest?"

McGee addressed the unseen male voice. "Seeing that you as a group are as reliable as Mexican tapwater, anyone who has to ask an idiotic question like that isn't competent to cover this campaign."

The other journalists turned toward the man who had made the comment with incredulity.

McGee turned and walked to the aircraft followed by a handful of campaign personnel. Bringing up the rear was Lieutenant Colonel Eastwood. They filled all seats equipped with seatbelts.

As the journalists behind the airport fence dispersed, one young man stayed behind. He wasn't really interested in the candidate, but he was interested in the aircraft. He wrote down the number painted on the side of the engine cowling and took a smartphone picture of the business jet. He selected an app on his phone and reported McGee and his security detail boarded a G-550 at the Elmira Corning Regional Airport. He included the N-number of the jet and attached the photograph of the pretty white aircraft with dramatic blue and gold streaks running from nose to tail.

•   •   •

Throngs of people waving American flags and wearing blue hats with a gold U.S. Navy's SEAL Trident embroidered on the front met the jet at the Warren County Regional Airport near Bowling Green, Kentucky. Bill McGee dashed out of the Gulfstream, bounded onto a platform, and stood behind a lectern to roaring applause. After leading the assembly in the Pledge of Allegiance he looked across the 30,000 people gathered near the airport's parking apron and shouted into the microphone, "I thank you for coming. I'm humbled by your greetings and support. Our country needs help. Along with you we will save our country from the enemies that have us by the throat. So, before we get serious let's have some fun; what do you say?"

Eastwood noted the crowd was borderline hysterical. He wrote, *Is this what it looks like when people who have wanted a real leader finally get to meet one? They waved and whistled and were over-the-top joyous. You could make the case they loved Bill McGee like the girls had loved The Beatles in decades past. They're going nutsy seeing him for the first time in person. He talked to them, not condescendingly but as equals. It will take a while to deprogram them from the left's Blatherskite.*

"...and we are going to learn a few things about our wonderful country and our Founding Fathers along the way. But tonight, we are here in God's country, the home of the National Corvette Museum and the factory that builds America's *out-of-this-world* sportscars."

The crowd erupted in applause.

"You're our first stop. Let me say for the record your welcome has been wonderful. We have Colonel Eastwood with us, the nationally recognized war correspondent. I know whatever he writes about us will be accurate. I wouldn't let the evil alphabet media aboard our jet just to lie to you."

The crowd booed and hissed and clapped wildly at the mention of *the evil alphabet media*.

McGee rattled off a string of politicians who were attending the rally. After the business of political introductions, Admiral McGee said, "Thank you; I thank all of you. Let's get to business. We know America is in dire straits. You see the riots, the cities burning, the violent protests in the states controlled by Democrats. I want to tell you why these things are happening, and no, it's not because you're a bigot or a white supremacist or an Islamophobe."

"What you're actually seeing and hearing, ladies and gentlemen, results from raw propaganda being put into action and funded by Marxist, Communist, and Socialist groups — in other words, a lot of folks from the Democrat Party. Americans like you are being forcibly distracted by the negative incessant push to convince you that you're the problem, that *we* cannot see that *we* are the actual threat. We are a threat alright! We are fighting back. We are in a silent war with Communism, Socialism, Marxism, and Liberalism! Their weapons are the silent weapons of a quiet war. They use mind control techniques to alter your thinking. It drives the left crazy when we tell you what they're up to and what their jobs are — to instill fear and induce mass hypnosis. They want you afraid; they need you afraid for their program to work."

"The government and the media have no business telling you how to think. And we are going to get after that crap!"

"If you think I'm joking you, you have smartphones. Look up *Using Behavioral Science Insights to Better Serve the American People*. I suggest you read it. Former President of the United States Mazibuike proclaimed by executive order the government would help you make better decisions through *Behavioral Science Insights*, or what the laymen know as *brainwashing*. Yes, that is your Democrat Party at work. They manipulate Americans to think they're the problem; they need help in making decisions. They manipulate you to think you must obey Democrats. They manipulate you to think Republicans are evil and wicked. Positively incredible. Here tonight, I'm asking President

Hernandez to rescind that executive order." McGee's voice increased in volume. "Government agencies shouldn't be in the business of using propaganda against citizens! They work for us! It's *We The People* who control them! Not the other way around!"

Eastwood was shocked. The crowd held on to every word McGee spoke. He was mesmerizing.

Applause from the crowd died down and McGee continued.

Sticking a finger in the air, *"Are you ready to take this country back?"*

The people from Bowling Green shouted, *"Yes!"*

McGee shouted, *"Are you ready for a change?"*

The crowd shouted, *"Yes!"*

McGee shouted, *"They're assaulting us with propaganda. Are you ready to learn some counter-propaganda techniques? To stop their nonsense."*

The assembly went delirious and shouted, *"Yes!"*

McGee introduced several women who had made their way onto the platform. He said, "We have here with us ten women from the Great State of Kentucky who couldn't defend their homes from invasion, break in, and burglary. In some cases, the police never arrived. Ladies, am I correct in saying that up until your unfortunate encounter with the criminals who terrorized you, you believed weapons were bad, no one needed an AR-15 to hunt deer, and other Democrat talking points on gun control? They projected their fear of guns on you; you are made to feel their fear. Correct?"

The representative group of women nodded or shouted, *"Yes!"*

"Gun control is a damned lie. If gun control worked, Chicago, New York City, Philadelphia, Washington D.C, and Baltimore would be the safest places in America. In Democrat-led cities, gun control not only means to disarm law-abiding citizens, it's the next step to losing your citizenship. I can tell you the Democrat Party has taught you to be afraid of weapons. They want you in a continuous state of fear of weapons and Republicans. They want you to ignore the criminality of criminals. And what they have done is pass laws in these cities that effectively disarms you."

"They want you to believe their propaganda when they tell you how bad the police are. They want you to believe the rioters who are burning businesses are mostly peaceful protesters. These are propaganda techniques to stoke your emotions, and if they can find the little controls that manipulate your emotions, they can and will control you."

"On a radio station in Washington the great Chris Plante says, 'Give a liberal a thimbleful of power by breakfast, and before lunch, he will have abused it.'"

The crowd laughed, and Eastwood thought the comment was an appropriate observation.

McGee continued, "We are here to deprogram you from the wickedness of the Democrat Party. They say, 'This is your future unless our gun control measures are implemented.' They say they have the solutions, but their solutions clearly show they do not care about you or your family. All of that is propaganda. What they really want is to disarm America and disarm you. Their goal is your vote. That is the prize. They will lie and cheat to get your vote. The Founders understood this aspect of human nature and that's why they put in the Second Amendment!"

"If we do things their way, if we listen to them, we will be voting for them even after we are all dead. You shouldn't trust them with walking your dog, and you certainly shouldn't trust them as they finagle your vote away from you under bogus pretexts. We can't have that!"

The crowd chanted, *"We can't have that! We can't have that! We can't have that!"*

"In an age when Democrat public officials' solution to rising crime is more gun control, gun confiscation, and defunding the police, here is our first lesson. Listen carefully." McGee leaned into the lectern. The crowd went silent. He said, "If violent crime is to be curbed, it's only the intended victim who can do it. The felon doesn't fear the police; he fears neither judge, nor jury, nor jail. The felon must be taught to fear *his victim.*"

The crowd was eerily silent for several seconds before breaking out in riotous applause.

"To start that process, we must do whatever is in our power to teach you not to fear weapons. We are not emphasizing military discipline or transforming citizens into fighting machines. Instead, we want to prepare civilians to be ready to deter and kill invaders when criminals attack. We will help you overturn unconstitutional gun control laws, but in the meantime, that is going to take time. The left will fight back."

"Ladies, you are smart, incredibly talented and accomplished women. You shouldn't be afraid of anything. If you look at all the evidence, you'll see if you are to survive, you must protect yourselves and your families. Our Founders were brilliant men who created the First and Second Amendments for law-abiding Americans. For you and me. The Democrats and the leftists in the media are on a crusade to destroy the First and Second Amendments. If they can make them go away, you'll be their prisoner. Then hello, *1984*."

There was hooting and hollering. The crowd was ecstatic for this *not-a-politician* politician.

"The left has programmed you to believe the police are the problem, the police are evil, the police are white supremacists. Of course, it's all a lie. That is their propaganda in action. The Big Lie! You don't even realize they're using propaganda against you. Whenever they pass a law that sounds like it will benefit you but actually befits them, they're using a *silent weapon* of propaganda against you."

"Defeating propaganda requires *counter-propaganda*. They pass a law that injures you or your family; defeat that law. The real problem is the Democrats' *policies* are detrimental to your health—like enacting gun control laws that strip you of your ability to protect yourselves and your families. Why is it that none of these riots with burning cities in the background are in Republican led cities? That is a legitimate question. This is on par with the idea America should give money to a Russian or Chinese bioweapons lab; maybe that makes sense to Democrats in Washington, D.C. But that isn't only wrong, that is treason."

"It's a sad commentary the Democrats have engineered these riots in their cities. They manipulate the media; they want you to see city blocks on fire on the networks just so they can blame Republicans. Democrats set Democrat controlled cities on fire, and then they blame Republicans. Can you see how that stirs your emotions to make you want to take to side of the protesters?"

"I ask you sincerely, how are Republicans to blame? These cities and towns are run by *Democrats*. If these riots were attempted in Republican cities, they would be stopped before they could even get started. This is their propaganda. They repeat *ad nauseum* Republicans are to blame so you'll continue to vote for Democrats. They will save you from the wicked and evil Republicans. But it's Democrats who set the fires and constantly divide us. I want to stop that nonsense."

The outburst of the crowd was deafening.

"This is an undeniable truth: criminals want to outlaw guns so they won't get shot when they commit crimes. That is a problem, but we have a way to fix it."

He continued, "I'm calling on President Hernandez to issue an executive order that provides firearms training and firearms to disaffected women like our ladies here. They should never again have to rely on hoping a Democrat administration send the police when they have an emergency." On cue, the women approached McGee and hugged him before they left the stage.

Eastwood wanted to shout, *I like the way he does business; one EO in, one EO out!*

The crowd was surprised but approved of the initiative with a roar. Eastwood couldn't believe what he was hearing. He recalled a photo of a shriveled up little old lady sitting on her doorstep in the Middle East cradling her AK-47. He wrote, *that is true, if given the opportunity, criminals will steal from you without blinking an eye. That image would make a wickedly cool campaign visual....*

McGee shouted, "I respectfully request President Hernandez provide firearms training for those families who have lost loved ones, have had their property invaded by criminals, or fear for their lives under Democrat Party rule. We can and will show there are weapons that can be used defensively, easily, and without harm to the operator. We have millions of surplus M-16s in armories. They do not recoil. I suggest a Presidential Executive Order to authorize the de-militarization of those weapons, turning those offensive fully automatic weapons into semi-automatic defensive weapons for civilian use."

He gestured to the crowd, "Our country is under assault. We have to change the way we look at this problem. Government power should protect all Americans, and we are the ones who can fix this problem. Our goal is to offer you immediate direct protection from the criminals, not a busy signal from a 911 operator."

The throng clapped for two minutes as McGee caught his breath and took a drink.

"You may not be convinced this initiative will work, because we are so spread out. Some people live on farms, some work at building Corvettes, some live in or near the city. Let me read to you some true stories." He held up a clipping, "Here we have a woman with children in her home when a group of armed men tried to invade her residence by force. She took her gun and fired on the invaders, killing one and scattering the rest of them. We know we live in a world where criminals prey on the unarmed. They feel they can waltz into any house and take anything they want. But they got nothing but a little lead from that house."

"Here's another one. In a South Dakota town a woman's ex-boyfriend violated a restraining order and confronted her one evening while she was with a male companion. Words were exchanged, and the ex-boyfriend assaulted the woman's male companion. She drew a handgun from her purse and chased the old boyfriend away. An hour later the police finally responded to the incident. This is what I mean. *The right to keep and bear arms shall not be infringed.*"

Momentarily basking in the adulation of the packed party of people McGee stated, "We will take America back from the criminals. Look around, you'll find our supporters working their way among you with hats for the kids and business cards I hope you'll put in your wallets and purses. On one side is the Second Amendment: *The right to keep and bear arms shall not be infringed* and on the other is the quote I used earlier, *If violent crime is to be curbed....* That one."

"Take several and give them to your friends. There will be more on this topic in the coming days. And look for Colonel Eastwood's articles about our rallies and this movement. He will report the status of our *Not Going to be Afraid Any More* initiative. But you, Bowling Green, are the first, and we need you to get the information out. Thank you, Bowling Green, thank you Kentucky, God Bless you, and God Bless the United States of America!"

The crowd was loud. They clapped, screamed, and whistled their approvals. Some people took dozens of the business cards.

On the way to the Gulfstream, Eastwood wrote, *Here is a politician who actually makes sense, and he's taking it straight to the Democrat Party and their media. Not only have they been feeding the American public a pack of lies through propaganda, but they have repeated those lies to scare Americans in perpetuity.*

CHAPTER 24

November 7, 2019

Newspaper editors and network producers were in an uproar over Candidate McGee's comments and actions. They worked furiously to rebut the former CIA Director's controversial comments, that the arming of women would lead to untold deaths. Media correspondents took a favorite line they used to denigrate Texans and threw the insult around newspapers and on the air; *he's all sizzle, no steak.*

As reporters and journalists crafted witty and devastating responses to McGee's rally, Demetrius Eastwood posted his piece from someone who had been on scene. His was an exclusive with quotes directly from the candidate. In newsrooms across the country, reporters hunched over computer screens or read Eastwood's article from flimsies being spit out of a printer.

By: Demetrius Eastwood
November 7, 2019
Former CIA Director and retired U.S. Navy Rear Admiral William "Bill" McGee held his first presidential campaign rally at the Warren County Regional Airport near Bowling Green....

•   •   •

That was last evening. This morning, President Hernandez announced he signed an executive order effective immediately that allows the de-militarization of surplus M-16s for defensive civilian use. Ammunition manufacturers have volunteered to provide training ammunition for the initiative at no cost to new gun owners in the program. The manufacturers of laser sights have volunteered to provide laser pointers at no cost to new gun owners in the program. The National Rifle Association will provide free firearms training to women at their request.

President Hernandez made the most stunning announcement from his desk in the Oval Office. He said, "The federal government will establish a legal defense fund for these women who receive a demilitarized weapon and training. If they stop an intruder with one of these weapons and need legal services, it will be provided. The legal defense fund will ensure women are protected against an unscrupulous local, city, or state Democrat government or a frivolous lawsuit that may be brought by the families of the criminals who perpetrate home intrusions and assaults. The U.S. government will assume liability if government furnished weapons are properly used to protect Americans. Democrats want to provide funds for free college to illegal aliens; this initiative will benefit Americans."

The Democrat Party immediately ridiculed Candidate McGee's initiative, claiming countless women and children would die needlessly because of this program. The Democrats cannot see weapons are a deterrent. In most cases when a woman brandishes a weapon, the criminal flees. McGee believes arming women is counter-propaganda to the left's propaganda. It's well known Democrats have been trying to disarm law-abiding Americans for decades.

A remarkable thing has occurred since Admiral McGee announced his *Not Going to be Afraid Any More* initiative last night. As of 9:00 a.m. Eastern time, the NRA and White House telephone lines and websites have crashed. A few newspapers and networks have interviewed frustrated women who wanted to sign up. But they said they would wait. They didn't want to be afraid any more.

Late last evening immediately after McGee's rally, a Democrat Party spokesperson claimed Rear Admiral McGee may have unintentionally shot himself in the foot with such a radical, nonsensical, and unsafe initiative. The same spokesperson said, "It will be hard for political analysts to see McGee as a credible contender for the Republican nomination. He's a big headache for the Republican Party. Bill McGee won't be the Republican nominee for president. His attempt to paint Democrats as Machiavellian mind control experts is the stuff of conspiracy theories." Noteworthy, the media didn't mention President Mazibuike's executive order: *Using Behavioral Science Insights to Better Serve the American People,* proving the axiom one of the foremost powers of the media is their power to ignore.

As this report goes to print, Rear Admiral Bill McGee has shot up dramatically in the polls. According to several polling companies' rolling average of polls, McGee now ranks first in the GOP field by a significant margin. He leads the top Democrats in the race by twenty points, towering over all the Democrat Party candidates.

The Democratic National Committee said they welcomed Rear Admiral McGee to the race. "Today, former CIA Director McGee became the latest major Republican candidate to announce for president. He will add some seriousness to the GOP field, and we look forward hearing more about his ideas for the nation."

Rear Admiral McGee told the GOP and the DNC he will debate any Democratic nominee, but he won't take part if the moderator is from any of the left-wing cable news networks. He said, "We will not have a national debate with a key Democratic activist moderator who spouts every single anti-Republican conspiracy theory Democrats have cooked up in recent years. We won't have a national debate with any Democratic activist moderator who has deceptively edited and personally participated in the censoring of real news and/or discussions that push for Democrat and left-wing policy positions such as gun control, teaching racism to young children, and scaring our women. We won't have a national debate with any Democratic activist moderator who is ignorant of our Founding Fathers' views. We won't have a national debate with any Democratic activist moderator who claims some Republicans don't 'believe in the Constitution' because they believe rights come from God. We will have a highly respected war correspondent preside over town halls where we take questions from the audience, where the point of the interview isn't to improve the stature of the Democratic activist moderator, but to have my message conveyed to you. That's how we are going to have discussions with the American people."

In newsrooms and networks across the country, the DNC ran negative reports on Bill McGee. They couldn't understand why women across the nation would want to arm themselves with an overly complicated assault weapon that could get them killed.

CHAPTER 25

November 10, 2019

The Supreme Allied Commander Europe (SACEUR) of all commands of the North Atlantic Treaty Organization (NATO) barged through the Base Operations doors to see who the hell was on Ramstein Air Force Base. If there was one thing that drove the four-star general nuts it was the CIA screwing around with the Air Force and abusing his airmen and his bases for their little projects. Even at almost 55 years old, the athletic Air Force general huffily raced across the tarmac in his flight suit, picking them up and putting them down like an Olympic speed walker. When he reached the cabin door of the C-17 General Walter Todd III didn't announce his presence. Sometimes he liked to throw his weight around and this was one of them.

General Todd III bounded in the door and came face to face with the unshaven *Maverick*. Whatever anger and frustration the general had suddenly fell to the ramp outside the *Globemaster II*. His frown was replaced with a smile.

Duncan Hunter shouted, "Attention on deck!" He offered his hand and said, "General, it's been a long time. And, congratulations, sir."

General Todd III shouted, "*Maverick! I should have known it was you, you old fart!*" He barked "At Ease" to those on the jet as he shook Hunter's hand vigorously. He inspected the contents of the C-17 and saw there was operational Agency equipment and a security contingent aboard. The pilot emerged from the cockpit, introduced himself, and explained the jet had required some maintenance and the aircrew had needed crew rest before they headed back to Andrews. "We had received our weather brief and clearance and were about to start engines when the word came down there would be no engine starts, you wanted to see the aircrew."

General Todd III asked, "Mission Complete?"

The pilot in command and Coffey looked to *Maverick* who chimed in, "Yes, sir. I can give you a debrief, sir. Your eyes and ears only." Before General Todd III could respond, *Maverick* asked Bob and Bob to open up the box as he led his old commanding officer to the rear of the shipping container. Hunter had been the number two civilian on a pilot training base in Texas when Todd III had been a colonel and the commander of the base.

As *Maverick* and the general stepped inside the YO-3A's illuminated container, both men recalled their strange meeting on the Texas ramp with a former CIA executive. Greg Lynche had explained to the colonel they were involved in a special access program and Hunter's Air Force job as the Deputy Director of Maintenance was his official cover. The toothpick-thin Greg Lynche, the true mastermind behind the YO-3A program, asked the colonel if he would allow Hunter to continue in his position, and the colonel agreed.

Hunter pulled back the sheet covering the nose and the almost-square, three-bladed propeller of the YO-3A. No words were spoken. General Todd III just smiled, nodded, and wrapped his arms across his chest. *That is just unbelievable!*

Maverick then described the different propellers used on the YO-3A. "This one is one of three designs that were specially engineered, fabricated, and tested in the late '60s by an acoustic laboratory in Massachusetts. All three prop designs ensure the tips of the propeller won't go supersonic at low RPMs. As you know, sir, tip speed is the source of 90 percent of all piston-driven aircraft noise. Each prop has a special function, and they're still considered top secret. TS/SCI." *Maverick* didn't think it was time to say the three-bladed short wooden propeller mounted on the YO-3A was used specifically for insertions and extractions in high-threat, noise-sensitive missions. "We have a six-bladed composite prop we install when dash speed is needed."

General Todd III nodded as if he understood perfectly. He finally unfolded his arms and slapped Hunter on the back. He said, "*Incredible, mon ami*. More fun than flying a T-38, I bet." Hunter leaned into the man's ear and said, "It also has a gun." SACEUR rolled his eyes and pulled on his nose, *Oh Duncan, stop it! Some guys have all the luck....*

As they walked outside under the wing of the massive cargo jet, *Maverick* said, "I don't know if there will ever be an official accounting to the Air Force of what we did. General, I can arrange for a debrief, but I don't think...."

"*Maverick*, during my intel brief this morning, I heard the IRGC shot about a hundred of their people for failing to do something. The intel shop wasn't unambiguous, but maybe...." General Todd III broke out into a huge smile. "... *maybe someone got away.*" He looked around the massive C-17 as if he could see through it to the little black airplane hiding in a box.

When Hunter grinned and nodded like a frat boy at a wet t-shirt contest, then General Todd III knew. *Maverick is more of a patriot that I ever would have considered.... I took him for granted in a way. He must be one of us, but I need to make sure.* He said, "You know *Maverick*, after this gig I could see myself in the top job at your place."

Maverick knew he was being probed, but it wasn't the time or the place to let the cat out of the bag. "Me, work for you again? Be still my beating heart!" They laughed and *Maverick* wrapped his arms across his chest, a subtle sign that maybe his words and desires were in conflict. "Sir, *wilco*. I will see what I can do. I *used to have* a little pull in that area, but you know, now I'm just an old washed-up F-4 pilot."

SACEUR quickly unfolded his arms, wagged a bony finger, and accused the old washed-up Marine F-4 *Phantom II* pilot, "*Oh, that's bullshit Maverick — you used me and everyone in the chain of command to get a U-2 flyover!*"

Hunter grinned and said, "Very respectfully sir, I don't remember hearing any complaints. Just a lot of tears running down the faces of nearly every patriot that day."

He has me there. That was such an incredibly special day it still sends chills down the spine. General Todd III caught his breath and thought, *So, you admit it! You're an Irregular! You are definitely one of the Bubbas!* The comment cracked the men up. It was like the last time they had been together in Hunter's office in Texas before the colonel left for his follow-on assignment. He had a question only the deputy maintenance director could answer. He had been serious that day and had never expected to see Duncan Hunter again.

"*Maverick*," the future SACEUR had said, "I know you can get things done like no other person I've met. You have a gift. I want to know, how is it I have never experienced a ground abort the whole time I've been at Laughlin? I talked to the other training wing commanders, and they all say they ground abort about fifty percent of the time. I never had one, and I've flown twice as often as they have. They said I was full of it."

Hunter had leaned back in his high-wingback judge's chair and told him with a deadpan delivery. "*Colonel*, sir, I *cheat*. Unlike the competition, I make sure you never get a bad or even a marginal jet. I do that by having a dedicated crewchief; his sole responsibility is your aircraft, 0008. He fires your jet up in the morning before you go out, warms up the systems, and checks to see that everything works. If he finds something wrong with your jet, we give you our best spare so you don't ground abort."

That day the man who would become Supreme Allied Commander Europe had howled. Uncharacteristically for a wing commander, he had carried on about how Hunter, a retired Marine Corps pilot and aircraft maintenance officer, a quiet Ph.D., sometimes had a different way of looking at problems and solutions, like how do you get a U-2 flyover for a bunch of retired officers? *Easy — let's have a dedication for a patriot! No one ever saw Maverick's quiet brilliance at work until the end, like a chess grandmasters' career of moving different pieces while forcing the opponent's king to move across the board into CHECKMATE.*

But more than that, Hunter had taken care of him and his instructor pilots when *Maverick* had never been asked. General Todd III had marveled at the man in the cramped office with dozens of F-4 *Phantom II* prints and photos and a half-sized Texas flag framed in barn wood on the wall. He knew Hunter spent his nights teaching grad students at Laughlin. His students — Air Force officers, mostly Texas-based instructor pilots from several Air Force bases within Air

Education and Training Command—would travel hundreds of miles to attend Hunter's classes.

General Todd III and *Maverick* shared a special bond, a friendship that knew no bounds. He remembered he was within weeks from his change of command when the retired Marine Corps captain erupted during his wing staff meeting, shaming lieutenant colonels and colonels, squadron and group commanders for not being a part of their junior officers' professional training. *That was another incredible day! Maverick knew exactly what to say and when to say it. I couldn't get them to do shit, but that day virtually every officer around that conference table made the pilgrimage to the education center and signed up to be a graduate school instructor.*

Coffey was intrigued by the men's interactions. He watched their body language and looked for the tells. *But there was something else at play.* As he observed the men's actions and gestures, Coffey discerned the four-star wasn't *that* type a guy, a criminal guy. Someone who would abuse their power. He was the obverse, a patriot, one of those long-lost heroes quietly doing what he could to serve America. The more he watched General Todd III, the more Coffey was convinced he was one of the leaders of the military forces for the good side. Not just someone doing his job during the day and at night, passing secrets to the Kremlin.

Coffey could see the Air Force general wasn't a *dark state* guy; he wasn't outwardly political. He was outwardly *apolitical*, and that threw him the curveballs. *The man is the anthesis of a dark state swamp creature; he isn't some bureaucrat from a nebulous organization within the government. That is why he and Maverick are friends, and that's why they're so comfortable with each other. Their interaction has a completely different vibe. Not just friends but…. What could it be? What is their history? Racquetball? I doubt it.*

The retired senior law enforcement executive slowly smiled at what he was witnessing; *Maverick* and General Todd III responded as if they were *resistance leaders*? They weren't behaving simply as old friends who hadn't seen each other in years. No. Their interaction was more collaborative, more conspiratorial in a good way. *Like what I know of Captain Pete Ortiz spiriting Goebbels' papers from the Ministry of Propaganda? Maverick extracting defectors from a fascist Islamic hellhole. You can't ask regular people to do jobs like that, no matter how much you check their backgrounds, no matter the level of clearances you have or the number of NDAs you sign. To operate in the enemy's back yard, that's not normal. You need someone special. That's not normal Fifth Columnist activities. I think I'm comfortable with Maverick acting like a resistance leader. There are problems in the government but he's not undermining the government. He's assisting the operation and good order and discipline of the government, and the feds don't even know it. Huh!*

That is exactly what the Irregulars did during the Pumpkin Papers Irregulars Dinner. Are they part of some shadowy group of patriots? Is their goal to counter dark state actors and prevent extremist ideologies from flourishing? Maverick? I believe so. Yes! Coffey now had more respect for *Maverick. Captain America* was real and operating in another world. Maybe he had been for a long time. *Was this meeting planned? Was there a message that needed to be transmitted? What do you call these people? Irregulars doesn't seem adequate and Fifth Columnists just seems inappropriate. Is there such a thing as a Sixth Columnist?*

With heavy sighs and handshakes, they exchanged challenge coins. *Maverick* gave him one of the good ones. General Todd III scrutinized the *sui generis* Air Branch coin and concluded *Maverick* had taken care of him again — with serial number 0008. The side number of his T-38 when he was a colonel and wing commander with *Maverick. That lad has a gift of doing the right thing at the right time.*

General Todd III said, "That is some *gift.* Thank you, *Maverick.*"

Hunter smiling, said, "Sir, I think it's a gift and a curse."

General Todd III replied, "It doesn't do any good to say what the Chinese said best: May you live in interesting times. Because *Maverick,* you are already living in interesting times."

•   •   •

After they had been airborne for a while, Coffey sidled up to *Maverick*. He made several efforts to talk about General Todd III, but *Maverick* demurred.

Maverick had been excited to see his old friend. He thought about the possibility of Todd taking the role of Director of the CIA. Some of the generals who had held similar senior intelligence positions in the past had been numbskulls at best, idiots at worst. The generals who had led the National Reconnaissance Office were rockstars, geniuses, Ph.Ds. But General Todd III, he was one of the *Bubbas*, a fellow member of the resistance, one of *the Irregulars*, and that was actually essential. Nazy's the Acting Director and McGee's hand-picked successor. *Even though Americans don't do things like that. Nazy can't be Nazy if she's tied to that desk.* Duncan would talk with her when they were together.

He would remind her it had never been her goal to be the Director. It was something she could do when the Director was out of town, but it involved too much exposure to the public and detracted from her work in Operations and the National Counterterrorism Center. To make his case, *Maverick* would cite the immortal words of Baltasar Gracian, the author of *The Art of Worldly Wisdom*, number 149: *Let someone else take the hit.* Hunter worried about her; the Muslim Brotherhood maintained several *fatwas* on her.

Maverick thought having someone else play boss, operating on the skyline, and taking the hits might not be such a bad thing. Could he do that to McGee? Could he do that to his buddy, General Todd III? *Well, hell, yeah! He's part of the team. He'll have a security detail. But above all, we could use him, and he just let me know he's not only amenable but eager.*

CHAPTER 26

November 10, 2019

After landing at Joint Base Andrews Duncan Hunter climbed out of the C-17 cockpit and thanked everyone for their help. He told them the mission had been a success and he hoped the crew would get some much-deserved rest and awards. As always, he had coins for them as he shook their hands. Not the Air Branch challenge coin but a solid gold $50 American Gold Eagle. Brilliant, uncirculated. Spendable. Untraceable. The airmen were amazed they had received something they could actually use. Several of them checked the spot price of gold on their smartphones and found they had hit the lottery.

Bob and Bob, and Joe and Tommy were busy loading the YO-3A's container and equipment onto a tractor-trailer rig that accommodated shipping containers. The *Yo-Yo* would be taken to a cargo warehouse on the Baltimore-Washington International Airport until the next mission. It had been handled and stored this way for the last fifteen years. The office door at the airport marked it was the shipping and receiving office of QAS – *Quiet Aero Systems.*

Coffey and Hunter said their goodbyes. Coffey had things to think about as he returned to his home in Stafford, Virginia. He was intrigued with the special access program and the secret aircraft. He could see himself doing the work. The real question was, would he? Was it enough?

Nazy didn't meet Duncan at the aircraft. Hunter hadn't expected her to, but she had indicated she could meet him later. Hunter had suggested a rendezvous; Nazy had said to look for her around six o'clock. The additional time allowed Duncan to get to the hotel and into disguise as Dante Locke.

At the Washington Capital Grill, Nazy and Duncan as Dante Locke shook hands as if they were business associates meeting for dinner. They were under the watchful eye of the Agency's security detail posted inside the steakhouse. Hunter asked Nazy to tell her personal security people to order whatever they wanted. Everyone had the most expensive items on the menu: the filet and the key lime pie. Hunter surreptitiously paid the bill for all of them in cash by peeling off twenty-five new $100 bills from his wallet.

After dinner the security detail took them to the JW Marriott across the street from the White House. The security detail was dismissed. They would return for her Monday morning.

As they approached the open elevator, Hunter shifted a long skinny can of hairspray from his inside suit pocket to the inside of his sleeve. A thin but powerful stream of the sticky fluid saturated the camera panel before they entered. The unscented hairspray obscured the surveillance camera that monitored the inside of the car. With the camera effectively disabled, Duncan kissed Nazy passionately from the ground floor to the top floor. When the elevator doors opened, Nazy remained inside the car. Duncan stepped out and kept his head down as he trained a stream of hairspray on the three ceiling-mounted security cameras in the hall. Inside their room, Nazy went to the bathroom while Duncan set up their security system of three tiny wireless cameras held tight by white putty wedged into three door crevices. He aimed one camera to monitor the door. The other cameras monitored anyone on the floor left or right of their room. Once the door handle was braced with a door security bar Hunter got his laptop up and running. He opened the surveillance app and the three cameras fed imagery to his computer screen.

CHAPTER 27

November 11, 2019

After a couple of hours in the hotel's gym, they breakfasted, showered, romped in the bed, and showered again. It was past noon when Duncan finished reading an article in the *Washington Times* about a NATO-led research group who had determined the Muslim Brotherhood's complex network in Europe constituted a grave and serious danger. He smiled. The Supreme Allied Commander Europe, General Walter Todd III, had initiated the counterterrorism investigation. With no other newspaper article to distract him Hunter said, "You know your way of taking a shower is a waste of water. Not that I'm complaining; it's just an observation."

"I suppose the next time you want to me to say, 'Hey, handsome, want to waste some water?'"

Duncan dropped the briefing materials he had received from Nazy into his lap and looked at his wife. "I don't think I want to change a thing. We get too few opportunities to do that, and if it means paying a little more for the water in order to enjoy a long hot shower with you, they can add it to my bill. How about that?"

She poked his nose and said, "You're such a big spender."

"Only when it's for a good cause." Duncan returned to the briefing materials and the President's thank you card. Over the years he had received many invitations and cards, but the Presidential Seal embossed in gold leaf centered on the front of this card was by far, the most impressive. President Hernandez's handwritten *Thank you* was heartfelt and not in any way prosaic. The note that followed at the bottom of the card was incredible. *What would you need for an Intrepid-sized extraction?*

There were extractions like going into Iran and bringing someone out, but those were always Agency sponsored, and the president didn't get involved in them. Then there were *extractions. What would I need for a presidential requested extraction? I'll have to give that a little more thought. No one has done anything about this one for 200 years. It's not like it's time sensitive.*

Hunter returned the card to its envelope and put it to the side. He returned to the file in front of him; he was head-down with a laser focus reading the Agency's brief sheets on Rho Schwartz Scorpii and Ahmad Khalid Saleh Hashash.

Nazy reminded him Hashash was the last one on the *Matrix*, and Scorpii was a special case, a financier of terrorism and the financier of candidates of the opposition party.

Hunter wouldn't ever make a go at Scorpii. The personal security protection on him was the best money could buy, and there was no sense trying to crack an uncrackable nut.

Scorpii appears to be funding terrorist organizations through non-governmental organizations or charities, and I'll bet he's running interference against Bullfrog. He's the top transnational criminal on the planet, and he's paying most, if not all the Democrat Party's Marxist and Communist candidates running for office in the U.S. He funded the voting machine companies. He funded social media networks to the tune of $400 million during the last election. He funded illegal immigration from South and Central America. All these funds run through his charities. He could buy politicians of every political party. A Scorpii-backed presidential candidate could have access to billions, which would make Scorpii the titular President of the United States if his candidate won. A diminutive old man who pulls all the strings because he's a Marxist with money.

Hunter paused and wondered, *Did Scorpii pull Mazibuike's strings by funding him or was 3M just a loose cannon bought and paid for by the Muslim Brotherhood?*

While storming Scorpii's fortress, wherever it was, it was not doable. Hashash was even more of a remote possibility if not an impossibility. First, he had to be found. If he hid in a metropolis, he couldn't be taken out with the YO-3A platform. Regardless of the priority of the target, Hunter and the Agency wouldn't have the *Yo-Yo* silhouetted over a city for anyone to see.

Duncan asked, "So, the latest intel is Hashash is in Algiers hiding out in the Casbah. Can't get him there. I understand it's a warren of apartments; he can hide there for eternity if he's even still alive."

"The best analyst in the business thinks he is."

"Alive or at the Casbah? I'm so *distracted.*" *You are soooo good looking!*

She threw a pretty pucker at him for being flippant.

He wanted to kiss those incarnadine lips again and again and again. *There's time....* "But darling Nazy, aren't you the best analyst in the business?"

She cooed, "It's some of my best work. Money sometimes opens doors that cannot be opened any other way." Sex was inferred to be the other way.

"Only the best for the President." Hunter smiled at the directed compliment. He held up the President's *Thank you* card.

"He's thinking of you. He wears that watch like it has always been on his wrist. The press wants to ask him where he got it but they don't dare. And he's making sounds like he would like you to avenge the death of your parents."

Some words trigger powerful memories that explode in a burst of energy. It was difficult not to think about those terrorists who blitzkrieged the aviation industry, but Hunter had kept those two men from dominating his thoughts. He raised an eye to his wife, nodded, and reflected with a faraway gaze: *the President's sister was a flight attendant aboard TWA Flight 800; my parents were aboard PanAm Flight 103. Jets knocked down by Abu Manu and Hashash. Murderous Islamic terrorists.*

Other than McGee and Nazy, no one at the Agency or in the federal government knew about that bond that linked President Hernandez and Duncan Hunter.

Hashash simply snuck a bomb he built aboard the PanAm jumbo. I still feel the pain my parents and the others falling six miles to their death in a shattered jet must have felt. Hashash scurried away like a cat-sized New York City rat. Nazy and her folks could never find him, that is until now. It was incredible work just finding out who did it. How am I going to get a shot at him, or will he be gunned down trying to escape like the Peter Lorre character in Casablanca trying to get out of Rick's cafe?

Nazy brought Duncan back to earth as she said, "I believe Hashash is still alive, and we think we know where he is. I have offered a $25 million reward for his capture; $1 million for proof of his death. The President will place pressure on Algeria's leaders to find him and hand him over."

"*Twenty-five* million dollars? That will get some action, I'm sure."

"Alive, preferably alive. We'd like to ask him a few questions."

"You and several other intel agencies. I just don't see him giving up. He keeps buying his way out of trouble."

"We don't want him abused by the Algerians. We will have to deal with the Algerian secret police network. With them it's still a hit-or-miss proposition."

Duncan said, "Let's see if my French is good enough...that is the *Département du Renseignement et de la Sécurité,* the DRS, I believe."

She said, "That's very good, darling. The DRS, or Department of Intelligence and Security is led by General Mohamed Mediene, also known as *Toufik.* Old FLN." (National Liberation Front.)

Hunter responded, "In French, *Front de Libération Nationale.*"

Nazy said, "Somehow, *Toufik* has survived all the treachery and intrigue within Algeria's vast security infrastructure. He's rich, and he'd sell his mother if he could get $25 million for her."

Duncan knew a little. "What I know of him is he knows all the dirty little secrets of their government's officials and where all the bodies are buried."

"That is because he buried them!" Nazy rolled her eyes. "*Toufik* runs the detention centers. When we pulled al-Qaeda out of Afghanistan, our field officers told the detainees we would send them to *Toufik's place* unless they talked. Most talked. They knew of *Toufik's* detention centers where detainees were subject to torture."

"So, they talked."

Nazy agreed, "They talked, but they were not the leaders we thought they were and rarely said anything useful."

Ignorance is bliss. Hunter nodded, "Algeria is like Pakistan and Syria. Their secret police have to deal with lunatic religious mass murderers, not regular criminals. Didn't he say, 'I am General *Toufik, the God of Algeria?'* Hasn't he benefited financially from his position? Doesn't he have stakes in Algeria's oil and real estate sectors?"

Nazy nodded and explained, "The rise of *Toufik* coincided with the emergence of an Islamic militancy that threatened to topple the long-entrenched FLN regime. *Toufik* directly took part in an election that was canceled by the government because of Muslim Brotherhood infiltration. That sparked a brutal civil war. Nearly 200,000 people, mostly civilians, were massacred by militants and government forces."

When Nazy stopped talking he thought, *Her Oxford accent reminds me of a British college professor. It's still intoxicating. She believes if Hashash is still alive that Tofu, er, Toufik will turn him over for the money?* After a moment Hunter asked, "Photographs?"

"Some. Positive ID. They're three years old. He wasn't the target of the photos, what they call a *photobomb*, but we have him in the Casbah. We believe the regular police have been paid off to protect him. We'll offer more for the DRS to take him alive."

He quietly nodded, soaking it all in. "A bidding war for a murderer. The things we do with taxpayer's money. Any other intel?"

"No, darling Duncan." Nazy was flipping her hair around to shake some body into it which was arousing Duncan. When she finished fluffing her hair, she seductively adjusted the earring in her right ear. He dragged her into his lap and kissed her for a long time, slowly and sensuously.

After a few more kisses, Duncan tried to put a stop to it by bringing up the eighty-year-old financier of terrorists. He asked, "And, uh, Scorpii?"

She ignored his question. She had other things on her mind. She draped her arms around him and pressed into him. She kissed him playfully, passionately. Hunter gave up on reading briefs; the files had fallen on the floor, anyway. He was prepared to really get with the program when Nazy pushed away and asked, "Is Coffey going to work out? I think Bill is waiting for you to train Coffey so you can help him on the campaign."

He allowed some distance between them. *Is Coffey going to work out?* "Since when has that SEAL needed help on anything? No darling, I'm thinking we need a vacation first and then some help."

You have ulterior motives? I'm surprised. She thought about the possibilities for a few seconds and asked, "Wasn't it your idea he run for president?"

"I shouldn't get blamed for that. Yes, I said years ago once all the terrorists were removed from the *Matrix*, he should run for president. Politicians' reputations are built on accomplishments and to say, 'When I came to the job there were sixty-seventy men on the FBI's Most Wanted Terrorist list and now there are none; the world is a better place to live with those criminals removed.' I mean, he's the perfect person to be president, but I was kidding. Or was I?"

Nazy looked as if her feelings were hurt. "President Hernandez values your counsel above all others. He wanted you to be his National Security Advisor, but you turned him down. Bill will be a harder person to turn down. We know honest, trustworthy help is rare in this town. He's not a political animal, and he will need help."

"Bill knows what he's doing. I'm helping. He's got the jet. Carlos delivered the motor coach. And my body armor. And he has a wife. What else does he need?"

"You."

"I don't think so." Hunter closed his eyes and slowly kissed her several times before asking, "How wedded are you to the Director's job?"

She gently shifted her position in his lap to look at him. She recognized he was probing. But could she tell him her innermost thoughts? They had been through so much together. She said, "Well, you know I'm not. I never wanted that job, even though I know why Bill designated me to take his place. *We* need continuity. Our work, *his* work, *Greg's work* over there is not yet done. Rothwell and Carey ruined the Agency's reputation and helped realize Mazibuike's vision of infiltrating the CIA with his radical Muslim friends. Greg and Bill stopped the bleeding, as you like to say, and I'm certain we are within one or two intelligence officers of being completely free of all of 3M's infiltrators. We still have some *dark state* actors but I don't think too many of them are in the decision-making process. Greg, and especially Bill, kicked them off the property; now we can get back to doing what the IC does best. Why the question?"

"I know a guy.... A *Bubba*."

"*Coffey?*" Her eyebrows almost touched in surprise. *There is no way he's a Bubba! Not one of Duncan's Bubbas!*

"Oh, hell no. White, Christian, male. Smart. A general who I actually like and have known for a long time. He's a fellow patriot. *A Bubba.* One of *the Irregulars*. He could tell I'm one of *the Irregulars* too. He even said so. Which makes me think we are not alone in fighting our battle with the Dems."

One of the Irregulars? The resistance? She nodded to convey she understood. "There are a lot of SIS (Senior Intelligence Service) over there who think they should be the next Director. They're not thrilled with me, and I'm so busy. I'm working a hundred hours a week as it is. We are working a hundred hours a week."

"See, we need a vacation." Nazy nodded. Duncan continued, "Your guys are not *Bubbas*. Not *Irregulars*. You would find none of them at the *Pumpkin Papers Irregulars Dinner*, and that is telling. You shot up the food chain and passed a lot of deadwood along the way. CIA is still a meritocracy, but Bill said he wanted you to be the Director. Replace one member of the resistance, one of *the Irregulars*, with another. It's not political grandstanding."

"I know. He just wants what is best for the country and the Agency. Continuity. Sometimes I think I'm the only member of the *resistance* over there. After going to the *Irregulars Dinner*, I recognize not only are we few, but we are *different*. We're older. We see things *differently*. There are not many of us, but Bill knows I'll continue his agenda. He's afraid we'll just get another political appointee. We know we don't want another infiltrator in there. Allegiance to the United States is always assumed; sometimes we are surprised how cleverly they hide their socialist backgrounds."

Hunter considered her insight. *McGee was afraid his replacement would just be another political appointee? Would POTUS really do that? We need one of the Irregulars in there. I need to talk to him.* Duncan had another more selfish thought. "I really think we should go on a vacation; get away from this place for a while. What do you think?"

Nazy thought about the question. *He wants to have some "us" time. This work can be overwhelming. We really haven't had a vacation. President Hernandez or Bill or Greg always summon us back for work.* She kissed him and cooed, "What did you have in mind?"

"I'm thinking a ski trip. There's a place in Canada. Ski all day, hot tubs and fireplaces at night. Maybe a European river cruise. Then I need to go to Belgium for an airplane."

"But, I don't know how to ski."

"I'll teach you."

"You'll teach me? I'm such a clutz when it comes to those things."

Duncan grinned. "You're athletic; you're coordinated. You have the best legs on the Eastern Seaboard! You'll make the perfect snow bunny!"

She loved his compliments even if she didn't believe them. "When are you thinking?"

"Maybe before Christmas when your place shuts down for the holidays. It's someone else's turn to be essential personnel."

"I don't know if I can do it. There is so much work since Bill left."

He pulled her closer. "Not trying to put words in your mouth, baby. Are you saying you don't want to admit you need help?"

Duncan could be right. She nodded.

"How about letting me see what I can do?"

You? How are you going to find me help?

Duncan grinned and said, "Isn't work over? Shouldn't you be focusing on us right about now? Do we need to waste some more water?"

Nazy smiled then playfully head-butted him out of the chair all the way to the carpet. By the time they got to the bathroom they had lost all of their clothes. Duncan reached out and turned on the water. Nazy stepped inside, turned around, closed her eyes, and let the water saturate her hair and cascade over her body.

CHAPTER 28

November 12, 2019

They said goodbye in the hotel room with kisses and hugs and promises to call. Time seemed to stop until the moment Nazy dragged herself away and threw up her arms. She was a working woman with incredible responsibilities. One more crushing kiss and a little pressure on her tongue. Then she just had to go; her security detail had waited long enough. Nazy had one more show to perform.

One of Hunter's saddest visions was watching his wife close the door behind her. *I helped shave those legs to make them the best legs on the planet, and on the callipygian scale that derrière is a ten!*

With Nazy gone, Hunter recovered his surveillance cameras, lazily packed his bag, shouldered his weapon, and finding new energy, took the stairway down with his hand on the grip of the semi-holstered Colt *Python*. Safely in the limo and into traffic, he lamented all he had to do in the next few weeks now that Link Coffey had agreed to enter the program. The CIA would have to update Coffey's background investigation, update his clearance, get him to take a polygraph. Then he could be officially read in on the *Noble Savage* special access program.

Hunter promised himself he would consider *an extraction*. He was unaware of anyone doing anything so outrageous; so daring, so audacious. *It would be one for the record books. And that's the problem. What did Baltasar Gracian say? Let someone else take the hit.*

Duncan had arranged for a charter to take him from Ronald Reagan Washington National Airport to Hondo, Texas. He needed to retrieve his other jet, an older Gulfstream G-4, specifically a GIV-SP, or Special Purpose. With McGee using the G-550 as his campaign aircraft, Hunter would have to fall back on the jet he had had since 2002.

He had optimized it over the years for use as a *rendition aircraft.* The GIV-SP's cabin was fairly sterile. There were two seats and places to lash down multiple stretchers for heavily sedated terrorists who were bound and gagged, wearing diapers for sanitary purposes and black bags over their heads. And they were shrink-wrapped. *Their names were immaterial. Some high value detainees the CIA wanted to interrogate rather than exterminate, a beard with a bad attitude with a million-dollar missile. These nameless, faceless murderers would get a gamboge jumpsuit, three culturally sensitive meals a day, their very own Qur'an, and a private room at America's terrorist holding complex at Guantanamo Bay, Cuba. GITMO was for the worst of the worst terrorists that American forces captured on the battlefield in the Middle East. And the Agency liked to interrogate them. Liked isn't the right word.*

On the way to the BWI Airport, he reflected on how he acquired both aircraft. The DEA watched and tracked the tail numbers of the jets of known drug cartel leaders. The GIV-SP had been registered to a company in Bogotá, but surveillance of the aircraft revealed it was a Colombian drug lord's private jet. It had been seized by the Drug Enforcement Agency when it landed in Florida carrying the drug lord's wife and children. For 17 years the GIV-SP had been on loan to one of the Agency's former front companies, a research laboratory with a new owner, a Texas enterprise, Quiet Aero Systems.

The G-550 had been a brand-new, virtually zero-time jet that was officially and legitimately changing ownership.

He shot me down and thought he had killed me, but I parachuted to safety. I surprised him and his security detail. What an insane night that was! He was the only one who ever seemed to know I was out there. He was briefed by the old CIA Director, that lecherous Democrat pig named Rothwell. After I blew Abu Manu's brains out, I found his inventory of shoulder-launched, surface-to-air missiles. And his containers of gold coins. I had no other way off the continent so I took his jet. My crumpled flaming YO-3A for his G-550 with that new car smell.

Hunter had flown the new Gulfstream to Texas. Since all the ownership papers were blank as required by the ransom demands, Hunter claimed it. And the ransom of $100 million in Gold Eagles was offloaded into his hangar in Hondo, Texas. Finder's keepers.

And over $3 billion in ransom payments were recovered that night and returned to the U.S. Treasury. President Hernandez considered Hunter a hero.

As Hunter reflected on McGee's need for aircraft, he realized the flying requirements of a presidential candidate must be significant. The G-550 was nearing its maintenance check and it would need new rubber. Tires. With a momentary frown he knew what he must do for McGee. *I'll have the mechanics install the seating we removed turning the GIV-SP into a rendition jet. I have other ways to travel incognito. Not as fast. Old school speed the commie tail watchers might look at but don't report and track as a government executive transport.*

I will not like trading my nights in Washington with Nazy in order to train Coffey in Texas. But the only remote landing strips to practice lights-out nighttime takeoffs and landings in the Super Cub, Schweizer, and the YO-3A are in Texas. And I haven't hit our old haunt, the Azteca in Hondo, in some time. McGee will be so jealous. Aw, hell. I know he could use a terrific meal. We have to do a jet swap, anyway. I'll send him the GIV-SP until the G-550 comes out of maintenance. We'll even send chimichangas with the jet. That's the ticket!

CHAPTER 29

November 15, 2019

Super Cubs can be frightfully difficult to fly if you haven't ever been behind the control stick of an airplane with a tail wheel. After fifteen touch-and-gos, *Maverick* instructed Coffey to land so they could get lunch and *Maverick* could debrief the flight. They drove into Hondo to the Texas landmark, the *El Restaurante Azteca* for exquisite Mexican food. Chips and salsa and water were delivered to the table as the men sat down.

Coffey asked, "What's good?"

Maverick, in his best impersonation of Elvis Presley, sneered and shook his head and said, "*Everythang!*"

"What do you usually get?" Coffey asked after he rolled his eyes at the terrible Elvis impression.

"The chimichangas, of course." After the waitress left the menus for them, *Maverick* surreptitiously pulled out a *Growler*. He flicked it on and observed the television sets in the room. Using a rheostat on the side of the green electronic device, Hunter turned the wheel until the televisions started to act up; the Mexican *novella* on the tube went from nice picture to interference as *Maverick* adjusted the minute inconspicuous rheostat. After a few seconds he had the *novella* back on.

Coffey said, "I've been meaning to ask, what the hell is that thing?"

Hunter moved the light-neon green rubberized device out of the way so no one would set a plate on it. "*Growler.*"

That still didn't tell Coffey anything.

Maverick explained in a whisper, "It generates a bubble of electronic noise and prevents anyone from eavesdropping on our conversation. When the lamp illuminates it indicates the device is energized." He handed it to Coffey to inspect. Hunter continued, "And it does, um, other *things*."

Coffey noticed it had multiple thumb-actuated rheostats that were not marked. He looked under his brows and asked, "Like what?"

Maverick smiled. "Well, let's see. If you put it on top of a transformer that delivers electricity to a house or a block of houses it will disrupt the power for a few minutes. If you put it near a voting tabulator, it will interfere with the computer inside causing it to not take any input. Things like that."

"You can screw with a signal from an insulated cable?" Coffey returned the device to *Maverick* who found the correct thumbwheel and the rocked it back and forth in perfect timing of the television's picture transitioning from clear to electronic noise. "That is just *stupefying!*"

Maverick smirked, turned the gain down until the television was again watchable, and put the device back on the table.

Coffey said, "That is quite the parlor trick. So, no one can listen to our conversations electronically?"

"That's right."

"What did you mean it could shut down a voting tabulator machine? I don't know what that is."

Maverick continued to smile between chips and salsa.

Coffey thought, *And, he won't tell me. Oh well, maybe the timing isn't good. But the chips are good and the salsa is terrific.*

Hunter began, "How does it feel to be back flying?"

"It's definitely different flying the Super Cub. It seems like my body and mind have been programmed for flying jets. This going slow and pointing the nose to where you want to land will take a while to get used to."

Maverick said, "It will. It's a completely new skill. You have to be reprogrammed. Our advantage is you're comfortable in the air; flying doesn't scare you, doesn't make you sick. You've had the best training and you lived to talk about it. You'll pick up the communication and navigation gear in no time. Instead of NATOPS manuals, you'll have to study navigation and communication and equipment manuals and handbooks. All you really need is practice and learn to use all the new technology in the old airplane. But it's intuitive. You're doing well. We'll spend some more time in the Cub, and then we'll go out for a day session with a Schweizer motor glider."

"A Schweizer motor glider?"

"Oh yes, the Air Force Academy kids flew them in Colorado Springs for several years. We have a Schweizer SGM 2-37; it's a side-by-side, fixed-gear, low-wing motor glider. Fun to fly. Once you master the 2-37 at night under NVGs, we'll transition into the retractable *Yo-Yo*. Sound, ok?"

"That actually sounds glorious, *Maverick*."

After the meal, *Maverick* talked with the owner who said he would comply with Hunter's request. Then *Maverick* debriefed each of Coffey's landings. They were friends; there was no animosity. Hunter mentioned when Coffey started too high, when he recovered too low, and when he put the airplane in the proper attitude for landing. *Maverick* said, "I'm pleased with your progress. Over time, you'll develop a consistent daytime sight picture and will automatically respond with appropriate stick and rudder when you're out of position for landing. Unlike the Air Force, we were trained for precision landings. Land in the box. So, when you are comfortable with the Cub during the day then we'll get some night landings with an illuminated runway. A couple more day sessions solo, then we'll do several night sessions dual. Finally, we'll go under the goggles for no runway light landings."

Coffey remembered the difficulty of night qualifying in the F-4 *Phantom II*. *First there was field carrier landing practice (FCLP) which comprised 200 precision touch and gos at night. If all went well, you'd go out to one the big decks for your first arrested landing at night. Nothing gets the heart rate up like a night landing on an aircraft carrier. All the pilots in the squadron except Maverick dreaded carrier operations at night. Hunter just considered it part of the challenge. Maybe that was the reason Maverick was always the number one carrier pilot on the boat and in the squadron. Precision night carrier landings separated the men from the boys. To him it was a game like learning to play racquetball like a pro. Coffey said,* "Kind of like FCLPs."

Maverick nodded, "The Navy's method works, and I'm not about to change it. It's what I had to do because there were no YO-3A pilots to serve as instructors for flying it at night. I was extremely cautious. The airplane wasn't mine and I would have hated trashing it during landing. I've been expecting training my replacement for several years. I never expected you to be the guy, but I'm glad you're here."

"I am glad I'm here, too."

Maverick and Coffey headed back to the Hondo airport for more day touch and gos. After another dozen landings *Maverick* noticed they had company; a rental car was approaching the company hangar. Hunter was expecting the vehicle and instructed Coffey to make the next landing a full stop and let him out at the hangar.

Maverick told Coffey he was ready to fly solo. "Get some touch and gos. I have some business to tend to."

After *Maverick* disembarked the Super Cub, Coffey taxied back to the runway for run-ups. He waited for the control tower's permission to take the runway, but he was more interested in watching *Maverick* talk on his *BlackBerry* and to the two men who got out of their car. The men were like twins, both were about six-foot tall, wore Oakley sunglasses and white short-sleeve shirts with standard issue captain epaulettes — four gold bars. From the back seat of the automobile, they took black leather flight bags and dark flight jackets like the Air Force issued their pilots. *Ferry pilots. Maverick said they were expected.*

He was in no hurry, so Coffey continued observing the interaction of the three pilots. The business jet pilots greeted *Maverick* heartily; he opened the airstairs for them and showed them the Gulfstream. The old GIV-SP had a somewhat faded base paint job; the formerly brilliant glossy white showed its accumulated hours in the air. The paint was dull with tired red and gold trim, but it had fresh tires. It looked as if *Maverick* was giving them a brief.

Link Coffey knew part of the brief. Take the GIV-SP to Kerrville, Texas where a team of mechanics would go over it from nose to tail. They would perform a scuff and buff, a new coat of paint and add new red and gold trim streaks. The pilots would have access to a rental car and enjoy the inimitable accommodations of downtown Kerrville. They were to remain until all the maintenance work had been done on the GIV-SP. They had McGee's campaign manager's cell number and would rendezvous with the campaign to perform the jet swap. *Maverick* had let McGee know about the plan.

Coffey decided he had seen enough and went flying. He could tell immediately *Maverick's* weight had been an additional drag factor. The Super Cub jumped into the air quickly at takeoff RPMs.

CHAPTER 30

November 15, 2019

The Executive Director, High Captain El Masri delivered *Die Lage* with his usual aplomb and professionalism and the buttery-like delivery of a Tijuana used car salesman. Every continent was discussed, including Antarctica. He saved North America for last.

Supreme Lord Chancellor Scorpii expressed some irritation he had been made to wait so long for information on the *Amerikaners*. His interest in former CIA Director McGee and the Acting Director, Nazy Cunningham was bubbling over.

El Masri read the analysis of the situation in *Amerika*. It was comprehensive but missed the mark. *Adherence to the Qur'an would restore national values.* Newspapers and cable news networks repeated the presidential candidate's every word, saturating the airwaves with Democrat Party propaganda to counter every move candidate Bill McGee made. Dispatches from local mosques detailed McGee's speeches and movements.

Scorpii wanted the essentials on McGee first. He was head-down, reading the summary when he asked, "Are measures being taken?"

"*Ja....*" El Masri's German was exceptional, yet still included hints of an Arabic accent. He was aware of what Scorpii articulated obliquely. He said, "*Das Amerikaner* Democrat Party and the media berate him every day, *mein Kanzler.*" Implied were the silent weapons of the media, the tools of propaganda. Scorpii held up an arthritic hand. He didn't want to know the specifics, and El Masri knew better than to offer them. Scorpii asked, "How is McGee responding to media pressure? Do we need to do more?"

El Masri provided, "*Das Amerikaner* is proving to be a formidable candidate. He's supporting candidates opposed to our agenda, and he's receiving more funding for them. He's well-versed in anti-propaganda. His voice and vision are outraising our contributions."

Scorpii slammed the papers down and struggled to stand up. He said, "Whatever it takes. We have been close before. We have lost all the leaders the Brotherhood said were essential to their plans. I feel we are losing ground." Scorpii found purchase and leaned against the edge of the conference table. He rolled his eyes and thought, *It feels good to be out of a chair, if only for a few seconds.*

El Masri stepped around the table and placed himself in Scorpii's direct vision. "Our people in *Amerika* have a track on him; we have his schedule and can predict where he goes. This is a good development; this is what *mein Kanzler* desires! *Overwatch* has superior intelligence on his transportation. His movements. We just need some time to organize an effective *interception.*"

Scorpii enjoyed the news. For a minute he forgot he was standing and reflected how he built *Overwatch*, what *das Amerikaners* call *Tailwatchers.*

Only I saw a need for tracking those capitalist countries' executive aircraft. Once Moscow heard of it, they wanted it. For the longest time I got nothing for my effort. I wanted complete control of the operation, but the Kremlin was correct, to do it right required resources which were beyond my scope. If I didn't capitulate, I would be left with nothing; they might have even killed me. They gave me no choice. There's great power in coercion. Another silent weapon....

There was a time where I could help them and they were appreciative. I received the benefit of registering the NGO, giving it a name, Overwatch. Das Amerikaners' bastardization of the name is vulgar. Tailwatchers. Bah!

We put the main office across the street from the Lubyanka. With my money and the KGB's people and organizational skills, Overwatch works. I knew it would, but I was surprised by other entities that were interested in our services! The KGB had a listing.... The Islamic Underground and the Muslim Brotherhood paid handsomely to know from which airport the evil Cee ah a aircraft were operating. And I could hide my involvement.

El Masri helped Scorpii back to his seat and finished his brief. El Masri said, "*Mein Kanzler,* as we feared the African and Middle East operations have collapsed. As soon as a new leader is identified and installed, they disappear or are eliminated."

Scorpii suddenly missed his old friend, General Roustaie, and blurted out, "What is the status of the device recovered from Iran?"

El Masri was familiar with all the circumstances of the device recovered from Iran. Scorpii had warned General Roustaie and the leaders of the Iranian Revolutionary Guard Corps not to gloat on *das Amerikaners'* inability to find the four *mujahedeen* in Iran. But Iran did gloat and the dreaded *Cee ah a* did find them and by killing them in a most unusual way, hurt the Islamic Underground movement. It signified the Iranian Revolutionary Guard Corps were not sufficiently protected in their own country from the *Cee ah a's* lethal drones.

Privately, El Masri had warned General Roustaie again that the Iranian Revolutionary Guard Corps invited many more unnecessary and unwanted reprisals from the *Cee ah a*. The four *mujahedeen* had killed hundreds of *Amerikaners*, and they had escaped punishment individually. It was a time to lay low. But *das Amerikaners' Cee ah a* didn't forget and was vindictive. There would never be a time for celebration. There would never be a marker or shrine to show Islamic conquest.

The Iranian leadership demanded vengeance. *Das Amerikaner president will pay with his life!* Scorpii advised against any retaliation. But the ayatollahs wouldn't reconsider. With the death of General Roustaie, Scorpii had lost a rational voice in a country full of madmen. An assassination attempt on a U.S. president by the government of Iran would be a death sentence for millions of Iranians.

Under the guise of a wedding, at the home of a newly promoted general in the Iranian Revolutionary Guard Corps they had feted the *mujahedeen* during a celebration extolling the Islamic Underground's success killing *das Amerikaner* infidels. Then while everyone was having a good time, eight tiny silent drones had flown over the compound's walls and attacked in a swarm the most famous *mujahedeen* to have ever escaped the vindictive arm of *das Amerikaners'* intelligence services.

It was sheer pandemonium for several seconds as onlookers were stunned at the spectacle, mesmerized by the swarming flying black devices that herded the men into a circle. What no one could know was during each pass in front of the faces of the *mujahedeen*, the tiny black and soundless drone's cameras and circuitries were systematically checking the faces of each *mujahedeen* against an artificial intelligence (AI) face-mapping program. When four of the drones had verified their targets, they shot forward, as if they were aiming for the *mujahedeen's* foreheads. An explosive charge detonated at contact. The report was graphic. The *mujahedeens'* heads blew apart.

The four *mujahedeen* lay in a heap in the center of a hundred stunned guests. They had been executed by silent flying assassins. One device lay on the ground, virtually intact. It looked to have been damaged from flying debris when the explosive charge went off. Its own charge had failed to detonate. General Mostafa Javad Roustaie picked up the *Cee ah a's* device and held it in his hand. He recognized its power as the future destroyer of infidels.

After the Islamic Revolutionary Guard Corps had studied the damaged device for over a year, taking it apart and reverse engineering it to the limits of their ability, General Roustaie hand delivered it to Scorpii. Scorpii passed the device to El Masri whose intelligence team had investigated and developed a working, flyable although ersatz copy. El Masri confirmed the recovered device had been replicated.

Scorpii barked, "Are you sure it's an *exact* copy?"

"*Ja, mein Kanzler.*" El Masri thought, *The device's facial recognition system was twenty years ahead of anything in German labs, meaning it was definitely made by the Cee ah a. We have a workable copy. It's not silent; we cannot sufficiently quiet the four rotors and we cannot get the others to swarm with it. There are some aspects of precision, coordination, and acuity we cannot replicate even through reverse engineering. We owe a debt of gratitude to General Roustaie for bringing it to us before he passed away.*

The old man looked at El Masri for a few seconds and wondered what he was hiding. After several laborious breaths, Scorpii asked, "What is the brief on the new Cee ah a Director?"

El Masri extracted a photograph that was in the file, he handed it to the Supreme Lord Chancellor. Its significance was not lost on him. *With this photo the AI program in the device will be completed. Maybe one of these days I'll use it.*

Rho Schwarz Scorpii handled the picture of Nazy Cunningham as if it was the most delicate paper he had ever encountered. He had seen a picture of her before when she was only an intelligence analyst. That was the day he had forced El Masri to put her on the list. *They protect her above all others. There is a reason. She is most dangerous. She could disrupt our operations in the Middle East and Africa.* Scorpii had dreamed of turning her, having her work for him at the highest levels of the intelligence community. But she wouldn't be turned, so he had ordered El Masri to have her neutralized. She should have died in Algeria. Professionals would have been successful, but amateurs had botched the job. Again. How did she get away? In his journal he wrote how disgusted he was that she hadn't been made to suffer. *Suffering sends a message. Rescue was not the message I wished to send!*

Scorpii made a teepee with his fingers and stared at the wall. He barked, "*Report!*"

El Masri knew when the Chancellor made that gesture, he was reminiscing. *But he would never share his private thoughts. He saves those for his journal.* He began the brief on Nazy Cunningham.

"*Mein Kanzler,* her given name is Marwa Kamal. She was educated as an attorney in the U.S."

"School?"

"Yale Law, like her father who was the chief justice of the Jordan Supreme Court. She was previously married; husband, Waleed, a wealthy Saudi. She left him, entered the United States on a student visa, Amman to Boston."

Scorpii almost fondled the photograph. He focused on a cross suspended on a delicate gold chain around her neck.

"As you can see, she's a striking beauty, an intoxicating combination of intrigue and innocence. She speaks with a British accent which she earned while attending school in England, Switzerland, and Oxford. She's tall with olive skin, high cheekbones, and a round nose. It's difficult for anyone to discern her nationality. Her mother was a relative of Mohammad Reza Pahlavi. Eyes; emerald green with hazel flecks."

Information I could do without....

"We have anecdotal evidence she was affiliated with a mosque in Boston ...."

"One of ours?"

"*Ja, mein Kanzler.* Most interesting. We have reports the imam coerced her to spy on two men at the Naval War College in 2003. Newport, Rhode Island. The imam wanted her to take their computers, but during that timeframe the mosque caught fire and burned down."

Scorpii looked up for a moment but ignored the fire connection. "Names?"

"The civilian named Duncan Hunter and Marwa Kamal met several times at an athletic facility and a restaurant before she disappeared. The Brotherhood's international students assigned there conducted surveillance on all the special operations personnel who had recently been in the field in Afghanistan. You'll find this interesting, *mein Kanzler*, it was reported this Duncan Hunter and Navy Captain William McGee were inseparable at the school. Professionally. Privately, McGee had a family and this Hunter liked the women."

Scorpii raised his head and furrowed his eyebrows. *That was totally unexpected!* He croaked, "*She was supposed to be surveilling this Hunter and McGee? She was to get access to their computers?*"

El Masri knew the man would be pleased. "*Jawohl, mein Kanzler.* Regarding this Duncan Hunter character, we are still gathering intel on him, but he was a Marine Corps officer, a pilot, and is buried at their Arlington Cemetery. But most astonishing, *mein Kanzler*, according to multiple reports the President and the *Cee ah a* Director attended his funeral; full military honors. This is unprecedented."

Scorpii said, "He must have been very special."

El Masri handed Scorpii the supporting documents.

A visibly troubled Scorpii coughed blood into a handkerchief, then put the monogrammed square away. He again made a teepee with his fingers, stared at El Masri, and raised a hand for El Masri to stop. *The woman and McGee's orbits intertwined? In 2003? Who is this, Duncan Hunter?* Scorpii lifted the article to read it and asked, "Where did you get this?"

"*Mein Kanzler*, our international intelligence services."

"This woman was...." Scorpii was searching for something. He knew he was close.

El Masri continued the thought, "She disappeared as Marwa Kamal and emerged in the *Cee ah a* as Nazy Cunningham. Her previous assignments were Analyst, Chief of the Middle East Division, Director of their National Counter Terrorism Center, the Director of Operations, and now the Acting *Cee ah a* Director. At various times local teams have tried to eliminate her."

Scorpii said, "They failed. They have failed directly or through surrogates. Failure." He calmed down after the outburst. He looked at a surveillance photograph. *Her beauty is understated. She looks like a painting, not like any of the women in the camps who did whatever they could to hide me and keep me from harm.* Scorpii returned the photograph to El Masri and looked up at him. For the second time in ten years, he cut his fingers across his throat. Scorpii nearly slurred his words, "She's the *Resistance*. She's brilliant and accomplished and has an eye for finding and interrupting the plans of the *mujehadeen*. They have kept her hidden. Out of the public eye. Unseen. Those are not the actions taken by government officials for normal employees. That makes her very unusual and incredibly dangerous. *Die hündin* must not escape this time."

El Masri nodded. *I want to get this picture of die hündin loaded into some drones. I will go to das Amerikaner's lair. We will do to her what the Cee ah a did to our mujehadeen. I won't fail.*

Once El Masri took his leave, and Scorpii was alone he huffed several times. He would need medicine soon. With trembling hands, he withdrew his journal from his desk and began to write. He recalled the events of the day chronologically. He let his mind and the quill wander across unsullied pages.

CHAPTER 31

November 17, 2019

Before daybreak hundreds of soldiers and policemen poured from their barracks, mounted trucks, were transported to, and took up offensive positions around the Casbah.

Residents of the Casbah who witnessed the invasion of armed men had seen it before. Every few years dozens of directors, cameramen, extras and movie stars from whatever motion picture studio came to Algiers for the city's marquee draw — the Casbah of Algiers. But this time there were no cameras, this time there were no extras. This time it was for real. Hundreds of law enforcement and military men in black uniforms bristling with black weaponry, black helmets, and black radios blocked the many exits and descended into the bowels and passageways leading to narrow apartments, some still marked with the fluted columns of original Roman Empire architecture. To visitors, it looked as if the police and military were genuinely looking for someone hiding in the Casbah and suddenly, dozens of smartphones were taking pictures or videos.

In the movies the Algerian Casbah was a strangely alluring and romantic place. Thieves regarded the impenetrable Casbah as their stronghold. It was also their prison, for they would surely be captured if they dared venture outside the citadel's mazelike, tortuous walkways of the eburnean walls.

The Casbah of Algiers was founded on the ruins of old Icosium, a Berber city that became an important Roman colony in the 10th century. It was built on a hill stretching towards the sea. Even today, visitors could find masonry and mosques dating from the 17th century and towering minarets with ovoid cupola points from the time of the Ottomans. The ancient Casbah was magnificent and encompassed several palaces that had housed the Pasha who had lived there for years.

Today's Casbah was mysterious and sinister, and was the area's greatest tourist attraction.

After several minutes of searching, the police net crackled with the news the superannuated, terrorist bombmaker from Libya had been found. No one had tipped him off. Ahmad Khalid Saleh Hashash was in custody.

Questions not for visitors but for residents: Would Hashash live another day? Would he talk if he was told he was going to *Toufik's* place? Would they take him to a Toufik-run detention center for transfer to Interpol? Would he be transferred to the Americans who would come and get him? The CIA had wanted him for a long time. Or would the Algerian secret police march him straight to the guillotine?

When Hashash was dragged through the headquarters of the secret police to the feet of General Toufik, he begged to be killed. *"Don't turn me over to the Americans!"* he screamed. *"Kill me! Kill me!"*

Resplendent in his uniform, Toufik condescendingly declared, "The Americans want you dead or alive. Scotland signed your death warrant. It makes no difference to me. You have already escaped one executioner. You'll not escape the law again!" General Toufik said to the group of gendarmes holding Hashash, "Take him to the courtyard, but wait until someone from the U.S. Embassy is there to witness his execution."

CHAPTER 32

November 17, 2019

The rally at the Des Moines, Iowa airport was attended by 30,000 men, women, and children. It was a raucous and boisterous affair; only a handful of presidential candidates could craft a truly esemplastic message. After the rally a motorcade took Rear Admiral Bill McGee and Eastwood to one of the local television stations for a town hall interview led by Dory Eastwood.

Bill McGee was warmly welcomed by the audience. Colonel Eastwood thanked the network for hosting and informing Iowans on the important political positions held by Rear Admiral McGee. Then he asked McGee if he was ready to take questions from the highly intelligent and politically discriminating people of Iowa.

The first question was from a college student. Her hair was pulled back in a ponytail; she wore oversized glasses, torn denims, and an oversized sweatshirt with the name of a university on the front. She also wore a scowl. "Admiral McGee, you have asserted there was cheating by the Democrats during the last election and they will cheat in this election. What proof do you have?"

McGee thanked the student for her question and turned to moderator Eastwood. "That is a good question, but not for the reason you think it is. Our very intelligent college student demands to know what 'proof' we have when she knows or should know that instantaneous '*proof*' is an impossibility. This impossibility also illustrates how the left controls and shapes the narrative. The wording steers the discussion into the desired area. Like verbal chess, they work to back the king into a corner where he cannot survive."

"It's raw propaganda to demand proof, because it takes months and years of investigation to assemble sufficient *evidence* for such proof. Our student demands an answer now, but that is impossible to give. Think of what it takes to build a Boeing 747. One can demand a jet but must wait a good long while for it to be assembled or for one to be flown into the Des Moines airport."

"So, let me be frank; no one has proof and the professional left plays word games. But look at what we do have, we have facts and evidence. That is what prosecutors need to build a case. Facts and evidence. Let's look at this rationally and logically — not words the political left often uses. A policeman comes upon a man lying in the middle of the road. Is he dead? Has he been shot or stabbed or did he have a heart attack? Is he unconscious? Is he drunk? Did he stagger out of the bar across the street and fall down? There's proof he's in the middle of the road because we can see him, but we don't know why. How did it happen? We have to develop and collect evidence in order to make a determination."

"This happens all the time. Just recently, we had a U.S. Attorney announce a New Jersey-based Democratic political consultant admitted hiring two men to kill a longtime associate who had worked for him on various political campaigns. The consultant pleaded guilty to one count of conspiracy to commit murder for hire. It was a callous and violent crime, and the defendant was as responsible as the two men who shot him. The defendant admitted to arranging and paying for a murder by two other people. His admission of guilt will bring some sense of closure to the victim's family who have been left to wonder — for nearly eight years — who murdered their loved one. It took investigators eight years of sifting through the evidence to find out what happened."

"In the absence of proof, lefties demand we go directly to their conclusion with no investigation and no analysis of the facts and findings. It's as if they want you to trust them, that their word is sufficient. Do it their way. But reasonable people see this is the wrong way. This also exactly demonstrates the difference in the parties. One party's goal is to find the cause and a conclusion; and the other doesn't want to find the cause. Their goal is to create chaos and confusion. Demanding proof is to create chaos and confusion."

"Remember, this is politics. Politics is a dirty game most often played between good guys and criminals. When the good guys are in power, they keep the bad guys away from the society the good guys have created, and when the bad guys are in power, they keep the good guys from stopping their bad ways. Follow me?"

"There are dozens of possibilities when an authority figure begins the investigation. Maybe someone has a photo or a video and demands immediate justice. Some policemen will provide that immediate answer, knowing they will probably be wrong. But with the addition of new evidence, the answer can be amended."

The men and women in the studio audience sat in rapt attention. Even the woman who asked the question was visibly loosening up.

McGee continued, "What is viewed in law enforcement circles as naturally occurring delays in the investigative process can be viewed politically, as if law enforcement is trying to hide something because they're not working 24/7. Around the clock. Humans are not infallible, but when leftist politics are injected into an investigation, then the investigation will turn into a circus, or worse. Insinuation is a tremendous tool of propaganda. We shouldn't seek the left's immediate and illegitimate cries of proof; we should seek the facts. Police departments shouldn't allow themselves to be manipulated with cries of where's the proof. *Demand* is a propaganda tool."

"A political party who has been caught doing wrong, cannot allow a full, open, and measured investigation into the accusation. They cannot allow the truth and the facts to lessen an advantage of the narrative they're pushing. So, we say the Democrats cheated during the last election, and that accusation is reported on the nightly news as another Republican conspiracy theory on voting fraud. The media skips away from any discussion into the truth, the facts, and the evidence. The media won't report an investigation has been started and the authorities are collecting evidence. When those lines are not articulated, people are left to make their own conclusions that there wasn't cheating as silence is proof the Republicans are lying or wrong."

McGee ended his response and handled a few more questions from the students. He was engaging and responsive.

Eastwood was amazed the process was going so well. There were no eruptions or protests as so often seen when candidates hit the campaign trail and expose themselves to questioning. *They're listening to McGee.*

McGee said, "Let's take another look at the original question. The Democrat Party and the media have a fifty-year history of cheating. They have a fifty-year history of covering up their political crimes. It's even in Wikipedia. They have a fifty-year history of malfeasance when they're in office, whatever the office. And they want you to forget their history. The media won't report it if they violate laws on the books. Fact: 98 percent of the media is run by Democrats. Media executives are prohibited by law from making donations to political campaigns, which sounds good on its face. What isn't publicized is these Democrat executives get around the law by having spouses make the contributions. Yet they castigate Republicans for breaking the law. That they cannot be trusted. In propaganda circles this is called projection, blaming others for what you are doing."

Eastwood chuckled, "I'm so old I can remember when the only fake news was the National Enquirer."

McGee smiled and said, "I'm so old I can remember when mentally ill people were put in hospitals and not Congress."

Twittering laughter erupted from the assembly.

McGee continued, "Do you think voting is so perfect a process it's beyond reproach? The left wants you to believe that. In the realm of higher learning, you shouldn't take what we say as politicians as the gospel. It's the politician's goal to advance their party's narrative. Find the facts and truth for yourself. It takes only seconds. If you do the research, you may be surprised at your findings. Do not prove your conclusion, for then you'll only research the areas which support your conclusion. Does that make sense? All of us have to resist the left's propaganda and resist becoming pawns and puppets for the left."

"Now I can answer the question. During the last election of President Hernandez, he had been polling exceptionally well in the battleground states. If those trends had continued, it should have been a blowout for the Republicans. It was well known the Democrat Party nominee thought she didn't have to run, that she should just be anointed."

"As you know, every week millions of lottery tickets are sold for a specific day. Within minutes of the drawing, lottery officials know how many winning lottery tickets there are and where those winning lottery tickets were sold, right down to the specific store location. But in our voting system, days after polls have closed, some voting officials don't know how many people voted, who they voted for, or what the accurate results are. We have the technology to know the results of a selection of numbers on a lottery card — virtually instantaneously. Republicans say the U.S. voting system is intentionally broken so it can be manipulated by unsavory Democrats. Think about it. Our voting system could be as responsive and as accurate as a lottery, but Congress chooses that it not be so. Democrats scream any change to the voting system is racist. We have to admit our voting system is broken, that a fixed voting system, a fair and balanced voting system doesn't benefit the Democrat Party. That is because of only one thing, a solid unimpeachable voting system is one where no one may cheat, and we have to fix the one we have if we are to have a republican democracy."

"When I'm elected President of the United States, we are going to fix the voting system so that it's fair, accurate, and fast for everyone who is eligible to vote."

CHAPTER 33

November 18, 2019

Nazy Cunningham delivered the President's Daily Brief with her customary professionalism. After the Monday PDB, the other senior members of the President's staff left the Oval Office. Nazy removed a file folder from a black Halliburton case and handed it to the President. "Mr. President, I respectfully submit a new *Disposition Matrix*. Ahmad Khalid Saleh Hashash has been removed, and we have an addition."

President Hernandez was caught unawares. He asked, "What is the disposition of Hashash?"

Nazy took a breath and said, "The Algerians executed him. Our Chief of Station confirmed it was Hashash."

"That's not what I envisioned."

"Yes, Mr. President, we had no idea they would comply with an almost forty-year-old Scottish execution order. They were incentivized to turn him over to us."

President Hernandez was quiet for several seconds. He pursed his lips. Nazy continued, "We have a new candidate on the *Matrix*, Adnan Abu Walid al-Sahrawi. He's the leader of the Islamic State in the Sahara."

President Hernandez nodded, stood, and asked "Background?" He went to the *Resolute Desk*, extracted an earlier version of the *Matrix*, and handed Nazy the old *Matrix*.

There was no more discussion on Hashash. That was old business. New business was al-Sahrawi. President Hernandez opened the new file.

Nazy said, "Mr. President. The ideology of the Islamic State in the Sahara didn't appear out of thin air; it has been preached by the Muslim Brotherhood in the book 'In the Shade of the Qur'an,' by Sayyid Qutb."

President Hernandez was impressed with Nazy's command of Arabic and said, "I understand. Continue."

"In Niger in 2017, we suspected but had no evidence al-Sahrawi led a raid that killed four U.S. Army Green Berets."

"I remember; I went to Dover and watched them come home for the last time." The memory of the coffins being offloaded silently was still powerful. And it stirred another memory. Something McGee had once said. Then Nazy interrupted his reverie.

Nazy continued, "Al-Sahrawi's ISIS operates in Mali and Niger and crosses the border at will to escape the French Foreign Legion. Now there are indications the Islamic State in the Sahara has infiltrated the French Foreign Legion."

"How did they do that?"

"Politicians of the French National Assembly felt there should be more Malian representation in the French Foreign Legion, but the vetting process of indigenous people is poor."

"So basically, they hire spies from the Islamic State. Like we did under Mazibuike, Islamic radicals, until you and Director McGee purged them from the Agency."

"Yes, Mr. President. Exactly. The French president doesn't want to announce their military forces in Mali have been compromised and he doesn't want to admit they cannot find and eliminate al-Sahrawi. Their situation is much like when the French DGSE—the Directorate-General for External Security—had to admit their airport security operation had been compromised by Islamic radicals. It took the crash of a French airliner and the collective outrage of French airlines' CEOs for liberal French politicians to come up with the political will to purge their airport security staff of Muslims. They used polygraphs to root out the al-Qaeda infiltrators."

"I remember. Their embrace of socialism and the replacement of the French people will be their downfall. What was that book?" He looked at Nazy quizzically.

"Mr. President, are you referring to Renault Camus' *You Will Not Replace Us?*"

Oh yes, Replacement Theory. "That's the one. The French are in trouble, and their socialists are taking them down the wrong path."

"Mr. President, if the French do not wish to fall to the Islamic invasion, they will have to strip their infiltrators of any citizenship given to them and deport their Muslims back to Africa. Nations know that is the only solution."

"And they won't do that. I've spoken with their president recently. France will be fifty percent Muslim by 2050 and a Muslim colony by 2100. They know what they should do; they know how to do it, but with liberal politicians there is no political will." For a fleeting moment, President Hernandez had images of Adolf Hitler signing the Nuremberg Laws, the heavy hand of government stripping the citizenship of German Jews. Then he just as quickly returned to the present. He continued, "About al-Sahrawi?"

"Yes, Mr. President. When the French Foreign Legion capture al-Sahrawi's men, they try them in Paris. The trials turn into spectacles. Their DGSE inquired if we could or would house their ISIS terrorists at Guantanamo Bay. The French and NATO believe al-Sahrawi's removal from the battlefield would cause the self-destruction of the Islamic State in the Sahara. Al-Sahrawi is the only thing that holds that organization together."

"I'll speak with the French president as soon as it's practicable. Nazy, are any Americans under threat?"

"Yes, Mr. President. There were the four Green Berets who were killed, and we have it on good intelligence an American businessman," she consulted her notes, "…a Mr. Jason O'Hair, was abducted in 2016 in Bamako. However, since there were no demands for ransom through private or official channels, we believed he may be dead."

"When Americans are involved…."

"Yes, Mr. President." Nazy continued, "We have some fairly good resources in both countries now. We have had *Noble Savage* try to locate Mr. O'Hair but the intel was insufficient. We have asked them repeatedly to observe al-Sahrawi and see if anyone knows the whereabouts of Mr. O'Hair or has knowledge of his demise."

"They sometimes keep hostages?"

"Yes, Mr. President. Especially if they're wealthy white hostages. I believe we have much better intelligence than our previous attempt and this would be an appropriate use of *Noble Savage*. If approved, we would like to mobilize as soon as practicable."

The President nodded and stood up. He said, "Let's do it. Do you have anything else for me?"

Nazy offered him a sealed envelope. "One final thing Mr. President. I will be quick."

"Take your time, Nazy. No factor, as you say." He deposited the envelope in the *Resolute Desk* and returned to his seat.

She smiled and said, "Mr. President, a routine follow-up investigation into the computers of Muslim intelligence officers and Agency contractors who were terminated for suspected trafficking of classified information turned up child sexual abuse images."

"That's different. Why would you investigate the intelligence officers and contractors?"

"Mr. President, they were found to have conducted inappropriate activities, such as simple mishandling of classified information or storing technical documents related to the Agency's systems on their computers. The Muslim intelligence officers were conducting espionage and stealing classified information. Those employees and contractors were terminated for cause. Their computers were confiscated and audited forensically to determine the extent of the security breach. I thought there may have been a greater problem and asked the Inspector General to investigate."

Nazy described the Inspector General's findings. "After the intelligence officers and contractors were fired and stripped of their security clearances, they were charged under the Espionage Act for activities such as revealing secret tools the CIA uses to hack into foreign computers. The IG indicated the security breach was likely much greater than we originally believed, and the child sexual abuse images on computers were found to be many times more pervasive than originally thought. And they pled guilty to the child abuse charges. They were sentenced and have registered as sex offenders."

"This is something other than a coincidence?"

"Yes, Mr. President. A software engineer was implicated as part of a much larger investigation into the largest leak of classified information in our history. Not only was he found to have child sexual abuse images on his computer, there was evidence he was being blackmailed. When he was caught *in flagrante delicto* with a minor, he agreed to trade classified information rather than be exposed to the authorities."

"I take it that wasn't the end of it."

"No, Mr. President. The Inspector General report shows a pattern. When Agency personnel are charged with sexual misconduct, federal prosecutors do not hold them accountable. Over the past fifteen years, the Inspector General has amassed credible evidence at least a dozen employees and contractors who committed espionage also committed sexual crimes involving children."

"I would say that is a problem."

"Yes, Mr. President. Being in Operations, I was not aware these cases were referred to U.S. attorneys for prosecution. Of the dozen people identified, only one individual was ever charged with a sex crime."

"One?"

"Yes, Mr. President. The IG said prosecutors would charge these employees and contractors with high profile felonious espionage, but would send the child sex crime charges back to the Agency to handle internally, administratively."

"So, these prosecutors tried to protect the image of the CIA by remanding those charges back to the Agency for disposition."

"Yes, Mr. President. And it appears so. Confident the greater charge of espionage would put a sexual predator away in a federal penitentiary for a long time, our deputy directors signed off on the prosecutorial strategy."

"Nazy, so what you are saying?"

"Mr. President, I suggest it means these charges may have masked the greater problem. We are an intelligence agency and our priority is the intel community. No one ever investigated if sex crimes involving children *is organized*. Is there an entity that entices people with the highest security clearances in the land, targets them specifically and facilitates them having sex with children? We know this is a problem in Europe where virtually every major city in every country has special brothels with child prostitutes who cater to military men and women while also targeting the intelligence community. This situation is known as a social construct, it's their culture. The quiet truth is there is an epidemic of NATO employees being charged with espionage, but there are virtually no mentions of their involvement in child sex trafficking or abuse. Espionage is a felony and punishments are severe and acknowledged, creating a high-level of deterrence. But child sex abuse isn't to be discussed. Not reporting it gives the appearance it isn't happening."

"Could something like that happen here?"

"Mr. President, Europe is the model. NATO is the target. The old KGB will do anything to get to NATO's classified information. Eventually, as social norms degrade under liberal rule, they will export it more than they are."

"Could it really be Russia?"

"Mr. President, the analysis suggests Rho Schwartz Scorpii is behind the child sex trafficking organization in Europe. He sells the products of espionage to the Kremlin for a premium. He's most likely the person responsible for targeting IC personnel in America. When the targets are in the IC, we call them *honeypots*."

President Hernandez was quiet for several seconds, absorbing the fresh intelligence. After a few nods, he said, "That's all for today, Nazy. Thank you. Good job." He stood up and moved to his desk.

Nazy stood. She was out of the door in seconds. The meeting was over. He didn't even watch her leave. His mind was now preoccupied with thoughts of Rho Schwartz Scorpii.

President Hernandez always had a full schedule and was grateful everyone had cleared out of the Oval Office. He plopped into his chair and buzzed his secretary that he didn't want to be disturbed for five minutes. Then he withdrew an unmarked file from a lower drawer of his desk and read more on the CIA's accounting of the saga of young Scorpii. He picked up the story where he had left off.

After the war ended there were countless homeless children on the street looking for their families. The East German social services placed these neglected children in foster homes. In 1947, at seven years of age Scorpii crossed the street alone and was hit by a car. He wasn't seriously injured, but he was hospitalized for several days. The medical staff conducted a physical. The results attracted the attention of the local youth-welfare office.

Caseworkers believed the injuries to his anus resulted from repetitive penetrations. The boy had also been castrated, suggesting he had been in the group of children who were part of a documented Ravensbrück sterilization experiment: Amputation of Enthusiasm. Studies of dominance and control. All the other Ravensbrück children who were test subjects for Mengele and Goebbels were believed to have perished when Allied soldiers liberated the concentrations camps. The Nazis shot all remaining prisoners in the camps before fleeing. We have no information how Scorpii escaped the Nazis final extermination orders.

Caseworkers at the office couldn't locate Scorpii's father or mother. His file annotated the caseworkers believed they were dead, casualties of Auschwitz or the war. He had survived on the street as a prostitute. He was known by the oversized driving cap he always wore.

Because of the extent of his injuries, caseworkers recommended he be given the emotional attention and that he be placed in a foster home with a family-like atmosphere. Once he could walk, he was discharged and sent to a day care center in his dirty clothes and his cap. He was left there. Caseworkers described Scorpii as an attractive boy who was wild and secretive but easy to influence.

After two years, because there were no available foster families, the nine-year-old Scorpii was placed in a foster home with a thirty-seven-year-old single man, Joachim Merkel. Merkel was a new member of the ruling communist party, known as the Socialist Unity Party of Germany (SED). He wanted to supplement his income as a foster father. Scorpii was Merkel's first foster son. When Merkel began fostering another school-age child, a teacher noticed Merkel was always seeking contact with boys.

In 1953, a caseworker observed Merkel appeared to be in a homosexual relationship with his foster son, Scorpii. Homosexual behavior was officially prohibited in East Germany, although tolerated in private. There were rumors industrialists kept many young men out of sight and employed in special brothels for their pleasures.

When a public prosecutor launched an investigation, Scorpii was at home alone and freely talked of his foster father. He said he hadn't been surrounded by regular couples, only male couples. His father's partners would drop in unexpectedly to eat and sleep in their home. Scorpii indicated he had been taken to meeting places in other communities and was exposed to various activities. The public prosecutor took his comments to mean they cared for him, but Scorpii corrected her. They didn't care for him until they had used him. Those were the terms he used to indicate they had sex with him. He said they took photographs of him in the nude, in group sex settings. He said they passed him around. Women took care of him after the men left him such a bloody mess he couldn't attend school. The public prosecutor returned the next day and found Merkel dead by hanging. Scorpii couldn't be found. In 1953, East German social services closed the Scorpii file.

President Hernandez spun around in his chair to look outside. He let his mind wander before his next appointment. He sighed and replaced the file in his drawer. He thought, *How does a sexually abused waif become a billionaire? Is it really possible he's the head of the Insiders, the one-world government crowd?*

President Hernandez buzzed his secretary, and she sent in his next appointment.

CHAPTER 34

November 19, 2019

The Abilene Police Department responded to a complaint a truck had been stolen from the parking lot of the Hendrick Medical Center South, formerly Abilene Regional Medical Center. The most noticeable feature of the white Ford F-150 was it had a tonneau cover. Like hundreds of others Ford trucks in Abilene.

•   •   •

The following day, inside the Islamic Social Center of Abilene, a dozen men with different colored spray cans painted an F-150 to look as if it were camouflaged. The paint job would be sufficient for their needs.

A robed cleric overseeing his followers said, "This is our country now; this tool will be a message from *Allah!* I call on Muslims everywhere to create the fear of *Allah!*"

A squarish, six-foot long composite container was carried to the truck bed by two men and slipped under a fiberglass tonneau cover. It had arrived from another Islamic Center in Dallas earlier in the day.

Once the truck and the cargo were ready, the cleric motioned for the men to assemble. He led them in prayer.

•   •   •

A man sat behind the wheel of the camouflaged Ford F-150 in the parking lot of the executive terminal. He had a perfect view of arrivals. Using high-powered binoculars, he even knew who got off the aircraft. He typed a text message confirming McGee had disembarked from the blue and gold trimmed Gulfstream. He confirmed the N-number of the aircraft was the same one that had been reported earlier. The Gulfstream's door/airstairs had been left in the down position.

He didn't confuse it with the other Gulfstream which had landed earlier. The paint on that jet was markedly brilliant as if it had recently been painted. That jet had bright red and gold stripes. It had a different registration number. After it had landed, he had watched the pilots leave the jet quickly, once they closed the aircraft's door. Their actions seemed to suggest they wouldn't be returning to that aircraft soon.

His smartphone vibrated with a new text message: "K." He drove out of the executive terminal parking lot. That part of his job was complete. It was time to reposition.

CHAPTER 35

November 20, 2019

They had been bouncing around the battleground states for days, sometimes stopping four or five times a day. *The McGee for President* campaign was in full swing. The campaign staff and security detail were told they would be changing planes in Abilene. Everyone needed to offload luggage and campaign materials from the G-550 and take them to the lounge of the executive terminal. After the rally and a town hall meeting, the campaign staff would collect their belongings and take them to the red and gold trimmed GIV-SP parked near the front of a service hangar well away from the executive terminal. There would be golf carts and trucks to help them move their gear.

Only a few cared to ask why the plane change. McGee answered off-handedly, "This jet will be taken to a maintenance facility and given a thorough inspection. I assume they will check the oil and the fluids, and they'll replace the main landing gear tires. I wouldn't be surprised if they change the brakes, wash the jet and detail the interior." He knew Duncan well. "I'll bet the owner of the jet ensures they finish it with a wax job."

The answer made the campaign staff smile. It was nothing they needed to worry about.

Unknown to the campaign crew, inside the GIV-SP there were thermal bags to keep chicken *chimichangas* and tortilla chips hot and ice chests to keep Julio's salsa cold. McGee would know what to do with the food from the *El Restaurante Azteca*. Chimichangas with a soupçon of guacamole from the *Azteca* were better than birthday gifts.

With all the dynamics of the campaign orbiting around him, Dory Eastwood's mind was somewhere else: in Germany. He severed the connection on his cellphone. A story he had been chasing for years, probably a once-in-a-career opportunity had just materialized. The doctor in charge of a mental health clinic in Berlin had offered him the exclusive opportunity to interview several survivors of the child sex slave trade in Europe. He agreed before consulting McGee. *This may be a problem.*

As Eastwood went off in search for Bill McGee, McGee's campaign manager took the stage and began, "This presidential candidate has found a wedge issue in training and arming disaffected women. It's being widely reported that within the first 24-hours after announcing his *Not Going to be Afraid Any More* initiative, the NRA and White House were all aboard. Armories across the country have taken obsolete weapons out of storage and are making the revolvers and rifles serviceable again. A million M-1 Carbines with a 15-round box magazine and M-16s with 20-round box magazines have already been delivered to program participants."

"Armories report they have located 100,000 new and used Colt *Commanders*, .38 Special revolvers with four and five-inch barrels. About 70,000 Smith & Wesson revolvers have been found in like new condition in an armory storage bunker in Pine Bluff, Arkansas."

The campaign manager emphasized, "The program is changing daily. If a woman doesn't want the M-16, she can ask for a revolver."

"Over one million women have signed up, and 100,000 women are already in some form of weapons training across the country. Police and sheriff departments across the country are already seeing *significant* reductions in crime rates, especially violent crimes against women. Gun shops are reporting record sales." Sheriffs and police chiefs took the stage to confirm what the newspapers reported.

While there was euphoria and jubilation within the campaign, the liberal media was trashing Operation *Not Going to be Afraid Any More*, calling it dangerous and predicting people would die because of it.

One wag quipped to the audience, "If you break into a house, now you can expect to be shot!" The surrounding people clapped.

Next, the Texas Governor finally introduced Rear Admiral McGee to thunderous applause. During his remarks about the program, McGee said, "One of my pilot friends reminded me the flack is always heaviest when you're over the target. And we are over the target! The Democrat Party and the media positively hate Operation *Not Going to be Afraid Any More*. That's how you know it's working. That's how you know it's effective for our side, the side of law and order, and not for their side, flakes trying to bombard us with flak."

"Ladies, you are sending a signal you will not take any more of the left's incompetence and indifference to your concerns of safety and security. The Democrat Party insists on kowtowing to liberals and radical groups. They insist on defunding police and sheriff departments. They insist it's good policy to let criminals go free without bail or jail time. Ladies, these are not only issues of safety and security; they are issues of life and death! We choose life! And we will train the felons to fear you. That like Texas, you are not to be messed with!"

Above the audience there was something new to see. McGee pointed out the black and white posters of a 106-year-old Armenian woman sitting in front of her home guarding it with an AK-47 assault rifle. He shouted, "If the little old lady from Degh village needs to protect herself and her home from armed conflicts, so can American women."

McGee continued with stories of armed women who had successfully protected themselves and their families. "A Manhattan couple was involved in a road-rage incident. The driver of the other vehicle followed them into a parking lot and angrily approached them with a tire iron. Fearing for her life, the woman pointed her weapon at the attacker and he fled. Her husband took down the attacker's license number and the man was later arrested. In North Carolina, two men, one armed, broke into a home around midnight. The single mother of two who lived there heard them and fired on the intruders. They fled, and both men were arrested afterwards. If violent crime is to be curbed, the felon must be taught to fear his victim."

As Demetrius Eastwood stood at the side of the raucous crowd, a young lady walked up to him and introduced herself as Celeste Germaine. She told Eastwood she was now a graduate student at Abilene Christian University. Eastwood immediately recognized the name but not the face. He had interviewed her five years ago and was nearly floored by her presence. He did a double-take when Celeste pointed at McGee and said, "I remember *him* that night in the Devil's Hole in the U.A.E."

Eastwood was flipping and jerking around as if he were having a seizure. He asked, *"Who do you remember?"* He knew Duncan Hunter had rescued hundreds of girls and women from an underground harem near Dubai that night. *But was McGee also in the mix?*

Eastwood had won several awards for his expose which chronicled Celeste Germaine's story. She and other women had been kidnapped and forced into the sex slave trade. When they were rescued by Americans most of the credit went to one unnamed man in black. Eastwood learned the secret savior was none other than his benefactor and friend, Duncan Hunter. America had been transfixed by Eastwood's special, *Escape from The Devil's Hole.*

He remembered every aspect of that telecast. He remembered saying, "The sex trade was alive and well in the United Arab Emirates until our guest and almost three hundred others escaped the underground prison they called '*The Devil's Hole.*' Celeste Germaine is her real name...."

Celeste had been a beautiful 16-year-old student at Abilene High School. Eastwood remembered Celeste had gone to the skating rink and had then woken up in a shipping container. She was terrified.

Eastwood remembered Celeste's story about how the men got Celeste and the others to comply. Five large men spoke a language she had never heard before. She and four other girls of similar age were brought to an underground commercial kitchen and stripped of their clothes and shoes. They were convinced they were about to be raped or tortured when one of the men brought in a black child, presumably from Africa, and killed the little girl in front of them. The men used long knives to dismember the child. They fed the girl's body parts into a meat processor. Celeste and the others were transfixed in horror. They screamed and pleaded for their lives.

During the interview, Eastwood experienced chills as Celeste recounted what had happened to her. She said she and the other women believed they would be next to be cut up; that there wasn't anything they could do. But one of the men covered in blood came close to the girls and said in heavily accented English, "You will do exactly as we say and no harm will come to you or your family. If you fail to comply, we will return to this room to deal with you. If you fail to comply, your families will be hunted down and killed."

Celeste shouted over the crowd noise and pointed in frustration, "Admiral *McGee. He* was there with *us*, with *Maverick*."

Eastwood had to be sure. "McGee?"

She yelled at him, "*Yes, McGee!*"

Eastwood knew what he must do. He took Celeste Germaine by the hand and led her through the crowd until they were directly in front of the lectern. He tried without success to get the Admiral's attention. Exasperation got the best of him so he stuck two fingers in his mouth and whistled — *loud!*

Rear Admiral McGee stopped talking in mid-sentence. He said, "Colonel Eastwood, that is so unlike you." Then he looked at the woman standing next to Eastwood, pointed at her and asked, "Is that *Celeste?*"

Fifty thousand eyes focused on the woman.

Celeste nodded.

"Oh, this is incredible. Please, please come up here. Make way, make way — we have a very important person here. Dory, you too."

Pandemonium broke out on the dais. The Secret Service didn't like an unvetted, unscreened, and unfrisked person getting anywhere close to their presidential candidate. McGee pulled rank and said, "Let them pass."

The crowd of 25,000 murmured as they watched the drama playing out before them. It was an incongruous sight, the huge black man hugging the petite white girl as Eastwood took the lectern and said, "Dory Eastwood here. I know some in the media will think this is staged but I'm here to say, it's not. Some of you may remember a television special I did years ago, *Escape from The Devil's Hole*. One of the girls who was rescued from *The Devil's Hole* is with us now. She's from Abilene, and she remembers Admiral McGee helping to rescue her and the other girls."

Admiral McGee and Celeste talked away from the microphone as Eastwood reminded the crowd of those events. He then stepped down.

Celeste told McGee she wanted to speak. McGee agreed and walked her to the lectern. He pulled out a stool for her to stand on and adjusted the microphone for her.

"My name is Celeste Germaine; I attend classes at Abilene Christen University. As Colonel Eastwood said, I was kidnapped here in my hometown five years ago. I had gone roller skating. I woke up in a shipping container. I found myself thrown into a room with hundreds of other girls and women from all over the world. What I experienced there still gives me nightmares. We prayed for someone to save us, to rescue us."

Hands in front of them, like a soccer player protecting his privates from a penalty kick, Eastwood and McGee stood on either side of the lectern with their eyes on Celeste.

Celeste said, "But someone *did* come for us. *America* came to rescue us, and the man in charge was Admiral McGee. *This Admiral McGee.*"

The crowd roared so loudly they could be heard downtown.

Celeste continued, her words gathering momentum. "I didn't know what was going on. I just wanted out. We all wanted to get away from evil. We were so frightened. I was pleading with the man I've come to know as Admiral McGee not to leave us. I didn't want him to leave us to die; to leave us to the bad men. I found out later Admiral McGee assigned a man in black *coveralls* to take us to safety. This guy, he was kind of old but handsome. He said his name was *Maverick.* I will always remember that night. *Maverick* had a funny looking black helmet with what I now know were night vision goggles. *Maverick* and Admiral McGee got us out!"

McGee turned so no one could see his grin. *She just called Maverick old! He'll squeal like a girl.*

Tears flowed down Celeste's cheeks, and she let them run. Eastwood leaned in and handed her a handkerchief. She wiped her eyes, then a huge smile appeared to light up rosy cheeks. She turned to McGee and started clapping. The crown wildly chanted, *"USA! USA! USA! USA! USA! USA!"*

Celeste Germaine returned to the microphone. The crowd quieted respectfully.

Celeste composed herself and continued, "We never knew the real name of our savior in black coveralls, just *Maverick,* and I want to thank everyone who came to rescue us. Every night I thank God for Admiral McGee, for *Maverick* for saving my life, and the lives of those other girls."

The assembly roared their approval. More shouts of, "*USA! USA! USA! USA! USA! USA!*"

She and McGee shared a few more words. Then she departed the platform, and McGee took the lectern one last time. He gripped the lectern and said, "That was wild. During my thirty-five years as a SEAL, sometimes I was in the right unit and we got to rescue someone. Doesn't always happen, and things don't always go as planned."

"That night I wasn't even supposed to be there. Celeste, I think there were three or four hundred girls and women with you. I don't remember the exact number, but you were being held in an underground prison. The rescue was a team event, but we got them all out. That was an incredible night."

The people of Abilene were nearly delirious. Women were crying, and men were pumping fists.

McGee smiled broadly; people told him he had a good, calming smile. He said, "Those of us who deal with the corrupt, phony media, those guys with the cameras in the back row, we know what they will report. They will take some of Celeste's comments out of context and twist her words. Remember, she said, 'I was pleading with Admiral McGee not to leave us. I didn't want Admiral McGee to leave us to die; leave us to the bad men.' That's all the evil media will report. They'll make it sound like I abandoned Celeste and the other women. That I was the most evil person on the planet."

"That is our dishonest media today. The dishonest media won't report the rest of Celeste's statement, that I assigned an old man in black coveralls to get them out. I and others needed to clear the area so they could escape. We got them out. Your U.S. Navy brought her home to return to living the American dream."

The crowd applauded for two straight minutes and shouted, "*USA! USA! USA! USA! USA! USA!*"

"I never expected to see Celeste again. In this business you live for the moment and never forget anything. I remembered Celeste because she opened the door; she was the first person I met that night, we were underground, and she spoke English. If she hadn't opened that door and asked for rescue, we probably would never have known she and hundreds of other girls and women were down there."

Suddenly McGee thought of something else and shouted, "Where's Colonel Eastwood? There you are! Dory, did you recruit Celeste to help with our campaign?"

Amid the rowdy and uproarious applause, Eastwood nodded. He shouted, "Admiral McGee crossed an ocean to rescue Celeste Germaine and hundreds of women, and now Admiral McGee is running for president to rescue Americans from the evil Democrat Party."

The crowd liked the impromptu political tagline and so did McGee. He clapped his approval at Eastwood's imagination.

Eastwood then yelled, "*I did and she wants a poster!*"

McGee shouted, "Someone get Celeste a poster! I think we need to put *her* on a poster. There is no more appropriate way to celebrate Celeste's freedom than having her grace us with her presence. My first 'thank you' goes to her. My next 'thank you' goes to you, the wonderful and patriotic people of Abilene." He stepped back from the lectern to allow the crowd time to savor the moment.

"*USA! USA! USA! USA! USA! USA!*"

When McGee returned to the lectern, he shouted, "Our plan is to take America back from the criminals who now have us by the short hairs. That includes the phony media. I don't know if we can fix this phony media…can we just call them *fake news*? But we are going to try. Look for our supporters who are working their way through the crowd. There are official McGee hats for you and your kids, and business cards I hope you put in your purse or wallet. If you haven't seen these before, I hear they're on eBay. On one side is the Second Amendment: *The right to keep and bear arms shall not be infringed* and the other is the quote I used earlier. And take a poster of our little old lady. If she could protect her home from bad men, so can you. If you have questions, contact our campaign. And please give thanks to President

Hernandez and the NRA for moving mountains to make Operation *Not Going to be Afraid Any More* a reality."

"Now is the time to call your representatives and write to your newspapers. Now is the time to drive a stake into the heart of this evil beast. Remember the words of the author Margaret Mead who said, 'Never doubt that a small group of thoughtful, committed citizens can change the world; indeed, it's the only thing that ever has.'"

"You don't need a group of SEALs to be your heroes; you can be the hero. Do your part, and you can make a difference. As your President, we will make a difference and take back our country."

"Thank you, Abilene! Thank you, Texas! God Bless you and God Bless the United States of America!"

• • •

Immediately after the exciting rally had finished, the airport control tower broadcast a *Notice to Airmen* that quiet hours on the airfield were canceled and routine flight operations were authorized. The ferry pilots for the Gulfstream G-550 completed their before takeoff checks and started the engines. They called for their clearance, contacted Ground Control, and taxied to the runway for takeoff.

• • •

From over a mile away he couldn't make out the number on the side of the engine cowling, but the distinctive blue and gold fuselage trim was unmistakable in the powerful flood lights surrounding the airport parking ramp. He watched the business jet taxi to the end of the runway for takeoff.

High-power binoculars are so useful!

The engine and lights were off in the Ford-150. *Such a beautiful night to watch the jets fly in and out.* He scanned the immediate area to see if anyone was nearby. He quietly slid out of the driver's seat and walked to the rear to the truck. He rested his arms atop the tonneau cover and with his binoculars looked toward the airport. He could still hear crowd noise in the distance. Some vehicles' headlights illuminated, signaling people were leaving the airport going away from where he was. The unimproved perimeter road where he was parked was a good spot. Neither the police nor the sheriff's department checked it often.

He brought the binoculars up to his eyes again just in time to see the Gulfstream moving onto the runway with the nose turning to point in his direction.

It was time!

He quietly lowered the tailgate and extracted the missile container from the truck bed. He unbuckled the four latches on top of the dark canister and opened the box. Inside was the dull green shoulder-launched *Stinger* missile and the coffee can shaped battery coolant units (BCU). At the Dallas mosque he had practiced the procedures to aim and activate the *Stinger*. In one motion he jammed a BCU into the launcher and twisted it to lock it in place. Argon gas was routed to cool the missile's seeker head. With his left hand on the Uncage button, his thumb resting on the Safety and Activator switch, and index finger resting on the trigger, he looked over the sight to find the aircraft visually. He would listen for the homing tone from the speaker near his ear; the Bone's Transducer would vibrate against his cheek, so he would feel the tone if the background noise was too great. He located and tracked the aircraft in the sights and then depressed the Safety and Activator switch, down and in.

The anti-aircraft missile was ready for launch.

As the Gulfstream cleared the fence at the end of the runway and passed in front of him, he could see the landing gear doors were almost fully closed. He waited a few more seconds for the jet to continue its climb.

•   •   •

The G-550 pilot trimmed the aircraft to climb more efficiently as the landing gear retracted; the copilot switched radio frequencies.

•   •   •

He aimed carefully and listened for the growl as the infrared seeker head acquired the heat from the jet's engines. When the tone came, the transducer's vibration on his cheek surprised him. He matched up the rear sight reticle with the range ring, depressed the uncage button to free the fixed seeker head, and allowed it to track the aircraft independently from the aiming scope. He super-elevated the missile and led the jet to the right so when the missile fired off, the launch motor would push the missile out of the tube and the missile wouldn't have to chase its target. He squeezed the trigger. The tone became louder and instantly the missile fired off.

Between blinks he saw the flames of the launch motor die as it detached from the missile, then the red-hot exhaust of the flight motor kicked in. He found the fire from the departing missile mesmerizing. He was so spellbound by the track of the missile that he jumped when two miles from the airport, the Gulfstream exploded in a spectacular fireball.

• • •

Dory Eastwood's head snapped as a streak of fire caught his eye. *WTH?* The green and red position lights on the wings of the jet were still visible, and the flash of fire seemed to streak in that direction.

• • •

The concussion from the missile impact and the exploding aircraft nearly knocked him down and made his ears ring. The man rolled over and recovered his senses. In one motion, he tossed the spent missile launcher into the truck bed and removed a gas container from under the tonneau cover. He splashed gasoline into the truck cabin and set the Ford on fire.

He paused for a moment to watch his handiwork. He shouted, "*Allahu Akbar!*" and ran to an awaiting vehicle.

• • •

Bill McGee ran to where the jet exploded. He was stopped by his Secret Service detail. They insisted he and his campaign staff go to their vehicles for transportation to Dyess Air Force Base for safety as they assessed the situation.

• • •

Eastwood didn't know why he ran toward the exploded jet. He stopped when he nearly collided with a woman driving a John Deere *Gator*. He yelled, "*DRIVE!*" as he climbed into the passenger seat. She was clueless. He pointed; she mashed the pedal and quickly realized what all the commotion was about. A vehicle was also on fire.

• • •

Crash Fire Rescue began rolling toward the off-airport incident. Police assigned to the rally called for firetrucks and ambulances. Thousands of people were crashing into one another trying to get to their vehicles.

• • •

Bill McGee remained on the platform commandeering the microphone and asking everyone to calm down and proceed to the exits quietly yet purposefully. "There is no need to run," he shouted. "No need to be afraid. We have to let law enforcement and the fire department do what they're trained to do."

A couple of veterans shouted it had been a missile. Several people were conversing with the candidate and pointing in the crash's direction, "There was a streak of fire, then the airplane exploded."

If it had been a missile, that changed things.

The Secret Service would institute new procedures. Now they had another threat to consider.

• • •

The airport manager and mayor declared the airport closed because of the incident. The police chief told the mayor he needed to call the FBI, for several people were emphatically telling him and his officers there had been a missile fired at the candidate's aircraft.

•　　•　　•

Dory Eastwood told the woman to steer toward the vehicle fire on the airport's perimeter road at the end of the runway. He talked to her like she was family arguing over politics. "A plane gets shot down and there's a vehicle fire?"

They found the front end of the truck fully engulfed. Eastwood got out of the *Gator* and took pictures with his smartphone. She said to stay away — the fuel cell could explode. When Eastwood maneuvered upwind of the flames toward the truck bed, he saw them. The military man recognized the spent missile launcher and the unmistakable shape of a shipping container for a *Stinger* missile. He took photographs just as the fire crept around the truck bed and set the missile parts on fire, consuming them in seconds.

Then the gas tank exploded.

•　　•　　•

The *Gator* driver pulled a disoriented Dory Eastwood out of the way, singeing her clothes. She put out the flames on Eastwood's clothes with handfuls of dirt and sand. He scrambled around and found his phone — still smoldering. He was grateful it still worked. Eastwood turned to the woman in cowboy boots and said, "Thanks for pulling my ass out of the fire. Literally. What's your name?"

"Dawn Howell. My pleasure. You're Dory Eastwood. I saw you speak."

Some parts of Eastwood's clothes continued to smoke. He and Dawn Howell drove back to the site of the rally. He pounded his arms and legs to stamp out embers and possible firestarters still on his clothes.

The Secret Service had convinced McGee it was time to go to the base. The campaign had left him.

Dawn Howell volunteered to take Eastwood to the executive terminal to recover his bag. She called a downtown hotel for him. When he returned to her, he had a Bluetooth stuck into his ear filing a report with the chief editors of the *Washington Times* and the *New York Post*. He sent them pictures of the Stinger parts before they went up in flames. He sent them photographs of the aircraft crash.

When all of his work had been done, he turned to Miss Howell and asked, "Dawn, do you think we could go to *Whataburger?*"

CHAPTER 36

November 20, 2019

The Chief Editors stopped the presses for the exclusive report. Their Internet Desk placed the story on the Internet while it was being loaded for print publication.

On-line headlines of the *Washington Times* and the *New York Post* websites read:

MCGEE ESCAPES ASSASSINATION!

By: Demetrius Eastwood.

After a successful campaign rally in the town of Abilene, Texas, the campaign aircraft used to transport former CIA Director William "Bill" McGee and his campaign staff was shot down by a man-portable, shoulder-launched, anti-aircraft missile.

Immediately after the rally as Rear Admiral McGee was walking off the stage waving at well-wishers, eyewitnesses and this reporter saw a single streak of fire heading toward an aircraft that had just taken off. This jet had been used to move the McGee campaign from city to city for several weeks. Two ferry pilots whose names haven't been released citing next of kin notifications had just taken off. McGee and his staff were not on board; the campaign chief of staff cited maintenance was due to be performed on the aircraft. A replacement aircraft had been positioned at the Abilene Regional Airport for the campaign to continue their schedule of rallies. The aircraft was reported to be a 2014 Gulfstream G-550.

It's believed that a purloined *Stinger*, possibly from the inventory of Gaddafi's Libyan army, found its way into the American heartland to destroy the corporate jet. Photographs of a burning vehicle with a spent missile launcher and a MANPADS shipping container were taken before flames completely engulfed the vehicle. The National Transportation Safety Board (NTSB) and the Federal Bureau of

Investigation (FBI) are en route to Abilene and the crash site to investigate.

U.S. officials have long been concerned U.S. military MANPADS (Man-Portable Air Defense Systems) could fall into terrorist hands creating a threat to U.S. military aircraft and commercial airliners. There are unofficial Congressional reports the number of MANPADS unaccounted for may be in the hundreds. Congress has taken no action since the reported shoot down of TWA Flight 800 in 1996. Off the coast of Long Island, New York eyewitnesses observed a streak of fire, consistent with an anti-aircraft missile launch, hit the aircraft. The NTSB declared an internal wiring problem had brought the 747 down. Investigative journalists in America should reevaluate the NTSB and FBI's activities for honesty and accuracy.

Presidential Candidate Bill McGee took questions from the media covering the rally in Abilene and made a statement. "We are saddened two exceptional Americans who were just doing their job were maliciously killed by terrorists. We are convinced this is the work of the Muslim Brotherhood."

The Secret Service ushered the McGee campaign onto the Dyess Air Force Base for security reasons.

End of Article.

• • •

It was well after two in the morning when Bill McGee and members of his personal security team drove to the front gate of the Air Force Base. Members of the press lined up in the visitor's parking lot seeking comments from the campaign. McGee was reluctant to meet with the press, but it was expected during a crisis. He recognized Colonel Eastwood with a wave and a head-nod. Eastwood shouted he needed a moment of his time.

Bill McGee, in suit trousers and a long sleeve shirt walked into the middle of the gaggle of reporters and journalists, Eastwood thought much too cavalierly. McGee said, "You probably want a statement. We don't know what happened, yet. We have dead pilots, and I weep for them and their families. I extend my humblest condolences. This was not their fight."

"Where is Colonel Eastwood? He's to be commended for capturing evidence our campaign jet was shot down by an anti-aircraft missile. If that is true, then whoever perpetrated this crime underestimated American resolve to find and punish those responsible. They can run and hide, but the arms of law enforcement are long. These criminals will be hunted to the gates of hell and back. They do not know what forces they have unleashed by such a cowardly and dastardly act."

"I'm grateful my campaign staff agrees this isn't a time to shrink into the shadows. We should redouble our efforts to bring sanity to America again. They mean to stop us by any means necessary. These are the domestic enemies our Founder's warned us about. We mean to find them, confront them, and defeat them."

Eastwood raised a hand and asked, "Admiral McGee, Dory Eastwood of *Unmasked & Unspun Network*, sir, do you still believe the Muslim Brotherhood could be behind this?"

McGee half-smiled. All eyes were on him. "Dory, thank you for your exceptionally fine reporting. Let me answer that this way. You know our old friend, Carl von Clausewitz, said, 'Politics is combat through other means.' We used to debate our rhetorical differences with the Democrat Party, but we can no longer do that because the Democrat Party has been taken over by radicals, Communists, and Islamists. If I thought they were responsible, I would say so, but you would never convince me anyone in the Democrat Party would use true weapons of war to gain an advantage by taking out their competition in such a manner. Cheating, cheap tricks to disqualify candidates, stealing elections — that is their bag of tricks. This wasn't about politics; shooting down aircraft isn't politics unless you are in the old Soviet Union. This has the fingerprints of a Muslim Brotherhood operation all over it. We'll see what the FBI finds out. But one thing is certain, while this was not an accident it's the first volleys of *war*."

"Let me also add, even Hitler and his ilk were cowards at first. They strongarmed legislation through the German parliament to emasculate their perceived foes, but they wouldn't consider carpet bombing their own civilians into submission. Just like hijacking commercial jets and flying them into buildings, anti-aircraft missiles used in an offensive capability against civilians are the tools of the immoral *jihadist*. It's my firm belief, culled from years in the counterterrorism world, this was the work of mentally defective *jihadis*."

The response brought a smile to Eastwood's face.

McGee continued, "So I will tell you right now, the FBI is on this case. But I also know from my days as the CIA Director the Federal Bureau of Investigation is wholly compromised. They couldn't find water if they were standing in a kiddie pool with a miner's helmet and a dowsing rod. FBI Agents used to be revered across the globe for thoroughness and toughness, fighting domestic and transnational criminals. But no longer. Their priorities are diversity, inclusion, and equity. That's 'DIE' for those following along."

Multiple hands raised, a cacophony of shouting from the gaggle of journalists tried to drown out the former CIA Director.

"FBI Special Agents need to support the United States, Israel's right to exist, and a free market economy. Today the FBI has Muslim Brotherhood members throughout FBI headquarters. This is a treasonous crime former Democrat presidents are responsible for."

"Listen closely, I call on President Hernandez, if he is listening, to correct this travesty by executive order requiring FBI Special Agents to be polygraphed like the CIA intelligence officers are. If they cannot pass the polygraph, they cannot be trusted. If their interests are with Moscow or the Muslim Brotherhood and not the United States, then their security clearances must be revoked. They should be escorted off the premises. Maybe we could deport them to someplace that thrills them, maybe they think of paradise as a place where there is totalitarianism."

"All government employees take an oath to defend and uphold the U.S. Constitution against all enemies, foreign and domestic. This oath applies to every employee of the FBI. Those who do not agree shouldn't work for the FBI. It's not a free speech issue – it's a national security issue. We can no longer look the other way when we find spies for the Islamic Underground have infiltrated the halls of the FBI. We can no longer allow spies of radical ideologies to infiltrate our law enforcement and intelligence agencies. We need to remember which is more important, supporting the goals of the FBI and America, or supporting the goals of Moscow or the Muslim Brotherhood. Goodnight."

Most reporters agreed McGee was an asshole.

As McGee and his entourage walked back to their vehicles, Eastwood uttered, "*Wow!*" He had recovered from McGee's outburst with, "Admiral McGee, a moment?"

McGee walked over to Eastwood. He had been thinking of another time when the Muslim Brotherhood attacked him directly and he responded in kind, with fury and violence. This time he was a public figure and couldn't, it was necessary to turn the cheek. McGee asked, "Dory, you have a question."

Eastwood said, "Admiral, I need to go to Europe for a few days. I have been chasing this story over there for a while and I was just notified the people I needed to talk to are ready and willing."

McGee said, "Go. I doubt we're going anywhere for a while."

"Thanks, Admiral."

"Dory, thank you. You were right on top of that truck fire." McGee smiled at him, the first time he had smiled in some time.

CHAPTER 37

November 21, 2019

Her security detail knew there had been an attempt to assassinate Bill McGee before Nazy entered her limousine. With no emotion, the Duty Officer briefed her McGee had narrowly escaped death the night before and two pilots had perished.

Nazy Cunningham sucked all the air from the vehicle. *Two pilots perished? Oh, God!* She severed the connection. She couldn't believe two pilots had died. She wouldn't believe it could be Duncan. Nazy ran through the possibilities in her head. She wouldn't call him; someone else's voice at the other end would destroy her. She checked her BlackBerry for the headlines from the CIA's *Early Bird*. *Attempted assassination means failure. Duncan was not flying a jet. He was with Coffey. Flying an airplane. Oh Duncan.* She didn't have all the information needed to make a rational decision. She tried to remain calm.

Nazy had to know. She called Duncan's number, and he didn't answer. Nazy was becoming more frantic as she scrolled through the contacts in her BlackBerry. There were new men; she couldn't remember their names. She remembered one sounded like an American pastry.

She gave up and called Bill McGee. Nazy woke him up. He could hear the despair in her voice. He said, "First of all, Duncan was not on the jet." Her relief was instantaneous. They talked freely as if discussing the weather. McGee provided the details of what he knew; she listened and when he finished, Nazy said she would call the White House.

"He may want to see you."

"Even if you are ok?" She was incredulous.

"It's more of a courtesy call. You are all worked up, and they will be too. In the big scheme of things, there's nothing you can do. It's a domestic matter. But a call from you will calm them down. The FBI should be on the scene. I put them on '*blast*' last night so there may be some fallout. But, your job is to offer any assistance necessary."

Nazy considered his words for the moment. *You put them on "blast?" Oh, Bill, what did you say?* She said, "Eastwood's article has pictures of a missile launcher."

McGee thought, *I love the way she said missile like the British do, with the long ī.* "It *was* a miss-*īle*. But, the Agency has more important things to worry about than me. At the very least, the Muslim Brotherhood is out of its cage. You need to be careful, Nazy. *Very careful.*"

"I will. Thanks, Bill."

"Duncan probably has things to do. I'll call him when we are done, if I can. I think he's teaching that FBI guy how to fly."

She nodded absentmindedly. "He is."

"Nazy, we really are ok. When I know more, I'll call you. We are shaken, not stirred other than venting my frustration at the FBI." He added other information that was more rambling than coherent; a sign even the puissant and redoubtable McGee could be rattled by forces he couldn't control.

"Ok, Bill, take care." Then it came to her: *They never stop.* She said, "You know, there may be more."

"I will and I know. I expected something but not a missile." Exasperated, "Not in America. If it's the Brotherhood, it means an escalation in hostilities. It could even be traced back to the *Insiders*. You'll have to work it because the FBI will not. I'll let you go. *Bullfrog,* out."

Nazy called the White House and told President Hernandez what she knew, that McGee and his staff were shaken but ready to hit the campaign trail when the airport reopened.

The President thanked her for the update and indicated that McGee had asked him to expand polygraphs for anyone in the law enforcement and intelligence communities who come into contact with classified information. President Hernandez said, "The Chief of Staff is drafting an Executive Order that polygraph testing is now the norm for all members of Federal law enforcement and the U.S.

intelligence communities. It will remain in effect until a new Security Executive Agent Directive can be published."

Nazy said, "Mr. President, that is fantastic. We have needed that, especially over at the FBI. That might be enough to alter the balance of power over there and help them recover. Thank you, Mr. President."

• • •

In her office, Nazy called Duncan again. He still didn't answer. She knew it probably meant he was flying and couldn't hear it or feel the vibration of the phone if it was even in his pocket. She called the number of the new mechanic whose name sounded like a pastry.

Tommy Barraclough didn't understand what he was seeing on the front of his smartphone — three zeroes. His first thought was that it was a robocall. He was about to punch it into the trash when he remembered who he was working for. He nearly fell over when he realized he was speaking to the Director of the Central Intelligence Agency. For a few moments he lost his tongue, as any bear would.

Nazy asked to speak to *Maverick*; Tommy confirmed "the PM" was flying with his student and should return within the hour. She asked Tommy, "Could you have the PM call the office. He has the number." She thanked the new man and disconnected the connection.

Tommy Barraclough thought, *I'm about to faint!*

• • •

After the final landing of the Schweizer SGM 2-37 motor glider, Tommy and Joe walked to meet the airplane and turn it around, which in aviation parlance meant to get it ready to go again, check everything and top it off with fuel. As soon as *Maverick* emerged from the cockpit Barraclough bounded across the tarmac and up to the airplane, and told his boss, "The boss called and she said you knew the number." *Maverick* gave him a thumbs up. He knew who the boss was. And the number.

Inside the hangar's office away from the wind and the airport noise, Duncan used the special program app which engaged all the CIA's encryption technology and called Nazy's private line.

Nazy recognized the number, dismissed those in the office, and when the room cleared, answered and said, "First, I need you. Second, Duncan darling, were you aware someone tried to assassinate Bill? It looks as if a missile was used to bring down his jet?"

"*What???* I hadn't heard a thing and I must have turned my phone off." He flipped through screens until he got to the call register. He had multiple missed calls. First things first. "Bill and everyone, ok?"

"Yes, there were eyewitness reports of a streak of fire that headed to the aircraft and then an explosion. Your jet was the only aircraft that had taken off. Eastwood was on scene, took pictures, and filed a report. Bill blasted the FBI's Muslim Brotherhood problem."

My jet? Which one? And I missed a call from Eastwood. Bill blasted the FBI's Muslim Brotherhood problem? Be still my beating heart. A little late don't ya' think, Bullfrog?"

Hunter composed himself, took a deep breath, and told Nazy what had transpired from his perspective. "Baby, wherever Bill was going, both of the Gulfstreams — the GIV-SP and the G-550 — were supposed to go to him. We had ferry pilots deliver the GIV-SP for the campaign to use, and then they were supposed to take the G-550 to the maintenance facility for work. QAS got the pilots from a service. I met them but didn't know them. I'll contact their company to see what they need from us. That is a real shame."

"*I know;* I was frantic."

"I can imagine. But all is well."

"All is not well. I miss you. It's times like these that make me think I'm not the right girl for this job."

Hunter wouldn't agree or disagree; he changed the subject for her. "So, do you need me or do you need a lift?"

"I do." She was back to playing word games with her husband.

He couldn't tell from the sound of her voice if she was still upset someone had tried to take Bill out of action or if the lift wouldn't be a pretty one. Duncan just knew Nazy didn't like giving him ugly lifts. He listened; she said, "Thomas Sankara, al-Sahrawi, Jason O'Hair."

Hunter rolled his eyes. *Definitely not a pretty one.* He asked, "Meet you on the BWI ramp tomorrow?"

"See you then. Be safe."

Thomas Sankara International Airport. Ouagadougou. Burkina Faso. There are shitholes and then there are shitholes. And I was just there in the area looking for O'Hair. Nazy must have better intel this time to send me back to Ouagadougou. The Grinch, Greg Lynche, always told me I had the carbon footprint of Ouagadougou. I think Greg just liked saying, Ouagadougou.

Let's see. The airport has commercial service and an unpretentious military contingent. French? No, I think we have some Air Force Predators at one end of the field. No U.S. Air Force jet to chauffer us around this time. We will need their comm freqs. It means we take the Hercules. That means we'll be gone a week, at least. Maybe ten days. And it'll take a couple of days to set everything up when we get there. We'll miss Thanksgiving. Again.

Maverick gathered everyone around him, then turned to Coffey and his mechanics and told them the bad news. "I didn't know until just now that eyewitnesses report our G-550's been shot down by a missile. Eastwood has pictures of a missile launcher in a truck on fire. That is incredible on so many levels. What that really means is that the Muslim Brotherhood has MANPADS here in the country and are using them to cull Republicans from the political process."

Coffey got serious. "It's an escalation of terrorism when they go after our candidates. If they really tried to assassinate the former CIA Director, that won't go unpunished."

I only hope so! The FBI cannot be counted on to do anything but lionize Special Agents who carry a Qur'an. Maverick rubbed his face to stall for some time to think. He exhaled and said, "I hired ferry pilots to move the SP to wherever McGee's campaign was headed, and they were to take the G-550 to Kerrville for maintenance. They were killed. That pisses me off. I don't know how I could have predicted *that!* McGee, Eastwood, and company — they're all ok."

Then *Maverick* asked, "Have the Democrats come out and condemned this act? I don't think they will." His mind was going a mile a second. *Was it really a Stinger? I need to talk to Eastwood and see what he really saw.*

The men were quiet. Nothing like this had ever happened to any of them before. *Maverick* then said, "We have to go out again. We are in the business of eradicating terrorists from the planet, and now they have showed they can punch back."

He thought of Nazy and was grateful she now had McGee's personal security detail.

With the men still in a half-circle, *Maverick* said, "This means missing Thanksgiving. That means premiums. I'll make it up to you when we get back. In the meantime, we have a set schedule of day landings in the Schweizer I'd like to complete. Then we'll have lunch at the *Azteca* and get this show on the road."

•   •   •

While *Maverick* and Coffey practiced landings at Hondo in the long-wing Schweizer, Tommy and Joe moved the flyable *Howard 500* that was in the hangar out of the barn by its tail wheel. They serviced the twin radial-engine aircraft to prepare for flight to Baltimore-Washington International and wondered aloud why they were prepping an antique that was slower than dirt for a mad dash across country. Joe drained water from the tanks onto the ramp until the clear water was replaced by a steady stream of purple fuel.

The mechanics knew there were other aircraft in the hangar. There was a disassembled *Howard 500* undergoing restoration. There was an F-4 *Corsair* in dark blue paint with Marine markings that looked to be in pristine condition, like the flying museum pieces in Elmira.

Then there was the *Starship*. In the diffused mercury vapor lights of the hangar, it had an eerie look about it, like something from the drawing board of Burt Rutan or the Horten Brothers. It was ahead of its time and looked like it could go like a bat out of hell.

Tommy and Joe knew Beech Aircraft Corporation had built 53 of the futuristic-looking eight-passenger *Starships*. It had a carbon fiber composite airframe with a front canard, vertical tails at the tips of severely swept wings, and engines pointing aft. The one *Maverick* had was one of the last remaining operational *Starships*. All the others had been destroyed by the manufacturer.

Link, Tommy, and Joe had talked about the aircraft in the hangar from the first day they had arrived in Hondo. They all wanted to get a ride in the *Starship* and thought today would be the day. They had assumed they would take the *Starship* because it was fast, not as fast as a jet, but still plenty fast. Hunter had burst their bubble. They didn't know why, but they were taking the *Howard 500*; the *Starship* wouldn't fly to Baltimore. *Maverick* said he would explain later.

• • •

Before entering the restaurant, *Maverick* called the LM-130J chief pilot in Elmira and relayed the mission requirements. He and the YO-3A crew would meet the LM-130J crew at the cargo loading area at the BWI airport. Tommy and Joe would load the YO-3A directly onto the LM-130J. *Maverick* advised the *Hercules* pilot they would probably arrive later than normal but would see them soon. *Someone shot down my jet! Killed some patriots! And I think I know who was responsible.* It would be a long time before Hunter got over the attack on his jet.

Over lunch, *Maverick* explained about a communist organization few people knew about. "We have reasons to avoid the *Tailwatchers*. The *Starship* is too flashy and even though there are only a few of them remaining, it's likely on their database; the *Howard* is an antique on the outside but isn't on the inside. It has satellite internet, a satphone, and a STU-III (Secure Telephone Unit) where the *Starship* doesn't. I don't like giving those commie bastards any information about our comings and goings. They will watch our every move if we let them. I don't want anyone knowing where we are, who we are, or what we are doing."

"It's going to be dicey as it is loading the *Yo-Yo's* container at BWI. But we have done it before—it's just cargo. The only good news is *Tailwatchers* normally watch business aircraft, so no one will shoot at the *Howard*. Now, we have a subscription to *Tailwatchers* for one reason, if they are notified one of our planes needs to be tracked, I want to know about it. And so, I would appreciate your help. I'll give you the link and the access code to QAS' *Tailwatchers* account. You can get alerts, like they will advise you when McGee is moving and know exactly where the Admiral's GIV-SP is."

Coffey said, "What you are saying is taking the *Howard 500* means the trip to Washington will take longer, but no one knows we have it. The best part, it's like camouflage and it will escape the notice of the *Tailwatchers*."

Maverick smiled, nodded; he was pleased they understood there were reasons for doing some things to protect yourself when the other side is making plans to kill you.

Tommy concurred and said, "That is wise *Maverick*." Coffey and Joe agreed, even if he thought it was melodramatic.

Maverick said, "If it's wisdom then it's from years of avoiding roadkill. The secret of life is to stay off the roads that can take you to your death. If there is any killing to be done, I want to be the one doing it." He tapped Colt Python hidden under his arm.

Tom Barraclough asked how *Tailwatchers* got started.

As the *Growler's* on-light kept pulsating, Hunter explained, "We think *Tailwatchers* is an old KGB front company. We know its headquarters is right across the street from the *Lubyanka*. A choice location, I'm sure. *Tailwatchers* is a sophisticated form of social media, that on the surface they track business aircraft like those websites where you can input a commercial carrier's flight number and up pops its flight track with ETA to destination, and so on but it's also one of those companies whose prime business is to spy on businessmen. Not only do they track an aircraft by its tail number *but who is inside*." The words hadn't left his mouth when he realized there could be other uses for *Tailwatchers*. Issues to explore for another day.

"The Agency got caught several years ago doing what they thought was a secret rendition of a high value terrorist from the Middle East and were horrified to find pictures of their jet and crew on the front page of the *New York Times*."

Tom said, "That sucks."

Everyone around the table nodded. *Maverick* continued, "What something like that does is eliminates those aircraft and aircrew from ever doing that work again. Reporters descend on the companies working for the Agency. It makes it harder to do those kinds of things. They're exposed. Do you think the Agency will ever use them again?"

Coffey asked, "So how do they do that?"

Maverick continued, "When leftist, communist, and anarchist groups spot business-type aircraft at feeder airports, like Manassas and BWI, but not Elmira or Kerrville, and they report it to the *Tailwatchers* website, those people receive funds electronically for their work. They take pictures or video of the fuselage and our N-numbers. They take telescopic pictures of who gets on and off the jets."

Coffey said, "So, the CIA leadership learned the hard way about these turds."

Maverick said, "After being reported on televisions and newspapers, and splattered all over the internet, courtesy of Al Jazeera, they shut down their program. But we started it back up and the sandal-wearing, goat-smelling, Al Jazeera hasn't discovered us yet."

Tommy asked, "How did you do that?"

Maverick said, "I cheat." The table erupted in laughter.

After lunch, Joe and Tommy put the Schweizer in the hangar and closed the doors. It was time to load the *Howard 500*. Hunter transferred his cooler and baggage from the Hummer2 to the front of the aircraft. Coffey, Joe, and Tommy did the same. After he closed the aircraft door, Hunter climbed into the cockpit and Coffey followed. Hunter asked with a grin, "Have you ever cranked up an eighteen-cylinder radial?"

Coffey looked at Hunter as if he had lost his mind.

Hunter lied, "Me either." They laughed.

They were soon airborne and headed to Baltimore. Those in the aircraft were thankful for noise-canceling headphones.

The assassination attempt was still on the minds of Hunter and Coffey. Once at cruising altitude, Coffey asked, "It's hard to believe the Gulfstream was shot down."

Maverick nodded. "There is no doubt *Tailwatchers* had a play as did the campaign publishing McGee's schedule. We can't flip tails numbers on candidate's aircraft, so we are kinda hosed in that regard. The real question is how did anyone get a *Stinger* in place so quickly and I reminded myself Dyess Air Force Base have some pretty big jets flying in and out of there, and shooting one down might make for an al-Qaeda *spectacular*. Stateside, on a training hop, no one carries countermeasures. No chaff, no flares, no missiles."

"You are right. It could have been a coincidence."

Maverick shook his head. "It's not that the Muslim Brotherhood wasn't disciplined enough to let it go. They could have taken out a bomber from the base anytime they wanted but they attacked a candidate. That's not Muslim Brotherhood shit. That's strategic."

They had been flying along for an hour when Coffey asked about Flight 800. "Apparently, you know something. All I know it was really weird at my place when that jet went down."

Maverick said, "It's my assertion the FBI faked the investigation into the shoot down of the TWA 747, Flight 800. For political reasons."

"I can see why you could think that. The leadership was firing Special Agents left and right who wouldn't toe the line. Those who wouldn't maintain the narrative. We had a Democrat president who looked to be soft on terrorists. When Flight 800 fell out of the sky, there was a rush to exonerate al-Qaeda and the Muslim Brotherhood. And to prove they knew it wasn't AQ or the Brotherhood, they hired Muslims to be agents. We were suddenly placed in what was tantamount to a re-education camp. Muslims were nice people, not all Muslims were bad." *What could go wrong with that?*

Maverick said, "That is because I have traveled all over the Islamic world and Muslims *are* nice people; they're great people. They have a terrorist problem in their back yard and we have a Democrat media problem in our front yard. What the left accuses us of is that it had to be obvious the FBI looked at all Muslims as bad and therefore that kind of thinking must be punished and deprogrammed. Someone at your place allowed the FBI to be manipulated. If the direction was coming from the White House and the President told the Director to retrain you guys, he should have very publicly resigned. And anyone else who was put in that position."

Coffey said, "You are right, of course. I was working other cases on the West Coast and was nearly pulled into that one. So grateful I wasn't. How do you know so much on that investigation?"

"Well, I taught the Aircraft Accident Investigations course for Embry-Riddle, so I looked at a lot of accidents. What the NTSB and the FBI said about Flight 800 was it was a bad wire, which is impossible. They lied for an incompetent president who was having the shit beat out of him because al-Qaeda and the Muslim Brotherhood had declared war on American aviation."

Coffey grimaced and nodded. *That's one way of putting it.*

Maverick continued, "The guy who shot me down over Algeria had an extensive cache of MANPADS. The Agency figured it out and tried to buy them back, but the Muslim Brotherhood screwed everything up when they stormed the consulate in Libya."

"*Benghazi.*" Coffey said it like it was a bad, vile thing.

"Yes, sir. We had Agency people and contractors there to make the deal. They would have taken maybe a thousand MANPADS out of circulation, but the timing was off. Republicans and Democrats had been too afraid to stop ransom payments. Afraid more jets would fall from the sky like confetti."

Coffey added, "Sort of like what Jefferson did with the Barbary pirates. Everyone paid tribute; President Hernandez said no more."

Hunter nodded and looked outside. "Flight 800 was probably a random aircraft; they got aboard; they didn't know it was their day to die." He thought of his parents and turned away again. "It just happened to be in the sky at the wrong place and time. That Democratic administration covered it up. If the FBI sends some good guys to Abilene, I'll bet that's what they'll find. Missile parts in the rubble. Then they'll have to figure out who has anti-aircraft missiles in America. I know who."

"Who?"

Maverick said, "The problem is much more difficult than anyone could believe."

Coffey waited patiently for an answer.

"Who has the FBI been currying favor with? Mazibuike stopped all surveillance of mosques in America. Where there is a vacuum, there are *Stingers*."

"Oh shit!"

CHAPTER 38

November 22, 2019

In the early morning hours, before securing for the evening, High Captain El Masri saw the light on in Supreme Lord Chancellor Scorpii's room. It was unusual; he knocked and entered and found Scorpii in front of a television.

He looked up and said, "I was hoping for some information on the *Amerikaner*." Once he delivered his line, Scorpii's attention was back on the BBC news.

El Masri forcibly inhaled; he wasn't used to delivering failure reports. *Amerikaners!* He was exasperated and irritated. He needed to get it over with. *"Mein Kanzler...."*

Scorpii looked up again.

With his heels together, El Masri announced he regretted to inform the Supreme Lord Chancellor, *"Der neger nicht gestoppt."* He explained that a missile knocked down the jet, but McGee was not on it.

"Er überlebte?" He survived? Scorpii was at once crestfallen then exasperated. *How is that possible?* Then he accepted what he dared not say: *The Arabs can only be counted on to fail....*

El Masri said they would have more information in the morning at breakfast. He remembered there was some good news, if they wanted to call it that. He said, "The man, the Libyan bomber was terminated, as you directed, *Mein Kanzler*."

The old man nodded in understanding. The money was immaterial. Scorpii said, "It wasn't in anyone's interest for the *Amerikaners* to interrogate the Libyan." The effort sent a spike of pain across his chest.

El Masri thought, *The Amerikaners offered $25 million to General Toufik to deliver them a live prisoner, but Herr Kanzler offered the Algerian $25 million to execute the mad bomber before the Amerikaners could get their hands on him.* El Masri pulled his lips into a thin smile. *I hear everyone* *was happy but the Amerikaners. Toufik took Herr Kanzler's and the CIA's money.*

Scorpii rocked his head and shut off the television. The pain radiating across his chest was subsiding.

El Masri wondered if Scorpii would explode in anger, but he only motioned for El Masri to help him to bed. *He must not be feeling well. Is it time for his medicine?*

Once he was beneath the bedcovers, Scorpii said, "He's a hard man to kill."

"*Ja, mein Kanzler.*" El Masri noticed the man's tremors were much worse than usual. He wondered if they got worse with stress, or if he had overextended his physical capacity for work. *Maybe both?*

"Maalik...."

"*Ja, mein Kanzler.*"

"I don't want to be disturbed in the morning. I want some positive news. I want to hear *die hündin wurde gestoppt.*"

Scorpii turned his back to him. The sign he had had enough for one evening. *One failed evening.* El Masri turned out the bedside lamp and stepped to the door. Before exiting, Maalik El Masri turned back for one final check. He stood in the doorway, one hand on the knob, the other on the doorframe: *You want me to tell you when the bitch has been stopped? We had the advantage of surprise, but we failed with the missile. The Amerikaners will be on their guard. But we will try again.* He directed the security man to administer morphine before he fell asleep.

•   •   •

Demetrius Eastwood and his one-person film crew arrived in Berlin to interview child sex trafficking survivors. He hoped it wouldn't be a bust.

CHAPTER 39

November 22, 2019

The scarlet and gold-trimmed, four-engine LM-130J landed after normal operating hours at the Thomas Sankara International Airport in Ouagadougou, Burkina Faso. Everyone associated with the operation of the commercial airport had gone home for the evening. After civilian ops ended, the U. S. military on the military side of the airport used the runway for conducting clandestine unmanned airborne intelligence operations over much of Western Africa. They were open for business and were expecting them; they had given the *Hercules* crew clearance to land. The *Hercules* crew asked to continue to the end of the runway and do a 180. The expeditionary air traffic controllers had seen it all with the special operations and unmanned aerial vehicles crowd. Because the airport was actually closed, they granted the aircrew's request.

Once the pilot had spun the LM-130J around and pointed the nose of the aircraft down the runway, he feathered the propellers so no thrust would be felt outside at the rear of the aircraft. The flight engineer turned the red lights on in the cabin for nighttime operations and lowered the cargo ramp. Joe and Tommy pushed the YO-3A fuselage out of its container with just enough force to get it moving. The tailwheel and main landing gear wheels tracked in the aluminum U-channels which ran down the middle of the cabin floor and down the ramp of the LM-130J. *Maverick*, wearing a half-million dollar black helmet, sat in the rear cockpit and depressed the toe brakes to stop the airplane when he thought he was far enough away from the rear of the *Hercules*.

As Joe and Tommy went back inside the container for a wing, Coffey, in a black Nomex flight suit like *Maverick's*, mounted the aircraft, strapped himself in the front seat, and connected his lap belt, integrated helmet systems and communication cords. *Maverick* would pilot from the back seat in case he needed to reload the airplane's TS2, which could only be done from the aft cockpit. But first Joe and Tommy had to put the airplane together.

The two mechanics wore night vision systems strapped onto their heads and constructed the airplane in two minutes; they dropped the huge pins into each wing's two clevises to mate the wings to the fuselage. Then they hooked up all the QDs (quick disconnect fittings) for the fuel, the control surfaces, and the electrical systems. There were no wingtip lights.

Coffey was overwhelmed by the night vision imagery and cockpit instrument symbology on his helmet visor. He kept his hands and feet off of the controls and kept quiet, allowing *Maverick* to go through his pre-takeoff routine with no interruptions. *Maverick* called for the canopy, and Coffey lowered the canopy. Joe and Tommy taped all the fuselage-wing seams with speed tape. When they were clear of the YO-3A, *Maverick* engaged the starter. The six-bladed *fast* propeller slowly chugged around; Coffey counted eight blades passing in front of him when the engine fired off. Coffey was getting a show.

Curiously missing during the engine start sequence was the low growl of engine exhaust. Coffey couldn't hear none of the hot exhaust gases being diffused through a pair of large conformal mufflers and long, perforated piping that ran down the starboard side of the fuselage. The engine at start and idle sounded more like a diminutive Lionel locomotive circling a tree at Christmas. *Maverick* had reminded Coffey that the strangely engineered muffler system was top secret.

With a sweep of the flight controls, control stick right and left, fore and aft, pedals left and right, *Maverick* was satisfied the aircraft was ready to fly. Green images from the integrated night vision system filled his visor. He had a clear view ahead. He eased the throttle to the firewall for takeoff, right out from under the LM-130J's tail and into the darkness. Unlike the Super Cub and the Schweizer, Coffey felt the powerful YO-3A jump into the air. He lifted his visor to see the three multifunction displays were awash with night vision imagery, instruments, and flight data symbology that were light years ahead of what he remembered from the round steampunk gauges in the F-4 *Phantom* II.

The Agency's Science & Technology Directorate had integrated the best demonstrated and available forward-looking infrared sensor from FLIR laboratories with cutting-edge facial recognition software. This capability enabled *Maverick* to load known photographs of Adnan Abu Walid al-Sahrawi and American businessman Jason O'Hair into the aircraft's mission computer. Before landing in Africa, *Maverick* had received GPS coordinates from Nazy. Once safely airborne, he aimed the *Yo-Yo* to intercept the GPS coordinates and handed the aircraft over to Coffey so he could get a feel for the aircraft while the air was settled and thermals were not a factor. *"Your jet,"* *Maverick* said, and immediately he felt Coffey take control of the airplane.

Coffey grinned, *"My jet"* as he placed his hand on the control stick and his feet on the rudder pedals. Looking through the helmet's visor he could see everything he would have seen in the daylight, but now in shades of night vision systems green. *Maverick* had handed him an aircraft perfectly trimmed.

*   *   *

There was a time when there had been hundreds of businessmen and crewmembers kidnapped from hijacked ships in Africa that were being held every year. Bill McGee was running a complex near Hondo, Texas training former and retired SEALs and Delta troops to accompany ocean-going commercial ships as protection against open-ocean hijackings. Attempted hijackings continued but with McGee-trained men aboard ship, those all failed. Some private sailing vessels were captured and the Somalis held dozens of people hostage. But after a few low-profile rescues, where vast numbers of Somali pirates were killed, the hijackings stopped for years, because *Maverick* had eradicated Somali pirates from the equation.

For the past two years Special Operations Command (SOCOM) mission briefs had placed special emphasis on finding and exfiltrating the one American businessman who was still missing in Africa. The trail had gone cold, and everyone at SOCOM felt he was likely dead since there had been no demands for ransom. If he was alive, he had to be surviving in unspeakable conditions.

Months of satellite imagery analysis and high-altitude surveillance from the airport in *Ouagadougou* yielded nothing; no clues or trace of the missing hostage. When President Hernandez asked Nazy to look into the matter using all means necessary, she understood he was instructing her to send Duncan's special purpose aircraft and crew into position to conduct the mission.

After three hours in the Lockheed YO-3A at several hundred feet over the Mali-Niger border, *Maverick* found the jungle prison and command center of the al-Qaeda affiliate, the Islamic State in the Sahara. It was in Mali and was well-positioned under a natural sandstone overhang along the Niger River. Satellites and unmanned aerial vehicles never would have found the compound. FLIR imagery *under* the overhangs ratted the terrorists out.

"If I had come this far north and east the last time, I would have found him," *Maverick* lamented.

Coffey's wasn't sure what he meant so *Maverick* explained, "It's not as if they have a sign proclaiming they're the Islamic State in the Sahara. We have intel, GPS coordinates, and I know what kind of pattern to look for."

"Pattern?"

"Yeah. That's the secret sauce. Recognizing the pattern. You can see this setup is cleverly hidden and was chosen to exploit the limitations of satellites and UAVs. Soldiers out on maneuvers do not comport themselves in such a way and are not motivated to hide from satellites and UAVs."

"Oh, you are so right when you point it out!"

Maverick asked Coffey to set up an orbit so he could observe the comings and goings of the men in the compound.

He provided a running commentary. "I'm getting set up to check for a match from the facial recognition software in the FLIR. If we can positively identify al-Sahrawi, the game is on."

"You can see in the FLIR they have cut some material from that shipping container to make it look like the bars on a cell. My guess is that's the prison. You would never know from a satellite or UAV photo. And there is a guard nearby. All consistent with someone being held against their will. And... and... there you are. *Tally ho!* There is a sliver of thermal energy of a man inside the container. We have arrived at our destination. Now we have to make them move."

Coffey was incredulous. "We have to make them move?"

Maverick said, "Well, we can't land here. We might get him out, but I'm afraid he's going to have to help."

Coffey was mystified by it all. "What are you going to do?"

"You fly the airplane; I have some programming to do." *Maverick* provided more commentary. "I'm throwing out *Weedbusters* and programming the mission computer not to irradiate the area around that CONEX. I'm also deploying the laser designators and the gun. You'll need some more RPMs with the additional drag. Standby. I'm going to take control of the aircraft in three, two, one—*my jet!*"

Coffey threw his hands up and relinquished control as *Maverick* jammed the throttle to the stops for two seconds; he counteracted the nose suddenly yawing and the additional thrust and torque with a hefty application of rudder. After the violent, almost spastic maneuver, he centered the pedals with his feet, returned the throttle to where it had been, and shouted, "*Your jet!*"

As Coffey tried to steady the slightly unstable YO-3A, *Maverick* was already sighting in the TS2 said, "Now watch what happens. We need to be lucky. I only have a finite number of bullets."

Coffey frowned, *You only have a finite number of bullets? What are you doing?*

Dozens of men poured out of ramshackle huts which wouldn't have won any cliff dwelling contests with the Anasazi. The men were half dressed, stumbling out with what Coffey thought were AK-47s with huge curvy magazines.

Maverick said, "As you can see, those are AKs. The terrorists' weapon of choice. And they do not have uniforms."

The men on the ground looked up to find the source of the strange noise. *Maverick* engaged the *Weedbusters* laser system, blanking the area where he believed the hostage was in the CONEX container, and blinded the terrorists with ultraviolet radiation. The men's eyes were fully dilated, wide open to better see at night. But their eyes were also unprotected. When the men were hammered with the UV-C, they immediately fell or went down on their knees, grasping their eyes. More men spilled out of huts and *Maverick* illuminated them with the laser designator, fired the TS2, and dropped those men where they stood; about one terrorist every six seconds.

Things happened so quickly, Coffey thought he had missed something.

Maverick came back up on the intercom and said, "Now I'm looking for a sign. All part of the pattern. The boss will make his presence known. Hopefully, it's our guy."

After 200 missions, *Maverick* knew the leaders of terrorist organizations nearly always come out after first contact, and they're always pissed off. They had been interrupted, and someone would pay. *Maverick* assumed al-Sahrawi was with a woman and would emerge after getting some clothes on and grabbing his weapon.

When al-Sahrawi came out and saw his men dead or writhing on the ground, their hands on their eyes from flash radiation burns, he took an aggressive stance with the AK as if there were an enemy in front of him. He aimed, but he didn't fire. He looked around cautiously, and then he looked up.

In one movement, *Maverick* slewed the FLIR to him and queried the facial recognition program. *Maverick* placed the infrared laser designator on the man's chest just as the program came back with the match: *Adnan Abu Walid al-Sahrawi. Maverick* verified the crosshairs were on al-Sahrawi and pulled the trigger on the TS2 controller. The exhaust from the rocket-propelled *Terminator* round temporarily obscured the FLIR image. Two seconds later, al-Sahrawi's sternum exploded. The AK fell from al-Sahrawi's hand, and he toppled backward. He was wearing a wristwatch; no one else on the ground had a wristwatch.

Maverick zoomed the FLIR on the watch on al-Sahrawi's wrist. He nodded and calmly stated, "Keep flying the airplane. More altitude is ok. Now we have to get O'Hair out of there." *Maverick* fired the TS2 every twenty seconds, then slewed the FLIR and saw the thermal images of human feet moving in the container. The FLIR image clearly displayed on his helmet visor was virtually photographic quality.

. . .

Coffey thought, *Maverick displays remarkable sangfroid as he sizes up the situation second by second. He's so cool under fire.*

. . .

The man in the container had been startled awake by the gunfire. He heard men groaning and shrieking. He wondered what had happened. Jason O'Hair was weak. He had lost most of his hair and over fifty pounds. He shuffled to the shipping container's door and looked between the metal slats.

. . .

Maverick could now see the thermal image of a man. He cautioned Coffey to keep flying the airplane as he punched buttons and typed a message on one of the multifunction displays, selecting the red laser designator and writing program. He transferred the message on the screen to the display program which projected the letters on the ground in front of the makeshift prison.

OHAIR, R U OK? RAISE UR THUMB IF OK

The thermal image of a man holding his arm outstretched between the container's slats with a thumb pointing skyward set *Maverick* to work on a new message. Coffey could see everything *Maverick* was doing electronically as the helmet displays were linked and showed what was being selected.

Maverick said, "Keep us in an orbit at this altitude." He swept the FLIR around the compound to see if there was anyone who could threaten O'Hair. Satisfied all the men were either dead or still on the ground holding their eyes, he returned his attention to O'Hair.

Coffey trimmed the YO-3A to maintain altitude. He watched the FLIR sweep the area until it locked on the shipping container. *This is incredible! So many things to learn....*

Maverick typed: *RAISE YOUR THUMB IF OK*. After receiving a thumbs up, *Maverick* typed: *AFRAID IF I BLOW OPEN THE DOOR I'LL KILL U I DON'T SEE ANY LOCK JUST A LEVER TRY TO GET OUT*

Maverick watched O'Hair force his arm through the slats to manipulate one of the two door closing mechanisms. He stretched until he could get his fingers on the lever.

The helmets' thermal image overlaid on the night vision system imagery of O'Hair struggling to stretch his arm and get closer to the handle, energized the men in the *Yo-Yo*. They yelled, "*Come on! Come on! You can do it! You can do it!*"

Then in one quick movement, O'Hair got a grip on the handle and pushed it up and away. The cage door opened, and O'Hair tumbled out. Coffey yelled, "*There you go! There you go! Nice job!*"

O'Hair stumbled trying to get his legs to work. *Maverick* typed a new message with the laser designator to project at the man's feet: IF HE TOOK YOUR WATCH GO GET IT NOW

Coffey tried to comprehend what Maverick was doing and remained quiet.

The *Yo-Yo* aviators watched the man on the ground struggle to walk. O'Hair got to his feet and looked for a sign.

Maverick used the writing program and the laser designator to create a red pulsating arrow to show the direction where al-Sahrawi had fallen.

Coffey was astounded at *Maverick's* composure. He was more astounded to see the thermal image of O'Hair bend over and remove the wristwatch off the dead man.

Maverick typed and the LD displayed at the man's feet: *TAKE HIS GUN N TRUCK*

Coffey said, "He learns quick."

In the flickering light of two large barrel fires under the overhang, the men watched O'Hair relieve al-Sahrawi of his weapon and then shuffle to the nearest pickup truck.

The first vehicle O'Hair entered had a screwdriver in the ignition. He turned it and the engine turned over. The truck was a standard, but he knew how to shift gears.

Maverick repeated the command which generated a shape of a basic arrow. O'Hair followed the thick 90° angle with a three-foot line emanating from the apex. "Link, parallel him on the road leading east. We are not out of the woods yet. We are about fifty miles from civilization."

O'Hair found it was easy to follow the bright red arrow tracking on the ground in front of him, even if it was intermittent at times.

Every few seconds Hunter slewed the FLIR ahead of and behind the moving truck. The imagery in their helmets indicated no one was following Jason O'Hair.

Coffey thought, *Still checking 12 and 6. Maverick, this is mind-blowing!*

●   ●   ●

The U.S. Air Force air traffic controllers at the Thomas Sankara International Airport jumped when a deep bass voice came across one of their secret operational VHF frequencies. None of their manned aircraft were out, so it was startling to hear English on the encrypted frequency. The voice gave an Agency codeword which got everyone's attention and then continued, "Sierra Hotel Triple Seven flight following one AMCIT held hostage; request immediate airlift and ambulance at Dori. Will flight follow to Dori then must RTB. Questions, contact Charlie Oscar Sierra at Ouagadougou Embassy. Sierra Hotel Triple Seven out."

●   ●   ●

Safely airborne off the coast of West Africa, Coffey found courage to say, "You had him go back to get his watch."

Maverick was making his bed. "That's right."

"How did you know al-Sahrawi had taken his watch?"

"They all do. That is what terrorist leaders do. The more gold, the better. When American businessmen are in an African town, they never think of their expensive watch on their wrists. But you can bet on the come someone notices. Except for pirates, I don't know of a case where an American was kidnapped in Africa and he wasn't wearing an expensive watch. Having him retrieve his watch from the guy who took it's a way of saying he was stronger than the man who tried to take his watch and kill him. They targeted them because they know he has money. And they will do anything for money. They targeted O'Hair for his watch, and al-Sahrawi paraded around his compound, brandishing that watch. Proof of Muslim power over the infidel. So, if I can, I try to reunite the watch it its owner."

Coffey shook his head in amazement. Hunter wasn't through. "You asked about the *Daytona* I had when I was on active duty — rose gold. Moon watch."

"I remember."

"Hardly anyone has ever heard of rose gold in watches but the Shah of Iran had heard of the moon watches and by royal order in 1972 he had 50 made, in rose gold, for gifts to his generals. These watches like the Rolexes are universally regarded as trophies, not timepieces. They're coveted by thieves on six continents."

Coffey was speechless for a few seconds. "*Maverick*, I will always remember you sending Mr. O'Hair back to get his watch. That was so incredible — the kind of stuff you would hope *Captain America* would do."

As he rolled over on his sleeping bag, *Maverick* grinned. *Just another day on the treadmill.* "We need to get some sleep. Goodnight, Link."

CHAPTER 40

November 27, 2019

The President of France held his weekly press conference and announced the death of Adnan Abu Walid al-Sahrawi, the leader of the Islamic State in the Sahara, and the rescue of a dozen women. He stated, "There are no further details on the operation other than the French Foreign Legion has finally brought al-Sahrawi to justice. Without their leader, the Islamic State in the Sahara has been routed and destroyed. I applaud the admirable work of the men of the French Foreign Legion in Mali."

The Associated Press reporter detailed the Islamic State in the Sahara had abducted many local churchmen, women, and foreigners over the last five years and was believed to have been holding American businessman, Jason O'Hair, who was abducted from his hotel in 2016 in the capital city of Bamako. There had been no confirmation from the U.S. Embassy in Ouagadougou Jason O'Hair had been returned to the United States via military transport within the last 24-hours.

•　　•　　•

After receiving the President's Daily Brief, President Hernandez welcomed Jason O'Hair to the White House and the Rose Garden. From behind the lectern with the Presidential Seal emblazoned on the front, President Hernandez said, "I officially welcome Mr. Jason O'Hair to the White House." To loud applause, President Hernandez shook hands with the former captive. His Rolex *GMT Master* would be clearly visible in the official photos when he raised his hand to wave at an attentive crowd.

"Mr. O'Hair was abducted by the Islamic terrorist group ISIS, the Islamic State in the Sahara, a Muslim Brotherhood affiliate. The French Foreign Legion working in Mali rescued him and a dozen local women hostages. I again call on Congress and the Federal Bureau of Investigation to declare the Muslim Brotherhood a terrorist organization."

"I have invited Mr. O'Hair to the Oval Office where I will sign an Executive Order that polygraph testing will be required for all members of the law enforcement and U.S. intelligence communities. This Executive Order will be effective immediately and shall remain in effect until a new Security Executive Agent Directive can be published. This new directive signals polygraph testing will be the *de facto* screening tool for all recruits, contractors, and government personnel who come into contact with classified materials."

"Specifically, all Federal law enforcement agencies and the intelligence community shall establish a new polygraph program if there isn't one already in place. Agencies with polygraph programs will expand existing polygraph testing in vetting staff members of the legislative branch, the executive branch, and Agency executive personnel as a prerequisite for security clearances or determining their eligibility for sensitive positions."

"Furthermore, the Administration rejects the innumerable erroneous studies about the validity of using the polygraph for employee screening. This directive mandates continued reliance on polygraph testing which has been the mainstay of the intelligence community for decades."

"Among all the occasions for use of polygraph testing, the Executive Order singles out suspected and actual 'espionage, sabotage, and unauthorized disclosure of classified information.' These diverse offenses are of comparable significance and concern and shall result in the employee's termination."

President Hernandez left the lectern with Mr. Jason O'Hair as dozens of reporters shouted questions.

* * *

The QAS LM-130J blew a tire on landing at Shannon International Airport in the Republic of Ireland. Since the civilian crew always carried spare tires, jacks, and tools for such an occasion, repairs were made quickly. Once the corrective maintenance had been completed, the crew couldn't continue their flight to the United States due to crew rest issues. They would stay at the Treacys' Oakwood Hotel for the night.

* * *

After signing the Executive Order, President Hernandez cleared the Oval Office for a few minutes. He was interested in the latest edition of the CIA's assessment of Rho Schwartz Scorpii. He had time for the few pages Nazy had left for him before his next appointment arrived.

Regarding the question of how Scorpii accumulated his wealth, there are several possibilities. Our best assessment is derived from a rabbi's diary we gained in 1959. Scorpii's name appears in several diary entries. The nineteen-year-old Scorpii had traveled with the rabbi and some Jewish people to escape from East Germany.

The timing of this movement is consistent with the Soviet Union's mobilization of materials and manpower to begin the construction of the Berlin Wall in 1961.

There were groups of Jews who had survived the war or had returned to Berlin after the war, but didn't want to give the Soviets and the East Germans another opportunity to eradicate them. The Jewish people were extremely suspicious of any unusual activity made by soldiers of the Soviet Union and fled to the Allied Sector to escape what they believed to be a more hostile and irreligious East Germany.

Key in understanding the dynamics of Scorpii's acquired wealth begins on Kristallnacht, the evening of November 9 and 10, 1938, before Scorpii was born. On that night the main building of Fraenkelufer Synagogue at Kottbusser Ufer 48–50, was reportedly badly damaged. By the end of 1941, Fraenkelufer Synagogue's address had been renamed Fraenkelufer 10-16. It was no longer an active synagogue; Nazis were working in the building. The building had never been repaired, so the bombing damage was still evident. That was a perfect camouflage which enabled the Nazi's to use the building to store looted Jewish property from the concentration camps around Berlin.

A diary entry of a Nazi colonel detailed that gold watches and teeth were collected from the extermination camps in Auschwitz, Buchenwald, Dachau, and Ravensbrück and were stored there until they could be processed into gold bars and coins. Nazis chose the site specifically because Allied bombers wouldn't intentionally bomb churches and synagogues, even those that were no longer active.

After a bombing raid on Berlin in 1944, the Nazi's were forced to abandon the old synagogue. It was reported all the Nazis who worked in the shadow of the damaged synagogue had been killed.

When the synagogue was scheduled to be demolished in 1957, the rabbi's last comment was, "Young Scorpii, who came to us from the other side of Berlin, who always wore a threadbare driving cap that was too big for him, who had worked so hard on removing the piles of debris from our beloved Fraenkelufer Synagogue, has abandoned us."

Thousands of pre-war Jewish gold watches and gold ingots, presumably hidden in the Fraenkelufer Synagogue, have never appeared on the black market, in pawn shops, or been identified in private collections. Rumors of Nazi goldsmiths working at the synagogue appeared to be just rumors.

By 1970, Scorpii appeared to have come into significant wealth and was living in the Schöneberg district. This Berlin district has been home to the gay culture for over 100 years and is well known for having "the first ever homosexual villages with a thriving queer attitude." The district also features small covert businesses which cater to pedophiles.

Records indicate Scorpii began his business career as a party promoter, hosting male-only fetish clubs around West Berlin. His trademark was a driving cap of the style favored by professional golfers in America. There is no known rationale for his preference of wearing a wool tweed driving cap.

He purchased nightclub establishments in the Schöneberg district of Berlin which catered to men. Profits from his nightclubs provided the seed money to acquire real estate and hotels that catered to an "underserved clientele" in Germany.

There is sufficient evidence he either directly or tangentially influenced the collapse of communism in Eastern Europe in the late 1980s and early

1990s, and took advantage of the chaos in the remnants of the former Soviet Union to secure ownership of several petroleum conglomerates. There is less physical evidence these petroleum acquisitions were facilitated through blackmail, i.e., rumors of photographic evidence that the Soviet officials who once controlled the petroleum industries, such as Red Star Fuels, had inappropriate or proscribed contact with minors.

Petroleum makes up the bulk of Scorpii's overall net worth of $250 billion. Ten percent of Scorpii's overall net worth is in real estate.

He is believed to have been born near Ravensbrück, Germany to a non-observant Jewish family. Analysis suggests Scorpii survived the Nazi's extermination camps as a child prostitute.

Scorpii is a supporter of progressive and liberal political causes, to which he dispenses donations through his foundation, the Ostgut Foundation. Ostgut was the name of the former railway depot from which Scorpii and his family boarded a train for the Nazi concentration camps.

He has donated over $10 billion to various philanthropic causes through the Ostgut Foundation "to reduce poverty and increase transparency, and for scholarships and universities around the world."

When President Hernandez finished reading the documents, he better understood what drove Scorpii. *Payback's a bitch.*

It was time for his next appointment.

•   •   •

The heavily accented Arabic voice came through the walkie-talkie receiver, "Just entering the parkway, one mile."

The man received the message and put the walkie-talkie into his pocket. He removed the utilitarian pot metal grenade launcher and the rocket-propelled grenade from his backpack. He assembled it quickly; the RPG's long cylindrical solid-rocket fuel motor slipped effortlessly into the launcher. He stroked it and beheld the power of Allah in it. He looked around once more to ensure he was alone.

He knew how to fire an RPG from his time in Palestine, and that was his mission. He was on another mission for Allah.

The RPG was the Tandem 95, a dual-charge warhead on a rocket-propelled grenade. There were a few that had been used in Israel; this was the only one in North America. It was derived from the immensely successful Yasin RPG developed by Hamas engineers in their Research and Industry Unit. The first charge of the dual-charge warhead was designed to disrupt the Explosive Reactive Armor (ERA) blocks that envelop a tank's body, allowing the second main charge to hit the armor of the vehicle. The warhead was designed to detonate on impact. He believed he was far enough away from the traffic below him that he wouldn't get fragged from the impact.

The Tandem 95 could destroy a tank, but the target was not a tank. It was an armored vehicle. He was beside the George Washington Memorial Parkway in a perfect location, hidden from view and waiting for the CIA Director's limousine to pass in front of him. He put binoculars to his eyes and repeated, almost as a chant, "*Tawkalt ala Allah, Tawkalt ala Allah, Tawkalt ala Allah....*" (I rely on God, I rely on God, I rely on God.) He took up tension in the trigger. When the black vehicle entered the reticle of the optical sight, he squeezed the trigger on the RPG launcher. After a microsecond delay, it shot off and he was immediately enveloped in white wispy smoke.

He didn't stay to assess his success. As he had done several times in Palestine, in one continuous movement, he turned, slipped the spent launcher into his backpack, and shouted as he ran up the hill, "*Allahu Akbar!*"

●　　●　　●

The trailing edge of the lead vehicle exploded in a red and yellow ball of fire; the vehicle was launched ten feet into the air and away from the roadbed, toward the Potomac River.

The driver of the middle vehicle reacted as anyone would when a vehicle in front of them erupts into a fireball. Conditioned by years of defensive driving, he hit the brakes, but the head of the security detail riding in the passenger seat screamed at the driver to "*DRIVE!*" She reached to his side of the vehicle and mashed the man's foot on the accelerator.

At the moment of the assault, Nazy Cunningham had been reading papers from her briefcase. The proximity of the blast's concussion hit her vehicle instantly; shrapnel was embedded in the windshield. The head of the security detail pulled her weapon and shrieked for Nazy to get on the floor.

Nazy had already been flattened; she wasn't wearing a seatbelt. She felt the vehicle speed up. All she could think of at that moment was the instructor of the defensive driving course yelling, "*Back up! Back up! Back up!*"

The trailing security vehicle caught up to the speeding Suburban as they rushed down the George Washington Memorial Parkway to the entrance of CIA headquarters. After Nazy was aboard the installation, the guards at the entry control point raised the crash barriers and stopped all traffic coming onto the facility. They took up firing positions and waited for instructions.

Nazy didn't immediately emerge from the Suburban. She asked what had happened, and the security chief told her an RPG had been fired at the vehicles, hitting the back of the lead vehicle. Nazy asked, "How do you know it was an RPG?"

The woman responded, "I've seen them in Iraq and what they do. I've had vehicles explode in front of me from IEDs and RPGs. That was an RPG. It tore the rear end off of the number one vehicle."

The Park Police and the FBI scoured the area where the RPG had been fired. The FBI Special Agent in Charge didn't know immediately what kind of weapon had been used.

No official word was uttered on the Washington D.C. cable television networks or in the newspapers. Later in the evening, according to an FBI official, the cause of the vehicle explosion was a bad wire in the gasoline tank had ignited gasoline fumes.

No one in the media asked the FBI spokeswoman, "Are there supposed to be wires in a gasoline tank?"

CHAPTER 41

November 27, 2019

News of the attempt on Nazy's life reached the White House before the fire department extinguished the fire on the destroyed security vehicle.

President Hernandez called her cellphone. She answered and put him on speakerphone. She told him she was still in the limousine, safe at headquarters. He asked what had happened, and she said she had been so engrossed in her paperwork she had seen none of it; she heard and felt the blast, and the concussion of the powerful explosion. "The vehicle was tossed about. After the blast wave, I tried to pick myself off of the floor, but the security chief told me to stay down, so I did. My ears are still ringing." Nazy said she was grateful for her security detail and hadn't received information on the condition of the security officers in the lead car.

"Nazy, I don't mean to be indelicate, but it appears you and Bill have both been targets for assassination. Any ideas?"

She took a few seconds to consider her reply. "Yes, Mr. President. We must have kicked over a fire ant hill. We hurt Iran, but we have also decimated the Muslim Brotherhood. I don't know who else could have been responsible. We can surmise who they are, but it's early. Someone doesn't like what we have done and are striking back. I expect the police and the FBI are on it. But that part of it, the investigation phase, is out of our hands. Domestic investigation."

She confessed to herself, *Oh yes, I know who it was. Duncan worries about me all the time, that the Muslim Brotherhood is waiting for the right time to do something exactly like this. If they had just taken a shot at Bill, I'd blame Iran. But both of us? We need more intel.* She suddenly got cold and wished she had brought an overcoat. It was always cold in the New Office Building and it was cold outside. She had a jacket there, but she had forgotten to put one in the limo. Nazy shivered then continued, "Mr. President, we have no answers as to who; we'll have to work on why questions."

"You have no intelligence as to why?"

"Not at this time, Mr. President. These were domestic attacks. Purview of the FBI. We know the CIA leadership are perennial targets. But the only thing that has really changed is Bill is running for president. And that may scare some people in high or even foreign places."

"*Foreign places?*"

"Mr. President. Iran hates Bill and the Muslim Brotherhood dislikes me with a passion. Some senior intelligence officers believe that when they're in these jobs, they escape scrutiny from terrorist organizations. While I have nothing at the moment to connect them to this episode, I wouldn't discount Bill's campaign as a causal factor. Someone may not be happy with it, or Bill, or me."

"Or all three. It might be because of our successes."

Nazy thought, *We crushed the Iranian leadership and slapped them in the face by killing General Roustaie. The Muslim Brotherhood couldn't fathom their mujahedeen being eliminated in Iran.* She let the obviousness set in and said, "That is entirely possible, Mr. President, but we need to investigate. We need an honest broker. I'm afraid it will be five years before the FBI finds anything." That was another way of saying she didn't trust the FBI.

Nazy was now shaking so uncontrollably she wouldn't have been able to write her name or keep the contents of a coffee cup from splashing out. She gave herself a mental pat on the back for selecting the speakerphone option, because she could barely hold her BlackBerry.

President Hernandez asked, "Where's Duncan? He's not home yet, is he?"

Oh no, Duncan! He will be livid. "Mr. President, I talked to him this morning. They stayed at Shannon. He will be home soon." She ran her trembling hands through her hair then wrapped her arms around herself tightly. "I appreciate your concern, Mr. President. I'll be alright." *I lie! I lie! I lie!*

"Nazy...."

"Mr. President, Duncan told me when pilots have to eject from an airplane, they get them back into another airplane as soon as they can. Work forced on you doesn't allow you to dwell on misfortune. I have so much to do; I think I'll really be ok. As long as I can get into my office without too much trouble. There's a couch in Bill's office; if I have to stay on the property for a few days, I'll stay here." *But if Duncan comes into town, he'll want to meet at the Marriott. And I can't go to the hotel looking like this.*

"OK. So, you want to get back to work... and you are not comfortable leaving the complex just yet. Ahem, umm, can you just send over the PDB tomorrow? Electronically. Please know that's an option."

She was hurt at the implication. Nazy chose her words carefully. "Mr. President, someone will be there tomorrow at the regular time."

"Ok, thank you Nazy."

It was warming up in the vehicle, as if the driver had turned on the heater. Nazy nerves were suddenly calmed. She took a deep audible breath and got out of the car.

•　•　•

I don't know if good news travels fast or bad news travels faster. Nazy entered her office much to the amazement of her secretaries.

Someone tries to kill you and you're back at work?

She left the door open. She expected a flurry of activity to occur on the seventh floor at CIA Headquarters. It wasn't every day the Director was targeted for assassination. *In Washington!*

Nazy then remembered the CIA was the likely target on September 11. The passengers wouldn't stand for more murder and mayhem; they interrupted the terrorists' plans and forced the jet to crash in Pennsylvania. *This is dangerous business. Not for everybody.*

A dozen members of the Senior Intelligence Service who thought they should have been promoted to Director came by to express their support and thanks she was safe. Universally, they were convinced that Nazy should question her dedication to *the Company*. Nazy indulged the visitors all the while thinking, *I've been targeted and I just want to see my husband.*

Public Affairs, the Director of the Science and Technology Directorate, and the Chief of Security all walked in at the same time. Nazy told the Public Affairs Officer, "We do not have a comment, and you should forward all inquiries to the FBI. Officially, I will be out of sight for several days."

Nazy told the Director of S&T what she wanted and when she needed it. The S&T woman couldn't conceive coloring Nazy's remarkable black hair and responded, "We can make you a wig; we do not have to color your hair. A wig can be any color; we can even reverse the color."

Nazy said, "I don't care—I just don't want to be a redhead."

As Nazy further explained what she wanted, the S&T Director concurred. "You are right. A wig probably won't do in that situation. You want to put it on and take it off without a lot of fuss. I have the perfect product for you. *Magnifico!* You can wash it in and wash it out. If you have a husband, he won't recognize you!" She raced out of the room.

Nazy thought, *Duncan won't recognize me? That's absurd! One look at my hand or my ankle, and he would know.*

The Chief of Security, Maggi Munro, told Nazy the security officers in the lead vehicle of her detail were badly injured but were expected to make full recoveries. Munro was thankful the shooter of the RPG was a poor shot, because the tank-killing grenade barely hit the aft part of the Suburban. Another microsecond of travel and the RPG would have passed entirely behind the lead car.

Whoever ordered it won't accept the failure. I'd like them to think they might have been successful for as long as possible, since there was a detonation.

Nazy knew the President was concerned about the injured. She would tell him in the morning that three security officers had been taken to the Walter Reed National Medical Center by Agency ambulances. Nazy said, "Maggi, I don't want a press release but one of the injured, under heavy guard was Nazy Cunningham. Until further notice, I'm in the hospital, in critical condition."

The Security Officer lifted an eyebrow and surmised intrigue was in the air. She asked if there was anything else; Nazy said she needed someone to go shopping for her.

Once everyone cleared out of the office, Nazy looked at the time and closed the door for a little peace. She had calls to make. The first one went to the former CIA Director, Bill McGee.

· · ·

Five zeros displayed on his BlackBerry. He knew who was calling. He had heard about the special symbology when he called Duncan and it always surprised him when he experienced it. Bill McGee answered on the first ring with his Barry White baritone, "Director Cunningham, to what do I owe this pleasure?"

She told him, "I'm ok."

"What do you mean *you're ok?*"

She said, "Officially, I'm at Walter Reed National Medical Center in critical condition, under heavy guard. Someone tried to take me out with an RPG."

An RPG? Oh crap! "But you are really ok?"

Nazy said, "I am. The President is wondering, who do you think could be responsible, besides the usual suspects?"

McGee repeated, "Besides the usual suspects? If it isn't Iran and the Muslim Brotherhood, I'll have to give it some thought. I would vote for Iran if it were just me but it's not just me that they are after. They have tried to kill two key Conservatives. It's safe to say fate intervened, otherwise we would have been killed. Nazy, this type of attack in America isn't approved at the Muslim Brotherhood level, although they're in all likelihood the shooters. We could investigate them for years, and we might never know who pulled the trigger. But our first clue is they're tactical. Tactical is the Muslim Brotherhood's *forte*; small-scale clandestine operations. Lackeys out of some local mosque. Trigger pullers. Bombmakers. Snipers. Now Iran, al-Qaeda, and the Islamic Underground are *strategic* by comparison. They put bombs on ten jets a couple of decades ago. Big picture planning; big picture stuff. Like Khalid Sheikh Mohammed, mastermind. My kneejerk reaction is I wouldn't put it past Iran. We hurt them rather badly."

"That was my assessment. Iran and the Brotherhood."

McGee continued, "Maybe someone gave AQ and IU the intel on our schedules and calendars, but it's unlike them to have those weapons in their possession. It's possible, but I don't see the AQ and IU moving weapons like that into the country. I'm leaning on another strategic power who has the means and methods. Uses surrogates for everything including Iran and the Brotherhood."

The encryption technology hissed in her ear as she blurted out, "Scorpii."

A thousand miles away he nodded. "Scorpii."

She asked, "What do you think of having Colonel Eastwood do an exposé on Scorpii as a person of interest? Something like *Who are the Insiders?*"

McGee was quick with the thought: *How about how Mazibuike and Scorpii conspired to destroy DOD and NATO through social engineering? Something tangential, not a direct attack.* "I'd say you are getting acquainted with the office. I like it. He's in Germany at the moment, but he'll do it, especially after he hears you've been targeted."

"Thanks Bill, stay safe and keep your head down."

"You too."

"I'm not leaving the office."

"Famous last words. I know Duncan's trying to get back to you. We're on the hook for dinner there in D.C. at the end of the month. I'll talk to him; if not there, then on the road. Good luck. See you soon. *Bullfrog* out."

Nazy snuggled deep in her chair and kicked off her shoes. The trembling was gone; with the door closed it was warmer in the office. All the telephone lines were blinking; someone important was waiting. Someone needing a decision. She keyed the microphone to the secretary, "Can you take messages for all of my calls?" One by one, the blinking lights went out. She asked the Deputy Director to handle the office; she needed quiet to make some calls.

Nazy called the satellite number for the LM-130J to see how long it was before Duncan landed. He was still several hours out. *I need a hug. I need you darling, Duncan!*

Nazy reflected on the vicissitudes of the day and her time at the CIA. Then, for whatever reason, she thought of President Hernandez, one of the unacknowledged members of the *Irregulars*, but one of the most important. For a couple of years, before he became the President of the United States, Duncan and Congressman Hernandez had been annual attendees at the *Pumpkin Papers Irregulars Dinner*. Kind of the Texas Contingent of Conservative activists.

But he had never known Duncan Hunter's CIA cover was his Border Patrol job until Duncan told him at one of the *Pumpkin Papers Irregulars Dinners*. That was the day Congressman Hernandez and the Border Patrol's National Aircraft Maintenance Director became Conservative activists. *Irregulars.* Two patriots in a political pod. And they looked at terrorism from other perspectives.

Nazy thought, *Some Presidents become smitten with the instruments of the intelligence community, but President Hernandez was more than smitten. His is an intelligence presidency. President Hernandez has been an active participant in our clandestine operations at a level that hasn't been seen before in a chief executive. Duncan called it being a clandestine Conservative activist. Working behind the scenes for America.*

President Hernandez leveraged the power of the Office of the President to facilitate our success. What we did was unheard of. Eliminating terrorists from the Matrix disrupted the chaos operations of the Insiders, Iran, and the Islamic Underground in the Middle East and Africa.

And Scorpii? Yes, and Scorpii.

And the dirtiest little secret in America was that the opposition political party worked to destroy America's democracy. What was said of the Nazis could easily be said of the Democrat Party.

A percipient expression on her face telegraphed her understanding. She recalled a story Duncan ad told her.

When the Nazi's marched into France, they found resistance. The French Resistance, the Maquis, but they were not organized. The OSS, the Office of Strategic Services, handpicked Captain Peter Ortiz to organize the Maquis. In the beginning, they were few. With Ortiz they learned to be clever, and as they became more organized, they became effective. And because of their success, they could create more and more Resistance groups. Under his leadership, they conducted and perfected irregular or what some call asymmetric warfare. It's incredible that OSS Director could see what others couldn't see: one man could turn peasants into patriots. Together, they changed the face of the war.

Bill and Duncan are correct; the left — the Communist, Marxist, Socialist, and Islamic criminal forces — are trying to overthrow America. We cannot allow them to do it. We need more help. We have no choice but to fight or die. Their goal is to exterminate us; they won't allow us to exist. We must provide Conservative leadership and organize the Resistance, otherwise we will lose the country. And then our lives, for they will come for us first. That's why Bill is running for president. He's taking on the mantle of the top Conservatist activist in America.

Maybe the only way to see that the country is in trouble is to have a certain perspective. I defected from Islam and a husband who was a radical. A jihadi. Bill has been fighting evil terrorists on three continents for four decades. President Hernandez lost his sister to a terrorist's missile and Duncan lost his parents. Duncan would say there's a pattern. We Irregulars have been scarred by the evil part of Islam.

Is it possible the left, the Insiders fund Islamic terrorism as a distraction to their one-world Marxist machinations? Hmmm....

I know what we must do; we must break the backs of the Insiders; Scorpii and the lot of them. We must stop them. I dare not articulate these thoughts to anyone but Bill or Duncan. Before I say anything to Bill, I will tell Duncan. He will understand.

• • •

Today was the day, today was the day! The Executive Director of Foreign Intelligence, Maalik El Masri checked his electronic devices for news. He wanted to give the Supreme Lord Chancellor Scorpii some good news, that the *Amerikaner, die Frau* had been stopped.

A stately grandfather clock in the hall chimed eleven bells. El Masri got up from his desk and proceeded to Scorpii's room to put him to bed. Three steps away from his desk, his smartphone sounded a ringtone that indicated a text message had come through. The message was from his duty officer; it was horrible news. It read: *Sie hielten die Frau nicht aufhalten. They didn't stop the woman. She's in the hospital near death.*

El Masri cursed under his breath: "*Scheiße! Scheiße! Scheiße!*"

Before taking another step, El Masri considered what this information would mean. *I must provide recommendations for the Supreme Lord Chancellor. First, we must halt the funding stream of the Arab organizations in Amerika. We have done that before teaching them a lesson when they couldn't eliminate die Frau. How many times have we tried? Acht? Zehn? Eight? Ten?*

When they overran the embassy in Algiers and took her, she was in their hands. El Masri rammed his fist into his palm to emphasize his frustration. *But, somehow, she miraculously survived. Then she was in the hospital in Italy. I lost count the number of times she was supposed to have been eliminated. The Arab Amerikaners always promised they could do the work, but they always failed us. Always, always, always! The Supreme Lord Chancellor will not be happy. If I tell him tonight, if it doesn't kill him, then no one will get any sleep.*

But if I do not, there will be hell to pay. We struck out at them and failed. My fear is completely founded. They're gaining the upper hand. They're smart enough to know when the tide has turned. That is when they will come for us.

CHAPTER 42

November 27, 2019

After a raucous rally at the Harrisburg International Airport, Bill McGee and Dory Eastwood, recently returned from Germany and fighting the jet lag, traveled to the arena at Drexel University for a question-and-answer session.

There wasn't even standing room inside. There were some protesters outside threatening to disrupt the proceedings, but the school police and the sheriff's department were keeping the peace. Colonel Eastwood handled the microphone like at expert, thanking the students and faculty for giving a warm welcome and a tremendous round of applause for Bill McGee.

Eastwood paused for dramatic effect, "Admiral McGee will be a President we will all be proud of."

After several questions from students and instructors, McGee was asked one in particular. He collected his thoughts and said, "Ladies and gentlemen, I think we are dancing around the issue. I have said repeatedly during this campaign Republicans must do a better job of countering the left's propaganda. The *LA Times* yesterday said I was the 'black face of white supremacy.' That is part of the problem. The media and the left have mesmerized America with utter nonsense. Some of you may recognize those words as propaganda, what the psychologists call mass hypnosis. You are in school to learn to think critically. For yourself. Not manipulated. You're not in a trade school learning how to be a plumber or an aircraft mechanic. A friend of mine who has a Ph.D. said, tongue-in-cheek, 'Ph.Ds figure out problems, MDs treat problems, and JDs typically cause them."

The arena roared with applause and laughter.

"That's probably why I joined the Navy. *I took care of problems before they became problems.*"

Again, those in the arena stomped their feet and erupted with applause and laughter.

"In a perfect world, everyone has a place in America. At home, at work, or at school you are most likely not aware of the organizations of federal government designed to keep you safe. We can debate the merits of budgets for some of those agencies. Congress was always in my chili regarding the CIA's budget, which I inherited, by the way. Democrats in Washington complained the Agency was mismanaged, and they questioned where the funds appropriated by Congress were going. To hear the Democrats in Congress tell it, we are always doing something bogus, something illegal, or something stupid. But what you don't hear from them, the media is what the Republicans say at these hearings. 'The CIA is to be commended for eliminating the terrorist threat by neutralizing hundreds of terrorists that were planning to do us and our families harm.' And just to bring this around full-circle, all government agencies have Inspectors General and internal audit departments all designed to account for taxpayer dollars. Does that make sense?"

The massive crowd nodded; a few clapped.

McGee took a drink and continued, "So what happens in Congress when there are reporters or TV cameras present is nothing more than public theater. Hollywood stars, network producers, newspaper chief editors, and others have become the latest version of Leni Riefenstahl, the German film director, photographer, and actress, known for her role in producing Nazi propaganda. In the 1930s and 40s, the Nazis exported propaganda to extol the virtues of Hitler, the promise of the Aryan race, the glories of fascism. Conservatives in Hollywood produced anti-Nazi, pro-democracy movies. There's a reason *Casablanca* is the number one movie all-time."

"With the critical thinking you are learning and developing here, I challenge you to look at these network reports and newspaper articles and see how the media in America used propaganda to extol the virtues of Maxim Mohammad Mazibuike and the glories of Islam. The Nazi regime was eighty years ago, and the left, the Nazis of today, are back at it. Leni Riefenstahl has been replaced by the ladies of *The View*, social networks, Hollywood, the media. I have always said, Joseph

Goebbels, the Nazi Minister of Propaganda would have given anything to have our media."

"The jobs I did as a Navy SEAL stopped the enemy's propaganda from affecting you, from influencing you in your day-to-day decisions. We were on duty to protect our culture and our way of life. Where moms and dads and their children are not subject to socialists' politics or political intrigue."

Thunderous applause raced around the arena.

"Some may think I'm pulling a fast one on you. I suggest you do a bit of research into Presidential Executive Orders. Specifically look at the last one President Mazibuike left for an unsuspecting American people. President Hernandez recently rescinded the secret Executive Order entitled *Using Behavioral Science Insights to Better Serve the American People*. This order authorized the U.S. Government to conduct behavioral modification *on the public* for the purpose of understanding how to nudge them into compliance with their public policy objectives."

"Think about that for a second. He directed the government to use propaganda on you to help you make better decisions, decisions in line with their agenda. Like who to vote for."

"Let me wrap this up. I gave you a little homework. My contention is the Democrat Party shouldn't be using propaganda on you in any circumstances. Some of our opponents are saying to frighten you, that Bill McGee is dangerous. Bill McGee is dangerous for the country. Who wants a president who puts walls up and discriminates against women and gays?"

"The role of the legislature is to serve you and improve your life. In a previous life, my role was to ensure the bad guys didn't come over the ramparts to harm you. And while the Democrats have put policies into place that threaten women, we have organized Operation *Not Going to be Afraid Any More*. We now have hundreds of thousands of women who have the training to handle a weapon so they can protect themselves and their families. Their side just throws rocks."

"We are a Party of Action. We have done a good job of that, but what we haven't done a good job of is keeping the propaganda away from you. So we are going to educate you on what they're doing. I plan to inform Americans of the dangers of propaganda and reject the Democrat Party's program of mind control and manipulation."

McGee stood up and told the assembly, "Thank you and go vote!" The congregation gave him a standing ovation.

Demetrius Eastwood thought, *And that, ladies and gentlemen, is why the Democrat Party, the Communist News Network, and the rest of the liberal media lapdogs are terrified of the former Director of the CIA. They might react with condescension, rage, or dismissal, but inside they wet their pants when Bill McGee goes all Bill McGee on them.*

CHAPTER 43

November 28, 2019

Dory Eastwood raced from Harrisburg International Airport to finish his latest exposé into the child sex trade. The cable news network producer said it was a powerful piece and his plan was to advertise with promotional announcements leading up to showing the special later in the day. With the story out of Germany done and in the can, he turned to the project he had completed on the return trip to the U.S.

He had never received correspondence from CIA Directors, present or past. They would usually bypass the media as media don't have clearances. But the request from Admiral McGee wasn't out of the realm. Eastwood was a *de facto* member of the campaign; somewhat historian, someone to interface with the networks and newspapers as necessary. So if Admiral McGee had an idea for an article or television special, he was all aboard with it.

It would likely be a controversial piece, concluding Rho Schwartz Scorpii was more than the master manipulator in American and European politics. As the top billionaire in the world, he had lots of money to protect his interests.

McGee suggested the American and European intelligence communities were being destroyed from within, influenced by the power of money and power, and he believed Scorpii and the lesser billionaires in Europe, his puppets, were also into political intrigue up to their eyeballs.

Before Eastwood submitted his proposal for an editorial page piece, he looked it over one last time.

To: Chief Editor, *New York Post*

President Mazibuike and Rho Schwartz Scorpii accomplished something no group had ever done. They facilitated the infiltration of sexual and mental disorders into the Department of Defense, the intelligence community, and NATO agencies. I respectfully submit this article for consideration.

Title: DOD's and NATO's Suicide Problem

By: Demetrius Eastwood

The Department of Defense has a suicide problem. NATO also has a suicide problem. But more than that, the intelligence community, domestic and international, has a suicide problem. They're killing themselves in more ways than you can imagine.

If you are a communist working toward the overthrow of the U.S. government, thank Democrat presidents, but mostly thank President Maxim Mohammad Mazibuike. The Kremlin can thank Rho Schwartz Scorpii. These two men are responsible for instilling policies that have attacked the very foundations of the good order and discipline for combat effectiveness.

Through one of his NGOs, Rho Schwartz Scorpii funded the legislation mandating DOD and NATO ban screening programs to detect candidates and employees with mental disorders. These screening programs had been the mainstay of western defense policy. They detected and removed people with personality or gender identity disorders and other mental illnesses at the source, before they could infiltrate the militaries of the Department of Defense and NATO and their intelligence agencies.

Prior to 1993 the Department of Defense screened recruits, officer candidates, and service academy entrants for mental, personality, and suicide behavior disorders. Over the strong objections of Republicans in Congress, in 1994 the policy was replaced with laws known as *Don't Ask, Don't Tell*. This deemed any potential recruit, officer candidate, or intelligence community candidate with mental, personality, or other behavior disorders as fit for service. We will be clear; a stroke of a political pen overrode seventy years of diagnostic and statistical analysis on mental disorders and disposed of significant disqualifying medical conditions for military service.

It has long been known people with mental and sexual disorders commit suicide in numbers far greater than the rate of normal people. The unintended consequence of these laws allowed people who were predisposed to commit suicide into the military and intelligence community. But the law also did something more ominous and deleterious to military forces. In virtually every case, the law prohibited the use of the polygraph as a screening tool. Previous blackmail targets, closet communists, socialists, gays, and lesbians were now eligible for TS/SCI clearances and could spy for their masters.

About the same time, the Democrat president and Congress demanded the militaries of the North Atlantic Treaty Organization (NATO) countries follow suit or face U.S. defunding. NATO countries capitulated. People previously prohibited from entering the intelligence agencies and accessing classified information were no longer subject to the polygraph and infiltrated NATO's intelligence agencies and military forces.

The DOD and NATO countries use the Diagnostic and Statistical Manual of Mental Disorders (DSM) as its source reference for psychiatric diagnoses and metal disorders. Most Americans and citizens of European counties have little knowledge of the DSM, its contents, and its implications. The DSM is published by the American Psychiatric Association (APA) and "offers a common language and standard criteria for the classification of mental disorders." It's used by clinicians, researchers, psychiatric drug regulation agencies, health insurance companies, pharmaceutical companies, the legal system, and policy makers. In the United States and European military services, the DSM serves as a universal authority for psychiatric diagnoses.

Prior to 1993 overt homosexuals were barred from the intelligence community because of the blackmail risks. The intelligence community administered polygraphs to anyone needing a clearance. People with overt personality disorders or mental illnesses are unstable and untrustworthy, and these behaviors were exposed during polygraphs.

Rear Admiral Bill McGee supports reinstating mental disorder screening for DOD and NATO to remove those who exhibit the traits of personality disorders or mental illnesses or those who are predisposed to commit suicide over confusion of their sexual identity. This would be a return to normalcy with Americans whose allegiance is only to America. Americans do not want military members with mental disorders piloting aircraft, standing watch in missile silos, or driving aircraft carriers or submarines. A return to normalcy would see those with mental disorders getting the help they need, while DOD and NATO might find their suicide problems substantially reduced.

Rear Admiral McGee proposes a commission to study liberalism. Liberalism with its extraordinarily high suicide rate has all the traits of a mental disorder and liberals are preoccupied with creating chaos. This commission will be organized in the same manner as the Center of Security Policy analyzed *sharia* as a national threat. Scorpii has given the APA millions to keep liberalism out of the DSM as the basis for a destructive personality disorder.

And maybe, just maybe a civilized society will look past the distractions of the attacks on DOD and NATO to find out what kind of monsters Scorpii and his billionaire friends have lurking under the beds of Europe's children. Various sources cite that on average, over two hundred thousand boys and girls go missing in Europe each year, never to be seen again by their families. It's difficult to believe Scorpii isn't involved in some way.

It's time to find some answers.

End of Article.

CHAPTER 44

November 28, 2019

President Hernandez remained seated at the *Resolute Desk* signing papers when a woman whose face he didn't recognize entered the Oval Office with the Vice President, the Chairman of the Joint Chiefs of Staff, the National Security Advisor, the Attorney General, and the President's Chief of Staff. It was time for the PDB.

The woman's outward appearance, her face, hair, and clothes suggested the Acting CIA Director had sent someone else to deliver the PDB. When the President finished his paperwork chores, he pushed away from the magnificent oak desk and joined the group on the carpet. President Hernandez started to sit directly across from the CIA woman who had commandeered the single chair reserved for the presenter of the President's Daily Brief, when he realized they hadn't been properly introduced.

His eyes dropped momentarily to the woman's ankles; they looked familiar. The woman stood to greet him as the room erupted in laughter. President Hernandez didn't get the joke. He finished greeting the woman and shook her hand. Then Nazy Cunningham said in her best British voice, "Good morning, Mr. President."

President Hernandez nearly jumped out of his skin.

Everyone said it was a fantastic disguise.

Nazy said, "It's the absolute latest in stereolithography 3D-printing of a polymer, disguise technology, and can be worn for forty-eight hours. It's designed to defeat any facial recognition systems. Even ours."

President Hernandez and company were impressed; they were thrilled to have been let in on one of the Agency's secret projects. Nazy presented the PDB and handed the President a separate POTUS EYES ONLY file. When she finished, she flipped the long, stringy, variegated gray hair out of her way, gathered her black leather briefcase, and began to take her leave.

President Hernandez interrupted the natural flow of the PDB and asked, "Can I have a few moments with Miss Cunningham? Then you can come back in." The other men left the office quietly.

When it was just the two of them, the President looked at his watch and said, "Nazy, I can't believe that is you." Then he tapped the POTUS EYES ONLY file and asked, "I don't like the CIA having to do the FBI's work, but under the circumstances I don't know how to get around it just yet. I take it you have done some analysis?"

Nazy said, "Mr. President, we can conceive and accept that drug cartels, the mobs, and gangs can operate in the United States without discovery, dealing in proscribed goods and services. Could there be another cartel that deals in children as a good or service? The FBI and law enforcement chase the internet pedophile. The laws against pedophilia here are very strong. But the left seeks to reduce the severity of those laws, and soften pedophilia to make it more acceptable to the public. Sexual activists are significantly stepping up their threats on the lives and families of the American Psychiatric Association membership to convince them to vote to remove pedophilia from the *Diagnostic and Statistical Manual of Mental Disorders*, the DSM. This is something Duncan has seen for decades, and it frankly opened my eyes to how significant the problem really is in the U.S. Remember, there was the Cleveland man who helped free three kidnapped Cleveland women from a decade-long captivity."

"I remember. Charles Ramsey. Amanda Berry ran into the rescuer's arms. She had been a child who had gone missing without a trace. Colorful interview."

My situation was not so dissimilar. "Yes, Mr. President. While our laws are strong, the professional left is trying to weaken them, Europe's' laws are virtually nonexistent. The U.S. is Christian and cherishes life. Europe is secular and doesn't."

"I sense you are about to hit me with the big reveal."

"Mr. President, the sex cartels have probably been operating in Europe for centuries in various forms. They have centuries of experience hiding their activities. There have always been men's clubs, we are not talking about the smoking rooms of London's barristers but men on the DSM spectrum in the sex clubs that cater to men on men and pedophiles, primarily men on children."

"Pedophiles."

"Yes, Mr. President. Where you find men's sex clubs in Europe you find organized pedophilia, children's brothels that have been operating in secret. It has been going on for centuries."

Nazy continued, "You could also say one of the reasons the left has issues with Christians is they interfere with their child sex trade. It's Christian values that is a deterrent and those values suppress the Islamic child sex trade in Africa and the Middle East. Europeans know what is going on and either condone it or feel helpless to do anything about it. In America, Christians have driven it underground."

The President said, "*Silence of the Lambs.*"

Nazy remembered the movie. A man with a mental disorder was snatching women and killing them in a gruesome way. It was based on an actual case and was made before the FBI had been taken over by the Muslim Brotherhood. She nodded.

"I think I can figure out the rest."

"Yes, Mr. President."

"Nazy, don't terrorists?"

"Yes, Mr. President. They do. Extensively. Boko Haram kidnaps children by the hundreds and sells them as sex slaves across Africa and the Middle East. The Taliban barter for children. Child brides for rich men are big business. Men dominate their culture, and women have no rights and are little more than cattle."

"One last thought, it's a good assumption that wherever you find terrorist organizations, there is a healthy sex slave trade and child sex trafficking."

"Child marriages?"

"That too, Mr. President. Largely confined to terrorist organizations today, such as the Taliban; Mohammad took a child bride. In the classic sense he was a pedophile and engaged in the child sex slave trade. The Islam of old fought and conquered other people for their children. Like the Taliban."

"So, the unspoken history of the Crusades was?"

"Yes, Mr. President. Polite history says it was over ideology. But Muslims invaded Europe for sex slaves, child sex trafficking of children with lighter skin."

"It wasn't always like that."

"No, Mr. President. Once Khomeini acquired the wealth of Iran, he completely changed the calculus in the Middle East. Islam after World War Two was becoming Westernized until he arrived in Tehran."

President Hernandez said, "I can see that now. You always have the best insights. Nazy, what do we do?"

"Mr. President. Moderate Muslims in Indonesia, for example, is working hard to give up on the old ways. In the cities, no child brides, no sex slaves, no child sex trafficking. They have modern laws and prosecutors. In rural areas they still embrace the old ways."

"The elimination of master terrorists from the *Matrix* has removed those who would engage in those ancient activities. Europe is a different can of worms. We think Scorpii and the *Insiders* use their billions to continue the trafficking of children for various purposes, including child sacrifice and espionage."

Child sacrifice; barbaric! He meekly asked, "Espionage?" The look on President Hernandez's face registered he wasn't exactly convinced.

"Yes, Mr. President. There is an unhealthy relationship between men's sex clubs, military installations in Europe, and the trafficking of secret material. We deduce the business must be greater than what we know to exist, but it's largely underground. We know the documents exist but unfortunately, we do not have them. We have informed our allies they must take measures to better protect sensitive materials. The FBI has tried to assist Europe, but they usually catch only amateurs, like the clumsy internet pedophile. Duncan sees an unintended consequence. We can insist Europe strengthens their security program to prevent espionage; the left responds with expanding child sex trafficking. In a strange way the U.S. presence subsidizes Europe's child sex trafficking business."

"I can see that." *But what do we do?*

"Mr. President, Duncan had an idea."

President Hernandez smiled. "Really? Are you going to tell me?" *Nazy, your husband is full of ideas.*

"It's fairly radical, Mr. President."

"Let's have it. No attribution."

Nazy told him. He frowned and then came to see the brilliance of it. He stood up and said, "This is exactly why I wanted Duncan as my National Security Advisor." They shook hands, the meeting was over. Nazy left the Oval Office and the security council returned.

Once the door was closed and the men were seated, President Hernandez checked the time on his Rolex and said, "I saw those ankles and that face and thought, there can't be two people with those ankles in this city. The different hair and briefcase also had me going. I was completely fooled."

The Vice President offered, "We were all fooled when she walked up to us. All I know is, if my wife looked like that in a mask, I wouldn't let her take it off!"

There was the usual cacophony of laughs as President Hernandez retrieved the remote and turned on the television. He invited the men to watch the Eastwood television special.

When the President of the United States invites you to watch a TV show, you find a good seat.

CHAPTER 45

November 28, 2019

"Hello from Berlin, this is your host, Demetrius Eastwood. A few weeks ago, I was contacted to see if we would be interested in interviewing child sex trafficking survivors. Of course, we would, and my film crew and I raced to Germany. We met Dr. Hans Schmidt who runs a mental health clinic in a suburb of Berlin. Doctor Schmidt explained he uses our exposé, *Escape from The Devil's Hole*, which chronicled how girls were kidnapped and forced into the sex slave trade in his therapy sessions with men who were used in the elite sex slave trade in Europe. Without further ado, this is *Trafficked as an Elite Child Sex Slave*."

With the Tempelhof Airport as a nighttime backdrop, Demetrius Eastwood, in a dark blue suit, while shirt, unbuttoned, no tie entered the screen and said, "In this three-part series, we were privileged to speak with four child sex trafficking survivors. In our interviews, they describe a remarkably consistent theme on how they grew up as sex slaves to high-profile aristocrats, politicians, and generals. These men also reveal when they were children, how they were part of a European operation. They were moved across borders for various purposes which included male sex prostitution, entrapment, and blackmail."

"Our story begins with Moritz Schröder."

Mr. Schröder spoke German; an interpreter provided the dialogue in English. He said, "I was born in Berlin in 1964. My mother was single and was not well. When I was three, we moved from Berlin to the Bavarian part of the country when she married. I was targeted right away. They groomed me for about a year. When I was six, they took me to an orgy. The grooming ended when they began sexualizing me."

Eastwood cautioned the audience Moritz's retelling was rough and filled with pain. People could see the pain and anguish in the man's face. He wouldn't look at Eastwood directly and often appeared to be on the edge of tears or a breakdown. Eastwood asked, "By grooming, what do you mean?"

"My mother turned me over to a man and a woman I didn't know. We went on many outings with other children, until one day the man raped me, and the woman screamed at me. Later I was led into a castle. I was humiliated. The man took me on a stage. There were people all around. Everyone was dressed as hippies, and they were taking drugs. But they weren't hippies; I learned later on that they were aristocrats and politicians. Most of them were so high they really weren't paying attention. I was naked, and he abused me on the stage. After he was done with me, he left me on the stage like nothing had happened. He thanked me; the woman talked to me like she was my friend."

"I was so afraid. I remember we went for a long walk, and I thought I was going to be killed. They said, 'We like you, and wouldn't want anything to happen to you.' Trying to connect with me. Calm me down. They said I shouldn't say anything. That if I wanted to talk about anything, to come to them. They wanted it to be kept a secret. Our secret. They gave me candy to keep me quiet. To keep me coming back."

"They bought my mother a car, and she began driving me to the places where there were these clubs. Men's clubs. Sometimes they were just houses. She would drop me off. There was always someone to take me inside. She would come back at dawn. Sometimes she had new clothes. If I didn't come out, she would just wait."

"When I was nine, we moved to a different place. I was driven to Switzerland with two other children. When we arrived there, we were sent into a tunnel. I remember there were torches on the sides of the walls. Very primitive. The ground and the cobblestones were wet. When we got to the end, we were turned over to the other handlers."

"One child would be sacrificed. I knew that girl. She was a little bit backwards, a little bit slow. I was extremely protective of her. I tried to hold her."

There was raw anguish in Moritz's voice and actions. He struggled to speak. When he regained his composure, he talked away from the camera. He couldn't look at Eastwood. His voice had become a dull monotone.

"She was torn from me. I was made to watch. I had never felt more powerless. Everyone was wearing black capes and robes. I learned later that it was a satanic ritual."

Eastwood said, "Moritz's story continues after this break."

President Hernandez had seen enough of Eastwood's special. He thanked everyone for coming. He asked the Attorney General to stay for a few moments and asked the Chief of Staff to ensure they weren't disturbed.

After exchanging thoughts with AG Burnt Winchester, President Hernandez shook his hand. As the AG left the Oval Office, President Hernandez retrieved the file Nazy had given him. He opened the double-taped TS file and withdrew the latest installment on Rho Schwartz Scorpii. He hunched over the desk and began reading.

Documents were obtained that Scorpii purchased nightclub establishments and hosted male-only fetish clubs in the Schöneberg district of Berlin. By all evidence, this was a project in the germinal phase and not a case of entrepreneurism. Scorpii chartered conversion operations which were done only by lesbian women.

Scorpii financially sponsored recruitment seminars given by gay men's clubs for teachers of middle schoolers. They provided workshops that encouraged teachers to create a safe environment that fostered exploration of sexual orientation and expression. Teachers were instructed how to survey students and deceive parents. Teachers would eavesdrop on bathroom and hallway conversations in order to target sixth and seventh graders. Children in this age group were especially susceptible to the propagandistic covert invitations to secret clubs.

From notes taken at the seminar, teachers were warned to ensure these clubs didn't keep rosters or record anything on paper. Parents were not to know their children were being recruited to the clubs. If parents became aware of the clubs, they would be bribed with money and automobiles to keep silent, or various forms of propaganda would be used against them to gain their acceptance.

Prepubescent minors in the clubs Scorpii ran depended on surrogates who recruited other children to the clubs. This tactic helped the children feel more comfortable.

Some teachers created and led seminars on, "How to run 'gay and lesbian' clubs in the heart of conservative and military communities," and "Massage as an Icebreaker." Intelligence and military communities were extensively attacked.

One teacher highlighted the objection of a mother who wanted to wait before talking with her middle school student about sex and gender. The seminar leader provided cash incentives and tips on how to ridicule the parents' reaction or use other tools of propaganda to achieve program goals.

While some parents moved their children to private schools and alerted the authorities, teachers were given access to legal representation to avoid being fired. In almost every community, local law enforcement had been bought off to allow the seminars and teachers to continue their work. It's believed Scorpii's money was used for these bribes.

Findings: On average, 200,000 children in Europe go missing every year, and law enforcement is incentivized not to research the circumstances or determine the whereabouts of these children. Some of these children may find shelter in gay and lesbian clubs. When properly targeted, children working in gay clubs were successful in extracting classified documents from gay and lesbian government employees. If gay and lesbian government employees were terminated when they were discovered conducting espionage, one of Scorpii's companies employed them.

President Hernandez had had enough of Scorpii. The Eastwood special still resonated in his thoughts. He closed the file, walked to a closet, and turned on his private paper shredder, affectionately known in intelligence circles as *The Disintegrator*. The super-shredder's rotating blades turned documents into quarter-inch-long strips, .5mm wide. It could turn a laptop into scrap in seconds.

Then President Hernandez reconsidered. He shut off *The Disintegrator*, returned to his desk, and thought about what Scorpii had been through and why he fostered the lifestyle he had been forced into.

But there is something else. It would probably take a phalanx of psychiatrists to figure out what made Scorpii finance terrorists and spies and leverage sexual disorders to spy on the government. I sense it's revenge. I sense Scorpii resented being labeled a mentally defective. Revenge of the mentally defective to punish normal people.

I remember Nazy called them honeypots. I wasn't entirely familiar with the lingo of espionage. But it was one of the dirtiest operational practices I had ever heard involving covert agents... to create a sexual or romantic relationship to compromise a male target with access to state secrets. That's what Scorpii did over the years, but he used sexualized children to compromise men and women for providing intelligence or for being a pedophile.

Scorpii-owned foundations have long been suspected of hiding special brothels that use male children in the male-only fetish clubs. First the one in Berlin, and then replicating those arrangements elsewhere. Scorpii bought police protection so those clubs could operate without interruption or harassment. Noteworthy, the clubs were always close to military facilities. Nazy said to manipulate that many people, they must have recording equipment. You don't have a business like that to be a public service, you have a business like that to make money. Secret off-the-books money.

President Hernandez closed his eyes for a moment and shook his head in disgust. He thought he had figured it out, but he had to tell someone his suspicions.

He called the Department of Justice. He looked over at the off-white Stetson under glass and smiled. When Attorney General Burnt Winchester came on the line, President Hernandez said, "Could you return to the White House? I need you."

"I'll be right over, Mr. President."

●   ●   ●

After a spirited meeting with President Hernandez, Attorney General Winchester again left the White House. This time he had work to do.

Their discussion had taken place next to the white Stetson he had given to President Hernandez years earlier. In his limo, Winchester recalled with a one-cheek grin how he and Javier Hernandez had gone to a San Antonio bootmaker's store to celebrate Hernandez being elected to the 23rd Congressional District. Winchester had just been appointed a U.S. Attorney for the Western District of Texas. The new congressman had stood by his word and paid off a friendly wager by buying black crocodile Lucchese boots for Winchester. The new U.S. Attorney had promised he would buy the more expensive top-of-the-line Stetson *El Presidente* if Hernandez ever became President of the United States.

• • •

Winchester extracted an unusually thin file from his briefcase. It contained no classification headers other than POTUS EYES ONLY. The traffic was heavy; he thought he'd read the document in its entirety before arriving the Department of Justice.

He made a few notes in the margins. The CIA file on Rho Schwartz Scorpii explained much about the man. Although he had only seen part of it, the Eastwood show on child sex trafficking explained a missing, almost inconceivable element. A half-million children go missing in the United States; a quarter-million in Europe. *Is it possible there is a connection?*

President Hernandez believes there is. He believes it's worth a shot to find out.

It will take some time to get all the players in the same room. The scale of the thing is the problem. Forty-four European countries; forty-four ambassadors. He scribbled notes to be used as leverage. *Lame duck presidents are generally thought of as being done with their time in office, but President Hernandez is about to go thermonuclear on Europe.*

CHAPTER 46

November 29, 2019

Dory Eastwood's newest special *Is it Terrorism?* was broadcast on the television networks. Following his highly successful special, *Trafficked as an elite Child Sex Slave*, it shattered records for the number of viewers in all demographic categories. The program began with Eastwood interviewing rank-and-file intelligence agency and law enforcement personnel in a Berlin suburb in order to capture the range and depth of what was happening in Rho Schwartz Scorpii's *Ostgut Foundation*. The interviewees sat in silhouette and their voices were electronically altered.

"The chief insists we do not patrol certain areas, especially where there are sex clubs. We may not conduct surveillance on these locations, even where there is an active drug trade. We believe child sex trafficking rings are operating in the open. In the past our offices were inundated with finding and rescuing dozens of children, arresting perpetrators, charging them with sex trafficking. There is nothing worse than finding a child prostitute and having to take that child to the emergency room because of sexual abuse by men."

"But this new Chief of Police directs we cannot go there. We cannot conduct surveillance. We know children are being raped and even murdered. They're essentially disposable. We begged the chief, the captains, and lieutenants, any supervisor who would listen to us to let us go in there, but we were threatened with our jobs if we persisted. Many of us took positions in other departments. Some were so frustrated they quit or retired."

Eastwood had empaneled a group of counterterrorism specialists to speak about Scorpii's misplaced philanthropy in funding terrorists. He said, "So, Scorpii has these foundations and charities, and it all sounds wonderful. But once you look into what is actually going on, these NGOs and charities are not giving microloans or grants to African women to start businesses. Embassy personnel see these foundations, Scorpii's foundations, are buying influence and weapons. After fifteen years of civil war in Liberia, the United Nations came in to manage a cease fire and the peace. The U.N. painstakingly removed the weapons from rebels and murderers. Then under the guise of charity, one of Scorpii's philanthropic foundations smuggled weapons back into the country and the capital city of Monrovia. These foundations gave money to opposition candidates to influence the government. Imagine trying to put a government together after years of horrible civil war and Scorpii funds radicals and communists to defeat the creation of a functioning government. Why would he do something like that? Easy, Liberia is Christian."

Eastwood concluded his special with, "The implication is that Scorpii's foundations and NGOs fund socialist leaders in police departments and district attorney and federal prosecutor offices in order to create chaos in the legal system in Europe and the United States. In the U.S., they fund socialists on city councils, school boards, and anyplace where illegal activities, socialism, Marxism, and communism can flourish. But more than that, these foreign foundations fund American candidates and programs that undermine American values and culture."

"How can Congress allow this? Easy. Americans are susceptible to their propaganda and have voted the most radical socialists and communists into high office. To turn this around, we need anti-socialists, anti-communists, anti-Marxists. We need to stop calling these people liberals and instead begin referring to them as exactly what they are: American communists who work for the destruction of America and western civilization."

"We need patriots who will expose these criminals. Patriots like Rear Admiral Bill McGee who is running for president."

"Eastwood out!"

CHAPTER 47

November 30, 2019

The off-site meeting was unusual, but presidents had been sneaking out of the White House and away from Secret Service protection for years. Today however, the President had snuck out of the White House with Secret Service protection. They had taken a detour from a Starbuck's run. Presidents get out of the office from time to time. Some in the Secret Service assumed the trip was for sex, but others reminded their buddies this was a Republican president, and adulterous sex was a game they didn't play. *Besides, what could anyone do in ten minutes?*

The Secret Service personnel were surprised the current and former CIA Directors were in the room along with a man they didn't know. There was a series of collective thoughts between the two Secret Service men who escorted President Hernandez: *Was that the CIA Director's husband? Why are they meeting here? Is it because there were two attacks on the CIA's top executives?*

Duncan Hunter had reserved several facilities at the Army Navy Club in Washington, D.C. With *Growlers* flashing in the middle of a petite conference table for four, President Hernandez, Rear Admiral McGee, Acting Director Nazy Cunningham, who had returned to her natural jet-black hair color, and Duncan Hunter held an impromptu and unofficial meeting. They discussed the attacks on McGee and Nazy and what to do to prevent future attacks. President Hernandez and Bill McGee suggested they needed to cut the head off the snake. There was no doubt the head of the snake was Rho Schwartz Scorpii.

President Hernandez said, "Time has a way of resolving most problems." The implication was if Scorpii was near death, there was no use killing him.

Acting Director Cunningham replied, "The most recent intelligence report on *The Black Scorpion* confirmed he's the individual most likely responsible. The intelligence is insufficient to declare he bankrolled the assaults. Also, available information indicates he should be in hospice. His doctor has prescribed morphine, the clearest evidence Scorpii's death is near."

President Hernandez stated, "The White House cannot be involved."

Nazy asserted the Agency couldn't be involved. Snatching a billionaire and subjecting him to a rendition from Europe was out of the question. Everyone concurred.

Hunter understood the challenge; it was out of his purview. He acknowledged, "I have done ground work in the past, but in this case, I'm the wrong person for the job. I don't have the means for ingressing or egressing the target undetected in the airplane." Again, they all concurred.

McGee suggested, "This is in the category of being too hard to do. Time will solve our problem."

Nazy thought, *His death in Europe won't help me. We still do not know where he is.*

That was the moment President Hernandez said it was time for him to leave. He stood saying, "Bon appétit! I wish I could partake in the post-Thanksgiving festivities, but officially, I'm not here. We never had this conversation and a *venti frappuccino* is calling my name." Hunter asked for a private word with the President, who agreed. President Hernandez shook hands with McGee and Nazy and wished them "Godspeed." Then he and Hunter departed the room.

McGee turned to Nazy and said, "Maybe we need to let nature take its course."

Nazy nodded with a smile and said, "I want his journals. That's the priority."

McGee squinted his eyes and whispered. "There may be a way to do that."

Nazy was surprised, and her eyebrows telegraphed her thoughts.

Duncan returned from his three-minute discussion with the President. When President Hernandez and Hunter shook hands, Duncan pressed an Air Branch coin into the palm of the President. Number 0007.

Nazy and McGee looked up; they had been waiting.

With no comment or expression from Hunter, McGee still saw intrigue in the eyes of his friend. McGee asked him, "Didn't you bring us here for a meal?" The men retrieved the *Growlers*.

The unofficial group of *Irregulars* — McGee, Nazy, and Hunter — fist bumped across the small table. They had done it before; now they were doing it again.

Hunter was hungry. He responded with a smile, "I did, good sir. I did. And I think Nazy needs to lead the way."

Nazy shot the men one of her most disarming smiles as they stepped into the hall.

•   •   •

The men of *Noble Savage* had missed Thanksgiving, so the Army Navy Club chefs put on another amazing spread of food for Link Coffey, Tommy and Joe, the aircrews of the G-IVSP and LM-130J, Nazy, Lt. Col Demetrius Eastwood, and the woman he had met in Abilene, Texas, Dawn Howell. Rear Admiral Bill McGee and his wife also attended with their girls, who were on leave from flight school in Texas and were looking especially sharp in their Marine uniforms. Dr. Lindell wore an orange tie and brought a date; a neighbor who claimed she saw the President leave the elevator and depart by the rear entrance. By the end of the evening, she was convinced she had been mistaken. *Presidents don't sneak out of the White House.*

After dinner everyone said their goodbyes in the lobby.

McGee asked Hunter if he could call him tomorrow. Duncan negotiated to the day after tomorrow knowing the retired SEAL would call any damn time he wanted.

The McGee girls hugged those they knew well and told Duncan they were going to kick his butt the next time they got him on the racquetball court. They took a limo to Washington National Airport. Bill McGee and his wife hugged Duncan and Nazy and were chauffeured to Washington Dulles Airport Executive Terminal to take Hunter's jet and return to the campaign trail.

Eastwood and Ms. Howell shook everyone's hands, took the hotel shuttle, and were dropped off at Washington's Union Station for the Acela to New York Grand Central Station. Before he left, he handed a manilla envelope to Nazy and said it was additional research of an intelligence nature he had done while in Germany, but it wasn't conducive for a telecast. She accepted it with a smile.

Coffey returned to his home in Virginia via taxicab.

Dr. Lindell and his guest returned to their homes in Vienna.

Tommy and Joe and the LM-130J crew commandeered a hotel shuttle to take them to Manassas, Virginia where the LM-130J had remained overnight. They would fly home to Elmira, New York.

Duncan and Nazy headed to the Presidential Suite on the top floor of the Army Navy Club. The plan was not to come out of their room for two days.

That was the plan.

Plans routinely fell apart when Duncan and Nazy got together after an extended separation.

•   •   •

The Secret Service stopped at Starbucks for *venti frappuccinos* and pumpkin bread slices before returning to the White House.

When President Hernandez returned to the Oval Office, he asked the Chief of Staff to set up a meeting with the Arab Republic of Egypt's Ambassador to the United States. By the end of the day, the Ambassador of Egypt had been received and had verbally invited the President of the United States to his country. President Hernandez accepted and suggested a date and time that was sooner rather than later. A private call was made to the Presidential Palace, and the two presidents talked. By the end of the night the President of Egypt, a former general who literally kicked the Muslim Brotherhood out of the Egyptian government, offered a state dinner in President Hernandez's honor in Cairo.

President Hernandez interrupted him and said, "Mr. President, the request I have is for your ears only."

Awareness instantly dawned on the President of Egypt. He said on the speakerphone, "Mr. President, we might schedule a visit to the Sphinx. Do you think that would be sufficient for your needs?"

President Hernandez withdrew a green *Growler* from his suit pocket and set it on the *Resolute Desk*. From the same pocket he removed the coin Duncan Hunter had given him and scrutinized it as he listened. When it was his turn to speak, he said, "Mr. President, that would be fantastic. My office will work with your office to finalize a date and a time. Please accept our meeting will be beneficial for all."

With silence once again reigning the Oval Office, President Hernandez marveled at the trinkets from his CIA. He pocketed the Air Branch coin and admired the gold Rolex on his wrist. He shut off and returned the *Growler* to his pocket. With no one else in the room, he was proud of himself for what he had just accomplished. He said, "It's about time to earn your keep, Javier."

•   •   •

The White House Press Secretary discussed a change in the President's schedule and informed the press pool of White House correspondents that President Hernandez would attend a State Dinner in his honor in Cairo, Egypt to discuss greater trade and security for Egypt.

CHAPTER 48

December 1, 2019

As expected, McGee called the following day and asked *Maverick*, "Can you make some time for me?"

Nazy and Duncan were in the hotel gym. Hunter wanted to say no, but McGee so rarely asked for time. He hinted he might have a solution to their problem, *The one I said I couldn't talk about.* McGee had something that couldn't be shared over the phone, regardless of the CIA's magical encryption technology.

Hunter told Nazy, "It's face-to-face work with McGee."

Nazy thought it could be anything and told her husband to go, she had work to do at the office. She reminded Duncan she also had Eastwood's envelope of research to process.

Hunter mouthed at his wife; *I'll be back! Couple of days.* He returned to the cellphone and responded to McGee with, "Absolutely. Where are you? I'll come to you." Duncan frowned, *This means more nights away from my bride – this better be good, Bullfrog.*

After showering and dressing, Duncan helped Nazy with the spider silk body armor. The torso protection would stop a high-velocity, armor-piercing round from penetrating the skin and was light enough the wearer barely knew it was there. She wore a silk camisole under the body armor covered by a long-sleeve silk charmeuse shirt.

. . .

Safely ensconced in the Agency's limo, curiosity got the better of her. She folded the metal tabs in order to open the envelope Eastwood had given her. At first glance the documents appeared to be thematically related to child sex trafficking, but when she read the part about how the East German government conducted research and experiments while claiming they represented the CIA, Nazy decided to re-read Eastwood's handwritten findings.

The Central Intelligence Agency was blamed for having secretly carried out experiments on hundreds of orphaned children in Europe in the 1950s and 60s. The charges were so bizarre as to be dismissed outright. It was well known that experiments were actually carried out by the East German Stasi on orphans from the war. The research was an apparent extension of the testing conducted by the SS-Hauptsturmführer Josef Mengele, M.D., Ph.D. It was true the CIA funded covert research on brainwashing after the war, but the dirty little secret was Joseph Goebbels expanded the aperture of propaganda research; the Soviets and the East Germans were conducting research on their political prisoners and their homeless and orphaned children.

The experiments were designed to reveal psychopathic tendencies and traits and to map out the link between normal sexual behaviors and abnormal sexual behaviors, such as homosexuality, transvestitism, transgenderism, and pedophilias. They also investigated the link between heredity and environment in the development of sexual proclivities. But the heart of the research was to determine what was in the art of the possible; explore the limits of what could they get someone to do through re-education.

According to the report, the children were tortured in clear violation of the Nuremberg Code of 1947 that introduced ethical restrictions for experiments on humans.

Hundreds of East German orphans were unknowingly used in experiments called Predictors of Sexual Proclivities. The children were orphans from schools run by the state government. They were not told they were involved in research. Not even after the experiments ended. This was the only known experiment in East German history that used children under state care for research.

The examinations and experiments took place in a basement of the Berlin Municipal Orphanage. Rho Schwartz Scorpii claimed he was a victim and was subjected to these experiments as a child before he was placed in a foster home. He recalled being placed in a chair, having electrodes put on his arms, legs, and chest around the heart. He then had to listen to loud, shrill noises, which attempted to incite a psychological response.

During their time with the children, the doctors conducting the experiments said repeatedly they were working for the CIA, which at that time, was only three years old. It was classic deflection. Blame the CIA for the depravity and violations of the Nuremberg code that they were actually doing.

Before the Berlin Wall was erected, it was reported CIA intelligence officers located 36 boxes of records at the Berlin Psychiatric Center that detailed the Stasi's unscrupulous child experiments. When the center got word the Americans had purloined 36 boxes of research, the center ceased their research and shredded any remaining documents.

If history is any indicator, no one will be held responsible for exploiting these children and it will be swept under the rug, likely escaping any scrutiny.

Nazy wrote in the margin: *If they still exist, where are the 36 boxes?*

CHAPTER 49

December 3, 2019

They met in the airport restaurant. McGee held out a hand that could have doubled as a catcher's mitt and said, "Welcome to Eau Claire. I know you say you've been everywhere; I say bullshit. I've never heard you mention you've been to Wisconsin."

"Wrong, good sir. I raced the Vette at Elkhart Lake half a dozen times. I also attended second grade here. Somewhere in Chippewa County. Old school, bottom of a hill, near the river. I got to ring the bell. That's all I remember."

"Seriously?" He patted Hunter on the back. Directed him to a booth. Hunter looked out of the window to admire the lines of the *Howard 500* as he pulled out a *Growler*, put it in the middle of the table, and turned it on. "Whaddya got?"

McGee pulled one of the menus stacked at the end of the table. He was in no hurry. When McGee wasn't in a hurry, Hunter knew better than to prod him along.

In their collective view the billionaire Scorpii was a problem, and it needed a one-way solution, the Osama bin Laden solution. Someone else takes the hit. They had discussed the level of effort it would take to knock the billionaire Scorpii off his perch as the world's chief sponsor of terrorism. Scorpii owned virtually all the socialist and communist politicians in Europe, just as he owned the nicest hotels in Germany. He also owned Democrat politicians in the United States through massive campaign contributions. As long as the campaign contributions flowed steadily into a candidate's coffers, those politicians protected Scorpii and his activities with a fanatical zeal.

Scorpii's *Ostgut Foundation* detailed public policy changes. It was always done clandestinely through legislation with the genesis coming from third parties, charities, and other NGOs. Rho Schwartz

Scorpii had learned early all terrorism is economic. When Osama bin Laden was eliminated from the field of battle, al-Qaeda and its affiliates lost not only their leader but their funding source. Al-Qaeda should have collapsed, but Scorpii continued to *seed* bin Laden's enterprises.

Over the top of the menu McGee said, "We've talked about *Broken Lance*, once."

Oh shit! Just like that, we are on! Hunter checked the airport restaurant for any unsavory characters. Confident the only unsavory characters were he and McGee, he nodded. "Once. I remember. When a president is kidnapped, taken hostage, or can't be recovered the *Executive Special Access Program* is activated. Only fifteen bodies on the program, if I recall. Stuff you did, and stuff I'm not supposed to know anything about."

"Yes. Only ten SEALs assigned. To go after the *Insiders* or Scorpii, Nazy's place won't help if you're in Europe. Scorpii's in Europe. And you're going to need help. Lots of help. The good news is I know people."

"You mean from *Broken Lance*?" *You have to be shitting me!*

"Since we are retired, I'd think it's more appropriate to call it an on call *civilian* resistance movement. More like asymmetrical warfare using militia reinforcements."

Hunter smiled with his mouth full of ghost white teeth, just like he did when Nazy stepped from the shower. He recalled the high points of the discussion about that night when McGee's SEAL Team members were being hunted down across America and killed by an experienced sniper.

As McGee continued to fiddle with the menu, Hunter recollected the nuts and bolts of what McGee had told him years ago. *If it was confirmed the president had been kidnapped or was being held hostage, the Secretary of Defense, the CIA Director, and the Attorney General were to agree to the provisions of a secret Executive Order signed in 1962 by President Kennedy. He was the original Lance or Lancer, living in Lancelot or some such BS.*

What the Soviets did to CIA pilot Francis Gary Powers was a crime, parading him around and staging a sham trial. President Kennedy knew if he or any president was ever captured, they would likely suffer the same fate. Or worse. President Kennedy determined the American people didn't want to see their president subjected to torture or humiliation if captured.

If the SECDEF, the CIA Director, and the AG agreed, Operation Broken Lance would be authorized. If the Executive Protection Team of SEALs were in-country with the president, they'd be notified of the Broken Lancers' decision and try to rescue the president. If that wasn't possible, they would execute their orders, which were to take the president out by the most expeditious means possible. Sniper teams.

Maverick also recalled Broken Lance was a suicide mission. Not everyone could be counted on for such an assignment. The SEAL Team members on Broken Lance didn't expect to get out alive if they killed their president and denied the enemy their political victory. It was a volunteer assignment that required special training with special weapons, the weapons that couldn't be envisioned by the most experienced warriors or gunmakers. Some believed they were otherworldly, only because they didn't have access to the Agency's secret weapons labs.

Years ago, McGee had explained the selection process, how it required a word-of-mouth recommendation by the SEAL Team Six Commander and a double polygraph administered by a CIA polygrapher. Routine counterintelligence and lifestyle polygraph questions were ignored in favor of penetrating psychological interrogatories. The goal of the polygraph was to determine if a moral man could murder a sitting president. Some failed the test. President Kennedy and his advisors had table-topped the scenarios and agreed if a president was ever taken prisoner, there must not be any equivocation from the sniper team. If a rescue wasn't feasible, a captured president must not be allowed to live.

No more than ten SEALs from Team Six were active and read in on the program at any one time, and they were all officers. They ran scenarios and practiced rescue operations two or three times a year. SEAL sniper teams practiced with experimental weapons and ammunition. When they received an exercise order, a two-man sniper team would jump from a Special Operations C-130 or C-17, parachute into an area under cover of darkness, make their way to the target, and shoot a facsimile of the president at a range of over one mile using night vision systems. McGee had said when he retired, he was read off the program, and someone else took his place.

McGee asked, "Have you talked with Nazy?"

"I have, but not about this. She has her hands full at the moment."

"I have some patriots who are ready for *one more go*. They've been providing security for the *Insiders* for decades. They'll be at the upcoming Bensberg Conference."

Hunter glanced at the *Growler*, then considered the implications of the information. "Seriously?"

"Seriously."

"The only target is Scorpii. I'm convinced he was responsible for the missile that took out our jet and the RPG that nearly took out my bride."

"As am I. I have contacts in the NSA and German Intelligence; they're convinced he was the belly button who ordered the hit. But they won't act on it because of politics. He owns the German government ten deep. They would do nothing to jeopardize their funding support. If someone gets to him the Communists, Marxists, Socialists, sexual activists and Islamists in the German government will hunt down the perpetrators and destroy their families."

"We can't have that. Do you have a plan?"

"I always have a plan. You can't be part of it."

"You have a plan, but I can't be a part of it? What am doing here, good sir?"

"I need someone to drive the get-away vehicle."

Get-away vehicle? Isn't that part of a plan? Hunter squinted as if he were in pain, then illumination came to him. He snapped his fingers and said softly, "*My students,* your pilots recently delivered a jet to him."

McGee's smile illuminated the greasy spoon. "That's right. See? Get-away vehicle. He takes one from you; we take one of his."

"You mean 'payback's a bitch!'"

"It is, and if you are going to be my National Security Advisor when we win this thing, I cannot have you under suspicion. I can't have you whacking gay German billionaires."

"Got it." *Uh oh, did I just agree to something?*

"For the last twenty years, my guys have provided personal security services for kings and queens, the rich and the famous, and they're above reproach. They have made a name for themselves. They can do this; you cannot. Mainly because the security at *these places* will be intense."

Hunter looked at McGee. *These places. These places? Oh shit! They infiltrated the security systems of the Bensberg Conference, Davos, the World Economic Forum, and others.* Duncan shook his head in amazement and smiled like a kid with a new Schwinn *Lemon Krate.*

McGee continued, "They're inside, and you'd never make it past the lobby. Nazy would be pissed at me when you didn't come home. No, you are not and cannot be a part of the kinetics, but you'll be needed for logistical support. And to make contact."

McGee could tell his friend understood but was a little bollixed up and said, "Do you know how many times Captain Pete Ortiz wanted to be part of a group that killed Nazis? I can tell you, he wanted to be in everything; he just wanted to kill Nazis. He felt so much responsibility to get the job done; he wanted to be a part of it all. He wanted to do it all. At the OSS his job was to organize the *Maquis*, men who had good hearts but were quite dysfunctional because they were not trained soldiers."

"Let me tell you another Ortiz story. Still classified. The SOE...."

"The British Special Operations Executive...."

"Correct. The SOE broke into the POW camp holding Ortiz. Ortiz was needed for a special project—one that wasn't just for anyone."

"Get Goebbels' papers."

"Very good. And when he got Goebbels' *pumpkin*, all three truck loads worth, out of the country, he went back to the POW camp. How to break in and break out of a POW camp was one of the SOE's specialties and one of Ortiz's challenges. General Donovan wanted him to stay in the camp and Ortiz didn't escape. Everyone has a part to play. Some missions required the special qualifications of other *Resistance* members while he provided logistical support. My guys can do a lot of things, but flying a get-away jet is for someone special. Maybe knocking the lights out in the hotel, that'll be your contribution.

You don't always get to be the hero. No girls to cry over you, shout your name. Celeste called you old and Nazy will still love you. Sometimes there is a better solution. That's all this is. Nazy just wants *the pumpkin*."

Hunter chuckled and then repeated, "That's all this is. Nazy wants *the pumpkin*."

McGee added, "There's not much you can do when the head terrorist is near death. You have to get them out of there, both the *Broken Lance* guys and Scorpii's *pumpkin*. And of course, you have to pay them."

"What do they want for their services? Suddenly, I feel like a mob boss."

McGee told him. Hunter didn't flinch. Some things are worth paying extra for, even for a mob boss. Hunter said, "I have gold coin for that."

"Perfect." *And untraceable.*

A waiter finally showed up.

Hunter asked him, "What's good?"

McGee scowled.

The waiter just stood there like a mannequin.

Hunter didn't open the menu and said, "I'll have the hot turkey sandwich, dark gravy if you have it. If not, then whatever you have. Piled high and then some more. Extra gravy. Green beans. Don't worry about what it costs; I'm buying."

McGee caustically said, "You like turkey, don't you?"

"I do. High in lysine; best stuff on the planet against a coronavirus. Besides therapeutics and curatives and vitamins, of course."

McGee chortled and said, "You sound like you know something." He turned to the waiter and said, "Make it two."

CHAPTER 50

December 3, 2019

The security detail at the entrance to the executive suite unlocked and opened the door at the arrival of the Executive Director of Foreign Intelligence, High Captain Maalik El Masri. After placing a few CDs in the vault and logging them in, he prepared himself for the Supreme Lord Chancellor. He had bad news, very bad news to start off the morning. The Supreme Lord Chancellor didn't take kindly to bad news, especially very bad news. Few things were more pitiful than an eighty-year-old man throwing a tantrum. He could buy *special services*, but sometimes the proper execution of those services was unexpectedly inadequate regardless of what was paid.

El Masri entered the suite and found the Chancellor was up. He was in white silk bedclothes and a black robe, sitting on the glass-paneled patio enjoying a breakfast tray of fresh fruit and fruit juices that would likely be sampled but not fully consumed. The old man pointed to another tray of food and coffee. They ate in silence in the chilled air of the patio. It was December, but it hadn't snowed; a sure sign global warming was real and life on the planet would be snuffed out like a candle in the wind in months.

Scorpii's flatulence was noteworthy and audible, and impossible to ignore. He often broke wind, and didn't realize it until he actually smelled himself. His sphincter control was virtually gone, a hazard of the gay lifestyle and life's reality for any octogenarian. The inside of the suite would have been a thousand times worse if not for scented candles and trays of cinnamon-saturated potpourri on virtually every flat surface.

The chilliness of the patio seemed to negate the old man's gases.

El Masri would speak when he was spoken to. He surreptitiously checked on the Supreme Lord Chancellor when he closed his eyes.

Apparently, Scorpii had had a rough night and couldn't keep his eyes open at breakfast. When El Masri thought Scorpii was about to topple over, he coughed lightly. Scorpii was sensitive about being touched. When his eyes were open, there were no issues, but when his eyes were closed, Scorpii would lash out at the slightest tap. El Masri delayed the bad news as long as he dared, he coughed again which roused Scorpii.

Old, red, rheumy eyes pivoted to the younger man. "*Danke, Maalik.*"

El Masri wordlessly helped the old man inside and helped him dress.

Scorpii chose odd gold coin cufflinks for El Masri to use to secure his sleeves. Maalik knew exactly what the cufflinks were and where they came from. Why the Lord Chancellor chose them over some of the others was never articulated. As El Masri easily buttoned the collar, Scorpii became exasperated his shirt didn't fit. Maalik knew it was another sign of the cancer.

He helped Scorpii to his office chair. The Supreme Lord Chancellor of the European Federation was officially at work, leading the empire he and his friends had built from scratch. He barked at Maalik El Masri; did he know the status of *das Amerikaners?*

We have known for many days. Is his memory failing or is he just remembering some things? El Masri asked tentatively, "*Herr McGee, mein Kanzler?*"

"*Ja.*"

He was succinct but courteous. "*Mein Kanzler*, the attack on McGee failed over ten days ago."

Scorpii raised worn out eyes which telegraphed, *I do not care when it happened, do you have details?*

"*Ja, mein Kanzler.*" Scorpii rested his chin on his chest as El Masri again read local and American newspaper reports from his intelligence service. El Masri was surprised that instead of erupting like a volcano at the thought of being told twice on McGee's status, the

Supreme Lord Chancellor Scorpii frowned and nodded, almost as if had been expecting the failure.

Scorpii dismissed the fuzzy old thoughts and asked, "*Die Frau?*"

El Masri said the attack on Cunningham was a partial failure. "There were reports of her being admitted into their national hospital, but no reports of her death. Operations at the spy house are normal. And we have confirmation a woman entered the White House at the same time the PDB is normally given. She's not afforded the same level of security, just one vehicle. We have no further news on *die hündin.*"

Scorpii's arm clawed the air. He said, "Leave me. I'll call you when I need you. Tell the security guard I wish to speak to him."

"*Mein Kanzler*, do you wish me to remain with you while he is with you?

"*Nein.*"

"*Mein Kanzler*, please allow me to add every aspect of the Bensberg Conference is on track."

"When is that?"

"*Mein Kanzler*, ten days."

"*Danke*, Maalik."

High Captain Maalik El Masri paused to consider the Chancellor's journals. *There will be time after he's gone.* He departed on polished boots. El Masri stopped at the entrance to the Chancellor's suite and spoke to the security men. They walked with him on the way out of the hotel as if he required personal security.

After escorting El Masri out, the big burly man, one of two such men in Scorpii's personal security team, entered the living quarters and *reported* as if he were back in the U.S. Navy. He looked straight ahead as the Lord Chancellor spoke. As he had done several times over the past few weeks, Scorpii demanded a promise of loyalty to him. The security guard promised he would protect him with his life.

Scorpii whispered, "I am certain there will be assassins or kidnappers coming for me. It's their way. I must know you'll do everything in your power not to let them take me away."

The dumbfounded security guard said, "Lord Chancellor, you need not worry, sir. We are here to protect you."

Scorpii asked the man to step closer.

Gothear Horst could see real fear in the Lord Chancellor's eyes. Scorpii knew enough that he was about to embark on the great sleep and it frightened him.

CHAPTER 51

December 3, 2019

As their meals were being prepared, McGee explained when he was a U.S. Navy Lieutenant Commander in the SEALs, he had submitted two men for consideration for a top-secret special access program; a clandestine infiltration program which would eventually provide personal security services for the leaders of the *Insiders* based in Europe.

Hunter turned away and chortled. *Of course, you did!*

McGee explained, "Once the men were approved for *infiltration* I, newly promoted U.S. Navy Lt. Commander McGee, I think I was the only black dude in the SEALs, at least on the East Coast, publicly fired the former *Broken Lancers* for homosexuality, a dischargeable offence under the Uniform Code of Military Justice. This was just days prior to implementing the *Don't Ask, Don't Tell* law."

Hunter said, "I saw that as the start of the internal destruction of the DOD. The camel's nose under the tent."

"Well, it was all that and more. The left masked their intentions all along the way to where we are today." McGee continued, "The SEALs I fired had marketable skills in personal security. Over the years they moved from one personal security provider to another, paying their dues and establishing new credibilities, personal qualifications, and solid reputations. Eventually they were offered the position of protecting the Supreme Lord Chancellor of the European Federation, also known as the head of the *Insiders*."

"Scorpii. Billions to radicals and terrorists."

McGee nodded in agreement. "Scorpii and the *Insiders* and their interests go all the way back to the fifties, sixties, and seventies. Scorpii was a minor player in those days and wasn't on our radar."

Hunter checked to see the *Growler* was still flashing. He said, "The *Insiders* were also known for their secular beliefs and liberal viewpoints on alternate lifestyles."

McGee nodded. "In certain cities, hotels and nightclubs owned by some members of the *Insiders* cater strictly to the gay, lesbian, and alternative lifestyle crowds. Scorpii dominated those in Berlin in the late 60s and early 70s, and later throughout Germany. But the millionaires turned billionaires tried to corner the gay, lesbian, and alternative clubs and hotels in Amsterdam, Paris, Brussels, Madrid, Rome, and elsewhere. Those rich men formed and then strengthened the *Insiders* as they dominated the lucrative drugs and prostitution, and we think, the even more profitable pedophilia businesses. Government employees who were patrons of these businesses were blackmailed to commit treason. They provided TS/SCI documents to the *Insiders* who had developed their own intelligence service. They turned those documents around and sold them to Moscow."

"They made copies?"

"Oh, yes. They would have filled dozens of *pumpkins*. Those government employees who engaged in homosexual trysts were targeted and photographed. They were pitched, and if they didn't play ball, they were outed and humiliated. Virtually all who were photographed and couldn't be turned eventually committed suicide."

Maverick shook his head.

"But not before they committed some espionage. Sometimes *some* was enough."

Maverick continued to shake his head in disbelief. He remembered saying, *Personality and sexual disorders killed themselves at a phenomenal rate.* "I take it the *Insiders* sold information to the highest bidder."

McGee agreed, "That's right. The Kremlin."

"That had to be a tough nut for the IC to crack."

"We had a few gays and lesbians we tried to turn to be double agents. They were not dependable. Most of them stayed in Europe because of the gay friendly environment."

"I can see that."

McGee said, "So as you can imagine, getting the right people into the position to spy on an adversary in Europe required years of planning and decades of execution before our people could function and survive as informers. Some people were lost in the process because of age or infirmity or discovery. But those who could wade through the minefield of procedures and processes designed to find a spy, like polygraphs, those deep *infiltrators* were often rewarded with positions of the greatest trust and confidence. They provided the highest-level intelligence and political information. Those people were part of the resistance movements everywhere Communists set up shop."

"And as you can imagine, in the beginning the KGB sponsored the gay, lesbian, and alternative cultures in Western and European colleges, clubs, and countries as a means of infiltrating Western and European agencies and organizations. The Democrat Congresses wouldn't allow reciprocity in this type of espionage, and for some time the CIA was prevented from sponsoring gay, lesbian, and alternative lifestyles to infiltrate Eastern Bloc agencies and organizations. Few things are more pitiful than a straight white dude in a gay bar."

"There was pandemonium on the seventh floor; knock down drag outs, I understand, on this topic. Some Agency executives thought some members of Congress were Bible-thumping puritans, while others recognized the KGB was playing them against each other. The left's propaganda often won out."

Hunter said, "I would have fired those clowns."

"Me too. Others saw it our way. When it came time to consider inserting infiltrators into the gay, lesbian, and alternative lifestyles of European governments and NGOs, all the way back to the 60s when this was first discussed, President Kennedy declared some members of Congress would leak the secret material to the media and by extension, American adversaries everywhere."

"Democrats proving Democrats are not trustworthy. Democrats are not on our side." Hunter wasn't snarky.

"This was one of those rare Director-only special access programs because you couldn't trust any Democrat presidents after Kennedy. Not even the current president would be cleared to know of the program. The infiltration required men of unusual conviction and character, and they had to be gay. Once they were in, we believed they would have unusual access. Like what is possible when an intelligence officer converts to Islam."

McGee grinned as their plates of turkey were served, mounds of turkey and gravy. The waiter shook his head in amusement and refilled their glasses before walking away.

He looked directly at Hunter and said, "We need to bring them home. They have one more job, maybe two, then they need to come home."

"That's why you need me to fly the jet."

"Far more than that, we need to get *the pumpkin* out of the country." McGee nodded, "We don't know what the size of it could be, but we believe they're hand transcribed. No computer. You'll have to brief *them* as to what is important. I'll give you a special coin so they know it came from me and these are my desires. They work as a team; you'll get one shot at them. Weapons are out of the question; getting a weapon inside the hotel where they are is impossible."

Hunter deferred a bite and aimed a fork at McGee. "I would think getting a weapon into Germany is impossible."

McGee nodded and parried with, "It's not worth being exposed. Remember they're versed in the martial arts. You do not have to worry about them. I'm free lancing here. I think you need to make contact, tell them to get as much as *the pumpkin* as possible, and then let them take advantage of the situation. They're in their environment. You have to be tangential to the op and just get them out. Oh, and you'll have to pretend you're gay. I mean, more than you already are." McGee chortled.

Hunter wouldn't bite. "You think we can do that with this?" Hunter pointed at the *Growler*.

From a suit pocket, McGee withdrew his own *Growler* and a challenge coin in the shape of an arrowhead. He said, "The situation may need two *Growlers*. They've been there a long time; they know where every camera is." McGee held up the coin. It was an unconventional challenge coin in every way, striated red translucent glass from a glassblower's shop, embedded in pewter in the shape of an arrowhead. When McGee was the SEAL Team Six Commander, this was his personal coin. He said, "This will get you to the dance. You'll have to make contact and ask if they're ready to come home."

"Seriously? How will I know them?"

McGee said, "I have old photos, and I'll let one of them know you are coming." He added, "I know you've wanted to live the life of a ground agent. Here's your chance."

Hunter frowned. *I've never wanted to live the life of a ground agent!* "You have experience in this area?"

"I have experience in this area. Sometimes you have to do unpleasant things for your country." *Like killing Mazibuike's vice president.*

I sure as hell know that's true. He and McGee shared several secrets. Hunter took the distinctive coin, studied it, and mouthed *Thank you.*

McGee continued, "This is one of one, the deepest penetrations ever attempted by the Agency. Gothear Horst and Rudolf Blohm are the chief security men for Scorpii."

"Grandparents escaped Nazi Germany, came to the U.S.? Raised to love America? And they're built like you?"

McGee nodded. Grinned. *Of course. Some special qualifications are not always on a resumé.*

The men ate in silence. When it was time for them to leave, Hunter slipped McGee's dirty *Growler* into one pocket, then shut off his *Growler* and put it into his other suitcoat pocket. He reflected on why men would volunteer for such duty until he realized he was also one of those men. He had volunteered to work for advancing American interests. Whatever it takes. He was operational, and for over twenty years he had been the only mercenary to eradicate terrorists from the air. Hunter understood that only a gay man who could pass a polygraph would be able to infiltrate an operation such as Scorpii's *Ostgut Foundation.*

They walked outside to McGee's waiting limousine. McGee turned to Hunter. He had one more point.

Automatically, Hunter stuck his hand in a pocket and clicked on a *Growler* just to be safe.

Bill McGee indicated, although his intel was dated, the target was reportedly in very bad shape. "If death is imminent from natural causes, we usually leave them alone. But if you can use him, use him to your advantage."

Hunter frowned. "I get it. If we need to use him to get his journals and diaries out of the country, I'll do it."

McGee said, "Nazy asked me if I had *the pumpkin* after I returned from Zhavrazhinov's place with all of his stuff. If we don't get them, Russia and all of Europe will be in a mad dash for them."

Hunter smiled, nodded, and shook McGee's hand. He saluted McGee as he drove away.

On his way through the building he stopped at Flight Planning to call for the weather and file a flight plan. He paid for his fuel and other airport usage fees. While the employees processed his billing and credit card, Hunter recalled the day President Hernandez had announced McGee would become the new CIA Director after Director Lynche resigned. One of Greg Lynche's last official acts was to show McGee and him the secret *Library of Diaries* that was offsite of CIA Headquarters. Hunter knew the CIA was interested in the diaries of the rich and famous and it had been the informal responsibility of the chief of counterintelligence, during the 60s, 70s, and 80s but that it was now the Chief Special Activities Group (SAG) who usually facilitated the acquisition of diaries. When the SAG couldn't for whatever reason, he would contact Hunter's Quiet Recoveries International company to see if a civilian approach would have better results than the strong arm or clandestine arm of the government.

After the previous election, McGee had confided to Hunter that Greg Lynche had asked him to recover the papers of Dr. Nikita Zhavrazhinov, the Democratic National Committee Chairman who had committed suicide for failing Eleanor Tussy as her campaign manager. The SAG had been compromised, Bill McGee was available, so if the CIA were to gain Dr. Zhavrazhinov's diaries, an outsider would be needed and fast. And it was done without a contract.

Hunter absentmindedly signed the credit card charges with an alias, a phantom employee at Quiet Aero Systems and thought, *Oh, that's right. The morning newspapers reported on the unexpected win of the incumbent President over his heavily favored rival, Eleanor Tussy, the turd that won't flush even though she had led all polls and had won the popular* vote by over two million votes. And most of the national papers published a tiny notice of the death of Dr. Nikita Zhavrazhinov, but never said he took a swan dive off the 22nd floor of the Times Square Marriott.

Out the door and onto the ramp, frigid wind in his hair, Hunter reveled in the highlights of that election night. *CIA Director Greg Lynche called the Chief of the Border Patrol and asked him to dispatch one of his ultra-quiet MD-600 NOTAR helicopters to CIA headquarters for a sensitive project. He said, Let's call it a training exercise and send your BORTAC unit.*

Bill McGee, still technically the CEO of Quiet Aero Systems and by extension Quiet Recoveries International was under his line of busness, had changed into black battle dress fatigues, stepped from the quiet helicopter, and entered the residence of Dr. Zhavrazhinov. The heavily armed members of BORTAC, the tactical and special response arm of the U.S. Border Patrol, had fanned out and surrounded the former Harvard professor's residence while McGee searched the premises. He quickly found what he was looking for, a poorly hidden five-foot tall wall safe. He blew the door with specially shaped wedges of C-4 and investigated the contents.

Bill said he wasn't surprised to find Communist Party of America documents including lists of contacts, donors, secret cells, apparatuses. But he was to remove all of Zhavrazhinov's papers, his files and books, and especially the DNC's chairman's journals and computer. McGee took everything he could carry and set the place on fire. By the time McGee and the Border Patrol tactical agents had returned to the helicopter, I heard Zhavrazhinov's house was totally engulfed.

Nazy said Zhavrazhinov's pumpkin contained the names of defectors, spies, sleeper cells, ciphers, spy apparatuses, senior Democrats in Congress, and the names of FBI and Agency men who worked for the old cigar-smoking commie. There were enough datapoints of information to solve hundreds of political murders in America. KGB and mob hit jobs. And we never sent the CIA a bill.

Maverick walked around the aircraft to ensure the fuel caps were on tight and the fuel access doors were secure. He crawled into the *Howard* and closed the door. He consulted the pilot's checklist to ensure he missed nothing during start, taxi, and takeoff. He reached behind him to ensure the satphone was secure in its holder. Once airborne, he set the autopilot. He was alone again in an aircraft with just engine vibration to keep him company.

His mind jumped ahead in the story as he recalled when he and Nazy had talked about it. She had said, *"Tip of the iceberg. While it looked as if the Russians were doing everything they could to run drugs into the country, Dr. Z's journal showed it was actually several of Rho Schwartz Scorpii's NGOs. Outward appearances, it was the Russians who backed the Taliban and the opium trade, but it was Scorpii. It looked like it was the Russians who backed the narco-terrorists in South America, but it was Scorpii's billions. It looked like the Iranian ayatollahs were funding Islamic terrorism throughout the globe, but some of it was Scorpii's billions. There was a dark side to the KGB. Scorpii funded what was essentially double agents at the KGB; agents who pushed work to hm for a price and he jacked up the price for regular KGB officers. Everyone won. Scorpii did it all, trying everything he could to destabilize our country."*

•   •   •

After landing at the Baltimore-Washington International airport Executive Terminal, Hunter paid to secure the *Howard 500* in a hangar. He raced into town to be with Nazy.

CHAPTER 52

December 5, 2019

After a long day of public appearances, most notably the Presidents of America and Egypt shaking hands and conversing in front of the Sphinx, President Hernandez and his wife were treated to a state banquet at the Presidential Palace of Egypt, hosted by the President of Egypt. Over two hundred guests attended the star-studded banquet. The guests included Egyptian media and industry and the military, American luminaries including Cairo University alum Dr. John Lindell, and one of the more curious invitees, the man who was the Supreme Allied Commander Europe of all commands of the North Atlantic Treaty Organization, General Walter Todd III.

The meal was beef tenderloin and potatoes *boulangere*; dessert was the American president's favorite, key lime pie.

As the President of Egypt welcomed the Hernandezs, he said, "Today we celebrate one of our most important allies. The relationship between Egypt and America goes far beyond our military ties. We have a special relationship; it's a partnership highlighted by friends who actively wish to see Egyptians succeed and North Africa flourish. Today we visited the U.S. Naval Medical Research Unit, America's preeminent overseas laboratory encompassing thirty buildings on thirty-three acres. A thousand technicians, both Egyptians and Americans are conducting research and surveillance related to infectious disease. They support the U.S. military deployed across Africa, the Middle East, and Southwest Asia, and they also investigate diseases that impact Egyptians from all walks of life."

President Hernandez offered elaborate toasts to the President of Egypt and both of their wives. He affirmed the strong alliance between the countries. He said, "We are proud of the exceptional collaboration between Egyptian and American scientists at our infectious disease research center. They work on vaccine testing, infection prevention, diagnostics, and insect control measures focusing primarily on viral pathogens common to the region. We are grateful for Egypt's assistance in the research center and other efforts. We look forward to a long and exciting partnership."

He concluded his comments with, "Mr. President, under your strong leadership the forces of evil are in full retreat, but we know they won't be deterred for long. As gifts from the people of the United States, America offers to add a C-130 cargo aircraft and several additional F-16 fighter aircraft to the inventory of the supremely capable and accomplished Egyptian Air Force. These aircraft will help the Egyptian Air Force to better protect the people of the Arab Republic of Egypt. It's time for Egypt to be considered for membership in NATO, the North Atlantic Treaty Organization."

Two hundred guests stood and cheered.

SACEUR, General Walter Todd III, wondered if President Hernandez was serious about Egypt being included in NATO, or if there was another reason for the nearly impromptu meeting and state dinner. *Was that why I was an add-on to the guest list?*

CHAPTER 53

December 6, 2019

With a boarding pass and a passport with additional pages sewn in and multiple stamps and visas indicating significant international travel, Dante Locke passed through the Dulles airport security system without incident. Fully in disguise, Duncan Hunter-Dante Locke occupied seat 7A, upstairs in the first-class section of Flight 419, the 5:35 Lufthansa 747-400 to *Flughafen Frankfurt am Main.*

He took advantage of the lie-flat seats. Wearing a sleep mask and noise suppression headphones, Hunter slept the whole way. His bomb and weapons detection technologies were now in virtually every major airport in North and South America and Europe. As long as the domestic and international federal airport screening services didn't hire al-Qaeda for the key positions, he could relax.

Upon arrival at Frankfurt am Main, Dante Locke picked up a black Halliburton Zero from baggage claim and entered the queue for customs inspection. He opened the Halliburton and his computer bag for the customs personnel to inspect.

Dante Locke declared that his phone and computer were for business use only, he offered the customs officials the electronics declaration documents and his passport.

Customs officials were a little curious about the contents of the Halliburton. It held eight tiny flying drones and a pair of round green rubber-coated devices. Locke showed they were his products for a tradeshow.

One customs officer barely raised an eyebrow as he thumbed through the thick passport when he asked in German accented English, "Nature of your business?"

Dante Locke answered in English, "I sell surveillance equipment for law enforcement and the intelligence community."

The response didn't register any concern. The customs official behind the bulletproof glass checked the terrorist database and handed Locke's passport to another officer who stamped it. The customs men had nothing else to say to the traveler; they motioned for Locke to proceed.

Dante Locke closed the cases and headed to the rental car counter.

A Volvo SUV XC90 awaited Dante Locke in a subterranean parking garage. As he entered the Autobahn and motored toward Cologne, the high-speed highway evoked the memory of what he really wanted to rent in Germany, something incredibly fast and flashy. But he was working and that meant subtlety was the order of the day. Hunter thought, *There will be another opportunity to go fast, if I survive.*

Traveling at 150 mph was nothing for the Volvo, and Locke arrived at the stunningly regal Althoff Grandhotel Schloss Bensberg in no time. He exited the car to check in as valets swarmed him to take his Halliburton case and heavy bullhide computer bag the manufacturer proudly claimed: *They'll fight over it when you're dead.*

Under the watchful eye of two large security men, Dante Locke was about to enter the Grandhotel when he noticed under a separate awning a rare Mercedes 540K Special Roadster tucked to the side of the hotel's entrance. He stood there amazed, arms akimbo. He knew a little of its history. 1937. Custom coachwork, pre-war vehicle. He had never seen one in person, and they were rarely offered for auction in America. In the United States, a car like that would have been stuck in a museum or brought out once a year at Pebble Beach or Amelia Island Concours d'Elegance. Here it appeared to be someone's daily driver or maybe the hotel's special limousine. Dante Locke admired it as a stunning example of German engineering and design and muttered, "You probably have to pay extra for a ride in that thing." He thought, *Bosky Europe must have so many exotic cars stuck away in barns and garages.* Then he added, *And probably hangars. I have cars stuffed away in a couple of hangars.*

Once through the set of double doors, he found his path blocked with screening equipment like one would find at an airport security checkpoint. Locke picked up his bags and put them on a conveyor belt, noticing that the manufacturer's data plates recorded the airport security equipment was from his company. As the x-ray technician checked his bags for weapons and explosives, Locke walked through a magnetometer without setting it off. The x-ray tech stopped the conveyor and asked to see the electronic devices in the briefcase. Locke opened the Halliburton Zero, extracted a drone and turned it on. Locke tossed it into the air and the device immediately unfolded; four tiny rotors spun noiselessly as the rotorcraft hovered in front of him. The x-ray technician wasn't amused and didn't ask about the pair of green rubber devices or the three innocuous-looking rectangular black-coated stainless-steel devices. He was more focused on the drones. He had seen electronic road flares before. The black rectangular devices and the flares didn't register any traces of explosives according to the sensors inside the x-ray machine.

When the hotel's security screening technician was satisfied the businessman wasn't a cleverly disguised terrorist assassin, Locke turned the drone off and returned it to the briefcase. Baggage handlers carried his luggage from the end of the conveyor, and Dante Locke made his way to the check-in counter.

The receptionist registered Locke, made a copy of his passport, and assigned him a suite. He cautioned Locke that he had the room for only two nights. The hotel wouldn't honor any extensions or late check-outs as it was sponsoring the Bensberg Conference. All their rooms had been reserved for that event. Dante Locke agreed to the conditions before the receptionist handed the valet the room key card. Electronic; modern for such an antebellum hotel. *What you can do when you have money.* The receptionist had also upsold the obviously fatigued Dante Locke a sauna and massage package at the hotel's famous spa; the baggage clerk guided Locke to his room. Inside, Locke went about his room like there were no cameras or microphones in the suite. He was Dante Locke, salesman of law enforcement equipment, and not Duncan Hunter, CIA contractor and airborne assassin of terrorists.

Locke checked the time to verify how much longer he had until his mask would start to slough off his face. He removed a vial from his shaving kit labeled after shave and headed for the water closet. He closed the door but didn't turn on the light. In the dark, Locke poured some of the vial's contents into his hands and spread the humectant in the clear liquid on his face and neck—everywhere the mask's skin was exposed. This refreshed the mask's material. Then he acted as if he were fumbling for the light switch, used the toilet, and washed his hands. He put his things away in a closet and headed out the door, double-checking his shirt pocket for the room's access card. He wanted another look at the men at the door and the Mercedes.

Locke needed to drive around town, find the Cologne airport and a camera shop, and get something to eat. As he walked through the lobby and approached the entrance, he saw the two security men standing inside out of the cold. He shoved his hand into his pocket and palmed the special challenge coin given to him by Bill McGee. As he came under the scrutiny of the security men, he extended his hand to shake one of the big men's hands.

Locke asked if he could get a closer look at the magnificent car.

The security man was startled to have received a coin during the handshake. He answered, "*Ja.*" The big man indicated with a gesture to *go ahead and look* as he slipped the coin into his pocket, surreptitiously feeling the distinctive arrowhead shape of a former SEAL Team commander's personal coin. He knew what it was but he would confirm its authenticity when he was out of the range of the hotel lobby surveillance cameras.

The security man with the coin asked his partner to follow Locke to ensure the vehicle wouldn't be molested.

Under a stern eye, Locke kept his distance and admired the sweeping fenders and handcrafted coachwork. He asked questions which were likely recorded by hotel security. It wasn't the time to blast a security monitor's ears or use the *Growler* in his pocket to turn the wall monitors in the security video room into an electronic snowstorm. The Halliburton Zero didn't leave his hand.

After five minutes eyeballing the 540K roadster, Dante Locke returned to the hotel entrance and thanked the men. The man with the coin nodded imperceptibly, acknowledging confirmation that contact had been made. All Locke's training in reading microexpressions was unnecessary with the guard's well-timed and well-placed thumbnail innocently scratching an eyebrow. *That's the signal.*

McGee's guys remembered the old surreptitious hand signals. Radar contact. All I need now is some time with one of them.

Locke offered his claim ticket to the valet parking manager, then from his shirt pocket, offered one of his business cards to the security man who had the coin.

He looked at the card and checked the obverse. On the back of the card was written, *I'd like to take you home.*

Hunter-Locke thought the message could have been interpreted as an invitation by a gay man to a gay man. But with the arrowhead challenge coin from McGee, the message was an invitation to return to the United States. *Your mission is over; if you want to come home, Bill McGee and America will welcome you home.*

When the valet delivered the Volvo, Locke tipped the man and half-waved at the security men. He placed the Halliburton on the rear seat. By the time he began driving away from the hotel, Locke was fighting jet lag with everything he had. He had slept on the jet and was glad he had made contact, but most of all he gambled he hadn't been discovered. Locke was convinced he hadn't overdone the counter-espionage and natural activities to give himself away. All of his actions and activities, even when viewed through the lenses of a microscope, should have painted him as an innocent salesman and shouldn't have given a trained intelligence officer any cause for concern. The only thing someone could think as odd were three black Minox subminiature cameras and a single white short-sleeve shirt with tabs on the shoulders at the bottom of his Halliburton case. If someone was interested in the contents of the Halliburton, they would have to dig to find the shirt.

The Agency expected significant scrutiny. Scorpii's intelligence arm could look as closely as they wanted. A digital photostatic copy of Locke's passport was already being analyzed at a nondescript office building in Berlin. They would find Locke had a long history of international travel as the salesman for QuietWorks Robotics, a division of QuietAero Systems of Fredericksburg, Texas specializing in patented, proprietary silent drone technologies. There was a law enforcement expo in Dusseldorf, and he was a registered vendor of surveillance equipment.

However, in a room the size of a house, the foreign intelligence arm of the *Ostgut Foundation* couldn't locate any facial recognition records of Dante Locke's travel. The head analyst lamented to the Executive Director of Foreign Intelligence, High Captain Maalik El Masri, that not all international airports had state-of-the-art facial recognition technology. Locke's passport and visas matched the airport locations where there were security cameras installed but no facial recognition software. Was this just a datapoint or was it something to cause concern? Or was the man simply staying at the gay-themed hotel looking for some action he couldn't get in America?

Even the best facial recognition system on the planet couldn't crack who was actually behind the CIA's disguise. Before McGee had left the Agency for political pastures, the Science & Technology Director had loaded Hunter's Dante Locke disguise and his other disguises into the FBI's National Facial Recognition System databank. Hunter's Dante Locke passport was the real thing, as were the others, but the visas were all counterfeit products from the Science & Technology Directorate. When it came to replicating documents an undercover intelligence officer needed to survive, there wasn't anything the Agency couldn't or wouldn't do.

One of El Masri's intelligence officers was detailed to monitor the output of several hidden cameras and microphones in Dante Locke's room. The only thing to report before the target left his room was *The Yankee couldn't find the light to take a piss? What an imbecile!*

Duncan Hunter-Dante Locke's BlackBerry directed him to a large camera store in town where he bought every roll of film and flashbulb in stock for Minox subminiature cameras. The GPS feature then directed him to a street where he followed the signs to the Cologne airport. As expected, there were dozens of business jets but hardly any general aviation (GA) aircraft. The handful of GA on the ramp were probably heavy fuel, diesel-powered airplanes. Someone in the German government quickly ascertained if you outlawed aviation gasoline in the name of global warming, you could kill off the piston-powered aircraft industry. But the government officials hadn't considered aviation people installing modified diesel engines into small airplanes. *Screw your global warming crap!*

Hunter-Locke thought, *There is just no good in socialism, and if it wasn't for the propaganda, Germany would already be communist. But they like the money the millionaires and billionaires provide in taxes as long as they can get a pinch of the action. Mazibuike had gotten his pinch when he signed an oil agreement with Iran. For every barrel of oil produced in Iran, 3M got a nickel. But that's not my problem, not my problem.*

He took the road to the executive terminal, noticing where all the power lines that led into the airport were located. He went inside to the flight planning room envisioning what he would do when the time came.

Initially, no one in the executive terminal paid any attention to him even though he looked like a movie star from a popular American submarine movie. But that was part of the disguise. He wanted as many people to see him and remember him in this setting. If he survived the setting, he would be back.

He strolled in like he had been there many times and followed the signage to Flight Planning. A curious employee of the flight operations department would think the jacketed man knew his way around the building since he went straight to the doorless Flight Planning room. A curious employee could walk by Flight Planning and see he was consulting approach plates, reviewing IFR Supplements, and plotting routes on charts and maps and such. A curious employee would see that the Scottish movie star was actually doing some flight planning. A curious employee wouldn't have been alarmed and would have returned to her work station behind the counter. He no longer interested her. He didn't speak to anyone, but he did smile which was more than any of the other transient pilots would have done after flight planning.

Those employees who had been there long enough knew who used the Flight Planning office routinely. After flight planning, pilots always stopped at the restrooms. Because there were so few pilots who used their facilities they wondered: *Which aircraft is his? We haven't seen him before, is he a new pilot for one of the corporations that have their corporate jets hangared here? He's older, athletic, and dressed in a suit. He could be a corporate pilot. Only the top tier corporate pilots sport a Rolex, and he definitely flashed a two-tone Rolex Submariner.*

Then one employee mentioned to the other they would soon be inundated with jets and airplanes coming in from across the globe for the Bensberg Conference. For a few days they wouldn't have time to wonder who was supposed to be in the executive terminal and who wasn't. The conference planners took care of the security for the terminal and would leave the employees alone to help the aircrews who needed assistance.

The executive terminal employees thought they had figured it out and were grateful they hadn't embarrassed themselves with extraneous accusatory questions. The man was probably part of an advance party for a billionaire. The billionaire's aircraft would drop their party off for the Bensberg conference and then fly to another airport in order to secure the jet in a hangar. That was it—he was a pilot for a billionaire.

On the way out of the double doors of the executive terminal, Dante Locke waved at the employees behind the counter. He had cased the joint and found what he was looking for.

CHAPTER 54

December 7, 2019

Duncan Hunter-Dante Locke had a great plan; it was McGee's plan. But at a quick meeting at a Cologne gay bar with Gothear Horst while a *Growler* defeated the work counterespionage teams practiced incessantly, the former SEAL and current head of the Lord Chancellor's personal security detail expressed his view of the situation. He quietly articulated they had other plans.

Hunter-Locke didn't panic or erupt in a paroxysm of anger. He made a "come to me" hand gesture. *Let's have it.*

The old man was near death and Horst had been at the job a long time. He and Blohm had been thinking about leaving for some time. His plan was straightforward and Locke was impressed with it. By comparison, McGee's plan was clumsy, brutish and arrogant; Horst's plan was simple yet sophisticated. *We will be on a mission of mercy.* Locke glanced around the room, nodded, and thought, *I love it at first blush, but all plans are defenestrated at first contact. Next question: when?*

"El Masri isn't expected to be back tonight. He believes the Lord Chancellor has passed being hallucinogenic and forgetful, he's sleeping and cannot function. El Masri has stopped checking on Scorpii before he retires. We have been relegated to *death watch*. He sleeps and we provide morphine injections as required."

El Masri? Not familiar with him. Hunter-Locke had been thinking about killing the man who had been responsible for so many American deaths. Now the man's death was imminent. "He's that *close*?"

A nod preceded, "Very. Your timing is impeccable. This is our opportunity. We must hurry."

Dante Locke asked, "I agree we must hurry. But for all of us to leave, we are going to need a couple of things."

"I don't understand."

Locke said, "Let me explain. *Bullfrog* expects all of his journals come with us. Diaries, records, everything."

"There are many but we can get them."

"I expect there are videos. Surveillance tapes of...."

"Say no more. I know exactly what you desire. I will get as many as I can carry. Now I must go." Under the tiny table, Horst handed Locke the electronic keys to enter the airport property and the aircraft hangar, and the keys to the G-900's door.

Locke was incredulous. "You are ready to go now?"

"*Ja, Herr Locke.* I must go. I have much to do. You cannot return to the hotel. I will recover your things from your room." Horst gave Locke the combination to disable the hangar's security system as he left. Locke memorized the number, paid the tab, and exited the club.

Dante Locke could see his breath in chuffs out in front of him as he quick-timed to the Volvo. *So much for plans and first contact!*

·   ·   ·

One of the electronic keys allowed Hunter to enter the airport property and it was obvious which one it was. An embedded chip energized the security gate to life. It trundled along its guide rail until it was fully open. Once Hunter had driven the Volvo inside an electronic beam triggered the closing mechanism, and the sturdy chain-link gate closed. Airports across the planet had similar security systems for owner-operators of aircraft; the only difference was mode of access — electronic key or touchpad.

Dante Locke inserted a card into the electronic card reader by the rear door of the hangar, opened the door, and disabled the security system with Horst's combination code. He carried the Halliburton like it was a necessary *accoutrement* of the *hoi oligoi*. He found light switches, turned on the hall lights, and headed for the hangar floor. Locke pushed the crash bar on one of the double doors and spilled out into one of the cleanest, newest hangars he had ever seen. The hangar in Hondo was a pig sty by comparison. Locke glanced at the jet. The G-900 beckoned him.

Locke's curiosity was piqued by three sports cars under car covers that were parked neatly out of the way along the far wall. One had the distinctive shape of an early Jaguar. He wouldn't hazard to guess what the other two could be. That would have to wait.

He placed the Halliburton on the seat of the tug and opened it. Dante Locke removed the insert with the drones and extracted the white short-sleeved pilot's shirt. He buttoned captain's epaulettes on the shoulders and donned the shirt. Now he looked more like the captain of a corporate jet, as long as he didn't hide the epaulettes. He would have to be cold a little longer.

Locke found the controls to open the hangar doors and was aggravated he had to hold the switch to ensure the doors fully opened. The segmented doors took their sweet time, intermittently clicking and clacking. While he waited for the doors to open Locke eyed the underside of the jet for oil or hydraulic leaks, the landing gear tires for underinflation, and the walls of the hangar for any tools he might need. The only things in the hangar were the Gulfstream on a white epoxy floor, a small tug, a towbar, and the three covered sports cars. Otherwise, the inside was sterile.

When the doors finally stopped moving signaling, they were at their stops, Hunter jogged to the left side of the aircraft, unlocked the door handle, lowered the airstairs, and tossed the Halliburton inside. He raced inside, ensured the parking brake was disengaged, and bounded out of the jet. In a minute, he had the tug running and the towbar positioned reasonably close to the nosewheel. Locke carried the end of the towbar the rest of the way to the nosewheel, attached the towbar, ran to the main mounts, kicked away the chocks, and returned to the tug. Locke was grateful to whoever had positioned the jet in the hangar. All he had to do was follow the painted line on the floor and pull it out straight. If Locke did it correctly and didn't freeze to death, the wings wouldn't collide with the hangar doors or the hangar or the parked sports cars.

The ramp was fairly well illuminated as Locke, with four captains' bars on his shoulders, slowly pulled the G-900 out of the hangar and stopped on the centerline of the parking area. He chocked the nosewheel, disconnected the tow bar, and drove the tug forward.

Locke turned 180° to return the tug and towbar to the hangar. *All motions a ground crew or chief pilot would make. No one is in a hurry. No one is trying to fly the jet right out of the hangar as if it were being stolen. No! If anyone is watching, if there are Tailwatchers in the area, all they would see is normal preflight operations for a normal departure. See my captain's bars? Would warning bells go off when I take off?*

As Dante Locke walked to the executive terminal and opened one of the double doors, he thought, *Thank God for the heat but now is the moment of truth.*

In the executive terminal all heads turned to see who had entered from the sterile side of the airport property. Entering from the flightline meant you had access; you were someone who was supposed to be there; you had the keys and codes to get through the security systems, fencing, and barriers around the airport.

In his pilot uniform, Dante Locke half-waved and stepped directly to the FLIGHT PLANNING office. After ten minutes, he emerged to use the facilities, and then presented his flight plan and passport to the clerks behind the counter. They checked his passport, flight plan and weather brief, initialed the document, and called the tower to expect an aircraft departure from the executive terminal side of the airport.

Back outside in the cold, Dante Locke returned to the warmth of the hangar. While he silently begged for Horst to hurry, the three covered cars beckoned him.

I have time for a little look.

•   •   •

As Horst entered the Lord Chancellor's private suite, Rudolf Blohm heard him and immediately dispensed a full eyedropper of liquid morphine into Scorpii's mouth. Gothear Horst worked to prepare the man for transport. Scorpii had been sleeping restlessly, but relaxed seconds after the overdose of the narcotic. He fell into a deep sleep.

The room with a bank style walk-in vault had been left open. Several weeks earlier the Lord Chancellor had demanded El Masri leave the door open because it had become too difficult for him to work the combination correctly. Scorpii was too tired to stand. His memory failed him every time he tried the combinations, and he didn't want to return to his desk to reference his journal where the vault's combination was written.

The interior of the safe was as large as an American garage. The wall opposite the door had wide shelves from floor to ceiling stacked full of international currencies. Blohm worked inside the safe with the precision of an experienced bank robber. He gathered all the journals and papers in the vault and stuffed them into several matching Gladstone bags. The amount of wealth inside the room was distracting, unbelievable for a mere mortal man.

One wall, from floor to ceiling, contained the sex tapes of royalty, aristocrats, politicians, and generals who visited Scorpii's hotels. One section of shelves held the boxes of rare watches. Another section held stacks of 1934 $1,000, $5,000, and $10,000 United States Federal Reserve Notes (FRN). It was a collection of watches and currencies the billionaire had been amassing from auction houses across the globe for three decades.

It was tempting to pilfer some of the wealth, but after securing Scorpii's personal papers, Blohm ignored everything in the vault except the sex tapes of the Secretary General of the North Atlantic Treaty Organization, an assortment of sex tapes of leaders of European countries, the old FRNs, and a section of the shelves which contained several rectangular leather satchels of aircraft logbooks and vehicle documents. He checked and double-checked the newest leather bag to ensure the books therein were for the correct jet, the G-900. Then Blohm filled one bag with sex tapes and two bags with the FRNs, momentarily regretting leaving the safe's inventory of international currency, collector timepieces, and sex tapes of the lesser rich and not-so famous. There was no room; there was no time. Blohm walked out of the vault carrying two black flight bags and the matching luggage full of diaries and journals and videos. Blohm shut the vault door and spun the combination lock. Making two trips, he deposited the luggage inside the entrance of the lobby under the casually watchful eye of the on-duty security man.

Blohm directed the valet to start the engines of two of the Mercedes 540K roadsters and reposition them to the front entrance. He gave instructions to ensure the heaters were on and the top was down on the front one and up on the other. Blohm's eyes were emphatic, *Don't ask questions, just do it!* The valet shot away from the check-in counter and complied.

Before he returned to Scorpii's room, Blohm told the security guard, "Apparently, we are going away." He rolled his eyes to convey he and Horst were carrying out the wishes of a sick man, tacitly acknowledging men of wealth were sometimes unreasonable, but they could afford to be unreasonable. The men who make up their support structure had no say in the decision-making process; they were just doing what they were told and what they were paid to do. It was unusual to go to the airport at ten p.m., but it wasn't unheard of. *The old man has a new jet. But what was strange was that they were going in an open-air roadster in freezing weather.* The security man was sympathetic. The good news was it wasn't snowing, and the sky was clear.

Horst dressed the sleeping old man for the weather like he was a child's doll. Scorpii was unconscious and couldn't complain about the cold or being manhandled as he was stuffed into his tweed coat and a matching driving cap. Horst pushed the old man through the hotel in the wheelchair like he had done countless times before.

Ten large saddle-colored handbags were deposited into the rumble seats and trunks of the two idling Mercedes. Scorpii was transferred from the wheelchair to the 540K's passenger's seat. Horst went through the process of talking to the man, gently scolding Scorpii for wanting to feel the wind on his face as he bundled the billionaire up in blankets. But Scorpii didn't respond.

The security man watched his friends with amusement. There were obvious feelings of *Schadenfreude* as Horst and Blohm worked against the biting cold to please the Lord Chancellor. He chuckled, *Better you than me!* He didn't offer to help them; he refused to leave the warmth of the hotel lobby. And there was no need to tell his friends in security "*Auf wiedersehen,*" for they would return someday, maybe when it was warmer. They would all laugh about freezing their asses off doing the ludicrous in service of the privileged.

•   •   •

As *Maverick* waited for his passengers, he checked the closest car to him and verified the Jaguarish shape under a heavy car cover was one of the first production open two-seaters, a 1961 E-Type Series 3.8 *litre* roadster. He recovered the Jag and walked over to the middle car. He lifted the cover off of the nose and stood there speechless. *I have never seen one of these in person! If this is what I think it's, I'm certain this had been reported stolen.* Without his eyes leaving the car, *Maverick* withdrew a vertex pen from a shirt pocket and a Moleskin notebook from his hip pocket. He leaned over the driver's side windshield and copied the vehicle's serial number. He returned the cover to its place, copied the Jaguar's serial number, and then lifted the cover off of the nose of the last car. Dante Locke had seen renderings of the concept EV, the electric vehicle. He copied the serial number of what he believed to be a Mercedes-AMG concept car. *Oh my.* He returned the cover to its place and muttered, "I'll deal with you guys later."

He walked to the hangar door with the control panel, energized the door closing switch, and walked with the hangar door until there was enough room for a car to enter. Several times his eyes returned to the three cars under cover. *What is wrong with that picture?* It was going to bother him but he didn't have time to analyze it.

Maverick heard the approaching roar of classic cars.

Now it's showtime!

•   •   •

The employees at the executive terminal raced to the flightline-side window to watch two rare Mercedes 540K Special Roadsters drive by the office. They had seen them before, months earlier. All they knew was they were special cars.

The clerks who monitored the comings and goings of corporate and business aircraft, aircrew and passengers, opined it looked like the billionaire Rho Schwartz Scorpii would finally take out his new jet. The pilot had filed a flight plan, and he had been to the toilet.

Said one employee, "Probably a good idea to get out of town before we are crushed with aircraft."

Said the other. "I can't believe a billionaire would allow himself to be driven around with the top down!"

Said the man, "Maybe he wanted the top down."

Said the woman, "That's crazy; it's freezing out there!"

"I'll bet he's bundled up in blankets like a newborn."

"Probably." *It must be nice having all that money to keep you warm.*

.   .   .

Once airborne, at a table in the G-900 cabin, Rudolf Blohm and Gothear Horst had two of the Minox subminiature cameras from *Maverick's* briefcase steadily taking photographs. The measuring chains on the cameras proved invaluable photographing Scorpii's papers, providing the required distance from camera to document to capture perfect photographs. The close-focusing lens and small size made the camera perfect for easy copying of letter-sized documents.

The question Horst and Blohm had was would they run out of film before they ran out of pages to copy?

Between photographs, Horst and Blohm discussed what they knew of the mini spy camera. They hadn't seen them in years but knew exactly how to operate them. They knew the original Minox was used by both Axis and Allied intelligence agents during World War II, and the model Hunter provided was exceedingly new. Horst recalled being issued one while in the SEALs; Blohm stated he just knew one should have been in every clandestine officer's go bag. That had been a long time ago.

Horst recognized halfway through the remaining film cassettes they had copied half of Scorpii's books.

It was another way of saying they wouldn't get any sleep until after they had landed.

CHAPTER 55

December 7, 2019

Two Egyptian Air Force C-130s landed at the Tripoli International Airport. A construction battalion of troops offloaded from the aircraft; the Libyan government provided buses to transport the Egyptian troops from the airport to a small Protestant cemetery overlooking the harbor in Tripoli. Another flatbed truck was loaded with pine coffins and several crates of testing equipment.

At the cemetery an Egyptian naval officer, a graduate of the U.S. Naval War College, found the marker:

> HERE LIES AN AMERICAN SAILOR
> WHO GAVE HIS LIFE IN THE
> EXPLOSION OF
> THE UNITED STATES SHIP INTREPID
> IN TRIPOLI HARBOR
> SEPTEMBER 4, 1804

A crew of three men used ground penetrating radar equipment to determine the location of the suspected graves. After several passes of the device, they concluded there were thirteen skulls and thirteen sets of remains.

All present and accounted for.

Four hours later, one Egyptian Air Force C-130 returned to an air force base outside of Cairo with the Egyptian personnel. The other aircraft took off for Ramstein Air Force Base in Germany.

•   •   •

On the parking ramp, a formal ceremony was conducted to transfer the remains of the thirteen sailors of the *USS Intrepid*. The highest-ranking U.S. military man in Europe, the North Atlantic Treaty Organization Supreme Allied Commander Europe, General Walter Todd III, solemnly accepted the remains for the United States on behalf of the Egyptian Air Force and the people of Libya.

The air base was put on QUIET HOURS while the ceremonies were conducted. As each coffin was removed from the cargo bay of the Egyptian Air Force C-130, General Todd III, SACEUR led the assembly of uniformed men and women in salute. One by one the wooden coffins were quietly and ceremoniously transferred from the interior of the C-130 to the interior of a U.S. Air Force C-17. Inside the huge cargo jet the wooden coffins were placed in large metal coffins secured to the deck, and each was covered with a U.S. Flag. After all the sailors' remains had been secured and draped with the National Ensign, the C-17's engines were started. The aircraft slowly taxied in front of General Todd III and the assembled masses as if it were a funeral procession. When SACEUR saluted, everyone in uniform saluted the jet as it trundled to the end of the runway and departed for Dover Air Force Base.

General Todd III took several steps toward the runway to get a better view of the departing aircraft. He saluted one final time and said to himself, "Is this why I had to go to Egypt? I don't know how the hell you orchestrated this, but this has your fingerprints all over it. Good job, *Maverick*."

CHAPTER 56

December 8, 2019

The Ambassadors of the forty-four European embassies were summoned to the Department of Justice for an emergency meeting. Never before had any Attorney General assembled so many ambassadors for a meeting. Senior DOJ personnel were suspiciously left out of the loop. Secrecy was paramount; rumors swirled around DOJ Headquarters like bats exiting a cave.

It was a spectacle. Reporters on scene counted the number of Ambassador's vehicles with their special Diplomat license plates issued by the Office of Foreign Missions. They lined up around the block to deposit their nation's leading diplomats at 950 Pennsylvania Avenue, NW. DOJ security personnel lined the streets directing the charge of limousines and then escorting the scores of Ambassadors to the auditorium. Completely breaking protocol, auditorium seating was not designated.

When all of Europe's Ambassadors to the United States were seated Attorney General Winchester entered from a side door; he didn't take the stage. He walked to the middle of the gathering of diplomats and spoke without a microphone.

"I thank you for coming to what is likely a historic event. As you know over 200,000 children go missing in Europe each year. We know your justice departments and law enforcement agencies have come to accept most of those missing children find homes in the sex clubs in your largest cities. These children are abused in criminal ways. Police departments in these areas and politicians are incentivized, either directly or through front groups such as the *Ostgut Foundation*, to avoid patrolling or responding to emergency calls at these clubs. You're here because every major city in every nation in Europe has these sex clubs, and imbedded within those clubs are special brothels staffed primarily with Europe's missing children."

"The President of the United States demands these activities cease. He demands the perpetrators who have preyed on these children for decades be brought to justice. We have the documents from Rho Schwartz Scorpii's *Ostgut Foundation* that detail how extensive these operations are, how children are recruited, how they're exploited, and how they use propaganda against these children's parents to get them to agree to these nefarious activities."

"We know the leaders at the highest levels of government and in your law enforcement agencies are fully aware of these activities, but they're compelled to look away and do nothing. Why? Because many times they're clients of the clubs. The U.S. Department of Justice has proof, not just evidence but proof, that political funds from the *Ostgut Foundation* have corrupted the executive leadership of your governments and your law enforcement and intelligence agencies."

"President Hernandez demands these activities in your nations cease and the infrastructure is destroyed so they can never again be havens for pedophiles. You're here to be officially notified of America's intentions. The United States of America will not be a witting party to these crimes against children. Europe — each of your countries — has forty-eight hours to rectify this travesty."

The diplomats murmured among themselves.

Winchester continued, "You can choose to maintain the status quo and become satellites of the old Soviet Union. As you well know, if America pulls out of your countries the Russians will fill the vacuum with tanks and troops. Also, as you all are well aware, there are U.S. troops and businesses in each of your countries. The President has tasked our ambassadors to your countries to monitor the situation. If your leaders choose not to correct these deficiencies, individually or collectively, you'll be expelled with all due haste. We know some of you and your family members may not return to your countries even under urgent humanitarian circumstances. This isn't our problem, and we will not allow it to become our problem. These actions are not retaliatory. You have a choice. Unless you take the actions necessary to stop exploiting children, your visas and the visas of your staff and families will expire in forty-eight hours."

"In summation, if your country chooses to be or is a haven for pedophiles and lackies for Rho Schwartz Scorpii and the *Ostgut Foundation*, you'll be removed from U.S. soil. President Hernandez will remove all U.S. presence from your country and void all bi-lateral agreements between our nations. This means all U.S. presence: military, business, tourists and diplomats. I repeat for emphasis, we will cancel any valid visas your citizens have. There will be no exceptions. If you do not act, we will no longer be associated with or be a party to socialist, sybaritic, and criminal governments that prey on children. You can reject and destroy government-sanctioned pedophilia, or you can learn to speak Russian."

"Thank you for your time and consideration. America looks forward to your government's official response." Attorney General Winchester turned and walked away without taking questions as the diplomats raced for the auditorium exits.

• • •

Attorney General Burnt Winchester stood arms akimbo at his office window, still breathing hard, and now sweating. The Deputy Attorney General raced into his office, joined the AG at the window and asked, "Burnt, we have documents from Scorpii's *Ostgut Foundation?*"

The AG turned, smiled, and slowly shook his head. He said, "I said three times we have documents from the *Ostgut Foundation*. Goebbels said if you repeat a lie three times, people will believe it to be true. So, we'll see."

The Deputy AG whispered, "*Holy shit, Batman!*"

CHAPTER 57

December 11, 2019

President Hernandez, the Joint Chiefs of Staff, and the complete regiment of the U.S. Naval Academy quietly positioned themselves to welcome home the men of the *USS Intrepid.*

Rear Admiral McGee interrupted his campaign to fly in for the occasion, and he brought Demetrius Eastwood to cover the event. The White House Chief of Staff saw McGee in the crowd, which was one of the easiest things on the planet to do. He was so big, he had been accused of having his own gravity. McGee was waved over to be part of the official party.

Eastwood took photographs and notes.

A Secret Service man unsnapped one end of a Royal blue velvet crowd control rope and allowed McGee inside. President Hernandez welcomed the former CIA Director. He extended his left arm slightly and shook the Rolex; it slid down his wrist, then he offered his right hand. Eastwood captured the moment of the two Republicans shaking hands with a Nikon electronic camera.

The ceremony for removing the thirteen coffins from the C-17 to thirteen identical Cadillac hearses was solemn and conducted in silence. President Hernandez didn't speak until the last of the vehicles departed and the flag detail marched off.

McGee wondered how they had gotten the remains of the thirteen sailors out of Libya. He was out of the loop, focused on winning an election. It wasn't the time or the place to ask for details, but when President Hernandez shook the Rolex gently and repositioned his watch on his wrist, he couldn't help but wonder if it was a signal. McGee acknowledged he might never know. He shook hands and softly said, "Thank you for inviting me, Mr. President."

President Hernandez replied, "My pleasure."

My pleasure. Maverick's favorite one-liner. Then McGee knew. *Maverick put a bug in the President's ear! Somehow, someway. Of course.*

Before returning to the campaign jet, Eastwood filed his report directly from his computer.

To: Chief Editor, *Washington Times*

Dover Air Force Base, Delaware

Title: *USS Intrepid Heroes Home after 207 Years*

The remains of the thirteen U.S. Navy officers and crew of the *USS Intrepid* who were killed in action while fighting Barbary pirates off the coast of Libya have finally returned home. Joining President Hernandez at Dover Air Force Base was former CIA Director, Rear Admiral Bill McGee.

Among those aboard the *USS Intrepid* were Capt. Richard Somers, the commander of the ship, and his second in command, Lt. Henry Wadsworth. The poet Henry Wadsworth Longfellow, the author of "Paul Revere's Ride," was the lieutenant's nephew.

Shortly after taking office President Thomas Jefferson ordered the Navy to destroy a pirate fleet operating off the coast of North Africa. Before sailors could set scuttling charges on the pirate fleet, the *USS Intrepid* exploded.

After the solemn ceremony, Rear Admiral McGee voiced his disappointment with Congress and the Navy, "They should have been concerned about the status of some of America's earliest heroes and worked to return the remains of the men of the *USS Intrepid*. But under President Mazibuike, the Pentagon was ordered not to get involved, infuriating many Americans and military personnel. President Hernandez is to be commended, for he succeeded where the Democrat Party failed."

A U.S. Navy Captain assigned to the Defense POW/MIA Accounting Agency (DPAA) announced the names of the casualties of the *USS Intrepid* upon their arrival on U.S. soil. Military officials said the remains will be identified using the latest DNA and anthropological analysis available. Being welcomed home after over 200 years of being hastily buried on foreign soil, their remains will be sent to the DPAA laboratory at Offutt Air Force Base in Nebraska for closer examination and identification.

The descendants of the *USS Intrepid* sailors and Presidential Candidate Rear Admiral Bill McGee have long sought to repatriate the men's remains. Years after the ouster of the Gaddafi government, the Senate was on the brink of passing legislation that would have required the Pentagon, under a provision in the Defense Authorization bill, to seek the return of the remains. But according to backers of the measure, President Maxim Mazibuike blocked it. There have been several groups who pressed to have the remains brought back, but President Mazibuike continually fought them.

Presidential Candidate Bill McGee explained, "For over two centuries, these American heroes have laid buried in a hostile land. The sailors of the *USS Intrepid* deserved better. The Tripoli cemetery is hardly Normandy. The sailors were not honored in Libya, and it was time for America's first naval casualties of war to come home. President Hernandez made it all possible."

Previously, the Navy had raised doubts about whether the remains could be found and identified after two centuries. However, shortly after the Presidents of the United States and Egypt met in Egypt over Egypt's possible inclusion in the North Atlantic Treaty Organization (NATO), the men of the *USS Intrepid* were returned to the U.S. government.

In a stunning display of international cooperation, the Egyptian president appeared to have accomplished in days what the American Congress couldn't do in years. Egyptian military forces coordinated with the Libyan authorities, respectfully disinterred the remains, and repatriated the sailors to Germany.

After the *USS Intrepid* sailors returned to American soil, Presidential Candidate Bill McGee said, "America is so grateful to the President of Egypt for facilitating the return of our fallen heroes."

President Hernandez announced construction is underway at Arlington National Cemetery for a special final resting place for the men of the *USS Intrepid*.

End of Article.

CHAPTER 58

December 16, 2019

A crowd of about two hundred senior executives, their family members, and many Ambassadors from the European nations sat in overstuffed folding chairs in the Rose Garden of the White House. Marine Security Guards stood ramrod tall on either side of the West Wing doors waiting for the signal to open the doors and salute the President of the United States.

President Hernandez's entrance was stiff and formal. He mounted the dais in the Rose Garden and took the lectern. The assembly of politicians applauded. Marines saluted smartly.

President Hernandez said, "Thank you very much. Thank you. Members of Congress, members of the Cabinet, honored guests, and fellow Americans. It's my privilege to address you tonight from the Rose Garden of the White House. We are gathered together this evening for a truly momentous occasion."

"We are thrilled to be joined this evening by former Directors of the Central Intelligence Agency Greg Lynche and William McGee. Director Lynche, Director McGee, America owes you a profound debt of gratitude for a lifetime of noble service to our nation. Thank you for coming. Thank you."

Polite applause rippled across the gathering.

"Very special and treasured guests tonight are Director Lynche's amazing wife, Connie, and Director McGee's equally amazing wife, Angela. Thank you, ladies."

"One of the most important appointments a president can make is the appointment of the Director of the Central Intelligence Agency. Leading the nation's intelligence agencies is a unique and critical responsibility, requiring special trust and confidence to protect the

United States of America. This nation has been blessed with the superior leadership of CIA Directors Greg Lynche and Bill McGee, and the Acting Director Nazy Cunningham. I'm confident our new CIA Director will be every bit as effective as the epitome of the intelligence community. Ladies and gentlemen, I'm so pleased to nominate another exceptional American, the former Supreme Allied Commander European Forces, General Walter Todd III as the next Director of the Central Intelligence Agency."

The assembly stood, applauded, and cheered. After President Hernandez recited the general's curriculum vitae, General Todd III took the lectern, gave President Hernandez thanks for his trust and confidence in him, and quickly gave a shout out to someone not specifically identified, just "a special thanks to all the *Mavericks* who helped me in my career."

President Hernandez returned to the lectern to answer a few questions. Foremost on everyone's mind were the spontaneous raids and the destruction of sex shops that had been occurring in the major cities of European nations. Demetrius Eastwood, a White House favorite, was called on. He stood and asked the question. The President's response was evasive.

"Dory, I would like to thank the leaders of the European nations for their support in bringing child sex traffickers and child abusers to justice. These criminals have abused children in the most horrific ways, and it took a coordinated, comprehensive law enforcement effort to disrupt and destroy the cartels that organized these heinous activities. One of the consequences of what is happening all across Europe is that well over a hundred thousand boys and girls who had been missing, in some cases for years, have been found and are being reunited with their families. Attorney General Winchester and the Department of Justice are looking to see if similar organizations could be operating in the United States."

Eastwood asked, "Mr. President, one more, if I may?"

"Last one — go!"

"There are rumors the Secretary General of the North Atlantic Treaty Organization committed suicide and Rho Schwartz Scorpii was brought into the United States for cancer treatment. Sir, can you confirm or provide any details into these? Thank you."

President Hernandez pointed an emphatic finger at the reporter. "That's two, Colonel Eastwood. Mr. Scorpii was desperately ill, at the point of death. The Anderson Cancer Center was the only medical facility that could possibly save his life. When all the circumstances were described to me, I agreed to let him in for humanitarian reasons. Mr. Scorpii was, in fact, transported from Germany to Houston on a mercy flight where he expired shortly after arrival."

The President continued, "It's well known that Rho Schwartz Scorpii leveraged his vast wealth to sponsor terrorism through Europe, North and South America, Africa, and the Middle East. He funded biological research in China and Iran. We believe he funded the products of espionage, secrets from any intelligence agency he could compromise. He sold those secrets to communist countries. It was a humanitarian flight to save his life, but his condition was such that there was no hope of recovery."

"As far as the circumstances of the death of NATO's Secretary General, investigators are doing their due diligence."

"Mr. President, what will happen to Scorpii's *Ostgut Foundation?*"

President Hernandez raised three fingers and said, "I think what you'll see in Europe and elsewhere is the *Ostgut Foundation* will be broken up and investigated. Its accounts frozen and assets confiscated. Countries and leaders that took his philanthropy will have to account for their actions. It's our sincere hope that major European cities will no longer be a haven for pedophiles and child sex traffickers. Many European governments have a long record of zealously trying not to unravel these cases. We hope terrorist organizations will see their funding cut off. I also believe European authorities will see Mr. Scorpii's influence and money will no longer fund Democrat politicians, prosecutors, teachers' unions, and the like. There is no doubt his foundation funded the smoke of the devil. Disease finally stopped him. Now we have to let the investigators of the European nations to do their due diligence."

After Eastwood's last question, the White House Press Corps was escorted out of the Rose Garden.

• • •

That night like every night, a crowd gathered along the Ellipse to admire the White House. Maalik El Masri walked with a group who slowly strolled on the sidewalk around the perimeter of the White House fence. He used binoculars to get a better look at the goings on in the area where there was the most activity. He didn't see the woman he was searching for; she was reportedly in the hospital, registered under another name. *That's what we would have done.* As the group of tourists moved, El Masri moved with them; when they stopped and stared at the brightly illuminated edifice, the personal residence of the President of the United States, El Masri also stopped and stared.

He was still in a state of shock. He gripped the uprights of the fence and reflected on a string of failures. *That American's papers were impeccable, but his face couldn't be verified with the facial recognition technologies. I should have gone back to the hotel to investigate him. But I didn't go back; I was so confident Mein Kanzler was safe with Blohm and Horst. He was so ill, and they had been with us for so long. It's just inconceivable they took him. But I let my guard down. I should have known. Die hündin was indeed very dangerous; Mein Kanzler was justified in fearing her. I want to punish the Cunningham woman for stealing Mein Kanzler, to kill her like they killed the mujahedeen in Iran.*

El Masri had raced from the intelligence agency back to the grandhotel to find Scorpii gone. Blohm and Horst were missing; the cars were missing. The vault closed and locked. And Dante Locke was nowhere to be found. By the time El Masri arrived at the airport, he was crushed to find he was too late. Blohm and Horst had flown the Chancellor out of the country.

He pulled the drone from his pocket and studied it. He looked toward the Rose Garden and envisioned the terror and mayhem that should have been there. *They killed the mujahedeen during a celebration; they should experience the same fright and catastrophe during a celebration.*

It was loaded with the face of Nazy Cunningham. She was not there. It was useless. He wanted to toss the device into a wastebasket.

When the group he was with moved, El Masri went along. He became more agitated. *I will punish them for stealing him, for killing him. Blohm probably closed the vault so I wouldn't know immediately they took his papers. But I know. It took a few days to empty the vault, but now I am a wealthy man. I must consider my future, and there is no future in chasing die hündin when she may die of her injuries. My mission isn't yet over. I must be careful.*

As the group of tourists approached the entrance of the White House many of them dispersed leaving him to mingle with another innocuous group. When he found where the limousines of the cabinet members were parked, he staked out a spot, as did several others. The Secret Service astride silver bikes or balanced on black Segways kept their eyes on him.

El Masri pocketed the binoculars and counted twenty armed men in black uniforms on the rooftops of the Eisenhower Executive Office Building and the Treasury Department. Three times that many were on the grounds of the White House.

Then he recognized the cleverly hidden anti-aircraft and anti-drone equipment mounted atop the fire trucks had been positioned on either side of the White House.

Impenetrable! El Masri would have been surprised if the building wasn't so well protected.

I must find another way, or I must go home.

•　　•　　•

The official announcement was made and the ceremony was complete. Former Directors Lynche and McGee were first to offer their congratulations as hundreds of people lined up to shake General Todd III's hand.

Duncan Hunter, disguised as Dante Locke stepped in front of Nazy, disguised as an Egyptian actress and wearing a silver fox coat to keep her warm. She tugged a synthetic earlobe as Hunter raked a finger across his rubber brow. They grinned at each other. Then Bill

McGee came trundling up and nudged Hunter toward some of the Rose Garden's shrubbery. Nazy followed. They watched the procession of very important people do the grip and grin from their secluded spot. Hunter energized the *Growler* in his pocket.

McGee asked, "Why is it you always have to be right?"

Hunter countered, "How was I ever going to have time with my bride if you and the President had her chained to that desk on the 7th floor? She never wanted that job, but just like the rest of us, she couldn't tell you no."

McGee clenched his jaws and stared at *Maverick* for a few tense seconds and then looked at Nazy's masked face. She mashed red lips together and nodded her head. Then both men crossed their arms and exhaled. After a few seconds, impassioned frowns were replaced with nods and smiles.

McGee said, "So you're saying you can't tell ne no."

Dante Locke growled with a smile, "You know what I mean."

"Yeah, I know, but I thought it would be good for Nazy to do it for a while. She would have found out she was already doing what she had always wanted to do. Intelligence analysis. She can do the Director's job, but it would never be fun for her. It takes a special person."

Nazy said, "Like you."

McGee was slightly embarrassed and said, "Yeah, like me, but like Todd too. You did well, *again, Maverick*. He'll be great. He's an *Irregular* too."

Hunter said, "I suppose the AG is too."

Nazy and McGee looked through the crowd to find the Attorney General. Nazy asked, "Winchester?"

Hunter was quick to respond, "Yeah. He was at the *Pumpkin Papers*. He's quiet but effective."

McGee said, "Oh, yeah. That's right. There is no doubt. Quiet and effective. And that man *is* a patriot. I heard he threatened the European Ambassadors with fire and brimstone if they didn't get off the pot and kill the kiddie sex clubs and child sex trafficking businesses."

Hunter faked incredulity. "Seriously?"

McGee grinned. "Serious as a heart attack. If you ever stayed in town, you'd know these things."

Hunter shot McGee one of his classical sarcastic looks and asked Nazy, "Did the AG get *his pumpkin?*"

Nazy nodded while McGee frowned, "What are you talking about?"

"One of your boys not only snagged Scorpii's and the *Ostgut Foundation's* papers, he took the sex tapes of the rich and famous in Europe before leaving Scorpii's pad. Pedophiles on parade."

McGee blew hot air, tugged at his chin, and then laughed. "I think I've created a monster. That's incredible. I think the leverage arrow is on our side, I suppose if we choose to use them for good." *There will be billionaires jumping out of buildings...."*

Hunter quipped, "Shouldn't you get back on the campaign trail?" The man behind the mask handed McGee his *Growler* and said, "I didn't use it."

"I'd rather be here. I wondered what the hell happened. You took Scorpii to Houston?"

Nazy's hands disappeared into her fox coat. She was curious, too.

"*Bullfrog. Your* guys insisted. It was their plan to turn a kidnapping into a mercy flight, and it worked to perfection."

Nazy asked, "Perfection?"

"Timing was everything. I gave them Bill's arrowhead coin; they confirmed he was dying and got him out of the hotel. I got us out of Dodge, and they photographed Scorpii's papers on the way to Houston. The AG now has more sex tapes than a *Blockbuster*, Nazy's got Scorpii's pumpkin, I got a new jet out of the deal, but I need to put some paint on it for you. What do you want? *Rainbows?*"

"You do that and I'll have to hurt you."

Nazy and McGee laughed out loud. Hunter yawned from a lack of sleep and said, "It's getting new paint, blue and gold. Just for you. I also found some stolen cars in his hangar when I took the jet. One of your guys picked up a bag with titles. There may be a hundred more."

McGee was suddenly interested and asked, "Recoveries?"

Hunter said, "They ran the serial numbers of the three I found to confirm. Our guys are over there investigating and to take inventory.

But more than that, one of the three wasn't stolen but it was odd being there. It was an AMG EV. Maybe a concept car. I can't find much on it. And it didn't have any records. Anyway, our guys have the three under surveillance, I gave them the keys to the hangar, so they installed covert GPS trackers. It may be a bust. We don't know if any of them in that hangar will still be there after all of this. I just don't want the press to know what we are doing. My point, the electric vehicle should not be there. Too new."

Nazy asked, "You think it's for someone special?"

"It's not a car Scorpii would be interested in. Maybe the number two guy? I don't know. We'll see if we can get that lucky. They are finding that so many of them are stolen that Bong said they ran out of the GPS trackers. We don't think they'll go anywhere but we don't want to lose them on our watch."

McGee remembered; *Bong runs Quiet Recoveries International.* He said, "That's smart." Nazy nodded.

"As long as we can keep our *Recoveries* activities out of the press." Hunter looked around to double check they weren't being surveilled. "Scorpii also had a few 540K Special Roadsters he used as hotel limos. I left them in the hangar and I want to bring those cars here. But the clock is ticking." McGee and Hunter, nodded, looked at each other, and then turned their eyes to President Hernandez.

Nazy was suddenly aghast. "I don't know if that is such a good idea. He has done so much for us — the men from the *USS Intrepid* are now home, he killed the child sex trade in Europe and thousands of children who had been missing for years are being reunited with their families, he agreed to let Scorpii into the country, and we have Scorpii's *pumpkins.*"

McGee said, "And he rescinded that executive order and released weapons for the ladies. President Hernandez has been incredible. Democrats are in a frenzy."

McGee and Nazy half-frowned at Hunter. Hunter said, "A Democrat president would have shot us. Yeah, not bad for a lame duck. I can't ask him for those. I'll find a way even if I have to steal them."

McGee said, "You're as incorrigible as a liberal is crooked."

Nazy grinned and said, "I'm going to get a drink. Do you need your drinks refreshened?" Hunter and McGee shook their heads and Hunter said, "No, thank you, darling. But, let me get you something."

"That's okay. Really. Everyone's always getting me something. I sort of like being incognito. I'll be okay. You two always have something to talk about. I know the President is curious about *pumpkins*." The men acquiesced and watched her walk toward the bar.

Hunter continued from where he left off. "They should be called American Communists."

"That is much better. Anyway, thanks for your help with bringing the boys from the *USS Intrepid* home. I *know* you talked to POTUS. I have to say, *Maverick*, I never saw that one coming. I was totally shocked."

Hunter said, "My pleasure."

McGee said, "I hope the Army makes them a nice place in Arlington." Hunter agreed.

Hunter and McGee turned to see if the crowd in the Rose Garden was breaking up. Suddenly a half a dozen men converged on the bar and surrounded Nazy. They both took notice.

McGee took a sip and said, "The last time there were that many strange men surrounding Nazy, I killed them all." He turned to Duncan and found a strange lack of concern on his face.

Hunter shook his head once and said impishly, "I can't take her anywhere."

That's when McGee shot Pepsi through his nose. Hunter laughed so hard he almost cried and ruined his mask. Once they recovered their composure *Maverick* commented, "That demonstrates how two groups of men can deal with her. American men want to please her, be around her, admire her while the men of the Muslim Brotherhood just wanted to inflict as much pain as possible on her. That is a culture doomed to fail, and no one will cry if it's eradicated from the face of the earth."

McGee said, "We tried. I tried to get Congress to declare the Muslim Brotherhood a terrorist organization."

Maverick said, "It's the Nuremberg Law. The left can do it because no one stops them and we have politicians who don't have the political will to stop them. You're going to have to change all that. If the U.S. could outlaw the Muslim Brotherhood as a terrorist organization with the stroke of a pen, then anyone affiliated with them could be considered terrorists and deportable…"

McGee said, "The Democrats would rather die than let that happen."

"I bet you were even called a racist."

McGee cleaned his nose with a handkerchief. Suddenly dry and sober, he agreed. "I was and you're too friggin' smart. Which reminds me, I read the mosques in Abilene and Dallas burned to the ground last night."

Hunter deadpanned, "I had some *Firestarters* before they expired. Blohm photographed the pages where Scorpii detailed the expenses of acquiring and moving a shooter and a *Stinger* from a Dallas mosque to one in Abilene just to get your jet. I thought it was the least I could do. Payback's a bitch because the FBI won't investigate."

From their vantage point, Hunter and McGee had watched caterers replace reporters as they brought out tables, finger food, and chips and salsa. McGee looked wistfully at the men in suits and women in dresses and the caterers in white. He said, "Those are great inventions."

"*Firestarters? Oh, yeah!*" Hunter nodded and then asked, "What about Project *Arrowhead*? That's one for the record books."

"I thought I was leaving. Project *Arrowhead*. Where do we start?" McGee paused and took several breaths, then said "How about this? Al-Qaeda penetrated airport security with Islamists and that led to September 11. They were able to do that for several factors, but the one barrier that mattered was having to get through…."

Hunter was automatic: "…the FAA's background check."

"You call it what you want. It's really the torpedo nets of security programs designed to stop criminals from gaining access to the most sensitive parts of airport security to get weapons or bombs on planes. The feds weren't interested in airline security; so from the beginning it was lowest bidder, technically acceptable airport security. Of course, it was a mess, and all the papers reported just how bad it was for years. That invited terrorists of every stripe to take notice."

Hunter added, "The FAA said it was the airlines' problem. You know my first job out of the Marine Corps was airport security in Cleveland. It took fifteen years until they could infiltrate sufficient numbers of radical Islamists as airport security personnel to move weapons through the x-ray machine and into the hands of hijackers or plant bombs on jets. And with those, they could attack the World Trade center, the Pentagon, and the CIA if the passengers hadn't taken that plane down in Pennsylvania."

McGee exhaled and nodded. *It could have all been stopped. But it wasn't.* "With *Arrowhead*, we tried something similar. It was an infiltration program designed to get our security people inside the personal security organization of the *Insiders*."

"Horst and Blohm?"

"Horst and Blohm. You know the DSM?"

Hunter said, "I do." *Man, do I!*

"There are people on the spectrum and people off the spectrum. You and I are off the spectrum. We're the normal ones."

"If they only knew."

McGee consulted his watch. He had a few more minutes before he had to leave. "Horst and Blohm were *barely* on the spectrum; they straddled it. Sometimes straight, sometimes bisexual, slightly homosexual on the spectrum where Liberace and Elton John are at the far end, the openly flamboyant end of the sexual disorder spectrum. Back then the polygraph equipment wasn't what it's today. They were in that weird middle ground where being on the spectrum meets the demarcation line of not being on the spectrum. Their ability to function in that gap allowed them to pass Scorpii's polygraph about their sexuality. We trained them to defeat their polygraph. They were looking for a Liberace-like character but they got, um, someone like you."

Hunter shrugged. "Thanks!" As he listened to McGee, he observed Nazy trying to extricate herself from her admirers. *Maybe those PETA sycophants had never seen a real silver fox coat before?*

McGee continued, "First the CIA wanted to penetrate the *Insiders*. Then the CIA wanted to penetrate Scorpii's *Ostgut Foundation*, but it was known they only recruited gays and lesbians, while they quietly hired some of the sexual disorders, the personality disorders. The CIA didn't have any people like that, because the routine CIA polygraphers found them to be untrustworthy. Any candidates the CIA had couldn't pass the Agency polygraph so they were shitcanned. They needed someone else."

Hunter added, "So they trolled the beaches at Dam Neck, caught you, and you said you might know someone."

"Something like that."

Hunter stopped admiring his wife, turned to McGee, and said, "So, Horst and Blohm were the *Arrowheads*; they had the essential qualifications to penetrate the *Insiders* and you trained them to defeat a poly. I know there's more to that story."

McGee said, "Some of these programs aren't the decision of the director alone. The CIA Director at the time actually said no. The polygrapher stood by his work and said they were honest and therefore trustworthy. As the potential PM, I was the deciding vote. The only black dude in the SEALs at the time. It was a huge deal. Who would stake their reputation on a black dude?"

"*Bullfrog*, you're not a normal black dude."

"*Maverick*, you're not a normal white dude."

Hunter and McGee laughed at themselves. *That's probably true but you aren't supposed to say it.*

McGee continued, "Anyway, the director could have just shut it down. I thought it could work if they were given enough time, but I knew it might not because of the CIA's culture. I told the director we were dealing with SEALs, and they're different creatures than intelligence officers. That it might take twenty years to get in and while the SEALs could do it without question, his folks weren't that dedicated."

"So, on your recommendation, he approved it. Of course."

"You have anything else going?"

"I have a team watching a car in Scorpii's hangar in Germany. They were able to place a tracking device on it."

McGee said, "You think it's his."

"I do. I'd take it but you know I'm not a fan of electric cars."

McGee said, "So, all you have to do is to go back to Germany."

"Europe. And not get caught."

McGee said, "Try not to. I need you."

"I'll need a new disguise." Hunter and McGee smiled and nodded.

"Another chapter of the Great Game. McGee grunted and nodded. He knew it was time to go. He stuck out his hand. "Again, congratulations, *Maverick*. Good job. I'm looking forward to those papers being released."

Maverick gripped McGee's hand for all he was worth. "They will be soon. I can't wait to get out of here. Now if Nazy will just hurry back so we can go." McGee nodded.

• • •

Hunter and McGee watched President Hernandez drag Nazy away from the horde of men, and the two of them talked for a moment.

President Hernandez said, "Nice disguise. I assume everyone got *their pumpkin*." He smiled and enjoyed being able to use some of the multifaceted lingo of the CIA.

Nazy pulled a *Growler* from her coat pocket, turned it on, and didn't miss a beat. She said, "Mr. President, they did. We're analyzing ours now. Probably fifty years' worth of insight. There's a lot of information to process. I'll give you a brief once they have been fully transcribed, translated, and analyzed. We will provide an executive summary after your PDB."

President Hernandez said, "Thank you. I still cannot get over that disguise." He thought, *Wow! What a voice!*

Nazy stood still, waiting for her dismissal but the President asked, "What have you found, if anything?"

"Mr. President, a preliminary assessment is all we have. Every left-wing program in America was run through the *Ostgut Foundation*, which was actually a functioning organization hidden inside the German foreign intelligence service."

President Hernandez cocked his head.

Nazy realized she wasn't going anywhere. She inhaled and said, "Our assessment of the European Federation's Bensberg Conference and their agenda was on target. Scorpii ordered the attack on Bill and me and used the Muslim Brotherhood to carry out his orders. His NGOs smuggled RPGs and anti-aircraft weapons into mosques. Documented."

"We are not surprised."

"No, Mr. President. Scorpii mentioned our CDC Director has been funding a Chinese bioweapons lab."

"You mean creating bioweapons?"

Nazy nodded. "The CDC Director is on record saying China must lead the new world order, creating it, owning it, and supplanting the United States as the world's economic superpower. We think it's bluster but our eye is on their bioweapons program."

Nazy continued, "Mr. President, the CDC Director also just told his people there is a strong likelihood a coronavirus pandemic will strike the United States and crush Bill's presidency if he's elected. The CDC Director guarantees it. I'm sure those people still have President Mazibuike's picture on their walls."

President Hernandez intoned, "They're not happy with me."

"The only way anything like that could happen is if the Chinese is in the middle of it."

President Hernandez shook his head and said, "I will fire his ass by morning. What else?"

"Mr. President, if I may. Photographic copies of Scorpii's papers will be released to the public. *Whistleblowers*. We do not want our fingerprints on them for obvious reasons. But if they're suddenly released into the public domain...."

President Hernandez said, "Maybe because we want to telegraph there was a whistleblower in the House of Scorpii...."

Nazy nodded. "Exactly, Mr. President. We don't want anyone to know we have *the pumpkin*. It's better if someone else takes the hit, if I may. I looked at Scorpii's more recent journals and the *Insider's* agenda. Their agenda is to instill fear across Europe, force radical climate change legislation onto each country, and drain the national treasuries of each country. Enrich the elites to the detriment of all others. Which is counter to U.S. goals."

President Hernandez shook his head in disgust. "Scorpii was one of the most despicable persons to have ever drawn a breath. We have to stop them. The *Insiders*."

Nazy said, "That may be true, Mr. President, but Scorpii also left us...ahem, er, some would call it *a gift*. If we choose to use it. I can put them away or I can send it to *Whistleblowers*."

"A gift?" *Whistleblowers?*

Nazy fondled the *Growler* in her pocket. She pinched her lips and nodded. "Mr. President, the AG's *pumpkin* contains what is reported to be the top three hundred wealthiest men in the world.... Democrat Party leaders.... World leaders...." She let the implication float in the cold air.

President Hernandez inhaled, mashed his eyes closed and thought, *Videos... blackmail videos.*

"...we believe.. engaging in...."

President Hernandez knew exactly what Nazy meant. He raised his hand. She didn't have to say any more. *You have Scorpii's blackmail videos of those people having sex with children. Scorpii's ultimate blackmail.* President Hernandez shook his head in dark wonder. He closed his eyes again for another long second.

Nazy continued, "Scorpii covertly recorded them over decades. He definitely blackmailed those in the intelligence field and he blackmailed the *Insiders* to do his bidding. Like forcing them to fund climate change initiatives disguised as foreign aid which were laundered back to Scorpii's foundation."

President Hernandez exhaled and blew all the air out of his lungs. He thought, *Now I understand, politics is combat by other means....*

Nazy continued, "Mr. President, I suppose the AG can use them. Or I can send them to *Whistleblowers*. The effect might be the same but the U.S. would lose incredible leverage over the *Insiders*."

Then the President smiled bigly, "You're right, and *you are* the best analyst on the planet." He laughed and nodded. "Nazy, we don't have to decide tonight. Europe is already in correction territory. I will think it over. If you can find them a home in the *Library of Diaries*, let's park them there for the time being."

"That will be my pleasure, Mr. President."

"Thank you, Nazy for a most *interesting* evening. I think I saw a Soviet submarine captain around here somewhere. Go find him and tell him Merry Christmas and thank you for all of us. I'll talk to him later." They shook hands as professionals do.

President Hernandez headed in the directions of his wife, and they joined General Todd III and his bride.

Nazy went in search of her man in disguise. She found him where she left him, hanging out with McGee; they looked ready to leave. She looked forlorn when she realized they all had empty glasses. They laughed and she said, "The President wished us a Merry Christmas and thank you."

They took the comment to mean their presence was no longer required. They could go.

Nazy hugged McGee goodbye. As McGee walked off in search of his wife Nazy whispered, "I'm off for a month. No PDBs for me. The Deputy is in charge, I have use or loose vacation on the books, and General Todd should be confirmed by the time I come back to wherever you plan to take us. The President will decide how to proceed with the AG's *pumpkin*. Do you have any ideas where we could go?"

Duncan's jaw nearly dropped to the dead grass lawn. He was tired of being masked, so he nodded and said, "I think we need to celebrate and waste some water somewhere."

Nazy winked and said, "Good! I want to get this thing off of me. Don't we know a place just around the corner with incredible water pressure?"

CHAPTER 59

December 16, 2019

El Masri had his Zeiss binoculars plastered to his face, trying to find the CIA Director, Nazy Cunningham. He glimpsed a man and a woman entering a white Suburban but he was certain it wasn't her. He had memorized the photograph of Cunningham and the gray-haired woman getting into the vehicle wasn't her. The man holding the Suburban's door open for the woman might have been vaguely familiar, but he spent little time looking at him. He was focused on finding Nazy Cunningham. El Masri turned his binoculars to scan the other women in the crowd still on the White House lawn. He recalled a detail, *The CIA Director had a security detail and a string of limousines.* His gaze returned to the white Suburban now driving through one of the White House gates. *Without an escort or lead vehicle. License number; not even close. So that wasn't her. There was definitely a good looking Arab in that car, but it wasn't her. And the man's face… I wouldn't remember it if I tried.*

He scanned and rescanned the remaining women on the White House lawn with the binoculars. El Masri was frustrated. The intelligence he received had suggested she would be there, that it was a function she wouldn't miss. If she had been healthy.

Maalik El Masri slipped the binoculars into a coat pocket and pushed away from the White House fence. He crossed the road under the watchful eye of a five-man Secret Service detail. He hated to admit failure. He flagged down a taxi to take him to the Ritz Carlton where he had been staying. El Masri sighed. Would surveilling the White House the next day yield any useful intelligence? Or was it time to return to Germany?

He held hope. There were two areas where there was significant intelligence to be gathered. The President's Daily Brief was delivered five days a week by the same intelligence officer, the Acting Director

Nazy Cunningham. *But she remains in the hospital.* Someone else has been delivering it. But no one knew who. The other bit of intel was the make and model and license plate numbers of the Agency's limousines that entered and departed the White House. For several years, the CIA Director's security detail had consisted of three identical black vehicles with three separate and distinct Virginia license plates. Reportedly, two of the vehicles had been damaged and presumably replaced.

The White House seemed to be operating on some type of holiday schedule. El Masri knew it was technically possible to transmit the PDB electronically and use a video conference call to brief the President in the Situation Room. That bit of information was all that was needed for El Masri to feel completely defeated. He wouldn't find her and kill her. He decided he wouldn't conduct any more surveillance but would return to Germany. In his room, El Masri accessed the website which scheduled charter flights.

• • •

Nazy returned from the cold bathroom and snuggled in Duncan's warm arms. They were in the penthouse suite of the JW Marriott and had an unobstructed view of the White House. She was a creature of habit and had awakened early, programmed to rush to the office to familiarize herself with the contents of the PDB before hurrying off to the White House to deliver it. The Deputy Director of Operations was more than excited to conduct the PDB, even by video conference while Nazy was away.

It was about noon when Duncan turned over to find Nazy staring at him with a seductive smile. She kissed him to waken him fully and then rolled him onto his back.

It was well past one when they traded kisses for talk about where to find lunch. Duncan said he had a hankering for Italian. Nazy knew that meant Carpaccio's in Annapolis. After a steamy shower, it took two hours to get ready, the time required for Duncan and Nazy to install her disguise. They agreed they needed to get her out of town without no one knowing she was gone. Duncan stepped back to admire his work as he quickly applied the final nose pieces and glue that widened the bridge and the columella, the strip of skin between the nostrils, and the alae, the portion of the nostrils that attach to the cheeks. Expanding those specific areas of the face would completely disrupt the algorithms of facial recognition systems.

After cleaning up the special glues used to hold the mask in place, Duncan helped Nazy into her spider silk body armor. Although it was December, Duncan wore a dark silk Tommy Bahama short-sleeve shirt, jeans, and black crocodile Lucchese boots. Nazy wore a huge rolled collar, ultra-ragg sweater, jeans, and New Balance running shoes.

As Nazy finished getting dressed, Duncan called the BWI Executive Terminal to have the *Howard 500* removed from the hangar and serviced for departure.

CHAPTER 60

December 17, 2019

After being deposited at the BWI Executive Terminal, Maalik El Masri dismissed the limousine. His charter jet was inbound. The international charter company wanted him there two hours before departure.

An elegant smooth black leather briefcase was slung over his shoulder and he pulled a dark blue Tumi roll-aboard inside to await transportation. He went to the lounge in a surly mood. Nothing had gone right since he arrived.

Since intelligence reports detailed the CIA's executive transport aircraft were based out of the Virginia airports, El Masri's didn't want to take the chance of encountering an Agency intelligence officer in Virginia who may have known him by sight. The Maryland executive terminal served general aviation and business aircraft from a single runway, almost perpendicular from the longer wider main runway dedicated to BWI's commercial traffic.

He had been disappointed with the number of hours he had to sit in traffic in Maryland before arriving at his hotel in downtown Washington, D.C. He became disappointed with the furnishings and functionality of the Grandhotel in Cologne; it paled compared to the American Ritz Carlton. He had mistakenly believed the Althoff Grandhotel Schloss Bensberg was the epitome of hotels; the American hotel was on so many levels several times more exquisite. He had been disappointed he could not secure one of the penthouse suites at the Ritz Carlton. El Masri had been disappointed when he was told those rooms were reserved for the heads of countries and foreign dignitaries, and the reservations had to be made months in advance.

Now he was disappointed he had to wait for a jet. El Masri seethed someone had stolen Scorpii's jet and the German government had effectively dismantled the child sex trafficking and espionage business in Europe that the Lord Chancellor had worked so hard in building. He stared ahead as if he were in a trance and reflected, *I arrived at the airport and watched the jet I knew Mein Kanzler was in disappear out of sight. It slipped into the clouds illuminated by the city lights. Why would anyone take him? Mein Kanzler was near death. There had to be a reason. Then I realized.*

The hotel staff unwittingly helped facilitate their treachery.

They carried luggage and flight bags to the cars. I knew what I would find when I opened the vault, Horst and Blohm had taken Scorpii's journals. Papers for the planes and cars. Every aspect of the enterprise was laid bare in his journals. And an armload of the tapes. Those could have been worth trillions. Account numbers, combinations of safes, safety deposit boxes. Everything. Things I should have had. I didn't think his death through. I assumed too much.

The smartest thing I did was to take everything else out of the vault. Technically, I'm a wealthy man but now I'm politically poor. I have to think of what is best for me. I escaped the Egyptian military a long time ago. Now can I escape the Cee ah a? I'm certain they do not know who I am. They have the journals, but I planned for this day. I have many passports. I'm certain they will look for me soon. Very soon.

I have the EV Gullwing and no one knows I have that and no one will look for me in it.

•　　•　　•

The Agency's security team took Nazy and Duncan from downtown Washington to Annapolis via Highway 50. They monitored the traffic ahead for congestion and flow, and the traffic behind to see if anyone was following them. The driver purposely overshot the first offramp for downtown Annapolis, crossed the Severn Bridge, and took Highway 450 to detour through the Naval Academy yard. Anyone who wasn't authorized access to the university grounds while attempting to tail the Suburban would be met with armed guards and barriers. In the parking lot of the Naval Academy Bookstore, Nazy and Duncan exited the white Suburban and got in an unmarked black

Chevy Tahoe with Maryland license plates. They continued on their way to downtown Annapolis.

In a secluded corner of the restaurant at a table with a candle in a wine bottle, Duncan placed a *Growler* in the middle of the table. Nazy started to debrief Duncan, but Duncan jumped in. "When I landed in Houston, I turned over Scorpii's pumpkins to the Agency pilot who was waiting on the ramp for me. Thank you for sending him and a *Caravan*. I knew you wanted those papers."

And the CDs and videos. Nazy said, "My pleasure. Yes. When he arrived at headquarters, he handed over *the pumpkins*. It was larger than we envisioned. So, thank you, darling. The CDs were supposed to go directly to the Attorney General but the President wanted them under lock and key at the *Library of Diaries.*"

"I suppose if the AG got his hands on those, that would not be a secret they could contain at the DOJ." *Sex tapes of the rich and famous. Another batch of propaganda's silent weapons.*

Nazy agreed. "Europe is dismantling their clandestine pedophile infrastructure and I suppose we set back their child sex trade fifty years."

"Halleluiah."

Nazy continued, "We didn't really know what to expect; there were a surprising number of Scorpii's diaries, journals, ledgers, and videos—but no computers. Our analysts began pouring over them immediately. There is about fifty years' worth of information. It's a remarkable trove. Thank you, darling." *And there are still 36 boxes to be found.*

"My pleasure." Duncan gestured he was sincerely interested in what she had found as he attacked the basket of breads and butter.

Nazy said, "Consistent with the analysis we provided the President, Scorpii recorded that he found the gold the Nazi's had been processing in the bombed-out synagogue. He indicated it took weeks to remove all of it and store it in a safe location. He parlayed those gold bars into an enterprise."

Duncan countered, "Did he mention if he found gold watches in the synagogue?"

"He did. You're much too fast, my darling."

"That's not what you said last night." *I'll be quiet....*

She ignored him. "He was a complex individual and we hoped to find what motivated him."

"Did you find something?"

Nazy said, "Several things. Overall, there was a common theme of anger that was carried through from the earliest journals. He essentially blamed men in uniforms for taking his life away, his childhood away. Scorpii said he was the only child left alive at the Ravensbrück concentration camp. When the Soviet troops entered the camp, he assumed there would be people to rescue him. But the Soviet troops didn't know what to do with a child who had been used for experiments. He didn't know who they were and they shunned him."

"And he was ignored as they ransacked the camp for valuable items. Scorpii wasn't valuable and was forced to learn how to survive on his own as the camp was liberated. He was five-years-old. In other journals he revisited being abandoned in the concentration camp and blamed America for allowing Hitler to kill his family and experiment on him. He never mentioned Mengele, but he credited the experiments they conducted on him with actually making him valuable later and keeping him alive."

Duncan asked, "I understood the Ravensbrück concentration camp was north of Berlin was mostly for women."

Nazy said, "The camps had laboratories to conduct experiments on women and children."

"Sick." Duncan thought, *But I'll bet the leadership of the Western intelligence agencies wanted the Nazi's research. Every country wanted their research.* He said, "I'll wager Scorpii was probably one of the children referenced during the war crimes tribunal at Nuremberg. The Nazi's didn't follow any code of medical ethics or standards. They conducted research with no limitations."

Nazy said, "Research without ethics. You're talking about the Nuremberg Code. That document defines the requirement of *voluntary informed consent* of the human subject."

Duncan nodded. "That's a start."

Nazy continued, "There was little analysis done during the first pass. We sought answers to basic questions first. Like how does a war refugee become rich? Nazi gold."

Hunter nodded. "Did Scorpii's writings mention Al Husseni?"

"There was nothing on Al Husseni." Nazy pronounced the Arabic name in perfect Arabic, without a British accent.

Hunter thought, *How could he know Hitler wanted to deport Jews while Al Husseni urged Hitler to kill them. He was just a kid. I saw some photographs with Nazis and Al Husseni visiting a concentration camp I thought was Ravensbrück. Oh well.*

After a drink, Nazy continued, "There were tens of thousands of transactions for various initiatives which filled up several journals. We have to explore those fully."

The curious statement caught Hunter's attention. "Like what?"

"They're coded; we'll have to decipher them. Some are likely business transactions. We've seen many of them before; they're lightly coded and could be individual requests for funding for espionage, anarchist, or terrorist activities. The generally accepted version of history is the Kremlin funded Gus Hall's candidacy for president. It appears it wasn't the Kremlin; Scorpii funded all of Gus Hall's runs for president."

Duncan said, "I'm very cynical and my spider sense tells me those coded business transactions are probably sexual transactions. Maybe child sex trafficking. I'll wager the CDs, the videos, are all related. Blohm didn't know for sure but those CDs were specially handled by the El Masri character, Scorpii's handler, and were segregated in Scorpii's vault. He sensed they were surveillance videos of the wealthy, royalty, the important people. Either way, I won't be surprised." Duncan nodded as he told the waiter, "We're going to need a little more time." They still hadn't looked at the menus.

Nazy continued, "There were several uncoded observations we found odd. For example, Scorpii mentioned gay men were happy and rarely committed suicide, but homosexual men were mostly unhappy, problematic, and often committed suicide. It was an odd observation. Like there is a difference between a gay man and a homosexual man?"

"You mean, like there is a *variant*?"

Nazy nodded. "Apparently he believed there were variants of lesbians too but most of the discussions on variants revolved around pedophiles."

"Pedophiles?"

"Scorpii mentioned he didn't condone pedophilia for pleasure, but the different variants of pedophiles were remarkable and each had their purpose. All of them were already so compromised they couldn't be rehabilitated, but he found they could be manipulated."

"Manipulated? Such as…."

"Such as Scorpii used children to compromise pedophiles in the military and intelligence services so they would conduct espionage for him. By controlling access to the children, Scorpii found he could manipulate the pedophiles as he saw fit. Scorpii was infuriated by the men who committed suicide once they began conducting espionage for him. Scorpii complained because he spent significant resources to groom them to provide him with classified documents, but they were fragile and they would break."

Nazy frowned. It was an unpleasant topic. She tried something new. "There were entries on the Executive Director of Foreign Intelligence, the High Captain Maalik El Masri. I believe I have his title correct. As you said, Scorpii's handler. Very unusual. But he may have also been Scorpii's number two man."

"*El Masri?*" He knew there had never been a man with that name on the *Matrix*. "Horst and Blohm mentioned him. You?"

"We haven't heard of him, but those organizations are big on titles and tightly control their cover names. Probably one of a dozen names on a fake passport."

"You would think Germany had enough *chancellors*." Then Hunter had an epiphany. "With that name, El Masri, maybe he was Scorpii's link to the Muslim Brotherhood or the Islamic Underground. Horst and Blohm said he was at the hotel every day and took care of Scorpii's calendar. He delivered their version of the PDB and those things not handled by Scorpii's attorney."

Very perceptive, my husband! Nazy smiled broadly before getting serious. "You may be right. El Masri is a common name in the Middle East and North Africa. I'll send a cable to our Chiefs of Station to see what they can find out. The High Captain Maalik El Masri may not be his real name."

Duncan said, "If he was Scorpii's Brotherhood interface, that might answer a lot of questions." *And others I'm trying hard not to think about. Scorpii's dead — who is in charge of his money?* Duncan's brown eyes returned to Nazy's green ones.

But with Scorpii gone, just how much pull does the Executive Director of Foreign Intelligence actually have? Is there a typical organization chart? Who is in charge now? Billionaire Insider dudes or the High Captain Maalik El Masri? Blohm said El Masri had access to Scorpii's wealth and the vault.

Nazy said, "We suspected a German agency called the Federal Telecommunications Group, of which virtually nothing is publicly disclosed, was run and owned by Rho Schwartz Scorpii. We've suspected it of being a *double-agency*, a front company that works for two intelligence services, mostly for Russia's Federal Intelligence Services and sometimes for Germany's Federal Intelligence Services. Like a *double agent*, it's difficult to know who they're working for. We asked internally, if Scorpii's European Federation's Federal Intelligence Service was the same as Germany's Federal Intelligence Services. Was it a double-agency?"

Duncan added, "In the U.S. the media and some politicians call the opposition side of these double-agency arrangements the *deep state* or the *dark state*."

Nazy said, "I'm learning they're more ubiquitous than we realize. One of the things I discovered as the NCTC Director was we have offices and organizations that fall under the umbrella of the CIA and the federal government, but secretly work for the Democrat Party or President Mazibuike even though he's dead. They have idealized him. The FBI was supposed to keep track of the international double-agency arrangements within the U.S., but instead of monitoring the Muslim Brotherhood as an internal opposition agency, they opened their doors to them."

"So Nazy darling, if I'm following along correctly, you say that these domestic double-agency arrangements are no different functionally, than some office at the CIA working for the Democrat

Party or the ideal of President Mazibuike instead of for the people or the U.S. government?"

"Absolutely. I saw it but thought nothing of it at first. After 3M resigned, I know there were offices at the CIA that refused to post President Hernandez's picture. They kept the picture of President Mazibuike in those offices for years. Technically, President Hernandez's picture would be prominently displayed when management entered those spaces. But when we left someone would flip the frame to President Mazibuike's photograph. That simple act telegraphed to others they were some part of the informal political resistance."

Duncan followed with, "You would expect the folks in those offices, folks with the highest security clearances in the land, to carry out the policies of President Hernandez."

"Exactly." Then Nazy interrupted his thoughts. "There were several entries that suggested Scorpii disliked women."

Duncan said facetiously as he pointed at Nazy. "How could anyone dislike *that* face?"

Nazy was frightfully embarrassed then momentarily confused. *Do you mean my face or this disguise? Is Duncan being playful?*

The waiter returned. Duncan ordered for them both. Baked lasagna for him and shrimp scampi for Nazy.

When the waiter left, Nazy countered with a thin smile and said, "He made several comments about me. In one line I was 'the bitch' and in one of the last entries I was 'a remarkable beauty.' In multiple entries over many years, he was fascinated with using a woman's beauty '*as leverage*' for espionage, as in some men would do anything for beautiful women."

"I bet he took one look at you and thought he had struck the motherlode!"

Nazy was certain Duncan's line was a compliment, but she was unfamiliar with what had to be an American term.

Duncan asked, "Did he try to turn you?"

Nazy showed wide-eyed surprise at her husband's perspicacity. "How did you know?"

"You were on the Lord Chancellor's radar. If they can't have the women they find fascinating, they try to own them in different ways. I'm not surprised. Do you remember any specific instances where you were approached?"

Nazy said, "Nothing *enticing*. But there were threats."

Threats!? "Seriously? Oh, baby. I had no idea."

"It also happened to the few non-practicing Muslim women in the IC. They were threatened indirectly, if they wouldn't work as a double agent their families would be harmed. Most would not be intimidated and simply quit. I've been isolated from any direct approach. I don't have a visible family they can use as leverage to threaten me. And I'm so senior now, if someone tried to threaten me, I'd have them fired. There have been a few probing actions. They occurred when I was on temporary duty, like when I was detailed to work with FBI agents during joint CIA operations. It was before Greg mandated that I have a security detail, I think."

"Greg dismissed those that were directed at me and others as ridiculous and disingenuous. A joke. But then I was immediately assigned a security detail. I believed none of them were sincere, and I was never interested in working for the Muslim Brotherhood. I know they are a criminal enterprise. But I think the Muslim men who were hired by the FBI effectively removed Muslim women from all the American intelligence agencies for that reason."

Hunter said, "And you would know."

Nazy thought, *Maybe. It was all so strange the FBI leadership allowed that.*

Hunter completed his thought, *And I probably wasn't around.* Then Duncan shifted topics. "Were there any direct references to child sex trafficking?"

"There was but there wasn't; Scorpii didn't call it that. He viewed them as *inventory*. You almost have to be versed in the language of the elites. He clarified those children he couldn't use to incite espionage he turned over to the pedophiles and Satanists. He distinguished between pedophiles who preyed on children for pleasure and the pedophiles who killed children for satanic rituals. One was considered a stable sexual variant, the other an unstable sexual variant. Scorpii also verified he funded abortion houses and trafficked in the fetal parts for research."

"Biotechnology labs."

Nazy nodded. "He invested heavily in European biotechnologies as they had greater access to fetal parts than American biotechnology firms. He felt it was better to abort an unwanted child than discard it to a life such as his, a life of misery. He also said, 'Children make the best recruits for other children.'"

Duncan was not following along and it showed. Nazy explained, "In Europe, it's more lucrative and much safer to sell children than drugs or guns. A pound of heroin can be retailed once; a shipment of AK-47s can be retailed once or twice; but children can be sold hundreds of times a year. A pimp on the street can sell young women 10 to 15 times a day and confiscate all their earnings. Pedophiles will pay tens of thousands of dollars or euros for discrete time with children; those are multiple transactions and those seem to be what Scorpii specialized in. Satanists will pay tens of thousands of dollars or euros for a child sacrifice or fetal remains; those can only be done once. The more children they have, the more inventory they have to make more money. Eastwood's special was heart wrenching. And it's not just the Europeans. Africa and the Middle East. Boko Haram, the Taliban and others."

"Mohammad too." *Aisha was six years old when she was given to the 50-year-old Mohammad; she was nine when the marriage was consummated.* Hunter shook his head in disbelief. A new question. "Anything on funding attorneys and school boards here?"

Nazy nodded, "Attorney General Winchester is determined to recall, remove, and replace every state attorney and prosecutor that Scorpii funded."

That would be helpful. For a start.

Nazy continued, "There were annual entries. Every year American activists from each of his NGOs working in Mexico and throughout Africa went to Germany to deliver a measures of effectiveness report. Scorpii funded protests across the country. He funded small businesses to create bogus documents for passports and driver's licenses in Mexico for illegal aliens seeking to come to the U.S. He funded anarchists and revolutionaries in Mexico, Central and South America, but not the anarchists that Bill encounters on the campaign trail. Those are communists, if the FBI is to be believed. Oh, Scorpii was livid when Bill began to arm women. Armed women."

"It's difficult to turn someone into a slave when you put a gun in their hands and they say, *hell no I won't go.*"

"When Bill announced his intentions, Scorpii apparently flipped out. He wrote that Bill's initiative would set the communist movement in America back at least fifty years."

"Well, I say, let's drink to Bill!"

CHAPTER 61

December 17, 2019

Duncan said, "So he knew Bill's initiative was very effective counterpropaganda. Isn't that fascinating? I'm not surprised Scorpii wasn't a fan of the Second Amendment. I'm sure he funded the communists' propaganda and their protests, and everything he could to negate the Second Amendment."

Nazy said, "And *mujahedeen*. In his journals he was clear where and how he wanted his money spent. El Masri seems to be the person who took the direction and implemented his wishes on the Muslim Brotherhood and anything related to Islam."

Hunter thought, *Well there you go! El Masri was Scorpii's Islamic bag man.*

"But we anticipated much of Scorpii's funding communists and their protests. Confidentially, under Greg and Bill's leadership we went around the FBI and used our own overseas resources to pay for larger counterprotests. Anti-communists protests. Those had a dramatic impact."

Duncan reached for her hand. He purred, "Is there anything else worth discussing?"

"Mmm. The European chapter of Suicide.org is reporting a massive uptick in the number of suicides in older European men. And they do not appear to be related to health issues."

Duncan said, "So let me get this straight. Our AG tells Europe's ambassadors they need to fix their child sex slave problem or there will be hell to pay. The old man dies, billionaires cannot find Scorpii's blackmail videos, Europe suddenly finds their missing children about the same time as we hear about old dudes flinging themselves out windows. I call that a good work day, Miss Cunningham."

Nazy allowed Duncan to vent. She said, "You know *we* wanted Hashash. Last person on the *Matrix*. President Hernandez wanted us to get him, but the CIA leadership was never willing to pay enough to find him."

"The President bankrolled it."

Nazy nodded. "He authorized it and we offered $25 million to General Toufik to deliver a live prisoner to us, but apparently *Scorpii* wanted Hashash dead. There was no explanation in his journal. A better analysis of that situation is it's entirely possible *El Masri* didn't want us to interrogate Hashash. Scorpii or El Masri could have found out about the deal; but with no comment on Hashash in Scorpii's journal, we are leaning hard toward El Masri. The connective tissue is both men were Muslim. Maybe Toufik told El Masri. It was definitely Scorpii's Federation that paid the $25 million to Toufik, and we paid the one-million-dollar bounty."

"Scorpii made his whole adult living using children to blackmail people."

Duncan has such a way with words. Nazy nodded. She wondered what he would say with her next spot of information. It was an ugly topic: the murder of his parents. She said, "We also had cause to believe Ahmed Jibril had been paid millions of pounds to come up with the plot to down PamAm Flight 103. We thought Scorpii funded the operation, although he done nothing like that before. So far, there are no entries in Scorpii's journals that indicate he funneled the funds to Libya. We believe Tehran was the banker. A General Roustaie link."

"I must be missing something."

Nazy explained, "We believed for years the attack on the airliner was because of the intelligence officers who were aboard. That part of the analysis was spot on, but we didn't fully explore the triggering mechanism. In his diaries, the timing was such that Scorpii was incensed that President Reagan, who would soon leave the White House, suddenly wanted Europe to shut down his child sex trade business. The U.S. knew Scorpii was bad for decades and then Sayyid Ruhollah Musavi Khomeini...."

"... also known as *Ayatollah Khomeini*...." As Nazy continued to talk, Hunter remembered. *The shah came to the U.S. so Khomeini returned to Iran from his exile. Immediately men and women stopped going to American universities in the Middle East. They were forced out of western-*

style clothes to wear traditional Islamic attire. High heels for sandals. And then the war on aviation came, and it's still going on now.

Nazy nodded and continued, "Scorpii said it was Roustaie. Tehran funded a double-agency in Tripoli; Gaddafi didn't know. President Reagan threatened Europe to either stop Scorpii's sex trade or face a U.S. withdrawal from Europe. But Europe—how do you say?"

Duncan offered, "Slow-rolled. They *slow*-rolled him. They weren't serious and knew he would leave office soon, so they slow-rolled him. This is all about the treachery of *double-agencies*."

Nazy nodded and said, "Yes, that is how *we* function as *Irregulars*, only for good. But those on the other side, that is exactly what they did. The European countries agreed to conduct studies and investigations to see if there really were crimes. Double agencies got involved to dictate an outcome. And on the surface, like some initiatives, it just looked like they lost steam and died out."

"There were no studies or investigations into Scorpii. However, there was pushback to punish America for getting into the sexual business of the *elites* in Europe. President Reagan went to Berlin for the 750th Anniversary of the founding of Berlin, told Gorbachev to *Tear Down That Wall*, and threw all of Europe and the Soviet Bloc into turmoil."

"President Reagan said he loved Whittaker Chambers' book and gave his family the Presidential Medal of Freedom in his honor."

Nazy smiled. "There are coded entries. We believe Scorpii funded assassination attempts and funded a propaganda war against America. Khomeini used the treasury of Iran to expand fundamentalism and completely change the dynamic in the Middle East."

"Scorpii funded 3M."

Nazy pinched her lips. "Totally."

Nazy was emphatic. "There is a single entry, that the time was ripe. The U.S. needed a new leader to implement *sharia*."

Hunter thought, *What were we just talking about?*

"There were many entries on the Democrats in Congress. Apparently, Scorpii completely funded Mazibuike's rise in American politics."

Hunter just nodded as if he was hearing the same news for the tenth time.

Nazy dropped her eyes as if she were embarrassed. "Scorpii was very detailed with 3M. He was enamored of the man's potential to destroy America. It seems Scorpii funneled several million dollars to Democrat Congressmen and Senators to legislate the 'natural born citizen' clause be stricken from the Constitution and amend it with wording that would essentially allow anyone to become president. He funded 3M's radicalization, and he funded his education. Scorpii's billionaire friends who owned the media in Europe funded psychological operations against right-wing causes and against Republicans. I thought it was Scorpii, but now I can see it was probably El Masri who relied on Khomeini's network of mosques in America to find the perfect candidate. They—Scorpii, El Masri, and Khomeini—funded propaganda efforts in America, from Beria's book-is-a-hoax...."

Duncan knew the title. He said, "*Brainwashing*: A Synthesis of the Russian Textbook on Psychopolitics. I did a paper on propaganda at the Naval War College."

Nazy continued with a sigh, "…the psychology of transforming a nation from freedom to communism."

Duncan added, "You have to know what the enemy is up to in order to fight against it." *And it was all in Scorpii's diaries.*

Dinner was served. Nazy finished her thought, "President Hernandez was prominently mentioned when he was the Speaker of the House. Scorpii hated him. Scorpii blamed him for killing the bills that would have made an ineligible candidate for president eligible through legislation. President Hernandez disrupted Scorpii's efforts to amend the Constitution."

Duncan thought, *Not all silent weapons of propaganda work. Good riddance to both Scorpii and the ayatollah.*

They ate in silence. Duncan paid the bill. That was an automatic event as was a healthy tip for services rendered. Nazy said, there was one more thing. "Scorpii mentioned his old friend, General Roustaie had brought a device from Iran"

Hunter lifted his eyebrows in surprise. "Device?"

Nazy said, "It was recovered after the death of the four *mujahedeen* in Iran. It appears one of the drones failed to detonate, the Iranian Revolutionary Guard Corps recovered it, and they tried to reverse engineer it. Then Roustaie brought it to Germany where El Masri's office did reverse engineer it."

Duncan was momentarily crushed. *They have a copy of our Blackwings? Oh shit! Now no one is safe!*

• • •

They blew out of Annapolis on the way to the Baltimore-Washington International Airport. The Agency Tahoe was caught in the northbound I-97 traffic near the Millersville exit when movement slowed to a crawl. Instead of making out with his wife under the scrutiny of the CIA's security team, Duncan pulled out his BlackBerry and scrolled through a few pages until he found Dory Eastwood's *Unfiltered News* and Eastwood's latest post. He read it to Nazy.

"Bill is at it again. Or I should say, Eastwood is reporting again. In his latest piece, the Diocese of Austin installed a nativity scene in the rotunda of the Texas State Capitol and the Satanic Temple of Austin filed a lawsuit for their Texas members, claiming the laws of the State of Texas violate their religious freedom to perform abortion rituals."

Nazy was confused, "Abortion rituals?"

Duncan said, "That's what Eastwood says. He says the Satanic Temple demanded a bronze statue called 'Baphomet with Children,' be installed at the Texas Capitol to counter the nativity scene and a Ten Commandments display."

Nazy asked, "Where does it say what Bill did?"

"I'm getting to that. An editorial in the Dallas Morning News from former CIA Director and Presidential Candidate, Bill McGee, said 'Similar displays of the Baphomet statue — hooves, horns and all — in Europe were associated with pedophilia, child sex trafficking, and child sacrifice. It has no place at this Capitol or any other place in America.'"

Nazy shook her head in disbelief.

Duncan continued, "The Satanic Temple stated in a press release the Satanic holiday, Sol Invictus, is a religious celebration which takes place on the 25th of December. There's a trivial pursuit question for you."

"Eastwood indicates Bill was outraged and said, 'Mocking the millions of Christians in the State of Texas and billions around the world by depicting the baby Jesus this Christmas with the satanic deity Baphomet is the very definition of evil. It ignores the long history of child sex trafficking and child sacrifice by the Satanic Temple of Austin. I call on the Texas Governor to investigate the criminality of the Satanic Temple of Austin. The United States was founded on Christianity; Christmas is the celebration of the birth of Christ. We should not be celebrating evil, and I urge all people of true religious faith to shun the devil.' That's it."

Nazy said, "That's an aggressive stance for Bill to take, but it's the right one."

As the limousine rolled up to the BWI Executive Terminal, Duncan said, "I think it's about time. That BS cannot be condoned, and I can't imagine the Supreme Court would ever allow that to stand. But you never know. Liberals."

•   •   •

After a period of reflection, El Masri returned to castigating himself for his failure. He should have known he would fail. *The American president acknowledged the Lord Chancellor was granted entry to the country for humanitarian reasons. We knew he wouldn't live more than a few days, if that. Who flew Mein Kanzler to America? Not Gothear Horst; not Rudolf Blohm – if those were even their real names. They had been with us for so long. They're missing too. With that Dante Locke. Were they part of it? It would seem so. So many questions, no answers.*

He barely noticed the man and three women who walked across the executive terminal lobby carrying computer bags and luggage. El Masri didn't recognize any of them because he ignored them. They stopped at the counter, conducted some business, and proceeded out the doors to the flight line.

El Masri turned his eyes away to allow himself to stew in the juices of hate.

•   •   •

It took about a half an hour to prepare the *Howard 500* for flight. Hunter suggested Nazy remain in the aircraft's cabin unless she had to go to the bathroom. The Agency security women assigned to protect her looked helpless, unsure of what to do until Hunter instructed them to place their things in the aircraft. He would give them further instructions when they were ready to go. As Duncan walked around the aircraft conducting preflight checks, he told the head of the security detail, "I ordered submarine sandwiches and chicken for the trip, and it will be delivered to the Executive Terminal desk. When I get notified it has been delivered, you can go pick them up."

One security officer remained with Nazy while the other made several trips carrying a case of water, bags of chips and candy, and then the subs and chicken.

When Hunter finished his pre-flight checks, he announced, "This is your last chance for a head call." Like girls at a slumber party, the three women raced across the tarmac to the Executive Terminal to use the restroom.

•   •   •

When three women walked from the flightline side of the airport and proceeded directly to the women's restroom, El Masri lifted his eyes to follow them until they disappeared into the toilet facilities. He noticed two of the women were deferential to the third. They were likely the woman's personal security. *Probably a movie star. I don't recognize her as an Amerikaner movie star, but she looks like the Egyptian actress who played Cleopatra, years ago. What was her name? Amerikaners are so ridiculous to have female security for actresses or female leaders. That's how you know das Amerikaners' culture is kaput, when protection becomes a function of gender and not capability.*

El Masri exhaled in disgust and just wished his jet would arrive to take him away from this boredom. He stood up and walked to the counter to check on his charter. As the counter attendant called air traffic control, El Masri heard women's voices behind him.

The three women spilled out of the women's restroom in single file. The two security officers followed by Nazy Cunningham sans her disguise. They hurried past the counter. The man who had been in the lounge was hunched over at the counter with his back to them. That was a green light for the women to expedite their departure from the executive terminal through the two sets of double doors and onto the flight line. They walked at a brisk pace toward the *Howard 500*. The weather was a cold humid, and the winds on the airport were gusting. It was a chilly afternoon before the expected nor'easter blew in and made life miserable.

El Masri detected movement out of his periphery with the noise of the women passing him. His subconscious forced him to look to the source of the movement. He had seen three women enter the building, and three women leaving in his periphery. The uniformed woman behind the counter announced his jet would touch down in five minutes. El Masri was overjoyed and had lifted his head in a demonstration of relief when his eyes caught the women passing in front of the large plate-glass window. He took a double and then a triple take before it registered he had seen one of those women before. He froze in place and blinked wildly at the clear profile of Nazy Cunningham. *That's her. How did I miss her? That's her!* He was so shocked he couldn't get his legs to move. Then she was gone.

After several seconds, he staggered back to his coat and luggage as if drugged. He threw open the Tumi as quickly as the fasteners would allow, extracted the drone, and ran out the doors on the streetside of the Executive Terminal building. *It has to be her!*

Nazy Cunningham mounted the aircraft's stairs, assisted by Duncan. She had removed her disguise and was looking as radiant as ever. Duncan then assisted the other women to step into the aircraft. Once everyone was aboard, Duncan crawled under the wing to kick the single chock from the main landing gear tire. He walked around the aircraft and scanned 360°, the complete airport environment. Satisfied there was nothing that could hurt him or his passengers, he entered the aircraft and closed the door behind him.

Nazy had settled in the copilot position, her seat and lap belts were buckled.

Duncan flipped the avionics master and the cockpit came alive with lights. He started the *Howard 500's* engines.

• • •

El Masri only caught a glimpse of Nazy Cunningham as she entered the opening of an antique airplane. He restrained himself from screaming. He hissed his exasperation: *I missed my opportunity! I have her photograph loaded! There was no time for the device to acquire her, to target her. I didn't have a chance.*

Where could she be going?

He collapsed against the fence, stunned at the revelation that CIA executives were using old aircraft to escape detection and thwarting the network of *Overwatch* personnel. He grabbed the chain link and rattled it in frustration. *That is how they get out. At least that is how she got out.*

El Masri was still castigating himself for failing his mission when one of the engines of the antique aircraft started. He recovered sufficiently to remember he still had work to do. He looked for and found the tail number painted in black on the rudder of the aircraft. El Masri withdrew his smartphone, selected the *Overwatch* app, and followed the instructions for inputting a tail number. Under "Comments," he typed in: CIA DIRECTOR ON THIS AIRCRAFT. PRIORITY FOLLOW.

He was flummoxed. El Masri's analysts had assured him if an Agency executive needed a jet to use in an emergency, it would be close to CIA Headquarters, not hidden in Maryland. He stared at the old aircraft as it trundled to the runway. El Masri tried to convince himself he hadn't really seen the CIA Director; he had made a mistake. *She was in a hospital.* The CIA Director would fly in one of the Agency's corporate jet aircraft, and it would be tracked by a network of *Overwatch* people. That was how it had been for two decades. That is what made sense.

The high-pitched whine of an arriving corporate jet's engines drowned out all other sound. El Masri's aircraft had arrived and taxied to the front of the Executive Terminal. The noise from the jet was deafening. He turned away from the aircraft on the other side of the fence.

Now he would have to begin again to get into position to kill her. He pulled the drone from a coat pocket, looked at it forlornly, sighed and mumbled, "*Ich bin gescheitert.*" *I failed.* He looked up and watched the taildragger disappear from view.

CHAPTER 62

December 17, 2019

Twenty minutes into the flight, Cumberland, Maryland passed under the nose of the *Howard 500*. When the satellite telephone went off behind the pilot's seat Duncan looked at Nazy in the copilot seat, and she returned a bewildered look. He asked, "I wonder who's calling?" She frowned as he lifted the receiver of the STU-III.

Link Coffey said, "That website just came alive. Apparently, you have a VIP aboard."

Hunter shot Nazy a look of concern. She scowled for she didn't know what else she could do.

Coffey continued, "It looks like their version of an APB. (All points bulletin). There will be a reward to those who find your next airport."

"Thanks *Chain*."

He called me by my callsign. That's progress. "I think you need another airplane."

Hunter replied, "Yeah, that's obvious. I have several, but few that I can carry pax."

"I take it you're full."

"10-4."

"If you need me for anything, let me know."

"Thanks. Maybe continue monitoring them?"

"I will."

Hunter said, "Great. Tha...."

Coffey interjected, "...I now know why...."

Oh yes, you wanted to know if we were married and why I said, Maybe one of these days I'll tell you. Duncan smiled. "10-4. G.I. Dog. Over and out." He hung up the receiver.

Nazy waited impatiently. He smiled at her.

You are so very special and must be protected. Duncan waved for the security detail to come to the front of the airplane. He turned the radio off, then turned to Nazy and the women and said, "I don't know how, but *Tailwatchers* knows you're aboard this airplane." The security women looked at each other.

Nazy asked, "How is that possible?"

"I don't know. They don't normally track these aircraft. Someone must have recognized you in the terminal building without your disguise or when you were boarding."

Over the roar of the radials outside Nazy said, "I shouldn't have taken my disguise off."

Duncan said, "I didn't think it was necessary any longer. No, this is probably my fault. I assumed no one would look for a prop plane and no one would look for us in Maryland."

One of the security women said, "There was a man in the lounge in the terminal."

Duncan replied quickly, "That's probably the guy. When you had your mask on we got away without no one knowing you were not in a hospital, that you hadn't gotten blown up. In the meantime, I have to do something with this plane. This one is compromised. I need another one."

Nazy thought, *Don't you mean "we" need another one? What are you thinking? I don't think I'm going to like where this is going.*

Duncan didn't think long on his predicament. He turned the radio back on, canceled his clearance, and descended to a lower altitude to proceed to a private runway in Virginia.

Then he handed the satphone to Nazy. "I don't think it's prudent at this time to gallivant around the country and go on vacation. The safest place for you, my darling wife, is back at your place. Please call your duty officer and see about arranging for helicopter airlift to return you to Langley. Let's let this settle for a few days, then we can go."

It wouldn't do to refuse or protest so Nazy asked, "What are you thinking?"

"Whoever they are, they're not after me. You're the one they want at all costs. You'll be safe at CIA."

"What are you going to do?"

"I'm going to find the asshole who wants to do you harm." *If I can.*

• • •

They discussed the merits of using her disguise. She had used it at the White House. Duncan didn't want to tell Nazy what he thought she should do; Nazy's safety was paramount and the priority. Nazy acknowledged, "It would be best if Nazy Cunningham was not seen at all." Duncan agreed and Nazy left the cockpit; she returned to the cabin and the women helped her get into disguise.

• • •

Five hours after landing at a private airstrip in Bridgewater, Hunter disembarked from the legendary *Columbine II*, the first Air Force One, at the Elmira Corning Regional Airport. The unscheduled nighttime landing of the four-radial Lockheed C-121 escaped the notice of local reporters but not the employees of the airport. They called their families who rushed to the airport to see the airplane President Eisenhower used as a presidential aircraft. After disgorging an unremarkable passenger, the historical aircraft slowly taxied from the airport's terminal to the runway.

The onlookers' focus was on *Columbine II*'s slow deliberate visit; Hunter was completely ignored as he rode a golf cart in the sub-freezing temperatures away from all the commotion near the terminal. The one-armed war veteran mechanic whose empty coat sleeve was pushed inside so it wouldn't flop around, drove Hunter to the door of the immaculately restored Pan American Airways DC-3 parked in front of one of QAS' several hangars. Once the aircraft door was unlocked, opened, and loaded with the provisions from the golf cart, Duncan thanked the mechanic and began preflighting the DC-3 for departure. When the *Columbine II*'s four engines were run up to takeoff power, Hunter and the mechanic stopped what they were doing and moved to a better viewing location. While freezing their asses off they witnessed something they hadn't seen before and would likely never see again, a magnificent Lockheed *Constellation* roaring down the runway.

Within the hour after Nazy informed the CIA duty officer of her predicament, the Deputy Director was notified his boss was in a sticky wicket. The Deputy Director gave the duty officer the order to do whatever was necessary to evacuate the CIA director from the private landing strip in Virginia. The duty officer said he would inform the National Security Council (NSC) of the situation. The NSC duty officer contacted the HMX-1 duty officer at MCB Quantico who notified the command element of the NSC airlift request.

An hour later, an extraction team assembled at Marine Base Quantico. It took another hour for the on-duty aircrew to be activated, the on-duty security team to be detailed, and the duty aircraft to be preflighted. Marine Corps Air Facility Quantico was temporarily opened for the aircraft to taxi into position and depart to the Acting Director's location. It was another flawless response from the HMX-1 organization to a White House request.

The Marine Corps MV-22 landed well before midnight. Several heavily armored Marines disembarked the aircraft and were escorted to the CIA Director's location.

Inside the company's main office Nazy thanked the CEO for being a gracious host and thanked the Marines for coming to help. She attempted to grab her backpack, a go bag Duncan insisted she kept near her for emergencies, and her matte black Halliburton Zero aluminum briefcase, but the Marines wouldn't hear of it. They carried her bags to the awaiting aircraft, rotors swirling overhead. The Agency's security detail trailed behind Nazy; their bags were also carried to the tilt-rotor's open door by the armed Marines.

Nazy had been active in the CEO's office while she waited for transportation to CIA HQ. She discussed her situation with the CIA's duty officer and the Agency's security director, Maggi Munro. The large buxom woman had been asleep when the duty officer called. Munro wasn't surprised with the call or the situation. She lamented she had been through several episodes with Nazy Cunningham before, all requiring immediate and priority security handling. And

Marines. And security personnel. Whatever she asked for, she received.

It's always something with her, but she's the Acting Director now, and I'm still the security chief. Ms. Munro said, "So, Director Cunningham, as before we're going to avoid getting any clothes from your house. If someone's watching your place, we don't want to give them any hope you'll be returning soon. I know you wear the nice stuff and I hate to be the bearer of bad news, but girl, you might have to have to dress like one of us trench diggers for a while."

Munro was one of the few at the CIA who would address Nazy by her first name. The security chief was not enthralled or intimidated by positional power, and Nazy always treated her like an equal. When Nazy pushed back, Munro said, "Wouldn't be prudent, Nazy. Wouldn't be prudent at this time. You have a couple of bags. We need time to surveil your neighborhood. You have a few things that will keep you in your own skivvies until we can get someone into town and shop for you. The contracting officer is one cheap bastard and will toss me in GITMO if I were to go to Victoria's Secret for your delicates."

"It'll be fine; thank you Maggi. Whatever you do for me will be fine. I apologize for the trouble."

"Oh, no girl...no trouble at all. All part of the job, although you keep some strange hours. I understand you have a disguise. Please tell me it's one of the new ones."

Nazy assured her the facial recognition countermeasures device was the latest thing out of the labs.

After getting off the telephone with Nazy, Munro wondered just why one person at the Agency required so much help so often.

•　　•　　•

El Masri had consulted his computer and received satphone updates while en route to Germany. He was crushed to learn the antique aircraft the *Cee ah a* Director boarded hadn't landed at any of the airports monitored by *Overwatch* personnel. A thundering satphone call to the *Overwatch* hotline in Moscow revealed something El Masri didn't know. There were 300 runways in Germany but over 5,000 in the United States. There were only a few thousand people worldwide who monitored airport traffic for *Overwatch*, and all the aircraft under surveillance were jet-powered. Only in an emergency would *Overwatch* attempt to monitor the arrivals or departures of piston-powered or propeller-driven aircraft.

That aircraft had disappeared. It had probably landed at a location *das Amerikaners* called an uncontrolled airfield or even an unimproved runway. *And it was probably put in a hangar for safekeeping.*

Exasperated, he removed the drone from his pocket and held it in his hand. *It was a good plan, to return the favor. The apostate bitch deserves to die for all that she has done to spite Allah and his warriors! I will use this drone to get that woman if it's the last thing I ever do.*

CHAPTER 63

December 21, 2019

Duncan Hunter texted Demetrius Eastwood to expect another box. Previous boxes from Hunter at Christmastime hadn't been dried fruit and candies from *Harry & David* but rare antique typewriters. As in previous years, a note on the office door announced a small shipping container had been delivered to the building manager.

Eastwood used a hand truck to move the black shipping crate to his office. FRAGILE and FedEx labels were affixed on every flat surface of the container designed to ship delicate instruments. After unlatching the fasteners and lifting the lid, he discovered an old and small black metal traveling case resting inside. Eastwood gently extracted it from the precision-cut foam.

It was a design he had seen before. The 1913 Corona folding typewriter case and typewriter were painted black. British Racing Green cloth with razor-sharp edges decorated the inside of the case. A fresh ribbon had been used to type a proposal for an article. The salmon-colored sheet of paper was aligned between the paper table and platen. The typed message read:

Dory,

Regret this one is a little late. But this is a story that needs to be told. Is this something you would finish researching and put your name to? This professionally restored 1913 Corona folding typewriter is another shameless incentive to engage your services, good sir.

The biggest nut from the CDC treehouse has recently warned America if Bill McGee is elected, the new president can expect a coronavirus pandemic to hit the United States and millions will be killed. Just in time for the election, the latest episode in pandemic porn will terrorize America. It's a good time to bone up on the *Nuremburg Code*.

The left is horrified by the prospect of another Republican president. Evil is marshalling its forces against America.

More than before, we will need your sound and rational voice to counter the bullshit from the Democrats and the media.

If I'm wrong, I'll buy dinner the next time I see you. Or, I'll buy lunch anytime.

Think it over.

Semper Fi.

EPILOGUE

January 20, 2020

At the National Press Club, former CIA Director Bill McGee took the podium. Demetrius Eastwood had a prime position, front row, center of the assembled press. It was a full house.

Off to the side of the presidential candidate, in full view of the members of the press stood an easel with several charts turned 180° so no one could see what was on them until McGee called for them. Their presence created a sensation with the members of the press. Dawn Howell, Eastwood's friend, tended the charts.

Bill McGee flicked on the microphone and began. "As you know, this morning many of the private papers of the late Rho Schwartz Scorpii were posted and released by the Hungarian-based, international nonprofit organization, *Whistleblowers*. Those documents are more than evidence, they prove foreign intelligence agencies have been manipulating and corrupting American elections for some time. These documents also prove foreign entities completely control the Democrat Party with billions of dollars in illegal campaign contributions going to Democrat candidates seeking high office. These activities are not new in our elections and have long been suspected by law enforcement and our Department of Justice. Now DOJ has access to those documents."

"Foreign contributions to any candidate are illegal, and our campaign will resist any efforts by the DNC to manipulate and corrupt our elections that are encouraged by foreign entities. Our campaign will join with gubernatorial, senatorial, and other candidates to fight these illegal foreign incursions in court. Today we are filing over a hundred lawsuits in federal courts to stop them."

McGee continued, "We will also file lawsuits against ineligible candidates seeking the Democrat Party's nomination for president. First chart."

"This chart is verbatim from the U.S. Constitution, Article II, Section 1. We often find some reporters cannot be bothered with conducting research. For those so affected, we have done your work for you. You can read it with me."

"No person except a natural born citizen, or a citizen of the United States, at the time of the adoption of this Constitution, shall be eligible to the office of President; neither shall any person be eligible to that office who shall not have attained to the age of thirty-five years, and been fourteen Years a resident within the United States."

McGee continued, "*Whistleblowers* recovered the documents from the late Rho Schwartz Scorpii's foundation. There are no chain-of-custody issues and these documents are being validated by the U.S. intelligence community. These documents detail how his foundation and foreign intelligence agencies in Europe funded Democrat Party efforts to amend the U.S. Constitution, to strike the 'natural born citizen' requirement from the Constitution specifically, and have the new requirement for the Office of the President read simply, a citizen of the United States for fourteen years."

Former Director McGee said, "The tranche from *Whistleblowers* make clear when Rho Schwartz Scorpii's Democrats failed in amending the U.S. Constitution, he used his awesome wealth to engage in psychological operations against the American people. He paid the media, Democrat Party candidates, congressmen, and senators to create an illusion of legitimacy for Senator Mazibuike. The Rho Schwartz Scorpii documents show he gave over $100 million to members of Congress for their attempts to amend the Constitution. He added a billion dollars in illegal foreign contributions to fund propaganda that proclaimed President Mazibuike was a natural born citizen."

McGee said, "Next chart. You can see on this two-by-two table President Mazibuike was the son of an American mother and a foreign father. By the laws passed by our Congress, *that* rendered him a dual national at birth. A person with two citizenships isn't a natural born citizen and isn't in any way eligible for the Office of the President. Yet because we have Republicans who won't do their jobs, I call on the Federal Election Commission to stop this nonsense."

A member of the press raised a hand, objected, and shouted, "Natural born citizen isn't defined *anywhere* in the Constitution!"

Bill McGee said, "Next chart. This is the trope used by propagandists to shift the narrative away from the fact. Our first Congress passed the first law on citizenship, the *Naturalization Act of 1790*, which clearly enunciated a person born of U.S. citizens shall be considered a 'natural born citizen.' That is another way of saying the Democrat propaganda that insinuates the U.S. Constitution is faulty is an absolute lie. Joseph Goebbels would be so proud of this media and other Democrats."

"Next chart. You can see all the boxes of this two-by-two table are filled. Two U.S. citizens produce a U.S. citizen, and that person is a 'natural born citizen' per the *Naturalization Act of 1790*. When a U.S. citizen and a foreign national produce a child, that child is both a U.S. citizen and a foreign national. This is defined in immigration law as a dual national. Dual nationals are not constitutionally eligible to the Office of the President. Next chart."

Bill McGee said, "For our Democrat Party members and their media friends, *dual national* is another term not defined in the U.S. Constitution. No less of an authority, a Supreme Court Justice said the U.S. Constitution isn't a living organism, it's a legal document our Founding Fathers gave their lives to create. It says what it says and doesn't say what it doesn't say."

"The information on this chart is from the U.S. State Department. The wording is a little small so I will read the State Department's definition: *The concept of dual nationality means that a person is a national of two countries at the same time. Each country has its own nationality laws based on its own policy. Persons may have dual nationality by automatic operation of different laws rather than by choice. For example, a child born in a foreign country to U.S. national parents may be both a U.S. national and a national of the country of birth. Or, an individual having one nationality at birth may naturalize at a later date in another country and become a dual national.*"

McGee continued, "Foreign influence, foreign money, propaganda, mass formation psychosis, and lack of Congressional interest all contributed to the election of Maxim Mohammad Mazibuike, an ineligible candidate. You should be outraged

Democrats usurped the Constitution. Next chart! As members of the press, you're aware of and are supporting at least five other candidates running for the Democrat Party nomination who are dual nationals, not natural born citizens. Therefore, they're ineligible for the Office of the President. My campaign is filing separate lawsuits this morning against these ineligible candidates. They cannot be considered for high office, and their names should be stricken from any ballots."

"I sincerely hope Congress will enact legislation to prevent another usurpation of the U.S. Constitution as when they conspired with foreign nationals in the election of President Mazibuike. That concludes my remarks. I will gladly take your questions on foreign influence on American elections."

•   •   •

Demetrius Eastwood and Dawn Howell left the National Press Club and took an Uber to Washington's Union Station where Eastwood purchased first class Acela tickets to New York Grand Central Station. While on the train, he told Dawn he had an article to write on McGee's explosive announcement and he had a radio broadcast to do before they could get back on the campaign trail.

•   •   •

The White House Press Secretary announced the creation of a bi-partisan Presidential Commission on Presidential Election Integrity. She quoted President Hernandez: "There is no excuse for any state allowing dual nationals or foreign nationals to be considered for the presidency when the Founders mandated the Office of the President is the exclusive purview of natural born citizens, the children of United States citizens. Children of U.S. citizens have special rights foreign nationals do not have."

•   •   •

As the Amtrak wheels rhythmically clicked under their feet, Dory Eastwood and Dawn Howell worked on his article for the *Washington*

Times. Eastwood marveled at her editorial skills; he realized his previous work, filed directly from his computer, was rather poor. There was a reason the chief editor of the newspaper loved Eastwood's stories but always edited them extensively for publication.

To: Chief Editor, *Washington Times*
Title: *McGee to Challenge Ineligible Candidates in Court*
The leading Republican Presidential Candidate Bill McGee cited documents newly released from the *Whistleblowers* website. These documents prove the Democrat Party took hundreds of millions of dollars from foreign countries in their efforts to amend the Constitution, and they conspired with the billionaire Rho Schwartz Scorpii from Germany to install an ineligible candidate into the Office of the President. Previous documents released into the public domain proved President Mazibuike was a charlatan, and he was forced to resign and flee the country. These documents cite the names of Congressional Democrats who accepted illegal foreign campaign donations for their work to elect an ineligible candidate into the Office of the President. They also offer proof of the illegal foreign funding streams which paid for Mazibuike's education and campaigns.

The Department of Justice is investigating.

•   •   •

Dawn Howell sat quietly in the soundproof room as Eastwood made adjustments to his equipment. She was excited. They put on their headphones, and he flipped the switches that made the sound booth come alive.

"This is Dory Eastwood, reporting for the *Unmasked & Unspun Network* from high atop some tower of commerce in New York City, the town that never sweeps. Let's start today's show. After years of being steamrolled by the Democrat Party and covert foreign influence in our elections, the American public finally has something to cheer about. Today the Hungarian-based truth-seeking organization *Whistleblowers*, released their first tranche of documents from the late billionaire Rho Schwartz Scorpii and the *Ostgut Foundation*. These papers prove Scorpii, the richest man in the world, influenced

American elections with details of campaign contributions to Democrat lawmakers. There are so many documents it will take some time to sort them out. If you go to the editorial page of the *Washington Times* for my most recent article, that will give you a good start."

"There is an interesting article out of the *Dallas Morning News* — at least I found it interesting. Federal authorities investigating the wreckage of the campaign aircraft used by the former CIA Director, Bill McGee, found surveillance camera video of a stolen truck, which was used to transport and hide the anti-aircraft missile that knocked down the *McGee For President* campaign jet. It was seen leaving an Abilene mosque and driving to Abilene's airport. When investigators went to investigate the mosque, they were surprised to find the Abilene Islamic Cultural Center had recently burned to the ground. There was no suspicion of arson. But apparently, the *Dallas Morning News* reporter noticed on the same night the Abilene mosque caught fire, the Dallas Islamic Cultural Center caught fire and also burned to the ground. It doesn't look as if anyone was hurt in these fires, but officials in the two cities told the reporter the Muslim community who frequented those places of worship have disappeared."

For two hours, Eastwood reported the news from around America and across the globe. A full thirty minutes was dedicated to the rescue of thousands of children across Europe.

"Some final thoughts emerging from the *Not Going to be Afraid Any More* initiative of the McGee campaign. Republicans would comment President Mazibuike was the nation's greatest gun dealer every year he proposed gun control legislation. More weapons were sold every year he was in office than in any previous years. Independents and Republicans were seen as the main purchasers of weapons. Now it appears Bill McGee is the new greatest gun dealer in America. As one gun dealer commented, 'It's a good time to be in the firearms business.' Record sales are attributed to primarily Democrat-controlled cities. Democrats and women make up the preponderance of new guns sales. That is amazing."

"Lastly, another good news story. Far from the boredom of politics, classic automobile aficionados are celebrating the recovery of the iconic 1963 Aston Martin DB5 car used in early James Bond films *Thunderball* and *Goldfinger*."

"Yes, recovery. James Bond fans across the globe were saddened when the unique movie car with all the movie gadgets was stolen over twenty years ago."

"For over twenty years Federal and State law enforcement agencies had collected only scant evidence surrounding the disappearance of the Aston Martin DB5 from a secure aircraft hangar at a Florida airport."

"We know an American businessman had purchased the DB5 at a Sotheby's auction in 1986 and was the registered owner at the time of its theft in 1997. Although he was compensated over $4 million from his insurance company, he wanted to find his car and the people who stole it. Ten years ago he offered a $1 million reward for the DB5's recovery, and last month, he increased the reward to $5 million."

"We don't know how it happened, but it did. It took less than thirty days for Quiet Recoveries International, a secretive group that finds and recovers stolen luxury items, to find the stolen DB5 last month. When the DB5 was located, other rare vehicles which had also been stolen were discovered."

"Quiet Recoveries International, in an unusually candid press conference, verified its serial number and confirmed the Aston Martin DB5 was indeed the one that went missing in 1997. The DB5 has been returned to its owner and the reward was paid, and James Bond's Aston Martin is valued at over $25 million."

"The exact whereabouts of the Aston Martin DB5 made famous by Sean Connery in the 007 films hasn't been revealed, but we and only we, the *Unmasked & Unspun Network*, can report it was located somewhere in Europe."

"Quiet Recoveries International is working with multiple insurance companies to reunite owners with the other recovered automobiles. Quiet Recoveries International has discovered over one hundred rare and iconic cars scattered across several airport hangars at multiple airports. Law enforcement authorities across multiple jurisdictions have been notified but haven't been forthcoming how these cars could have been smuggled onto these airports and remained undetected for so long."

"Lastly, we don't hear of electric car fires in Europe for it's bad publicity for their electric vehicle market. The European media is working overtime trying to squash reports of Mercedes' newest electric vehicle, but we have a whistleblower. Apparently, a Mercedes-AMG GT R Pro Gullwing—whatever that it—was completely consumed in a fire outside of Antwerp, Belgium. The journalist coving the story said the driver was trapped in the vehicle because the electric gullwing doors wouldn't open. The fire burned for hours. That's going to be a bad day for Mercedes."

When Dawn Howell slipped off her clothes, Eastwood barked into the microphone, "And wouldn't you know it, another *Whistleblowers* tranche has just been released, I have work to do. Eastwood out!"

The suddenness of Eastwood terminating his radio broadcast coincided with a very nude Dawn Howell opening the studio door, and padding off to the shower. Dory Eastwood turned all the power switches off, ripped off his clothes, and rushed to follow her down the hall to the massive shower which could easily hose down a Clydesdale.

· · ·

After a half-hour of thrilling turns around the Belgian countryside, Duncan Hunter set up the 100-year-old airplane for landing. He was an accomplished taildragger pilot, with many logbook hours behind the stick. Although the black and white *Fokker Dr.1* was stunning to look at, it was a handful to fly, and the owner of the aircraft cautioned Hunter to avoid the chance of ground-looping the airplane, he recommended doing a three-point landing.

Which is exactly what *Maverick* did. With no brakes, the diminutive WWI fighter rolled to a stop in the grass. As *Maverick* climbed out of the open-air cockpit he was not only covered in leathers: wool-lined leather pants and flight jacket and flying cap, he was covered in oil, courtesy of a couple of gallons of castor oil used as lubrication and slung from the 100-year-old rotary engine. Even *Maverick's* teeth were covered with castor oil when he smiled, which now that he was on the ground, could have been permanent and wide.

Nazy clutched gloved hands to her chest and laughed. She had never seen Duncan emerge smiling from any of his aircraft while drenched in dark oil. *Is he smiling because he landed safely?*

The *Dr.1* owner had regaled her with a running commentary on how he built the aircraft from salvaged remains of the little *driedecker* made famous by the bloody Red Baron of Germany. He explained, "What makes this *Dr.1* unique among all the other replicas is it is the only remaining operational *Oberursel Ur.II* nine-cylinder air-cooled rotary piston engine we are aware of. It makes 110 horsepower. There are two *Dr.1s* with the *Le Rhône 9J* rotary engine and there are several *Le Rhône* engines in museums. These motors are virtually identical; they were just made by different manufacturers."

"Why is Duncan covered in oil?" she asked.

The old man smiled and said, "The 100-year-old rotary engine case isn't mounted to a firewall, and the propeller doesn't turn on a shaft like other aircraft. The nine-cylinders were engineered to *spin* and convert that energy to turn the propeller. It's a 100-years-old, and when a rotary engine spins, it throws oil everywhere. If Duncan wasn't covered from head to foot with oil, there would be a major problem."

Nazy thanked the man and waited for Duncan. With eye-goggles smeared with oil, he walked up to their smiling faces and said, *"That... was... incredible!"*

All *Maverick* could do as he tasted castor oil and smiled was say, *"Oleg,* we have a deal, good, sir."

•   •   •

Two hours in the shower apparently exhausted the hot water supply in the hotel. It was barely enough time to eliminate all the castor oil from Duncan's body before the water ran cold. Nazy was more than happy to help scrub her husband clean. They dressed together and he helped her with the spider silk vest. Duncan hid a shoulder-holstered Colt *Python* .357 magnum under a jacket. While Nazy finished up in the bathroom, Duncan perused some of the article's headlines on the front page of the *Brussels Times*, an English print newspaper. *CDC Director Fired, Children Reunited with Families Throughout Europe, Mercedes EV Production Halted with AMG-GT Fire, President Contemplates China Travel Ban, World on Pandemic Watch as China Locks Down Cities,* and *Virus Emerges from China.*

Just as Nazy emerged from the bathroom and announced she was ready to go, Duncan shook his head and threw the newspaper in a trash basket. She asked, "What have the Democrats done this time?"

"Trying to set the world on fire, as usual."

After the hotel's ancient Rolls Royce delivered them to a Brussels steakhouse where raw filets were served on an oven-hot square stone cooking the meat at the table, Duncan and Nazy lamented their travels were about to end. Her vacation time was up. Duncan said he had been productive. *Very productive. I got the bastard who was after Nazy.*

Nazy said, "I don't know how you'll top the *dreidecker*. Oleg was such a nice man. You could tell he did not want to let it go."

Duncan had visions of the *Dr.1* being disassembled and carefully packed in a storage container and flown home in QAS' LM-130J. He said, "I have been after him to sell it to me for some time. He knew I would appreciate it and take care of it until it was time to let someone else play with it or stick it in a museum. He did a fantastic job with that unique motor, but he knows he's too old to enjoy it now."

"And you got the Mercedes'."

Duncan smiled, "We did, at least Bong did." *The two 540Ks in the hangar in Cologne. It's a shame the one in Antwerp caught on fire.*

"Did you ever figure out how they stole those cars?"

"They stole those cars just like we stole those 540Ks from a master criminal. A C-130 on a ramp at night, a car under a cover pushed into the cabin, and off they go to deposit those cars on another airport. It wasn't hard to figure out. What was difficult was finding out who had a civilian C-130. There are few of them. The militaries that use them also use up all of their useful life before dismantling them and sending them to salvage. So rarely are there any in private hands. Ours is new and we had to wait five years for it."

"Lockheed keeps track of all of them, even the crashed one in the middle of the airport in Luanda, Angola. There are a few but they're all accounted for. What took some time was figuring out if there are C-130-capable aircraft available. Then it was obvious. When the old Soviet Union fell in 1988 Soviet cargo pilots stole the Soviet Union's Il-76s and An-12s to evacuate their families and friends from what was likely going to be a murderous hell. Coups and revolutions are not pretty. A lot of those formerly military cargo aircraft have been operating in Africa and the Middle East, and surprisingly, Canada."

"When Russians have revolutions, people die; people with contrasting views die first, and if they cannot be controlled, their families go to gulags."

Nazy said, "Talking with you is so illuminating."

Duncan was lost in platinum green eyes by candlelight.

Nazy ignored him for the moment. She remembered something important. "Oh yes, Scorpii. He created *Tailwatchers* or what he called *Overwatch* in his journals."

"Correct. Thank you, baby."

Nazy smiled and took a bite of beef. Duncan was much more relaxed. Was it acquiring the *Dr.1* or was it something else? It occurred to her to ask, "Do we know what happened to El Masri?"

Duncan said, "He and Scorpii were both cremated."

Nazy sighed for a moment and nodded. "You know how they did it? *Tailwatchers* was key?"

Duncan continued, "So, think about the ability to follow corporate and business jets from airport to airport. The richest men in the world drive their favorite cars to the airport, park their pride and joy toys inside what they consider a secure hangar on a secure airport. They get on their bizjet and go do business somewhere. When they return, they find their vehicle isn't in the hangar. It has been stolen." *El Masri found the Mercedes AMG-GT still in the hangar.*

"And, I thought I was a good analyst." She smirked at him in admiration and love.

He didn't know it had a tracking device. "Thank you, baby but you're the analyst. So, *Tailwatchers* or *Overwatch* follow not only aircraft. They use telescopic lenses to identity and track corporate jets, and they follow the rare cars of the rich men who travel in those jets. While they are gone, someone — probably several someones — flies in on a C-130 or an Il-76 or an An-12, defeats the hangar's crappy security, steals the car or cars, loads them aboard the cargo aircraft, and flies away. The bad guys are using airports and aircraft to steal and smuggle hot luxury items."

Nazy was fascinated with the topic and with the stone cooking pieces of beef.

I shot him, shoved a Firestarter in his mouth, and dumped a couple of Firestarters in the car. Duncan looked over the candle between them. He was about to propose a new place to visit when his BlackBerry went off. He shut his eyes. He didn't want to answer it. He was afraid to even look at the face of the phone. Duncan showed Nazy what he saw on the face of the BlackBerry when she called him for a lift.

A single zero in the tiny screen suggested it was from the CIA. The office of the Director. *But the Director is right here!* He looked at Nazy and sighed. *Who in the hell?* Hunter answered with all the enthusiasm of a man being led to the gallows, "Good evening, good sir. How my I help you?"

The voice of CIA Director Walter Todd III was unmistakable. "Hey *Maverick*, it's time for you to get your fanny back to work. I need you."

ACRONYMS/ABBREVIATIONS

AG — Attorney General

AGL — Above Ground Level

AI — Artificial Intelligence

AK — Automatic Kalashnikov

AMCIT — American Citizen

AMG — stands for Aufrecht, Melcher and Großaspach

ANVIS — Aviator Night Vision, night vision goggles

APB — All Points Bulletin

AQ — Al-Qaeda

ATLS — Automatic Takeoff and Landing System

BBC — British Broadcasting Corporation

BLM — Belligerent Leftist Mob

BS — Bullshit

C — Cargo aircraft

Cal — Caliber

C-band — Ultraviolet wavelength from 100 to 280 nanometers

CCP — Chinese Communist Party

CDC — Center for Disease Control

CI — Counter Intelligence

CIA — Central Intelligence Agency

CEO — Chief Executive Officer

COMM — Communications

COS — Chief of Station, Chief of Staff

CT — Counter Terrorism

CTC — Counter Terrorism Center

CV — Curriculum Vitae

DB — a British luxury grand tourer (GT) made by Aston Martin,
under the ownership of David Brown

DB5 — the best-known cinematic *James Bond* car, first appearing in
the film *Goldfinger*

D.C. — District of Columbia

DEA — Drug Enforcement Agency

DELTA — 1st Special Forces Operational Detachment-Delta

DEVGRU — U.S. Naval Special Warfare Development Group
DHS — Department of Homeland Security
DIC — Distinguished Intelligence Cross
DNA — Deoxyribonucleic acid
DNC — Democratic National Committee
DO — Director of Operations
DOD — Department of Defense
DOJ — Department of Justice
DPAA — Defense POW/MIA Accounting Agency
ERA — Explosive Reactive Armor
EV — Electric Vehicle
FA — Fighter aircraft
FAA — Federal Aviation Administration
FARC — Fuerzas Armadas Revolucionarias de Colombia; the
    Revolutionary Armed Forces of Colombia
FBI — Federal Bureau of Investigation
FCLP — Field Carrier Landing Practice
FDR — Franklin Delano Roosevelt
FISA — Foreign Intelligence Surveillance Act
FLIR — Forward Looking Infra-Red
FLN — *Front de Libération Nationale*, the National Liberation Front
F Troop — A satirical American television sitcom western about U.S.
    soldiers and American Indians in the Wild West
F-4S — Phantom
F-4U — Corsair
G — Gravity, Gulfstream aircraft
GIP — General Intelligence Presidency
GITMO — Guantanamo Bay Naval Base, Cuba
G-IV — SP Gulfstream Model 4, Special Purpose
G-550 — Gulfstream Model 550
GM — General Manager
G-Man — Government Man
GOP — Grand Old Party
GPS — Global Positioning System
GT — Grand Touring
HQ — Headquarters
HR — Human Resources

ID — Identify/Identity/Identification
IED — Improvised Explosive Device
IARPA — Intelligence Advanced Research Projects Agency
IC — Intelligence Community
IFR — Instrument Flight Rules
IG — Inspector General
IO — Intelligence Officer
IR — Infrared
IRGC — Islamic Revolutionary Guard Corps
ISIS — Islamic State of Iraq and Syria
IT — Information Technology
IU — Islamic Underground
IV — The Latin number four
J — Jet Engine
JDAMs — Joint Direct Attack Munitions
JFK — John Fitzgerald Kennedy
JSOC — Joint Special Operations Command
J-79 — An axial-flow turbojet engine produced by General Electric
     Aircraft Engines
KGB — Komitet Gosudarstvennoy Bezopasnosti; the foreign
     intelligence and domestic security agency of the Soviet Union
LD — Laser Designator
LED — Light Emitting Diode
LGB — Laser-Guided Bullet
LM — Lockheed Martin
LNG — Liquefied Natural Gas
MANPADS — Man-Portable Air Defense System
MCAS — Marine Corps Air Station
MCB — Marine Corps Base
MD — McDonald Douglas, Medical Doctor
MEMRI — Middle East Media Research Institute
MIA — Missing In Action
MiG — Mikoyan
MIT — Massachusetts Institute of Technology
MM — Millimeter
MPH — Miles per Hour
MTA — Maryland Transportation Authority

MVP — Most Valuable Professional

M-16 — M16 rifle, officially designated Rifle, Caliber 5.56

NASA — National Aeronautics and Space Administration

NTSB — National Transportation Safety Board

NATO — North Atlantic Treaty Organization

NATOPS — Naval Air Training and Operating Procedures
Standardization

NCS — National Clandestine Service

NCTC — National Counter Terrorism Center

NDA — Non-Disclosure Agreement

NE — Near East Division

NGA — National Geospatial-Intelligence Agency

NGO — Non-Governmental Organization,

NCIC — National Crime Information Center

NM — Nanometer

No. — Number

NSA — National Security Agency

O — Observation aircraft

OBL — Osama bin Laden

OPCON — Operational Control

OPS — Operations

OSS — Office of Strategic Services

PAC — Political Action Committee

PanAm — Pan American World Airways

PAX — Passengers

PD — Police Department

PDB — President's Daily Brief

Ph.D. — Doctor of Philosophy

Pk — (P-sub k) Probability of Kill

PLO — Palestine Liberation Organization

POTUS — President of the United States

POW — Prisoner of War

PSYOP — Psychological Operations

PT — Physical Training

P-51 — Mustang

Q — Drone

QAS — Quiet Aero Systems

QD — Quick Disconnect

R — Radial engine, rotary engine

R&D — Research and Development

RCS — Radar-Cross Section

RNC — Republican National Committee

RPG — Rocket Propelled Grenade

RPM — Revolutions Per Minute

RTB — Return to Base

SA2-37B — Schweizer single-engine low-noise profile aircraft

SACEUR — Supreme Allied Commander Europe

SAD — Special Activities Division

SAM — Surface-to-Air Missile

SAP — Special Access Program

SAR — Special Access Required

S&T — Science and Technology Directorate

SCI — Sensitive Compartmented Information

SCIF — Sensitive Compartmented Information Facility

SEAL — Sea, Air, Land

SED — Socialist Unity Party of Germany

SIS — Senior Intelligence Service

SL — Sport Leicht (Light Sport), a line of Mercedes cars

SOCOM — Special Operations Command

SDT — Specially Designated Terrorist

SS — Secret Service, *Schutzstaffel*

STD — Sexually Transmitted Disease

STU-III — Secure Telephone Unit

SUV — Sport Utility Vehicle

Tally Ho — A very old traditional cry made by huntsman to tell others the quarry has been sighted. Used by aviators to indicate other aircraft or targets have been seen.

TASC — Trans-Atlantic Security Council

300 SL — Mercedes sportscar, coupe has gullwing-opening doors from the roof

TIDE — Terrorist Identities Datamart Environment

10-4 — Message Received, from Ten Code

3M — Abbreviation for Maxim Mohammad Mazibuike

TOPGUN — The U.S. Navy Strike Fighter Tactics Instructor program

TS — Top Secret

TS2 — Terminator Sniper System

TS/SCI — Top Secret/Sensitive Compartmented Information

TV — Television

TWA — Trans World Airlines

280 SL — Mercedes sportscar with a Pagoda-like roofline

U — Unmanned

UAV — Unmanned Aerial Vehicle

U.S. — United States

USS — United States Ship

UV — Ultraviolet

UV-C — Ultraviolet-C band, wavelength from 100 to 280
nanometers

VFR — Visual Flight Rules

VIP — Very Important Person

Wilco — Will Comply

WWII — World War Two

Y — Prototype aircraft

YO-3A — Prototype Observation aircraft, model 3, series A

Yo-Yo — Nickname for the YO-3A

XKE — Jaguar E-Type; the most beautiful car ever built by no less of
an authority than Enzo Ferrari

ACKNOWLEDGEMENTS

I owe a special debt of gratitude to Barbara Hewitt, my editor and wife, for her careful reading and editing of my manuscripts, and her many excellent suggestions for their improvement. Her continuous good advice and encouragement has been invaluable throughout the making of my books. I'm not afraid of her red pen.

I'm also deeply grateful for U.S. Air Force Colonel George "Curious" Fenimore, Retired, and the brilliant "recovering attorney" Rosemary Harris for their unfailing patience and good humor that helped turn my very rough ramblings and ruminations into a set of coherent thoughts and a better story. George must be a genius for his reviews and precise penetrating insights often leave me muttering to myself, "I am not worthy." Any errors found in this novel are my responsibility.

ABOUT THE AUTHOR

I consider myself one of the luckiest men on the planet. For half of my
military career, I worked on helicopters; the other decade-plus was
served as a U.S. Marine Corps officer, where the highlight of my time
was to be able fly the aircraft of my childhood dreams, the amazing F-
4S Phantom II. I served in leadership positions with the Marines, the
U.S. Border Patrol, and the U.S. Air Force before leading and
managing aviation activities and aircraft operations for international
corporations in the Washington, D.C. area. I fixed a few airports along
the way, like Monrovia, Liberia after fifteen years of war. Somewhere
during my professional journey, I became a member of the intelligence
community, with a top-secret security clearance with SCI and had to
take a polygraph. One of my greatest thrills was the time I entered CIA
headquarters and saw the models of the Agency's "black" aircraft
suspended from the ceiling in the atrium. That is another way of
saying I am on an NDA and my manuscripts have to be approved by
the CIA Publication Review Board. My interest in spies and spyplanes

began when Francis Gary Powers, the U-2 pilot shot down over the Soviet Union, splashed onto the headlines. I was just a kid in Germany but I followed the case as closely as I could. I found out the Director of Central Intelligence declared the CIA would no longer put men in surveillance aircraft over the Soviet Union. We lived eight miles from the East German border and their MiGs routinely flew over our house. While my family was stationed in West Germany, I was guilty of smudging the windows of my neighbor's 1963 Corvette Sting Ray virtually every day and became enamored of sports cars, American and European. My mother read everything in the base library and I read the Hardy Boys and everything I could sneak into my room, primarily Alistair MacLean and Ian Fleming. My Duncan Hunter books reflect my various life experiences and my love for all things aviation. I've logged time in gliders, jets, props, radial-engine aircraft, helicopters, and qualified as an aircraft carrier pilot. Take it from me, being shot off the pointy end of an aircraft carrier is the most fun you can have with your clothes on. I wrote what I knew and saw that was unclassified, and it was a natural fit to see my protagonist as a CIA pilot flying a rare spyplane to get deep behind enemy lines, to hunt down the world's worst terrorists. More than one CEO has called my novels "a case study for conducting counterterrorism missions with special purpose aircraft." I have traveled extensively, to places that were dangerous (Afghanistan, Iraq, Colombia) or just hellholes (Liberia, Nigeria, Angola). When passing through U.S. Customs with a thick passport full of visas, I was often asked, "Just what the hell do you do?" For 12 years I served as an Assistant Adjunct Professor for Embry-Riddle Aeronautical University. I earned a Master of Arts degree in National Security and Strategic Studies from the Naval War College and I hold an MBA in Aviation from Embry-Riddle Aeronautical University.

Note From the Author

Word-of-mouth is crucial for any author to succeed. If you enjoyed *Infiltrated*, please leave a review online—anywhere you are able. Even if it's just a sentence or two. It would make all the difference and would be very much appreciated.

Thanks!
Mark A. Hewitt

We hope you enjoyed reading this title from:

BLACK ROSE
writing™

www.blackrosewriting.com

Subscribe to our mailing list – *The Rosevine* – and receive **FREE** books, daily deals, and stay current with news about upcoming releases
and our hottest authors.
Scan the QR code below to sign up.

Already a subscriber? Please accept a sincere thank you for being a fan of Black Rose Writing authors.

View other Black Rose Writing titles at
www.blackrosewriting.com/books and use promo code
PRINT to receive a **20% discount** when purchasing.